"I couldn't put *Consequence* down! [...] Francisco's radical sub-culture in this [...] finely-crafted novel. *Consequence* asks thorny, essential questions about personal responsibility and the role of violence in movements for social change."

—Sam Green, Academy Award-nominated
director of *The Weather Underground*

"Here is a carefully crafted book about the necessity, and danger, of taking personal action in the 21st century. ... Steve Masover's characters ooze humanity. ... The villain of *Consequence* happens to be genetic engineering but it could have been any current social or environmental issue. The premise, absolutely believable today, is that life on the planet is threatened and that battle waged by this novel's characters will make a difference. ... This is a human story shot in the ass with ideas."

—Doug Peacock, author of *In the Shadow of the Sabertooth*

"*Consequence* is a great read, full of building tension and excitement, written by someone who really knows the activist scene, with its moral dilemmas and its ideals. But this isn't just a book about activists—Masover writes about conflicts central to the human situation."

—Starhawk, author of *The Spiral Dance*
and *The Fifth Sacred Thing*

". . . exciting . . . a great read . . . reminiscent of *The Monkey Wrench Gang*."

—Scoop Nisker, author of *If You Don't Like the News,
Go Out and Make Some of Your Own*

CONSEQUENCE

A NOVEL

Steve Masover

Salted Rose Press
Berkeley

Published by Salted Rose Press
Berkeley, California
www.saltedrosepress.com

First edition, September 2015

Grateful acknowledgment is made to The Free History Project for permission to paraphrase interviews from the documentary film *The Weather Underground* (© 2003), directed by Sam Green and Bill Siegel.

Book design by The Book Makers
Cover design by Damonza Book Cover Design

Publisher's Cataloging-in-Publication data

Masover, Steve.
    Consequence / by Steve Masover.
    p. cm.
    ISBN 978-0-9864263-0-8 (pbk.)
    ISBN 978-0-9864263-1-5 (e-pub)
    ISBN 978-0-9864263-2-2 (Kindle)

1. Political activists—Fiction. 2. Bioterrorism—Fiction. 3. Genetically modified foods—United States—Fiction. 4. Agricultural industries—United States—Fiction. 5. San Francisco (Calif.)—Fiction. I. Title.

PS3613.A8188 C66 2015

813.6—dc23   2015900461

For Susan and Bob

ONE

March 2004

If he was going to play secret agent, Christopher Kalman needed to head for the bus. It would be simpler to log into online chat from where he sat in the Triangle's third-floor library, but he couldn't put his home and political collective at risk. The chat could be traced. Besides, he'd given Chagall his word.

It would cost an hour to take a circuitous, backtracking route to the Daily Grind, a café on the far side of San Francisco that sold internet access for cash. Chagall was fixated on that sort of paranoid rigor. Christopher didn't see the need, not if they were careful with security protocols. But he'd promised to take precautions against being tailed to their first real-time appointment.

The prospect of "meeting" the self-proclaimed saboteur made Christopher antsy. If his anonymous contact was a setup, or if Chagall were seriously dangerous, internet chat would place Christopher—and everyone he worked with—that much closer to an unknown threat.

He stared at the progress bar on his monitor. The Moscone Center's floor plans were nearly finished downloading, but he wouldn't have time to look them over until later. Not a problem. The coalition organizing to disrupt the International Gene-

Synth Convention wasn't meeting until Sunday. Still, the pressure was on. A month and a half remained before the conference opened, but the Triangle was planning a clandestine action in addition to their part in the public protest. The dual-track activism had been straining Christopher's limits even before Chagall came knocking.

Ninety percent complete.

Logistics research lacked the chaotic zing of an actual demonstration, but at least it satisfied his urge to put the world in order. The mantel clock showed 2:40. An hour and twenty minutes until their online rendezvous. He needed to hustle.

Christopher switched off the monitor when the download finished, and unkinked himself from a chair rescued years before from some forgotten curb, a sturdy, Mission-style piece that he could never quite adjust to fit his tall, barrel-chested frame. He descended the wooden stairs quietly, in case Marty was asleep. Christopher stopped to check on his housecomrade, leaning in through the half-closed door of the bedroom next to his own, at the front of the collective's century-old Edwardian.

"Who's that?" Marty grunted.

The curtains were drawn across the bedroom's bay windows. Christopher could just make out a ghostly arm raised against the light leaking in from the hallway. "It's Chris," he said. "I'm heading out. It'll be an hour or so before Jonah's back from school—can I get you anything?" Marty had taken a nasty fall off his bike the evening before, just a few blocks from home. He'd resisted a trip to the emergency room, but when Nora brought him home from the hospital the back of his shaved head was quilted with stitches and surgical tape.

"No, Chris. Nothin'," Marty said. "Just waitin' for the drugs to kick in."

Marty's Irish brogue, faint but discernible after a dozen years living in the States, sounded thicker than usual. Christopher figured it was the painkillers. "I'll leave the door open a crack," he said, "so Jonah remembers to look in."

"That's good. I'll be okay, just tryin' to sleep it off."

Christopher loaded up his messenger bag, crept another flight down to the front stoop, slipped quietly through the building's steel gate, and turned onto the tree-shaded street. Just short of the metro stop, he pivoted up Fillmore, then zigzagged around the hulking US Mint before heading north again.

Someone had postered the neighborhood's telephone poles with calls to march on the anniversary of the Iraq War. The flyers demoralized Christopher, one staple-studded wooden pole after another. He crossed the street to avoid them. Direct Action to Stop the War had mounted the Bay Area's share of the biggest protests in human history—eleven million people around the world, two hundred thousand in San Francisco alone—and five weeks later the US launched an airstrike on Baghdad. The Triangle, everyone they knew, every leftist group they'd ever organized with, had given everything they had. And they lost.

—

Three buses and two transfers later he set out on foot in the wrong direction, then circled an unnecessary block as he looped back toward the café. Christopher was drawing on techniques he'd picked up over years of evading police after rowdy demonstrations, or after wheat pasting agitprop on bus shelters and banks. He stopped in front of a jewelry store window to watch the street's reflection. The glass mirrored a face that was beginning to seem more his father's than Christopher's own: sharp, wide-set eyes planted amid blurrier features, dark hair receding as inexorably as the polar ice caps. He would turn thirty-five in May. A milestone, but was he on the right road? "Nothing ventured, nothing gained," he muttered to himself. The cliché did little to settle his nerves.

If anyone had been following, he'd shaken the tail. Retrieving a battered, gray fedora from his messenger bag, Christopher approached the Daily Grind. He never wore hats and felt sheepish playing dress up, but the café ran a webcam aimed out from the counter. He hoped to find an off-camera table. The hat was just in case.

In case of *what* remained fuzzy.

So far, all he really knew was that an anonymous persona had contacted him, insisted on taking elaborate measures against police surveillance, then asked him to draft a manifesto about Frankenfood. Chagall refused to supply even a nom de guerre; Christopher settled on naming him after a painter his mother had loved. From Chagall's guarded first contact through an intricate set of formalities involving encryption keys and single-use e-mail addresses, it took weeks for the saboteur to get to his point:

> We're looking for a writer to produce a political manifesto on genetically engineered agriculture. Publicly posted material suggests your views are close to ours. In the wake of spectacular political theater, my partners and I offer a staggeringly large and broad audience. All actors to remain anonymous, including writer. Action's logistics stay secret until it happens. The audience for your manifesto is everybody who reads news and anybody with an e-mail address.

As Chagall kept reminding him, there was nothing illegal about writing political screeds. And the task was right up Christopher's alley. He was an activist. He wrote. Genetic engineering was already on his publicly discoverable docket because of organizing against GeneSynth. None of which explained the hypervigilance. Unless Chagall meant *spectacularly destructive* when he bragged about political theater, his caution around drafting piecework propaganda arced way over the top.

Any activist would covet a *staggeringly large* audience, but Christopher remained skeptical. Odds were good that his anonymous contact would turn out to be a blowhard, the type who imagined that being targeted by police proved revolutionary cred. He could be a reckless fool. He could even be a cop himself: Chagall's approach might ultimately boil down to an FBI phishing expedition. Christopher was the one who insisted they communicate over IRC, internet relay chat. In real time, he stood a better chance of taking Chagall's measure.

Leaving his bag at a vacant table, Christopher kept the fedora pulled low, shielding himself from the webcam above the register. He paid for a double cappuccino and an hour's wireless. Back at the table he booted his laptop into a secondary operating system. Linux loaded, and he verified the machine was spoofing a counterfeit network card.

At the tail end of the dot-com boom, Christopher had taken a secure activism workshop taught by an affinity group called Rebel Geeks. There hadn't been much call for expertise in network protection over the years since, not among his crowd. But without some kind of background, Chagall's instructions would have tied him in knots. He fired up chat software, engaged his encryption keys, and typed the URL Chagall had supplied.

Six minutes 'til the scheduled meet-up. His table was beyond the camera's field of view, so Christopher stuffed the fedora into his bag.

He looked around the café. The Marina was a far cry from the Castro or the Haight. Only the women wore makeup; none had their lips pierced. A melancholy track from Beck's *Sea Change* played on the sound system.

A woman in a flashy ski jacket and worn sweatpants sat by the window, staring as if frozen at a gruesome photo on the front page of the *New York Times*. He'd seen it online that morning. Four commuter trains had been bombed in Madrid the day before, their carriages ripped open, jagged with savagely torn steel. The news was a jumble of blame and speculation: Al Qaeda, Basque separatists, unknown fanatics. Even seeing the image from a distance, he felt suffocated by the horror. Nearly two hundred dead. He shifted his gaze to a burly Central American lugging a bus tub into the back room.

Chagall logged in exactly on time.

CHAGALL: All clear?
CHRIS: Present & accounted for.
CHAGALL: If you need to stop this session for any reason, don't wait to explain.
CHRIS: Understood. Everybody in my part of the world is looking at news of yesterday's incident in Spain.
CHAGALL: That type of incident has nothing to do with us. I don't want to know about your part of the world. Let's keep to necessities.
CHRIS: Okay. Strictly business then.
CHAGALL: Right. And it's your move, you requested this.

Nothing to do with us was the response Christopher wanted to hear. But Chagall was as gruff in real-time as in e-mail. Christopher would have to stay on point and hold his ground.

CHRIS: Let's say you screw up whatever it is you're planning to do. What protects me from taking your fall?
CHAGALL: Fair question. Begin with this. First contact through your public address was a needle in a large hay-

stack. Now messages are anonymized, encrypted, deleted after reading.

CHRIS: What if e-mail is intercepted, or archived and hacked?

CHAGALL: Highly improbable. Even so, your part is just words. Theoretical. Justification for types of action taken for types of reasons. Worst is you'd be reviled for ideas. Admired too, by some.

CHRIS: Hope springs eternal. But I'm a conspirator via our contact.

CHAGALL: Conspiracy to express political speech. Delete communications as agreed, and even that much is speculative.

CHRIS: So my protection is to remain in the dark.

Christopher sipped at his coffee while waiting for Chagall to compose, encrypt, and send his response. Security slowed their pace. The pauses left him time to think. The saboteur's ideas about insulating Christopher from prosecution were naïve or disingenuous, overlooking how due process had been gutted in the few years since the Al Qaeda attacks. Chagall was ignoring John Walker Lindh, the so-called "American Taliban," who was railroaded into a twenty-year sentence after the attorney general publicly distorted a confession compelled by torture. And he seemed blind to José Padilla, a US citizen being held without charges in military prison, for an unproven role in a bomb plot that never got off the drawing board.

CHAGALL: That's a component of your protection, yes. But, again, your identity can't be linked to ours given attention to security.

CHRIS: Let's focus on message, complexity, style. Audience

remains undefined. You keep saying "everyone." That's not helpful when trying to set tone and depth.

CHAGALL: Aim for reading level of nationally circulated newspapers or magazines. Must reach diverse sectors, speak across the usual divides. Christian Right to Sierra Club. City and farm. Address human basics, avoid partisan trigger words. Write about rules against identifying GMO food in grocery stores. Regular people have reason to be scared, for their own safety and for their children's. Don't write for professors.

CHRIS: I need to confirm again: no one gets hurt. No one.

CHAGALL: This is fundamental. Same commitment as Planetary Liberation Front and allied groups. Years of hard-core political sabotage and their hands are clean. We adhere to the same principles.

CHRIS: That's fundamental for me also. No compromise on this. But I need to press for at least the category of action. Are you going to burn genetically engineered crops? Destroy a grain silo?

CHAGALL: Will not say.

CHRIS: Bust up a lab, like the Plowshares Eight?

CHAGALL: Priests taking hammers to nuclear weapons is dramatic. Chaining ourselves to microscopes in a soybean research lab would look ridiculous, like a high school science fair. The Plowshares Eight were setting up a courtroom drama. We're not seeking jail time, we intend to be free to act repeatedly. Look, it doesn't serve anyone to describe the plan. Would only increase danger to each of us.

The Feds classified destruction of property as terrorism, whether anyone was injured or not. In the opposite corner,

Chagall had compared his own group to the Planetary Liberation Front, which held that attacks on grain silos and fields of genetically modified crops were defensive so long as no one got hurt, defensive because gene splicers were pumping poison into the food supply and the greater biosphere. Because the damage might never be undone, and biotech had to be stopped.

Christopher agreed with the PLF, in principle and from the sidelines. He had never committed hard-core exploits himself. For better or worse, the Triangle's direct action tactics rarely edged past symbolic effect. It wore him down that for all their years of commitment, to their household and to their work, there was so little to show.

But he still had no idea what Chagall meant to do. Or whether he was a cop. Or, if he wasn't, whether he could be trusted to plan and act conscientiously.

Christopher steered their online chat into questions of political philosophy: Subcomandante Marcos and the armed Zapatistas' deference to civil society, Václav Havel's critique of capitalism and communism as two faces of the same technocratic coin. From there he began to tease out the spin Chagall wanted to put on biotech agribusiness. There were any number of approaches possible—contamination of the planet, corporate "ownership" of life, health dangers, hubris. It was a matter of which angle to emphasize.

The politics rolling off his correspondent's keyboard looked genuine. No cop who'd gotten that fluent in progressive arcana would waste his time on the Triangle's brand of nonviolence. He'd be looking for a bigger bust to justify the investment.

Flexing his shoulders, Christopher looked up from the laptop.

It took a second to register her attention.

A dark-eyed, oval-faced woman was gazing right at him. She

sat two tables over, and she didn't look away. Instead of lowering her eyes, she offered a dazzling smile. "That looks engrossing," she said.

British accent, he thought. Her voice filled the space between their tables like velvety caramel. "Old college buddy," he improvised. Her teeth glowed, polished ivory against walnut skin. "A lot of instant message bluster for very low stakes."

"And here I thought I was witnessing the birth of café-based day trading."

Christopher grinned. "Honestly, I wouldn't know a bull market from a short sale." Could she possibly be hitting on him? He had to disengage, whether or not. He'd made promises to Chagall. Their elaborate security rites would amount to nothing if someone ID'd him at the Daily Grind, geeking like a madman at such-and-such a time and date. His screen flashed the arrival of a message. "I, um . . ." He gestured toward the computer.

"I'm sorry, I shouldn't have intruded."

"No, no—it's—Paul and I haven't managed to connect in forever." Paul? Who the hell was Paul?

She gave a kind of sideways nod, and returned to her pint glass of milky tea.

Christopher dragged his attention back to the laptop.

CHAGALL: Multiple angles best for inviting all readers to see they have a stake. Your task to balance these as aspects of a single argument.

CHRIS: You can express yourself. Why add me to the mix?

If the saboteur was leveling with him, this was the biggest piece missing from his puzzle. Yet Christopher could barely force himself to keep looking at the screen. Why had a complete stranger struck up a conversation? Could she be a cop?

Don't go there, he told himself. No tinfoil hats. But he couldn't remember the last time a beautiful woman chatted him up. If romance was like weather, his life was a drought. Longing for rain, occasionally taunted by anemic drizzle.

CHAGALL: Our action isn't trivial and there aren't very many of us. Operations require full focus.

CHRIS: So you'll take nontrivial risks but can't be bothered to explain your own political motives and goals?

CHAGALL: We admire your articles in activist press. We're isolated, you'll reach our audience better than we can. As described in prior exchange we'll develop the text with you, over multiple drafts. We have the final edit, ensuring manifesto says what we mean.

CHRIS: Bringing me into your closely guarded secret takes a big gamble for marginal payoff. I don't get it, and I'm *not* convinced to sign on. I would need better assurances before letting you use my work. But let's say I mean to write something on this topic in any case. Let's say I start on my independent project, and if you don't persuade me, I'll use it some other way.

He glanced up surreptitiously. The woman was still buried in her newspaper. Could he end the IRC before she finished her tea? If nothing else, he needed to divert her interest in his over-zealous session with Chagall. The saboteur wouldn't approve of his tangled motives, but maybe that didn't matter. Chagall would never know.

CHAGALL: An independent start is acceptable for now. But we'll continue to recruit alternates. Must cover contingencies.

CHRIS: Fair enough. Suggest some specifics. How many words, on what deadline?

CHAGALL: As many words as it takes. Keep it short and sharp enough to avoid losing readers. For deadline, best not to imply when action will occur. How long for a first draft?
CHRIS: Maybe two weeks? Maybe three?

Again, carefully pretending to stare at his laptop, Christopher stole another quick look. What paper was she reading?

CHAGALL: Let's make contact in two weeks. You initiate, at next address in sequence. Send draft if ready and willing.
CHRIS: I'll have more questions before sending draft, but will propose next steps.
CHAGALL: Over and out then?
CHRIS: Appreciate real-time dialogue. Until next time.

Hands hovering over the keyboard, Christopher vacillated. He and Chagall had agreed on a protocol for securely deleting the IRC transcript. But the woman with the velvet voice might up and leave while his computer looped through random overwrites of each incriminating byte. And he wanted to read through the exchange again. To study Chagall's responses, to mull them over. Compromising, Christopher let his fingers fly, encrypting the file as temporary protection. He could follow the protocol later.

As the machine shut down he snuck another peek. The woman wore a thin gold necklace, no rings, and she didn't look up. Her ears were small, accented by a pair of dangling pearls. An intricately lacquered barrette held her jet-black hair. Her newspaper wasn't the *Chronicle* or the *New York Times*. Not the *Washington Post* either. Puzzling. Between layout and typeface he usually recognized broadsheets at a glance. When the laptop powered off, Christopher snapped the clamshell shut. He looked up again and met her gaze.

"Done with all that, then?"

"Sorry to be distracted." He scooted over to the table beside hers, still out of the webcam's range, and nodded at her newspaper. "What paper are you reading?" he asked. "It doesn't look familiar."

She raised a quizzical eyebrow. "*Sunday Times.*"

The penny dropped. Her accent. "Are you from London, then?"

"Brighton, really. I went to university in London. Do you know newspapers by gestalt?"

"I do layout for a living," he said, waving a hand vaguely. "You get sensitized. But why the Sunday paper on a Friday?"

She shrugged. "The news is stale, but Fridays are when I have time to catch up with what's going on back home."

"I've never visited the UK."

"But you inhabit the language. And the music? The Beatles, Elton John . . ."

Christopher smiled uncertainly. He didn't want to give a dull impression, but a taste for pretentiously obscure bands wouldn't flatter him either. "I've listened to my share of the Beatles," he said. "Though the truth is I lean more toward the Clash."

She examined him for a moment. "The Clash politically, or the Clash musically?"

"All around, I guess."

"When I came to this country a couple of years ago I landed in Kentucky," she said. "I have an aunt in Lexington. I didn't sense the Clash got a lot of play in the bluegrass state."

"I can imagine. Are you visiting, or is San Francisco home now?"

"I'm in medical school, at UCSF. You?"

"Born and raised in the Bay Area."

"I haven't seen you here. At the Daily Grind, I mean."

"I live in a funkier part of the city," Christopher said. "Well, it was funkier before the dot-com bubble. Maybe we'll get our groove back now that all that's over. Anyway, I don't often get out to the Marina. My name is Chris, by the way." He offered his hand.

"Suvali," she said. "Pleased to meet you."

Her hand was slim, delicately boned, but her grip was stronger than he expected. Christopher couldn't place her in the café before Chagall came online, but that didn't prove anything, let alone that she was an agent assigned to watch his IRC. He wasn't going to get worked up over baseless conjecture. Suvali was a friendly medical student, looking to talk about something other than malpractice insurance. End of story.

"I'm sorry I interrupted you earlier," she was saying.

"It was nothing."

"I have a brother who gets wound up over his computer."

"I—really, I'm not like that."

Suvali laughed. "But you were! You reminded me of Satveer, exactly."

"Is he a gamer?" Christopher couldn't imagine striking up a conversation with anyone who evoked his own brother. But his family was a special case.

"Oh, no. Satveer liked that stuff when he was a kid, but now it's all programming for banks and government ministries."

"Well, I couldn't program my way out of a wet paper bag. Rehashing glory days with your college roommate isn't exactly programming for banks."

"It looked very intense. But why don't you just phone?"

Christopher reached for the name he'd made up just minutes before. "Paul lives in Australia," he said, "so between the time zones and the cost of a call . . ." He needed to change the subject. "Don't you e-mail back to England?"

"Sure, but e-mail is like writing letters. 'Dear Mom, the

weather's terrific in California, wish you were here.' It doesn't pull you into the screen the way internet chat does."

Christopher flinched. Seven years on, but he still shied at even the most oblique assumption that he, too, had a living mother. "Everybody has a nomination for most annoying technology," he said. "For me it's cell phones. I refuse to carry one. I even hate to call people on their own cells."

"Really?" When she tilted her head, the pearls in her ears swung like eager little pendulums. "Why is that?"

"You never know what you're interrupting."

"But it's on them, really, for picking up."

He shrugged. "The interaction makes me feel clumsy."

Suvali smiled as if to herself. Christopher wondered if she'd pegged him that way already.

"I guess—I suppose London must be calling," he said. "I should leave you to your paper. Maybe I'll branch out this way again."

"Maybe I'll be 'behind the *Times*' if you do."

"Friday afternoons at the Daily Grind?"

"So long as the weather's nice enough for walking. I like to get some distance from the med center on my days off."

Christopher gathered his things, wondering whether she could really be interested in some random buffoon banging on a laptop. Maybe he did remind Suvali of a brother. Could that be a good thing?

He took his leave, wound through the tables, then turned back at the door. She was watching. She'd caught his eye, they had talked, she was watching as he left the café. He waved, and she returned his salute.

Suvali.

He wondered.

As he turned onto Chestnut Street, he was giddy with wondering.

T W O

October 2003

Chagall rolls up his ski mask, listening to the guard's Jeep recede down the logging road. A crisp autumn breeze dries the sweat from his face. The engine's noise echoes faintly off an escarpment to the north and west.

He stands and stretches. Chagall scatters brush across his spy post, and turns to the equipment yard across a scraped and graveled clearing. Halogen lights illuminate feller bunchers, grapple skidders, brush cutters, and knuckle-boom loaders inside the locked compound. Mud-crusted instruments of pillage and blight. Facing the cold steel, what he sees is slaughter. These ponderous beasts have ripped forests whole from the living Earth. In the quiet, Chagall hears an echo of venerable trees screaming.

Donning a pair of thin gloves, he circles to the back corner of the yard. Chain-link fencing gives way to his wire cutters. He snips a vertical incision, two feet off the ground. Then another, parallel to the first. The tool bites into the woodland hush, sharp and steady as a metronome.

A six-cylinder thrum, rising. The saboteur freezes.

The Jeep's engine is getting louder, straining back up the hill, close enough already that he should see headlights ripping across the trunks of mill-bound trees. There are no headlights. The guard is driving dark.

Chagall steps back from the fence, scanning to see how well its vertical tension hides the damage already done. He pockets the cutters, grabs his pack, and beats a retreat beyond the reach of the compound's lights.

The security vehicle clatters over road ballast and lurches to a stop. Chagall breathes humidly through his ski mask, crouching behind a manzanita thicket. The rent-a-cop shines a spotlight on the gate and its intact lock, then sweeps the equipment inside. A grapple skidder stands between Chagall's handiwork and the Jeep. It's the same guard as last night and the night before that, a slope-shouldered hulk with a wrestler's low center of gravity.

Chagall has been casing the site for three nights running, hiking in from a camouflaged campsite six miles south and east. Tonight is the first time the guard doubled back to the yard.

The uniformed man emerges from his vehicle, leaving the engine running. Swinging a flashlight as long as his forearm, he paces the length of fence. The beam skims a half-million in heavy machinery. Not a close inspection. His attention is slack, he's following a boss's orders. The poor bastard's job is tedious until the moment it's not.

The guard remounts his Jeep and guns away into the dark.

Chagall settles himself behind the manzanita. Best to wait a good long while before finishing his business.

—

Tonight he's putting a different spin on routine that has played out hundreds of times, in a dozen variations, over decades. Chagall's motive has little to do with gumming up the work of a local gang of forest slayers.

Like others before him, he has wrecked diesels up and down

the coast to hinder insatiable lumbermen. He has broken mink and chinchilla out of factory-farm prisons, burned construction sites at the edge of city sprawl, toppled electrical towers that rip through remote wilderness. Popgun sabotage, all of it. He understands by now that industry hardly registers a solo saboteur's attacks. It doesn't matter where in the great chain of annihilation Chagall and those like him strike. The predators ignore their toothless nibbling.

Chagall has always acted alone, planning for as long as precision takes. Opportunities to partner up are easy to find online, but saboteurs in his mold have proven over decades of eluding law enforcement that their best protections are isolation and independence. Chagall shuns unknown quantities sniffing around his avatars on the net. Or he did, always, until several months before. At the tail end of summer, a digital phantom who signed off with the naked letter "R" approached with a bold proposal. Romulus, as Chagall calls him in the privacy of his own mind, has set his sights not only on a high-value target, but on a new paradigm. Information, Romulus writes, is more volatile than gasoline, and he can hack an online media blast at thermonuclear scale. A brick-and-mortar attack that means little in and of itself might loft a propaganda blitz to heights Chagall can never realize solo. Or so he claims.

Romulus offered proof of his skills. A series of artful database incursions yielded confidential medical records belonging to executives of a half-dozen corporations, demonstrating not only ability, but also willingness to step farther over the line than an undercover lawman would dare.

But even if Romulus isn't card-carrying FBI, he could be an unmasked hacker run by a clever cop. Just as risky, he might be wet behind the ears. A postcollegiate misfit with little experience outside his electronic playground. Or a habitué of darkened rooms, surrounded by multiple screens and frustrated by the limits of his virtual reach.

Unwilling to trust any partner, Chagall has chosen their political focus himself: genetic engineering, for the scale of its threat and the readiness of an opposition movement to crystallize. Romulus initiated their conspiracy, but Chagall will pick their target too. He'll demand further criminal proofs of the hacker, and he'll draft the communication that will follow in the wake of their physical attack. It occurs to him, as he waits to be sure the rent-a-cop is done with feints and dodges, that he ought to recruit a third-party writer, neither Romulus nor himself. Their political justification should be drafted in someone else's voice.

How much will he need to expose to the hacker? What will Romulus guess about him? That he's a disaffected child of the cities, radicalized by liberal arts faculty at some obscure university? A forest-loving solitary, maddened by encounters with clear-cut? A farm boy disgusted by life indentured to poultry processors, trained as an Army sapper, embittered by officers blind to his talents?

Any of a hundred stories that lead to fury might be ascribed to Romulus or himself. Psychological profiling is useless to cops and saboteurs alike. Chagall could have come from anywhere, could have been almost anything, before he burrowed underground. The same is true of the anonymous bit jockey, who will get a taste tonight of what Chagall can do.

———

He listens from his manzanita blind, but registers only nocturnal scurrying through fog-dampened duff, only a breeze sliding through treetops across the land's dips and curves. The valley is haunted by emptiness that persists long after men and equipment knock off for the day. The sound of wildlife ebbing. No trace remains of elk like those Chagall stalked as a boy, never mind the bears and wolves that flourished before his time.

A winged thud and a tiny, terrified scream roil the stillness. A long-eared owl on nightly rounds, he guesses, or perhaps a great gray. Another deer mouse plucked from nest and litter. He is brutally comforted. The web is not wholly wrecked.

Gathering his equipment, Chagall approaches the compound again. He completes the rectangular breach, bends back the wire fence, and hoists his pack through the opening. Rubber overshoes, same as the plunderers wear, ensure that even his footprints leave no clue.

Crude matériel has no place in his repertoire. He won't haul jugs of gasoline, or shovel sand into crankcases. He's beyond cutting brake lines and slashing tires. Garden-variety monkeywrenching is useful enough, and he is unashamed to have done his share. But Chagall now plays for higher stakes.

Selecting a brush cutter alongside the fence, Chagall jimmies open its gas cap, releasing a cloud of refined petrochemicals. A tool he has forged for the purpose catches on a filter set deep in the fill pipe. Twisting, Chagall reams open the tank's throat.

He removes a handcrafted device from his pack, and inspects its timer and trigger. His hands are sure as he fastens wires to a soldered cradle, yet Chagall performs the rites of war attentively, as if this were his first time in the field. Exactness is all that stands between success and martyrdom. He slots a blasting cap into place, and slides a gauze sleeve over the cradle to guard against accidental sparks. Now he lowers the device into the brush cutter's fill pipe, pulling back a centimeter when the detonator touches liquid.

He repeats his drill, rigging two knuckle-boom loaders farther down the row, then a clot of skidders at the center of the yard.

—

At just shy of three thirty Chagall circles the perimeter, checking for evidence he doesn't mean to leave behind. The timers are counting down to four fifteen. Satisfied, he shoulders a lightened pack and exits the way he came in.

There's no need to wait for the fireworks. He'll see the glow as he crests the southern ridge, heading deeper into the wild than heavily equipped pursuers can follow.

THREE

Sprawled against the trunk of a budding sycamore, Brendan James watched the Triangle's front porch through half-shut eyes. He was scrawny as a speed freak, gritty as Duboce Avenue used to be before the neighborhood gentrified. Mothers with toddlers, hipsters with iPods, even the occasional gutter punk stepped around him gingerly, hugging the inside edge of the sidewalk. No one answered the collective's doorbell when he'd rung, maybe a half hour before. He didn't mind. He wouldn't say prison had been an enriching experience, but Tlaxitlán sure as hell taught him to wait.

After a while longer, Jonah turned the corner, sun glinting over his long blond hair. He'd grown it out just like his mom's, Brendan thought. And he was taller by a foot since Brendan last passed through San Francisco. Approaching home, Jonah scowled at nothing in the manner of coddled *norteamericanos* who have little to scowl about, and scuffed clear of Brendan's legs. Didn't even look up.

Brendan cleared his throat as the kid fumbled for a key. Jonah stopped. Turned. Looked like he was deciding whether the sun-scorched man outside his gate posed an actual threat.

Crusty denim and muddy boots. Reddish stubble blurring bony features. Hair cut to bristle.

"Where the hell've you been, kid?"

He watched recognition dawn as he stood and let himself grin. Joy, incredulity, and cool battled for ascendancy in Jonah's face. The boy stood paralyzed, hand hanging slack in his pocket. Brendan did the math. Thirteen years old. "How 'bout you open the gate, Jonah Rayle?" He stepped forward to wrap Allison's son in a bear hug. "I gotta take a wicked piss."

Jonah laughed. "Nobody said you were coming. Nobody even told me they let you out of . . . Mexico. Does Chris know?"

Brendan shrugged and turned to his beat up motorbike, parked by the driveway. He unbuckled a pair of saddlebags.

"That's all?"

"You know me," Brendan said. "He who travels light—"

"—travels far." Jonah held the metal gate open, then let it clang shut behind them.

Brendan winced at the sound of steel on steel, of the latch snicking into place. He forced his breath steady. The kid hadn't meant to startle him.

He stood aside as Jonah unlocked the inner door, at the bottom of the Triangle's steep staircase.

———

"Cheers," Jonah said, raising a bottle of ginger beer and keeping his voice low. They were sitting at the table in the third-floor kitchen, an artifact of the building's past life as separate flats, and a mindful distance from where Marty lay sleeping downstairs.

"To long-awaited Ithakas." Brendan tilted his porter in Jonah's direction. The kid looked puzzled but let it go. "So Marty's been sacked out all afternoon, you think?"

"The bathroom looked like a slasher movie before Mom and Nora took him to the emergency room. Mom said he got eight stitches."

"From a bike accident? And now he's sleeping off painkillers?"

"I guess so. But if he heard you ring the bell he probably thought it was Jehovah's Witnesses." Jonah reached for a bag of tortilla chips.

"Damn . . ." A single frying pan and a lightly rusted wok hung from the rack over the stove. A dented kettle sat atop a back burner. It looked to Brendan as though no one had cooked a meal in the upstairs kitchen for ages. "So what else is news around here?"

"Nora was on TV twice after they lost the case of those guys in Eureka," Jonah said around a mouthful of chips. "Those protesters who got pepper sprayed at that congressman's office? She's doing an appeal."

"Doesn't the Triangle have a ban on TVs?"

"It's not a ban," Jonah said. "We just have better things to do with our time."

Brendan laughed. "You sound like you're training to be a press spokesman."

"Ha ha. We watched Nora on the internet, I can find it again if you want. Did you know Gregor moved in downstairs?"

"That kid with crazy-long dreadlocks?"

"He's going to City College now. Gregor cut off his dreads when he moved into the downstairs flat. He might shave the rest, like Marty, and get a tattoo on his head. It's supposed to hurt, but at least he can grow his hair back."

"Guess it's too early to worry about male pattern baldness," Brendan said. "So what's Marty up to besides getting stitches in that thick skull of his? Is he still doing computer support for that healthcare outfit?"

"Yeah, same job."

"Chris never mentioned Nora's pepper spray case," Brendan said. "But he kept me going, really, all the stories he sent about you guys."

"What did he write about me?"

Brendan thought for a moment. "How everybody flipped somersaults about picking out your middle school."

Jonah rolled his eyes. "Yeah, it's bad enough if you have only two parents."

"So where's Chris now? At the *Reporter*?"

"I don't think so. Friday he's usually off work."

"Anyway." Brendan knocked back a mouthful of porter. "The house must be feeling pretty empty these days."

Jonah was tapping a complex rhythm on the tabletop.

"Only six of you left."

"Yeah."

Brendan saw he was meant to ask about the performance. "Last time I was here you were way into skateboards. Now you're taking up drums?"

"Tabla," Jonah said, withdrawing his hands. "Ever since this guy Ravi Shankar it's this major instrument for Indian music."

"You know, your mom and I saw him in a concert over in Berkeley, when we were in college." When we were lovers, he thought, and wondered whether he should have said that, whether Allison had already clued her son in. The Triangle made a conscious practice of welcoming Jonah into fully adult membership in the collective. Not pushing him, but not boxing him into an airbrushed childhood either.

"Seriously?" Jonah asked. "You guys saw Ravi Shankar live?"

"At the Greek Theatre," Brendan said.

"I can't believe Mom never told me that. You know Zac's really into mythology stories from India, right? He took me to see this movie, *The Mahabharata*. It lasted all day, but they had an intermission for lunch and we went to this awesome *chaat* place. After that we went to a bunch more Bollywood movies. The love stories are corny, but the war ones are crisp. You can get the soundtracks as MP3s."

Brendan must have looked puzzled, because Jonah began explaining the craze for music over the internet. He might as well have been speaking in tongues. Compression protocols, Grokster, Kazaa, LimeWire, 64-bit players, the RCAA.

"How's your mom doing?" Brendan asked after a pause. "You guys getting along okay?"

"Yeah, I guess." Jonah glanced at the clock over the stove. "She'll be home from the preschool around five."

"What kind of political work is she doing?"

"Um . . . death penalty, genetic engineered food, stuff like that. And she's teaching karate at the dojo." Jonah grimaced. "My dad had to get a new job after his dot-com went broke, but it didn't matter because of stock options from the one before that."

"Since when are you interested in finance?" Brendan was careful to mask his irritation. Never mind that Seth had stolen Allison's heart. They'd been young, freer then with love and loyalty. But the fact that Seth had ditched her and the kid both, not four years later—it still made him want to smack Jonah's father.

"I'm just sayin'. Dad talks about stocks all the time, Mom says I pick it up like lint."

Jonah emptied his bottle and jumped up to put it in the recycling bin. Opening the refrigerator, he stared inside for a while. Then he closed it again. He poured a glass of filtered water from a pitcher on the counter and sat back down.

"What about you?" Jonah rubbed an imaginary spot from his glass. "What was it like in . . . where you were?"

Brendan looked out at the backyards behind Hermann Street, at satellite dishes aimed into a sky ribbed with wispy clouds. "Lonely," he said, doing his best to sound cavalier. "Hungry. Boring more than anything else." He tongued a space in his mouth where there'd once been a premolar, until a guard they called El Dentista performed unsolicited surgery with a right hook.

"What—so—why did they bust you?" Jonah was asking. "What was in the truck?"

Brendan held the boy's eyes for a moment. Jonah looked back at him, steady and assured. He knew exactly what he'd asked. "Radio equipment," Brendan said. "Medical supplies. Stuff like that."

"For the people in Chiapas, right? For Subcomandante Marcos?"

Brendan shrugged, looking away again. "For the Federales. That's who took it in the end." The Mexican government couldn't touch him now, but it wasn't easy to shake rigidly schooled habit. His lawyer could never have cut deals for a gringo revolutionary.

"But—"

Brendan knew what Jonah really wanted to ask.

The press in Oaxaca reported that he'd been carrying more weaponry than could fit in a fleet of pickups, let alone the single truck he'd been driving. It was anybody's guess what Jonah had been told, or what he'd found online.

"It's over," Brendan said. "It doesn't matter anymore." He watched the light fade in Jonah's eyes. Himself, diminishing. "I'm not even sure I know the facts myself."

Jonah sat still. "Whatever."

"It's not like they tell you anything. The cops, the system. The real business happens in a judge's office, to spare everybody the embarrassment of passing bribes around in open court." Brendan imagined how he must sound to the boy. Lame. But it was true: he'd been locked up fourteen months and still had no idea how he'd been screwed, or by whom.

"If they . . ." Jonah swallowed. "If you don't know what's going on, how can you decide what to do?"

"I'm not sure I get what you mean."

"Everybody protests one thing, then some other thing. Mom and everybody else goes to million-hour meetings. People get beat up by the cops, you get majorly busted. And nobody knows what's going on? What's the logic of that?"

"Those are hard questions, kid. Hard questions with long, convoluted answers."

"Dad says we're tilting at windmills. Like Don Quixote."

"Some people think anything that's not about self-interest is foolish." Brendan sighed. "I don't think that, and neither does your mom, or Chris, or anybody else at the Triangle. Maybe Seth is still trying to talk himself out of something he once believed in. Maybe stock options are the windmills."

Jonah looked down. "I better do homework," he said.

"Okay." Brendan wondered if he'd overstepped.

Jonah pushed away from the table and disappeared into his bedroom, a converted porch between the kitchen and the back stairs. He shut the door behind him, harder than he needed to.

———

Brendan tiptoed through the second floor for a cigarette out back. When he returned upstairs an Indian raga was floating down the hallway from Jonah's room. He turned to the front of the building. A wall had been knocked out since his last visit, sacrificing the old guest quarters to expand space used for meetings. Little else had changed since the collective connected the building's top two floors some ten years before, shortly after moving in. Brendan recognized the same leaky sofas, the beanbag pillows sewn out of remnants from Berkeley's now-defunct Fabric Land, a scarred coffee table. Opposite the fireplace, a Che poster hung in the same aluminum frame that once graced the Carleton Street kitchen, south of the campus. Where he and Allison had shared the sunny front bedroom, and still believed that her talent for galvanizing a crowd of students on Sproul Plaza vaulted them into some utopian vanguard.

Neatly bundled wires snaked out from pocket doors that separated the front room from the collective's library. Brendan examined them closely. The bundles ran along the molding and fanned out to tiny polypropylene speakers fixed to the bay windows. Like translucent jellyfish, he thought. The setup had to be Marty's. Part of his endless snoop-proofing, not that the Triangle ever discussed political secrets in the house.

He leaned against a window frame and idly counted BMWs parked along the curb out front, then along Sanchez Street around the corner. After Oaxaca, Brendan felt the city's wealth as an almost physical hurt. On the sidewalk his battered Kawasaki seemed to wriggle and wave through the sagging windowpanes. A dark-haired woman paused to stare quizzically at the bike. It took a moment through the foreshortened perspective for him to recognize Nora coming home at the end of a workday. All kitted out in lawyer's drag.

He listened as she climbed the stairs. A thread of familiar inflection whispered up through the floorboards. Marty was awake, then. Brendan took a deep breath. He crossed toward the staircase and began to descend. Nora must have heard him. She stood in the hallway, stifling a cry when he came into view.

"What?" Marty asked from their room.

"It's okay," she called back to him.

Always disciplined, Brendan thought. He drank her in, her hand slowly sinking away from her face to reveal dimpled cheeks that softened the severe, analytical set to her mouth. Like coming into harbor, back among his oldest friends. He stepped off the last stair and opened his arms wide. Nora nearly squeezed the life out of him, neither of them making a sound. Then she led him into the dim bedroom.

"Marty," she said.

"Mmmmph."

The invalid's eyes were covered. Dim light shone off his shaven head. Brendan couldn't see the bandages from where he stood in the doorway.

"Marty, don't sit up. You don't have to move, even. Brendan is here."

"Brendan?" Marty fumbled the towel away from his face. Nora pulled Brendan to his bedside. "Jesus Christ, boy, where'd you come from?"

"Thought I'd head north for a spell. Jonah let me in."

"Fuck, Brendan."

"Yeah. At least that. What's with the Mad Max act?"

"Stupid," Marty said. "Tourist in a Land Rover came up on me, wheel slipped into the gap along the Muni rails. Fucking inelegant."

"We can have a contest. You'll win on stitches but I'm gonna kick your ass on days out of commission."

"They let you out?"

"It's a long, crooked story. Plenty of time for all that later."

Nora let go of his hand, reluctantly, Brendan thought. As if she were afraid he would fade as suddenly as he'd reappeared. "When was your last pain pill?" she asked Marty, pulling a prescription bottle out of the chaos beside the bed.

"Two thirty, maybe. I'm done with 'em, it's like thinking through sand."

"Percocet?" Brendan asked.

"Vicodin," Nora said. "The hard stuff. Do you hurt now, Marty?"

"The stitches sting. Everything else is just cramped up. Nothing a drop of whiskey wouldn't fix."

Someone was coming up the stairs. Nora cocked her head. "Allison," she said.

Brendan straightened. She stopped at the landing, then approached the bedroom door. As she entered, her mouth puckered, words all but formed. No sound came. Brendan watched her register his emaciated frame. The same sharp attention Jonah had shown; Allison had taught him that.

He couldn't say whether she'd changed. Brendan thought he detected a faint etching at the corners of her steady blue eyes, a crease beside her mouth that might have been new. Perhaps it was only the light. She stood as easy and sure as ever.

> With beauty like a tightened bow, a kind
> that is not natural in an age like this,
> Being high and solitary and most stern . . .

Yeats, but he couldn't put his finger on the title. Maud Gonne cast as Helen.

Allison broke the silence. "When?" she asked.

"Last week. Mom dragged me home for a few days, to fatten me up."

She made an overt show of inspecting him now, head to toe. "Your mom's a good cook. She couldn't do any better than that?"

"Cut me some slack, okay?"

She set down a canvas bag and gathered him in, holding on as tightly as Jonah had, and Nora, only longer. "You could have called when you got past the border," Allison rebuked him softly.

The smell of her hair, after all that time.

"I . . . I picked up the phone, Al. More than once. I couldn't think what to say."

FOUR

Christopher took the first outbound train that came through Montgomery Station, disembarking at Church Street. The short stretch from Market to Duboce was packed as ever.

Marty had taken his spill somewhere on these blocks. Christopher didn't see any stains on the asphalt that screamed "bike accident," though there were plenty of candidates. One could have been the dregs of somebody's mocha, another a spilled ice cream cone, several the dirt-crusted drippings from leaky oil pans. One furry patch by the inbound J line tracks looked suspiciously like flattened rat. What goes down on a busy city street fades fast, he thought.

Christopher pushed through a knotted crowd where the Muni lines surface from their downtown tunnel, and turned out of the human riptide. The pedestrian crush thinned just a few steps into the Duboce Triangle, the neighborhood from which his collective had taken its name. Three-story Edwardians extended granite steps from worn front stoops; scruffier stucco buildings slumped and peeled as if mourning their once-splendid flats, now carved into cramped apartments. An N train screeched up the gentle grade, too heavy for its rails.

The way those pearls swung from her earlobes.

What was he supposed to do? It seemed wrong to obsess over Suvali when he should be worrying about Chagall. But did that even make sense? He'd punted hard choices on trusting the saboteur by declaring the manifesto a personal writing project. For now. So did he owe it to Chagall to avoid the café, and Suvali because she could place him there? Or would precaution at that pitch be neurotic? How could he weigh promises about Chagall's security against the uncertainty that anything even happened at the Daily Grind? Suvali could have been making idle conversation. He could have misread her signals through a fog of wishful thinking. It wouldn't have been the first time.

Christopher unlocked the security gate that screened the Triangle's entrance from the street, then stepped across the narrow stoop to let himself in. A tangle of voices tumbled down the stairwell as he shut the door behind him. Strange. He'd expected to find Marty suffering one hell of a headache, and the collective walking on eggshells. Upstairs, Marty and Nora's door was open, a lamp burning beside their empty bed. Christopher ducked into his own room, easing the bag off his shoulder. Zac's giddy laugh echoed down the hallway, followed by a riposte he didn't try to make out. Sharp red pepper and an earthy richness of fermented black beans wafted in from the kitchen. Christopher caught a swirl of Marty's baritone and sprays of Jonah's sorties in the jumble. Then a long-missing voice.

Christopher listened.

There—again. He couldn't catch the words. But the voice was Brendan's. Damned if it wasn't, mellifluous and rough, and completely unexpected. He slipped into the hall.

Their long-absent comrade sat with his back to the doorway, rail thin, hair clipped to a thin wash of rust over his sunburned skull. Conversation faded as the others noticed Christopher standing there. Allison eased back in her customary chair at the head of the dining table, suppressing a smile. Brendan turned. "Look at you," he said, breaking into a grin. "Like a bigmouth bass that just got a taste of hook."

"Look at you," Christopher countered, winding up to ask how the weather had been in Dachau that morning. But he couldn't get the words out. Brendan stood and they embraced. Like late-stage AIDS, Christopher thought, appalled by the knobby fleshlessness beneath his friend's loose clothes.

"Jayzus and Mary, fellas." Marty doffed his ice pack. "Break it up before somebody starts weepin' again."

"Martin, be still." Zac's voice quavered. He stood in the kitchen doorway, a checkered apron tied over a plain white kurta he favored for meditation, his long hair gathered in a bun. A few leaves of cilantro clung to the chef's knife held loosely at his side.

Zac's emotion echoed Christopher's own shock. They all knew that Brendan had set out to do right by the *indígenas* in Chiapas. Now he was . . . wrecked. Was that the prize for graduating from political theatrics to real resistance?

"Somebody better set that table," Nora called from the kitchen.

Responding to her calm authority, a tone her friends had come to know and love long before Nora sharpened it up in law school, Gregor jumped to answer her summons. Christopher hadn't noticed him sitting quietly in a corner, drawn upstairs by the commotion, he figured. Gregor had visited the Triangle with his moms countless times over the years, for meetings and banner painting and holiday dinners. He was already at home amid the collective's chaos by the time he moved into the first-floor flat at the start of his freshman year. Without the dreads he had cultivated since elementary school, and still carrying traces of a chubby boyhood, Gregor somehow reminded Christopher of a lost puppy. Disoriented but hopeful. Pushed by a look from Allison, Jonah followed Gregor into the kitchen.

Nora brought out a six-pack of Chinese lager and set it on the table. "Go easy," she urged as Marty reached for a bottle. "Save it for dinner?"

He retreated with a sigh. "They don't even let you mix drink with downers anymore."

Christopher edged behind Marty and took the corner chair beside him. Brendan returned to his seat at Allison's left. From the opposite side of the table, Christopher watched for signs of Brendan's perennial hope that he and Allison might rekindle their long-dormant relationship. She had rebuffed Christopher only once, gently but certainly. He had pretended it was the tequila talking at that party they'd thrown on Carleton Street some dozen years before. Then he had buried his feelings, unwilling to risk their friendship in pursuit of hopeless romance. "I'm amazed to see you sitting up," Christopher said to Marty.

"Ah, it's just a little bump," his injured housecomrade replied, touching his bandages gingerly.

"The hell," Zac said, on his way back to the stove. "Resurrection is contagious at the Triangle tonight!"

—

Amid the chaos of Marty's bike accident no one had cooked the night before, so Nora and Zac had the run of the Seaside Organics delivery. They emptied the weekly co-op box in Brendan's honor, making fried rice with black trumpet mushrooms, spicy new potatoes with black beans and scallions, hot and sour bok choy topped with garlicky breadcrumbs, and fresh noodles stir-fried with squash, red cabbage, and water chestnuts.

Zac set the last steaming platter on the table, untied his apron, and sat opposite Christopher. Nora clinked a fork against her plate and nodded to Marty at the foot of the table. The mob fell more or less silent, as Marty raised his bottle high. "Brendan," he began, "welcome back to the land of the living."

"Hear, hear," Zac said, tilting his lager in Brendan's direction. Marty mimed solemnity for a few long seconds. "However," he said. "However. If you pull a stunt like that again—if you ever again talk yourself into carrying contraband across a national border, north or south, for good reason or on a fool's errand? I'll have no choice but to hunt you down, skin you with a dull knife, and tan your hide myself."

"I'm in," Allison said. They all drank.

"I'll help too, if Marty scrapes the meat off first."

"What meat? Look at him!"

"Let's just hope he's not actually rehabilitated."

Brendan's voice emerged out of the cacophony. "You greedy *cochinos*," he said, an impious glitter in his eye. Platters and chatter stilled. Christopher put his appetite on hold, and sat back to watch the performance. "The food on this table would feed twice as many people three times as many meals where I just came from, and never once—not one single time—did I eat even the humblest supper in the great state of Oaxaca without first saying grace."

Ahead of the inevitable groans, Gregor's arm shot straight up, an intrusion of classroom etiquette so startling that Brendan yielded the floor without argument. Gregor bowed his head over a chipped yellow plate and mismatched silverware.

Nora rolled her eyes. "I trust your mothers raised you better than to pray in mixed company," she whispered across the table.

"We thank our lucky stars that Nora and Zac don't cook like Stalinists," Gregor began, whereupon Brendan cut him off with a fervent and categorical "Amen."

The decibel level dropped as they turned to the business of eating. Christopher kept an eye on the far end of the table. Was he trying to charm her already? Was she letting him?

Between mouthfuls, the prodigal fielded questions. "There

was nothing to do. Nothing but read and gamble. Most guys stayed loaded on knockoff pharmaceuticals. The big excitement happened when they herded us into the courtyard for a search. This whistle blew, like an underpowered freight train, and in seconds you'd have guys frantically swallowing every pill in the prison. I don't think the guards ever once found drugs they didn't plant themselves."

"Did they house you with the other politicals?" Nora asked.

"They lock up hard-core Zapatistas in a prison outside Tuxtla Gutiérrez," Brendan said. "Maybe five hundred kilometers east. In Tlaxitlán the politicals were local Oaxacans, most of them *simpático* with the movement in Chiapas. Anyway, they had their own tank and the guards didn't like mixing. As for me, I wasn't broadcasting what drew me south."

"Why not?" Allison asked.

Nora drew back in her chair. "Wouldn't housing in the political tank have been safer?"

Brendan cast a questioning glance in Christopher's direction. The women were grilling him about plain and simple prudence. "Just the opposite in my situation," he said. "The safest thing was for nobody to be sure who I was or what I was doing down there. For all kinds of rumors to fester."

"Were there other Americans?" Allison asked, setting down her fork. "Other American politicals?"

Christopher watched uneasily. Brendan had dropped plenty of hints in letters shared with everyone in the Triangle. He'd walked a thin line in Tlaxitlán.

"There were a few gringos," Brendan said, "but not the type that go south for solidarity work. I steered clear. Hung with the Spanish-speakers and hid behind the language barrier. Like I said, attracting attention would have . . . complicated things."

Allison frowned and went back to her dinner.

Everybody just ate for a while.

"There was this one *cabrón*," Brendan said. "This guy who called himself Tex."

Zac let out a high-pitched laugh. "Oh, please," he objected.

"No, I swear. Who knows what was on his passport, but Tex was the name this guy went by. Sixty-something, skinny and mean, a right-wing, badly lapsed evangelical. Busted for running drugs, like most of the guys. Had a crazy line on anything, like this theory that coded messages in *The International Jew* proved the Israelis are running the whole South American continent as a training ground for Mossad. Sixteen, eighteen hours a day, the guy never shut up. Brawls, whores, vengeance, betrayal. Sneaking kids over the border with heroin-filled balloons in their bellies. Weapons transport to the Contras in Nicaragua. A real poster boy for twentieth-century imperialism."

"So what happened to him?" Gregor asked.

"Tex pissed off a guard. Got his jaw busted, then they threw him in the hole."

The room went quiet for a moment. Christopher couldn't begin to imagine the world Brendan had endured. Day after day, every moment taut with the threat of feral violence.

"Come to think of it," Zac said, "a guy named Tex used to hang out at Emily's when I was bar-backing there. Rangy guy, with wrinkles like he'd been hung up between a couple cactuses and left out to evaporate. And an overbite from hell. The dykes around the pool table used to call him 'Faxman'—'Hey, Faxman, stripey-nine to the corner.'" Zac mimed a sheet of paper sliding out from under his upper lip.

They all laughed. "Different Tex, for sure," Brendan said. "Tlaxitlán Tex had crooked little teeth, eaten away by shitty plug tobacco."

Jonah wrinkled his nose. "That's disgusting," he said. "What happened after they put him in the hole?"

"We never saw him again. It all came down around a major shakeout, some bureaucratic thing rippling out of Mexico City. A few guys speculated they were going to let him out off the books so they transferred him north, closer to the border."

"Pass the noodles to Brendan," Allison said.

Nora reached for the bowl. "And the veggies," she said. "The rice too."

"Nora, Zac, this dinner's phenomenal," Brendan said. "If y'all are kind enough to let me stay on for a bit I'll be a gringo *gordo* in no time."

Allison placed a hand over his. "You're always welcome, Brendan."

Christopher's breath caught. His autonomic response was eclipsed by a chorus of agreement, but not before Zac noticed, his elfin features brightening with alert sympathy. Then the moment passed. Christopher corked his untenable sensitivities, and Zac looked away.

FIVE

Surrounded by bookshelves, the oak table in the Triangle's library lay buried under drifts of newspaper and stacks of flyers that had accreted in the week since Christopher's chat with Chagall. On March twentieth, the anniversary of the war, he was working through an outline for his manifesto, and missing the march from Dolores Park to the Civic Center. Zac had said he didn't mind a housecomrade bailing on his speech at the kickoff, but the small disloyalty gnawed at Christopher. He typed a citation from *Scientific American* into his growing bibliography. Balancing the convenience of research at home against Chagall's paranoia, he made no handwritten notes. Encrypted bytes and the table's scatter were the only traces of his labor.

Christopher wasn't the only one skipping the march. In the week since his return, Brendan had never once gotten up before noon. From the guest room he'd been broadcasting prison-inflected nightmares, a hallucinatory soundscape of muffled shouts and moans reverberating along the second-floor hallway in the wee hours of morning. Tangled in his covers, Christopher would hear Brendan pacing around the dining room at two or three or four a.m., his cramped trajectories perturbed by forays to the back porch for long, brooding smokes. Brendan sometimes paused at the foot of the stairs—thinking—thinking what?—that he should try his luck with Allison?

In any event, Brendan wasn't going to surprise him that morning in the library. Christopher would hear him coming. And even if the entire collective were looking over his shoulder there would be no need to hide. With the GeneSynth actions less than six weeks away, it wouldn't surprise anyone to find Christopher buried in focused reading about biotech agriculture. He was drafting his own manifesto, after all. Not Chagall's. For now, anyway.

He was finding plenty to cull from the household clippings file on genetically modified organisms. Just that week reports had emerged of Mexican farms tainted by the spread of GMO corn. Nora had clipped and initialed a wire-service article that told an even broader tale:

> Over two-thirds of traditionally cultivated seeds for major US food crops are contaminated with engineered DNA, according to a study sponsored by the Union of Concerned Scientists. The results point to the failure of methods currently used to segregate genetically modified seeds from unmodified varieties.

Christopher cited the article in his outline as fodder for "human impact on environment." When a door opened downstairs he lifted his fingers from the keyboard. Another door closed. The pipes rattled as Brendan started the shower. Then the phone rang, and he reached over his laptop to answer it.

"Chris? It's your father."

"Hey, Dad, long time." He neatened the clippings file, cradling the phone against his shoulder. "What's up?"

"It's been a while, I suppose. How are you? I've missed a few issues of the *Reporter*; any big stories lately?"

"Nothing major." Christopher registered a labored undertone in his father's interest, and wondered how many years Professor Kalman meant by "a few issues." "How's the lab?" he asked. "Any Nobel Prizes on the horizon?"

His father chuckled, ignoring the barb. "Not likely."

"And Marshall?"

His father's voice dropped to a near whisper. "The truth is, I need your advice. Your brother is withdrawing again. He rarely comes upstairs when I'm home. When we do have a few words, all he talks about are stock trades."

"Sounds like business as usual."

"Worse, I assure you. But he agreed we could invite you to dinner. You can see for yourself. Marshall suggested a week from Monday, would that work?"

Christopher searched his mental calendar. "Yeah, I think so. What time?"

"Oh, I didn't ask. Hang on a second."

Professor Kalman put down the phone, and Christopher heard the creak of the door to his study over the otherwise-silent line. He could easily go another six months without crossing the bay to visit family. The shower stopped downstairs. He initiated an encryption program on his laptop, preparing to wind down.

"Chris?"

"Yeah, Dad, I'm here."

"Marshall says come between six and seven."

"Consider it done."

"Shall I pick you up from the BART station?"

"No need, I'll enjoy the walk."

Christopher hung up the phone. If history was any guide, an evening in his brother's company would irritate him no end, but he had time to resign himself. In the short term Brendan would want breakfast. He was due for lunch himself. Then they might as well head over to Civic Center, where the antiwar march would end with a rally on the plaza.

—

"So I've been thinking," Brendan said. "Since we talked about GeneSynth the other day." They were walking slowly downtown, after stopping at a crêpe shop in the Lower Haight.

"You sound skeptical."

"A little. I still don't see how stopping traffic on the Bay Bridge is direct action. The bad guys are meeting at the convention center."

"This is the biggest applied biotech meeting in the world," Christopher said. "Thousands of scientists and marketing guys are going to show up, and hundreds of them work in the East Bay. Chiron, Novartis, a load of little startups."

"Okay, that'd be direct, if you stop them from getting to the meeting. 'Course they'll mostly take BART."

"Not all of them. The sales guys ferrying over last-minute brochures and swag aren't going to lug it over on public transit." Christopher took note of his own atypical boosterism. Brendan's doubt, he figured, was crowding him over to the sunny side. "And there'll be the public protest outside Moscone Center. A broad coalition is planning actions that are going to fill the streets."

"Who's involved in that?"

"A lot of small players from all over. Affinity groups, each one sends a representative to a spokescouncil—same model as antinuke organizing in the eighties."

"Sectarians?"

"Only to the extent that the Trotskyists show up for pretty much everything. The bigger distraction is a nonprofit, Global

Justice. The woman who runs the organization is something of a control freak."

Brendan nodded. "Allison and Nora were telling me about her. Meg something or other?"

"Meg Wyneken. Allison can't stand her. Meg's trying to hold the reins, but the scale of the thing will keep it relatively decentralized." Christopher paused while a delivery truck rumbled by. "Point is, the police are going to put fences around Moscone, trot out the horses and the motorcycles, the whole containment scene. Like the economic summits, the G8 or WTO. Like they did here, for that matter, during the Democratic Convention in '84."

"I was still an innocent in the suburbs of Baltimore then," Brendan said.

"An innocent?" Christopher asked, throwing Brendan a dubious look. "In any case, somebody'll try to bust through, there'll be skirmishing—"

"And that's what the news is going to show."

"As always. Kids fighting cops, never mind the point of the protest. We need a message we control and that media can't ignore, to keep the coverage political."

"Hence a banner on the bridge."

"A banner as big as a billboard. And they can't ignore us if we shut down the main artery into the city."

Brendan took a hit of coffee from his to-go cup. "Allison started to tell me about this carpool thing."

"Fifteen vehicles aligning into rows just past the toll plaza, three deep by the time we get to Treasure Island," Christopher said. He drew a diagram in the air as they walked. "The front rank is the biggest cars we can muster. They stop, the buffer cars stop behind them. Our merry pranksters jump out of the first row and form a human blockade in front of the buffer rows. The front cars split. The buffers are masquerading as commuters, but the point is to form a cushion against drivers who are tempted to try something stupid."

Brendan thought for a moment, nodding. "So nobody's car gets impounded, and nobody gets run over."

"It's basically what people did in '89 on the Golden Gate Bridge. An ACT UP spin-off organized it. They called themselves 'Stop AIDS Now or Else.'"

"I remember that," Brendan said. "When we were in college. They stopped traffic for nearly an hour, right?"

"And got massive press. National."

"Okay, so what about the banner?"

"We're going to have a van out front, maybe two. The climbers, the banner, bikes to get the climbers off the bridge if the cops are slow enough showing up. That'd make it harder to press heavy charges."

"And Marty's a climber? With that pile of gauze taped to his head?"

"The stitches'll be out by then," Christopher said. "There's a lot of safety gear involved. Harnesses, carabiners, belay devices. That's where the tower crew is today, out bouldering for practice." He paused. "It seems plausible when Marty tells it."

"Allison said nobody knows what's on the banner yet."

"Not yet." They were stopped at a light.

"Does that worry you?"

"Hell yes, it worries me."

Brendan polished off his coffee and sank the cup into a trash can. The signal turned green. "And this is totally underground? No connection to public organizing?"

"If we planned this thing in an open meeting, the cops would catch on and stop it."

They took the next block in silence. "What if you buy cars that're ready for the junkyard?" Brendan asked. "Cheap. Barely enough juice left to wheeze onto the bridge. You could add half an hour to clearing the road, then just let the cops keep 'em."

Christopher looked over, surprised. In fact, he found himself a little irritated. It had taken him weeks to dream up a scenario that would require tow trucks to clear the road, and a lot of wrangling to convince the others to try to make it work. Brendan had been their best tactician from way back, and he apparently hadn't lost his edge. "We'd make a lot of annoyed commuters angrier," he said, floating Nora's initial objection to see what Brendan would make of it.

"True, but you're playing to media, not to drivers on the bridge."

"That's pretty much what we decided," Christopher said. Brendan's argument was the one he had advanced. "I had the same thought as we started planning this thing, so we're checking out whether we can make it happen. Eddie Bourgeaut is scouring Mendocino County for wrecks."

"That's perfect! Everybody along those twisty little roads has a rustbucket parked out back. How's Eddie doing? I saw he's still got a room upstairs but nobody said anything."

"Same as ever," Christopher said. "Happy to stir up trouble so long as he can wake up in the woods. Still renting us the building for next to nothing."

"That remains the luckiest break ever."

"Like Dickens. Our whole scene happens because some flower child inherited real estate."

—

The march was still pouring into Civic Center as Brendan and Christopher arrived. Traffic had been diverted, and a flatbed truck with a sound system was parked between the domed edifice of City Hall and a sea of protesters. A twelve-foot puppet of

Mahatma Gandhi towered over the throng, waving a hand-lettered sign: "Victory by Violence is Defeat."

Brendan spotted the others first. "Allison and Jonah," he said, pointing across the lawn.

"Good eye. There's Zac too, by the guy with the Bush mask."

Allison was speaking with a young woman of ambiguous ethnicity, coppery brown skin stretched taut over high cheekbones, epicanthic folds hooding dark, sardonic eyes. Allison crossed her arms, frowning at the well-groomed grass. Jonah was watching the crowd.

"Who's Allison talking to?" Brendan asked.

"Leona Kim, last year's student body president at SF State. She turned out thousands of students at the antiwar demos. Also my colleague at the *Reporter* since late last year, on the distribution crew."

They worked their way over, past a cluster of protesters wearing leather and kaffiyehs. Several were hawking newspapers for the Revolutionary Communist Party while a woman bristling with spiked wristbands shrieked into a bullhorn.

"Serious turnout," Christopher said when they reached the others. Allison looked up and gave a satisfied nod. A dozen musicians in fluorescent colors blared a rough polka for tuba, trumpet, and snare drum a few yards off, competing with the polemic droning from the sound truck.

"Whassup, Christopheles?" Leona said. Christopher self-consciously bumped her proffered fist.

"Leona, this is our old friend and comrade, Brendan. Brendan, Leona."

"How was the march?" Brendan asked.

"Impressive," Allison said. "Dolores Park was wall-to-wall, I'd put the crowd at twenty, twenty-five thousand."

"Zac's speech went okay?"

"He riled 'em up," Leona said. "Zac was on fire."

"Only a fraction of the people were paying attention," Allison added. "As usual. You guys should have come out for it."

"I was listening," Jonah said.

Brendan laughed. "But you've got a dog in the fight. If Zac messed up, the whole collective would be humiliated."

Jonah looked at him distrustfully. "It's not like that."

"He's teasing you, Jonah," Christopher said.

"So Leona just shared some surprising news," Allison said.

Christopher heard a strain in her voice. "What's that?" he asked.

"I ain't seein' the surprise in it," Leona said. "Meg hired me on at Global Justice."

"Really?" Christopher looked to Allison, but she was staring at the grass again. "I know you've been sitting in on that weasel's meetings, but you'd work for her?"

"Y'all really got to go frothy at the mouth over her? It ain't nothin'. Meg got her steering committee. Now she needs Youth Outreach and Street Protest Coordination." Leona enunciated her duties precisely. "Who else she gonna find fits the job?"

Christopher sighed. Leona was right. Meg was just following her flip-charted logic, the nonprofit Left's perennial script. Control the committees, rope in media, then line up activists hungry for exposure they couldn't generate without a seasoned organization's infrastructure. "Fair enough," he said. "I can see where you fit into the Red Queen's plan. She wants Global Justice to hold all the cards when the GeneSynth protest goes down. What I don't get is why you'd shill for her."

"Shill? Be careful, Christopheles. You know how desperate Little Miss Wyneken is to dye-versify that hippie haven, an' if I'm already organizing 'gainst GMOs, might as well have a desk and a paycheck."

Zac sauntered over, costumed in a credible imitation of John

Lennon's satin coat from the *Sgt. Pepper's* album cover, complete with daisies for epaulets. "Hey guys, what do you think?"

"Pretty good," Christopher said, grateful for the interruption. "Not like February before the war, but still. We heard you were awesome at the park."

"It went okay. Don't look now," Zac said to Brendan, tilting his head back toward the group he'd just left. "That guy in the silver tank top? Gideon Freedman from Queers Against Occupation. He thinks you're a babe."

"Oh, for Christ's sake." Brendan reddened. "You know, last February is not what I'd aspire to," he said, replying to Christopher. "Eleven million peaceniks who couldn't stop Bush from bombing Baghdad?"

Allison looked up, eyes flashing. "What *would* you aspire to?" she asked. "Are you going to judge the worth of a struggle by how the government responds to it?"

Brendan raised his hands in mock surrender. "Not the worth," Brendan said. "Maybe the efficacy."

"That's it," Leona said, nodding agreement with Brendan. "Power don't give a damn how many freaks are shakin' signs on th' other side of the fence. Makin' eleven million happen was huge, but it ain't real 'til we move that muscle to where decisions get made."

Allison shook her head. "Turning out eleven million people—eleven *million*—moves muscle to exactly where decisions get made. We did our part. We created enormous space for insider dissent. It's the media that failed, and Congress failed harder."

For a moment Brendan looked as if he would say something more, but he didn't.

"The argument is infinite and circular," Christopher said. "Nobody knows what's going to work until it does." He wondered whether Allison was really annoyed with Brendan, or just on edge after hearing about Leona's new employment. He wouldn't mind if she kept a wary distance from her former lover. But he'd be an idiot to get between them.

"Look," Jonah said, pointing toward the back of the plaza.

Several hundred demonstrators were milling around the steps of the public library. Most were dressed in dark clothes and wore bandannas or ski masks. A formation of riot police by the Asian Art Museum, and another in front of the Civic Auditorium, were positioned to cover a charge in either direction.

"Black bloc," Christopher said. "The young'uns are getting bored with speech making."

"Any bets the cops are going to overreact?" Zac asked. "I don't think they'll stand for a replay of last year."

The anarchists were splitting into two groups, and beginning to slip around the library's north and south façades. "Clever," Brendan said. "Scramble the cops, then join back up. Odds on the Burger King across the plaza?"

"Plate glass ain't got a chance," Leona said.

Christopher nodded. "Should we watch?"

"Sure," Brendan said, "if we don't get too close."

"Me too," Jonah said.

Allison shook her head. "I don't think so."

"Why not, Mom?"

"We're here to make a political point, not to break windows and provoke the police."

"But Chris and Brendan are going—"

Allison cast a baleful eye on each of the bad examples in turn. "Chris and Brendan are beyond being influenced by confrontation for its own sake. You're not. And I don't want you to get hurt. You never know how that kind of breakaway is going to end."

"That's totally unfair—"

"I ain't gettin' near that foolishness," Leona said. "That ain't what today's about."

"I'm going to pass too, Jonah," Zac said. "The black bloc kids are stuck in an endless loop. A girl can only take so much *samsāra*."

—

On the far side of the library, the breakaway crowd pressed toward barriers set up to protect the chain store's windows. Motorcycle cops from the tac squad formed a rolling guard on either side.

"No easy wins for the forces of chaos," Christopher said as they neared UN Plaza.

Brendan nodded. "Looks pretty locked down. The cops have seen this movie a few times before."

Revving their engines, the motorcycles fell back as the anarchists surged against the barricade. Police on the other side stood with helmet shields down and batons held ready. An aggressive few feinted in the direction of masked rabble-rousers, but most of the riot cops gave no sign where they might strike, or when.

From the middle of the crowd, a stubby red cylinder arced over the police line and slammed into the restaurant window. A cheer erupted, and the police took a choreographed step closer to the barrier. The window remained intact; if the glass had cracked, damage was too slight to make out from a distance.

"What was that?" Brendan asked.

"Coke can?"

A woman beside Christopher snorted dismissively. "Typical," she said.

Christopher looked over. Fifty-something, he guessed. She wore an embroidered blue peasant blouse over black spandex, and pink running shoes piped in silver. An armful of library books, Jodi Picoult's *Second Glance* topping the stack. "What's typical?" Christopher asked.

"These peace-and-love people lobbing rocks and bottles as if they've never heard of a brain concussion."

Christopher nodded, but he didn't reply.

"The cops ought to beat some sense into them."

He looked to Brendan, who elbowed him gently, egging him on. "Do you really think so?" Christopher asked the woman.

"They're asking for it. I went out with one of those types once. On and on about Vietnam and the draft, but he really just wanted to break things. His mother should have spanked him when she had the chance."

Christopher stared, incredulous. "Seriously?" he asked. "They're kids, and they're pissed off. Busting windows may not be effective politics, but it's what happens when government lies and kills and makes itself unaccountable."

She turned to face him, hardening her expression. "That's just the kind of thing he used to say. The boyfriend. And you know what? That's why the police are licensed to carry guns and you're not. We vote in this country, we don't govern by riot."

Christopher shook his head sadly. "People don't riot unless and until elections aren't working. And governance has always been messy in this country, ever since the Boston Tea Party." He turned back to the confrontation at the barricade, but the woman wasn't finished.

"Show me one of these bandanna-wearing buffoons who can even spell governance. The minute they finish their temper tantrum they'll hire lawyers to whine about free speech rights. That's as far as they can imagine when it comes to governance."

He turned toward her once more, giving her library books a significant glance. "This crowd is past spelling. They're here because they've concluded that statist governance is broken. I bet you could find a dozen in that crowd who've read every word Peter Kropotkin wrote."

"Who cares? I never even heard of him."

"Kropotkin was a Russian prince," Christopher said, wondering what the average Jodi Picoult fan thought of titled nobility. The woman didn't even slow down. "What do these hooligans care about Russian princes?"

"They're not hooligans," Christopher said. "They're anarchists, and I'd wager most of them have read more political philosophy than you're holding in that stack of library books. In addition to being a prince, Kropotkin was an intellectual—"

"Oh, please—"

"—and an anarchist," Christopher continued. "Your categories are way off target. You don't want to assume people are ignorant or unthinking just because they've come to different conclusions than you have."

The tac squad wheeled around to cut off the crowd's retreat. A formation of riot police approached the breakaway, from the street side of UN Plaza.

Brendan edged nearer, and Christopher followed, happy to step away from a pointless encounter. A shrill whistle sounded. "You think they have undercovers in there?" Christopher asked.

"Hell yes. But what're the chances they saw anything? By the way, you better hope your friend with the pink shoes isn't caught behind any bridge blockades."

Christopher laughed. He realized his hands were balled into fists. Self-consciously, he unclenched. The far edge of the crowd began to fray. "It's over once they get mobile," he said.

The mob accelerated toward Market Street. A phalanx of riot police remained behind the barriers, guarding against a sudden about-face. The tac squad eased their motorbikes into a single file escort, rolling along both sidewalks, between the marchers and anything worth breaking.

"Looks like Burger King gets a pass," Brendan said.

"You want to chase after them?"

"Naw. Zac was right. Whatever they do, it'll be a Hail Mary play."

"Agreed. I'm not in the mood for a nightstick massage." They turned back as the cops behind the barriers broke ranks.

"You really think those kids have read Kropotkin?" Brendan asked.

Christopher shrugged. "Some of them, sure."

They veered left, around a bronze statue of Simón Bolívar mounted on a rearing horse.

"It's pretty hard to ignore the déjà vu," Brendan said. "I keep thinking back to '91. Those endless blockades of the Federal Building during the first Gulf War."

"Remember that Union Square breakaway," Christopher asked, "speaking of black bloc anarchists?" Brendan wasn't any more likely to forget than he was. The tac squad had formed a line shoulder to shoulder across Powell Street, batons drawn, with no barricades to cushion confrontation. For a few tense minutes it had looked like the breakaway was going to get creamed.

"Thirty ass-naked mud people," Brendan said. "Of course I remember, like a tribe straight out of some rain forest. A gaggle of neohippies turned those riot cops to jelly."

"What blew me away was the timing. That was before people carried cell phones, right? And they managed to get onto that cable car, rolling down from behind the police at the exact moment." Christopher could see it clear as IMAX. When the mud people headed for Macy's, ululating like extras in *The Battle of Algiers*, the cops had no idea what to defend or attack. The ungovernable masses poured through their tattered line. "The Westin St. Francis," he said.

"And then Neiman Marcus. We never found out who those guys were, right?"

"Never did. Nobody got caught."

"But I'll tell you, Chris . . ." They came to the library and sat on the steps. "You know the difference between then and now?"

"Lay it out for me."

"Diddly." Brendan paused, challenging Christopher to react. "In 1991, no organized movement, the rest of the country thinks San Francisco is whacked," he said. "Fast-forward to 2003, eleven million show up worldwide, but there's still no movement. The politicians don't give a damn because people are going home afterward to watch *Survivor*."

Christopher absorbed the weight of the comparison. Not a new thought. But his friend was wallowing in it. "That's recklessly cynical," he said.

"Everybody out here knows how powerless this shit is. They found out a year ago if they didn't read the memo beforehand."

It was hard to argue against Brendan's despair. For Christopher, it struck way too close to home. They watched people come and go, a slow stream walking into the demonstration and a greater number heading for Muni. "So have you reached . . . the guys who set up your southern adventure?" he asked.

Brendan busied himself with a cigarette. "I put out feelers," he said. "Organizers who can contact the contacts, discreetly. It's only been a week, the ATF might still come banging on the Triangle's door. Better to sound things out before leading heat to people they don't know."

It was the second time Brendan had called out the Bureau of Alcohol, Tobacco, and Firearms. Not the FBI. "So you're pretty sure it's ATF who'd want to find you."

"Chris, it's no secret. The Federales said there were guns. Not what I enlisted for, but I didn't load the truck. I could have been carrying anything. Only the guys who set this thing up can fill in those blanks."

"I get it. And I don't mean to pry, I'm just interested. You tell what you want, when you want. Can I ask something else?"

"You can ask anything else. All those letters? Letters nobody else managed to write? You're the one kept me sane down there. I owe you answers if I owe anybody."

"You'd have done the same," Christopher said, embarrassed.

"Maybe. Not everybody came through."

"I want to hear stuff we couldn't put into letters." Christopher wondered who Brendan was angry at. Allison? "Like why you decided to go south in the first place."

Brendan took a deep drag, and exhaled slowly. "I was tired of feckless First World protests," he said. "I wanted to have real effect, at a global scale. The Zapatistas embody radical democracy like no one has in decades, and Marcos knows how to work the media. The chance might not have come along again."

"I get it about Chiapas and the Zapatistas," Christopher said. "And real effect, I sure as hell get that. But I can't give up on engaging here. Even our smallest victories make a huge, amplified difference elsewhere. In the countries we exploit, in the biosphere we're crapping on."

Brendan stared into the middle distance. He didn't reply.

"Given what the Federales said you were carrying, did you ever wonder if your contacts played you for a patsy?" In truth, Christopher was asking for himself. Without spilling the story of Chagall's approach, it was as close as he could get to angling for advice about the saboteur.

"How do you mean?" Brendan asked.

"I don't know, exactly. What if they planned all along to run

weapons? How do you know they're really Zapatistas? I mean . . .
what if they were fronting for some drug cartel?"

Brendan snuffed his cigarette, visibly pained. Christopher
swallowed.

"I hope I wasn't suckered that badly," Brendan said. "It'd be
hard to live with."

SIX

November 2003

Miles from home, Chagall climbs rain-slick stairs and enters a stuccoed public library, low and drab as the leaden sky. He wears a curly brown wig over his crewcut, and a baseball cap that calls out unremarkable loyalties. A pair of tortoiseshell glasses squares his features. Under worn denim, a knee brace encourages an adopted limp, and an army surplus jacket completes the masquerade. Shabby veterans are rife in this past-its-prime city, men whose prospects were tested and spent by the time they racked up thirty years. No one gives the invisibles a second glance.

He shuffles toward the back of a carpeted room. Only one of the library's internet terminals is being used this morning, by an old man, sparrow-thin in a blue windbreaker. There are no staff in sight. Chagall chooses a terminal, sitting with his back to a wall of gardening books, and surveys the equipment. He inserts a flash drive into an available USB port.

Chagall cycles the computer's power, boots the machine into MiniBot Linux, and points a web browser at a Civil War reenactment site sized to fill most of the screen. Opening a secure terminal window, Chagall positions it low on the monitor. He navigates through a series of anonymizers to an IRC host where he and the hacker who found him online have agreed to convene.

CHAGALL: Assume you have verified my claim?
ROMULUS: Indeed. Thanks for the b-day wishes. Loved the candles.
CHAGALL: Good. Let's move on then.
ROMULUS: Have you arrived at a preference?
CHAGALL: Leaning toward Corn.
ROMULUS: Surprised. Figured you for English Breakfast. Aspirin too hot in wake of recent activity, IMO.

Chagall stares hard at the screen, considering whether to dwell on the targets they're setting aside. He types a response, encrypts, sends.

CHAGALL: Agreed re: Aspirin. English Breakfast is densely populated. Corn carries less risk of unintended consequences.
ROMULUS: Understood. Will follow your lead.
CHAGALL: Need three items to determine feasibility. First, architectural diagrams. Structure only, interior plans not necessary yet. Readable w/o specialized software. Transmit via asynchronous drop.
ROMULUS: Have already begun to explore access points. Drop transfer is trivial. What else?
CHAGALL: Construction schedule for target. More detail than on public site.
ROMULUS: Shouldn't be a problem. #3?
CHAGALL: Agreement re: how you will physically participate. Risk differential is too great between virtual vs. physical roles. No action possible when entrapment possibility exists.

ROMULUS: This is new.

CHAGALL: Task assignment not yet worked out, so the question isn't settled. Suggest modes of participation that suit your capacity. There needs to be some activity beyond virtual.

Romulus takes a while to reply. Chagall surreptitiously observes a middle-aged librarian now sitting at the reference desk. Bobbed gray hair, prim white blouse buttoned to her throat. When she looks up he averts his eyes, focusing again on the chat window at the edge of his screen.

ROMULUS: I'm not prepared to respond now. This may require negotiation.

CHAGALL: I can wait.

ROMULUS: Let's come back to that. Have begun to collect addresses. Have tested capacity to send e-mails, previously discussed goal is attainable. Progress re: content?

CHAGALL: I want to recruit a writer.

ROMULUS: Why another party?

CHAGALL: I need to focus on mechanics to hit agreed date. And we need a fresh voice. Our message should not link to previous activity.

ROMULUS: I can draft.

CHAGALL: Your responsibilities are also nontrivial. Drafting can be done by an anonymous recruit without disclosure of action's nature, location, date. We finalize writer's draft.

ROMULUS: How would we recruit?

CHAGALL: Securely. Candidate identities need-to-know only. I will manage solo. Identifying evidence to be scrubbed once secure contact is established, for obvious reasons.

ROMULUS: You are distrustful.
CHAGALL: Of everyone.
ROMULUS: Proofs have been offered between us.

Chagall registers the hacker's petulance. A good sign, he thinks. Seasoned FBI would show a tougher façade, more bluster.

CHAGALL: Proof is in the execution. Nothing is proven until it's done.
ROMULUS: How can we proceed on this basis?
CHAGALL: No benefit of working together can outweigh caution.
ROMULUS: Some trust is inevitable. Example: how will you verify accuracy of plans? I could supply garbage. Or you could be a cop, lurking in chats to attract genuine actors.
CHAGALL: I'll take precautions. You'll watch your own back. If this is a problem, now is a good time to abort.

Again, the hacker pauses before he responds.

ROMULUS: Back to #3. Options for participation are unclear.
CHAGALL: Consider supply, transport. Consider target infiltration to place equipment. Beyond remote surveillance, beyond remote control. Need evidence of your boots on solid ground.
ROMULUS: I can hack. Physical break-ins are beyond my expertise.

Chagall, casting and dapping like a fly fisherman, dispassionately watches Romulus thrash.

CHAGALL: Our collaboration is not a video game. The project is worth some risk in working with an unknown part-

ner. You know how to obtain diagrams, build a bot net—I don't. Still, it's not worth a frivolous risk to freedom. Burden is on you to assure this is not a sting, you contacted me. Need you to do something no cop would contemplate.
ROMULUS: I'm discouraged by this interaction.
CHAGALL: I'm not a shrink.
ROMULUS: You're one cold MF.
CHAGALL: I'm good at what I do. Nothing else offered.
ROMULUS: Let's return to this later.

Chagall looks up from the screen. The librarian is scanning bar codes from a pile of books on the reference desk, absorbed in her work.

CHAGALL: Make no mistake. I want and intend to do this. Nothing personal. Bottom line, I don't know you.
ROMULUS: Understood. But consider the possibility we're both genuine. Why would either of us invest effort if we don't trust the other?
CHAGALL: Distrust is practical.
ROMULUS: I don't want to spend my best effort then be dumped.
CHAGALL: Action is incomplete until you broadcast our message. You hold the reins in the final lap.
ROMULUS: Perhaps. But these are unanticipated twists. I say we delay recruitment of 3rd party writer until after next contact. I need to participate in selection.
CHAGALL: No back and forth for selection, it's too cumbersome. I'll select. Opportunity for your influence in giving direction to writer through multiple drafts.

The hacker takes a full forty seconds to reply.

ROMULUS: I insist at least on contributing one or more candidates, to be considered on equal footing to yours.

CHAGALL: You have someone in mind?

ROMULUS: Will research.

CHAGALL: Strict conditions. No candidate can be connected to you in any way. You have never met or been in the same room. You have never participated in online exchange of any kind, not e-mail, not IRC, nothing.

ROMULUS: Of course, what do you take me for?

CHAGALL: I have no idea who or what you are. Makes no difference, conditions are invariant. I will accept writer candidates if submitted within the next two weeks. Structural drawings will enable further progress on my end.

ROMULUS: Two weeks for candidates, fine. Will obtain drawings, at least partial set, by then as well. That or call off collaboration. You are not easy to work with.

Chagall judges the threat is empty, that Romulus is blowing off anxiety.

CHAGALL: Via drop 17f?

ROMULUS: Roger that. Until then.

He watches Romulus exit the chat, shuts down his Linux instance, then starts the machine booting back into Windows. The librarian looks up. The chugging disk must have caught her attention, and now she sets aside her books. Footsteps strike the floor with dull precision.

"Are you finding everything you need?" the librarian asks in a whisper.

From where she hovers, the woman can see only the back of the monitor, but the screen's blue wash will reflect tellingly in his glasses. "Yes, ma'am," Chagall says, mumbling into the keyboard. "I'm about finished now."

"I noticed you turned the computer off and back on again. That's not necessary. Do you know how to log off from the internet?"

"Oh, yes, ma'am. I'm sorry to be troublesome." Chagall wants to bark at the woman's self-important sincerity. As if her shitty computers matter.

He steadies himself.

"It's no trouble," the librarian is saying. "Next time, please ask the person at the desk for help."

"I'll remember that, ma'am."

She moves along to the old guy.

"Good morning, Mr. Farrell. How are you today?"

Chagall rises and gimps his way toward the door.

—

The drizzle has let up. Streaks of blue show through cloud cover to the west. Hobbling toward the bus stop, Chagall is careful not to break character. He'll catch a ride several stops beyond where he parked one of the pickups he uses to project a blur of identity toward whatever persons, security cameras, and databases might register his existence. He has stashed a change of clothes a few blocks from the truck. The man in the library will cease to exist.

It's tempting to continue fishing for clues to whether Romulus is a cop. As he lowers himself slowly onto a bench, cold but dry under the slanted roof of a bus shelter, Chagall turns the question over in his mind. At this stage the answer doesn't matter much. There's nothing to be gained by trusting an unknown accomplice. Romulus may make good on all claims, but Chagall will retire before he lets anybody else calls his shots.

It riles him that Romulus imagines he would target a livestock cloning startup in Boston, the company they've been calling

English Breakfast. He failed to account not only for population density, but also for the fact that research on Boston's Route 128 is overwhelmingly medical. Yes, it's true that amateurs planting bombs at biopharmaceutical campuses in the Bay Area have put West Coast targets on guard. Romulus got that right. The startup they nicknamed Aspirin is located less than a mile from Chiron Corporation, where an animal rights group planted explosives less than two months ago. But the medical angle would compromise their message whether they struck Boston or Emeryville. Only fascist wingnuts win converts by attacking doctors. You might as well blow up a hospital.

If Romulus is naïve enough to aim at fuzzy targets, he's not qualified to draft their manifesto. Chagall sees their opening in grassroots rejection of growth hormone that taints commercial dairy products. Parents have already demonstrated they'll shun rBGH in milk; it follows that they can be convinced their kids are threatened by mutant grains and the animals that eat them. Protecting the food supply is a goal that can gain support if their target is sharply focused. Hence Nebraska. Corn.

Will his coconspirator deliver? Chagall will be interested to see what Romulus suggests as material contribution.

He needs blueprints and a bot-driven propaganda typhoon from a nimble-fingered hacker. If Romulus gets the diagrams and participates physically in their conspiracy, Chagall will take his own game to the next level. He'll run every play in his book—and likely some new ones besides—to mount their attack on a university research facility under construction on the outskirts of Lincoln. A building consecrated to agricultural biotech: the AgBio complex, as a campus spokesman names it in the local press.

The bus is coming, in a miasma of diesel smog.

Chagall, still playing the beaten-down vet, rises arthritically to his feet and digs in his pocket for change.

SEVEN

Allison sat in the salvaged wooden banker's chair at Jonah's desk, rocking gently forward and back. Jonah sat cross-legged on his bed. "Did you have any dinner?" she asked.

"Chips and salsa." Jonah kept his eyes on the history textbook spread open on carelessly straightened blankets, but the performance wasn't fooling his mother.

"That's not much," she said, keeping her voice even, her tone light. "Didn't Brendan offer to take you on a burrito run, or for pizza?"

"Yeah."

"And?"

"I didn't want to."

"But we agreed on our walk to school—"

"He's all freaky now."

Allison sighed. Parenting had been so much more straight-forward before teenage diffidence took root. "Jonah, I think he's turned inward a little bit, after a rough time in Mexico. But he's still the same Brendan."

"He's not." Jonah shook his head decisively. "Not like before. He doesn't even say what happened."

"What do you mean? Does he make you afraid?"

"I'm not scared of him, he's just . . . weird. All spacey and distracted. And . . . like that first night, when he told about that guy getting his jaw broken and stuff? It's like he was totally cold. Like he could care less."

Jonah looked up, his eyes pleading. Allison softened. Her own feelings for Brendan were complicated enough. Why wouldn't Jonah be getting mixed signals too? "I'm going to pay closer attention," she said. "You've known Brendan your whole life. I need to trust there might be something you're picking up on."

"Next time I could chill with Buzz."

Allison held back a smile. "Now that'd be double trouble."

"What's wrong with Buzz?"

"There's nothing wrong with Buzz, but he's not an adult. How about if Natalie or Gregor came upstairs when no one else is home?"

"Whatever." Jonah shut his book and flopped back against a heap of pillows. "How was karate?"

"I enjoyed it, though I have to admit it's hard to change gears after work. It's generous of Sensei Okano to let me teach, but pivoting from preschool to sparring can be a little odd."

"But you've been teaching that class since summer. Aren't you used to it?"

"Nine months isn't so long in the scheme of things."

Jonah tapped a quick rhythm across the pages of his textbook. "Did I tell you what Buzz and me thought of?"

"'Buzz and I.' Tell me now," Allison said.

"You know how Duboce Park is all full of dog poop, right?"

"Like a minefield."

"Exactly. So me and Buzz want to countermine."

"Um . . . I hope you don't mean what I'm thinking."

Jonah's eyes opened wide. "Mom, that's disgusting!"

"So what's your idea?"

"We're going to sprinkle powder on the grass to make all the dogs go bald."

"Mmmm . . . that seems kind of unfair."

"To who?"

"To the dogs."

Jonah leaned forward. "It's unfair to mess up the park."

"True, but the dogs are just being dogs. They don't know any better."

"Yeah, but the owners do. And they'd go totally nuts if their dogs went bald."

"They'd be really worried," Allison said. "But the dogs whose owners pick up would go just as bald as the ones whose people leave messes. And you'd probably kill the grass. Collateral damage."

"Okay, those are problems." Jonah considered. "But Buzz'll want to do it anyway."

"Do you think?"

"What would you do about the dogs?"

"It's not about the dogs," Allison said. Better, she thought. He was asking for advice now. She stood and started a series of leg stretches. "Do you mind?"

Jonah shook his head.

"If you want the owners to change," Allison said, "I think your best bet is shame."

"I don't get it."

"Say you've got a digital camera, one with a zoom lens."

"Okay . . ."

"So you take pictures of dogs pooping next to their owners. If the owner picks up after the dog, you delete the pictures."

"And if not, we put up posters of who's making the mess!"

Allison switched from her right leg to her left. "That'd work."

"We can make captions . . . like Dirty Dog."

"Crappy Neighbor."

Jonah giggled. "Filthy Fido!"

"Incontinence is for the Birds."

"Huh?"

"Never mind, that one's a throwaway."

———

She came down the back stairs after getting Jonah settled. As she entered the kitchen the others were engaged in heated discussion. Nora turned to her. "Al, you remember that mouse, right? With an ear cloned onto its back?"

"Of course I remember." Everybody was sprawled around the table, except for Zac who was still at work, pulling espressos at Café Royal. She lit a burner under the kettle.

"Grafted, not cloned," Brendan said.

Allison caught the wink he threw to Christopher, having beaten him to the punch. Boys and their rivalries. "But a soul-shaking image," she said.

"Grafted, cloned—whatever." Nora's round cheeks dimpled with exasperation. "That photo boosted visibility of the danger in biotech more than anything before or since. That's the point. Am I right, Allison?"

"What are you guys scrapping about?" Allison asked.

"But the mouse wasn't genetically engineered," Christopher said, sidestepping Allison's question.

"The mouse was bred for low immune response," Marty said. "You're right on the fine print, Chris, but—"

"Let's stay real," Nora said. "Technical correctness matters, but it's only a fraction of what we do. People who know nothing about tissue engineering remember that poor little mouse. On a sign or a banner, the right photo is worth ten thousand footnotes." She held Christopher's gaze for a long moment, then turned to Allison. "That's what we're scrapping about."

Christopher looked down into his lap. Allison raised an eyebrow and gestured faintly toward his end of the table. Nora pretended not to notice that she had stung Christopher sharply.

"You're all right," Brendan said, smoothing the label on his bottle of lager. "Give the papers a juicy picture to put on the front page and they'll use it. People form political ideas around images. But if industry PR forces a wedge between your image and your message, the whole thing backfires."

"I'm not so sure." Allison turned away from the others, speaking over her shoulder as she spooned green tea into a pot. "It comes back to the question of role. Is our action about getting attention, or about making an argument? And we're not actually considering the mouse image, are we? We need something fresh."

"Definitely not the mouse," Christopher said quietly. "The question is whether we can come up with an image that's fresh and honest. If we get attention for making a phony argument, we set everybody back."

"Maybe that's true," Allison said, crossing back to the stove, conscious that she was shepherding her housecomrades no less deliberately than she'd talked Jonah down from his dog park conspiracy. "The question is, what's 'phony'? There's a point of no return. My take is that we can make progress with a metaphor, short of qualifying every slogan. Once people get a picture in their head it's hard to talk them out of it."

"Exactly." Nora crossed her arms defiantly.

"Ever since UMass showed off their three-eared wonder, nobody else has made the same 'mistake,'" Christopher said. "So where's this miracle image going to come from?"

"All I'm arguing is that we have to look," Nora said "We have to look hard."

"No harm looking," Brendan said. "But say we develop materials that rely on having clear, graphic evidence of the slow, subtle threat of GMOs—and then suppose it doesn't fall into our hands. If we lean too hard on finding an image, we're screwed if it doesn't pan out."

Allison smiled to herself as she poured boiling water over her tea leaves. Brendan was including himself now: "we" instead of "you."

"An image could put us over the top," Christopher said, "but mainstream media isn't going to be snookered by a home-hacked digital job. *Attack of the Killer Tomatoes* was a hilarious spoof in the seventies, but B-grade spectacle won't pass as serious politics. And if we rely on a photo but don't find one, home-hacked is going to look like our only option at the eleventh hour."

Nora was looking down at the table, picking at a paper napkin.

"How long can we take to look?" Allison asked.

Marty rubbed his eyes. "Five weeks 'til GeneSynth opens. But I gotta fold laundry tonight."

Brendan looked around the table. "A week or two for a search?"

"I can live with that," Nora said. "Meantime the media committee drafts the pamphlet and press release. As agreed at tonight's meeting."

"How come you're not writing this stuff?" Brendan asked Christopher. "Used to be we had to duct-tape your hands to give anybody else a chance."

"Talk to the red pen."

Allison pulled up a chair. "Chris, don't be sour."

"I'll edit," he said, shrugging. "I'm too overbooked to draft. Luis, the other guy in layout, is out on vacation."

"Speaking of the *Reporter*," Allison said, "is Leona quitting her gig at the paper? Now that she's working for Meg?"

"I'm still in shock," Nora said. "Leona's the last person on Earth I'd have pegged for a Meg Wyneken stooge."

"I saw her yesterday at the office," Christopher said. "She's taken the exact temperature of Meg's fire. Leona's not going over to the dark side." He stood. "I need to get some stuff in the wash myself."

"She's young and she's aimin' for bigger prizes than Global Justice," Marty said. "What the hell? I'd rather have fools with street cred in government than fools with degrees in business and law."

Nora eyed her lover dubiously.

"Present company excepted, darlin', you know that."

"If she's less than straight up we need to keep our distance," Allison said.

"Isn't it a little late?" Brendan drained his beer. "She knows . . . a partial plan, right?"

"Not enough to cause a problem," Christopher said. "I'll get commitments when the time's right. And we can always pass faulty intelligence."

"We want to point her away from the action," Marty said.

"We've got timing, we've got target, we've got . . . the complexities," Christopher said. "Let's not talk about it here. Diversion shouldn't be an issue."

———

Marty preceded Christopher down the back stairs and into the basement's murk. The dryer's heat took no edge off the chill; their laundry room was ten degrees colder than the air outside. He reached for the light switch and the long, dank space filled with shadows. The sump pump cut out, leaving a heavy silence. One of the students from the first-floor flat had emptied the dryer and piled Marty and Nora's load on the folding table. Marty began to sort through the tangle. Christopher set down his basket and separated whites from colors.

"I don't mean to be a pedant," Christopher said.

Marty turned. "I know," he answered. "We all know that,

Chris. I suppose it's true a doctored photo could blow up on us, even after it got in the papers."

"We'd be no different than neocon scum lying their way into a war."

"Maybe. Maybe. But there's also the good in getting anything up on the . . . on the structure there. That'll boost up the volume, and volume's what we need. We're right, but nobody's paying attention."

Christopher sprinkled detergent over his clothes and started the machine. Then he leaned close to Marty, murmuring beneath the washer's racket. "I have a feeling Nora's already got something?"

"Not yet," he murmured back. "Something tentative, one of those whistleblower things. The source is skittish."

"Understood." Nora was visible enough as an activist lawyer to be sought out by a graduate student, or a disgruntled technician—someone with a story to tell and a career to protect. "Any idea about the visual?" Christopher asked.

"Don't know. The source says it's dramatic."

Christopher nodded, but he remained skeptical. Limiting the time to look for an image was a decent compromise, but they'd have to hold fast against delays and extensions. The ambient noise dropped abruptly as the agitator began to churn. Marty handed Christopher one end of a bedsheet. "Nora told me that your da was in touch," he said as they shook out the wrinkles.

"'Fraid so. I've been summoned."

"Anything wrong?"

They folded the sheet in half, then in half again.

"Marshall," Christopher said. "The usual. Dad wakes up every six months and sees we're all living parallel lives. That we're not much of a family anymore. 'You disappear into that goddamn commune, and I can't pry your brother out of the basement with a crowbar.'"

"Marshall's at home?"

"Since just before Mom died."

"How come I didn't remember that?" Marty set the folded sheet in his basket, then lightly fingered the edge of the gauze still taped to his head.

"When do the stitches come out?" Christopher asked.

"A couple more weeks. But I thought Marshall got rich. Some IPO or other?"

"Supposedly. Instead of working he plays the stock market out of an office he set up downstairs. He doesn't talk numbers."

"That TV room underneath the street level?"

"Yup. He remodeled it into a kind of in-law unit. Pretty good memory there, Martin."

"We were over enough times, escaping our own college-days cooking. So what does Professor Kalman want his wayward activist son to do about his wayward capitalist son?"

"Show up for dinner. Not so urgent now that we've learned how to cook, but—oh, fuck—"

"What?"

"I just realized—they want me to come Monday. The twenty-ninth." Christopher slumped back against the dryer. "It would have been my mom's birthday."

"But . . . that's not so bad, right?"

"Marshall gets sentimental. It creeps me out."

"But you'll go?"

Christopher sighed. "Yeah, I'll go."

Marty began to roll socks. "Did I tell you, the other week I heard my granny is giving up her place?"

"You didn't. Granny Flynn? The place in Connemara?"

"That's her. Aunt Mary'll take her in, they'll sell the sheep. My cousin Eamon'll keep an eye on the property while they decide what to do with it."

"It's been a while since you've been back to visit."

"That's what I'm gettin' at, Chris. Time's short, you know it as well as anybody. Go easy on your brother and your da."

Christopher helped with a fitted sheet, then they both folded towels. "You're right," he said. "Only it's easier to say so than to make it real."

"Always will be."

EIGHT

With an eye on the café's wall clock, Christopher sank into a slow funk. He'd staked the afternoon on Suvali's casual remark that she visited the Daily Grind on Fridays. Eager not to appear too eager, he'd skipped a week. Yes, he'd spied through the café's webcam the Friday before, and decided not to draw conclusions when he failed to spot her. In person he had a wider field of view, but it gave no advantage. Suvali wasn't there.

His schedule for Chagall's manifesto had slipped. A tsunami of photocopies and printouts littered the café table, as if materializing Christopher's anxiety about getting it right. A less determined propagandist might have thrown in the towel, but Christopher stayed focused on the facts. He'd been struggling to explain why splicing genes from bacteria, daffodils, and silkworms into food crops has nothing at all to do with hunger relief. He had to simplify if he wanted to counter the specious, feel-good claims of agribusiness PR hacks—especially if he meant to reach Chagall's "staggeringly large and broad audience."

To Christopher it was obvious that fiddling with molecules doesn't deliver food and water to where hungry people live. But convincing readers who don't live and breathe policy would require a careful walk through the logic. He had to explain how industrialized farming is hobbled in places that lack roads, oil, electricity, and irrigation. To describe that First World agriculture is driven by scientific practice, so transgenic crops solve nothing without an on-site cadre of educated agronomists. To detail what it means to farmers when markets are disrupted by war. And all without coming off as a condescending wonk.

For readers who follow the science, it wasn't hard to debunk agribiz PR. But think tank briefs didn't make writing agitprop any easier. Nora was right about the worth of an image: persuasion hates complexity.

Christopher read fitfully.

The café door opened, with a metallic scrape and a burst of street noise.

Yet again, Christopher looked up.

His heart raced cartwheels up his rib cage as she took her place in line.

Christopher resisted the urge to call out as Suvali slowly advanced toward the counter, engrossed in her stale *Sunday Times* and every bit as lovely as he remembered.

She added milk to her tea from a steel pitcher. Stirred it in with a wooden stick. Christopher stared deliberately at his papers when she turned toward the room. He looked up slowly as she scanned for a place to sit, doing his best impression of a man surfacing from deep intellectual reflection. At the moment he caught Suvali's eye he cocked his head, just so. Smiled. Beckoned her over to share his table.

"The place is jammed!" she said, edging into Christopher's corner of the room. Suvali sported a yellow cashmere sweater, jeans, and the same pearl earrings she'd worn two Fridays back.

"You're welcome to stake a claim here," Christopher said, gathering in his things. "Last weekend's London awaits you in perfect tranquility."

She set down her tea and the *Times*, laughing. "That's a new one. London and tranquility in the same breath. Are you sure you don't mind?"

"Perfectly sure."

Suvali made a show of noticing what he was reading. "That looks awfully sober."

"I suppose." *World Hunger: Promise and Risk of Biotechnology* topped his pile. "I warned you . . . politics."

"You did. You also said this isn't your neighborhood. I'm surprised to find you here."

"It's nice to find a new place," he said sheepishly.

"But no laptop today. No mad internet chats."

"Escaping the tyranny of the web, I guess."

She frowned.

Skepticism became her, Christopher thought. The pearl hanging from her left earlobe swung fetchingly in its harness. "So how's med school? Have you saved dozens of lives?"

Suvali thought for a moment. "I don't think I did any damage," she said. "I'd call that a moral victory."

"First do no harm."

"*Primum non nocere.* Our first lesson." She gestured toward his heap of articles. "I trust you follow a similar principle?"

"Rigorously," he said. "But I won't bore you with my sober obsessions."

Christopher had trouble returning to his photocopies. He watched out of the corner of his eye as Suvali sped through the front section of the *Times*, slowed when she got to local news, set aside sports and business, and settled in with arts and entertainment. She looked up to find him peeping over her shoulder at a four-color spread.

"I'm afraid I'm ruining your concentration," she said.

Christopher shook his head. "It's not your fault that Van Gogh is more interesting than golden rice."

"Oh, I've heard of that." Suvali folded her paper and pivoted to face him. "Isn't that the rice that cures blindness?"

"That's what the press releases say. The fine print tells a different story."

"I guess I haven't followed closely."

Twenty-five words or less, Christopher warned himself. "The 'gold' is vitamin A. Whether it'll be concentrated enough in GMO rice to make a medical difference is one question. Another is whether farmers can save their own seed, or if they'll have to pay the multinationals every season."

"Right." Suvali nodded. "I did read something about the seed banking issue."

"Vitamin A deficiency strikes hardest in Southeast Asia and Africa—you're probably up on that too. The article I'm reading is from the Nutritional Studies Institute." Christopher checked the title page. "It's in Birmingham, actually. They've got an interesting angle, kind of a big-picture look at the ongoing scrap."

"So what do they conclude?"

"It turns out distribution of golden rice can't happen without an infusion of private foundation money," Christopher said. "The grants are already secured, but the funds are earmarked for payments on seventy separate patents. Not for farmers or distribution centers. For seventy separate patent owners who demand return on their investment in this one genetically tailored grain."

"Isn't that reasonable? If they paid for the research?"

"I guess that's not the question I'd ask. The red flag here is that the poster child for genetically engineered agriculture is being marketed to nonprofits. So the story behind the story is that four billion dollars in annual R and D is aimed at generating charitable donations? That seems pretty implausible to me."

"I'm not sure I see."

Christopher hesitated. What the hell, he thought. "That's just not how capitalism works. In the best possible case, if farmers grow it and eating the stuff causes blind kids to see, the game is still rigged. Golden rice as a miracle cure isn't what's in play. It's a smoke screen. You can tell because there's no real profit to justify the research investment that brought it to market. Golden rice is a feel-good story that distracts from the leg irons that Monsanto and Novartis are trying to clap onto every farmer on the planet. What they really want is to sell patented seeds that require patented chemical fertilizers to achieve the promised yield, and forbid growers from banking the seeds they harvest so they have to pay again next year, then—watch the birdie!—once-independent farmers are indentured to agribusiness for life."

Suvali took in his argument. "I don't know, Chris. I can see how you're fitting that story together. But I wonder if your inferences might fall out differently in another telling."

"I suppose they might," Christopher said. "It's hard to sort spin from fact when the issues are complex. In my experience, following the money and the information that's downplayed by the press is your best bet. But it's work."

She nodded, considering. "Okay," she said. "I'll credit you this much: I knew several underinformed members of the reactionary Left at university, and you're certainly not in their camp."

"Thanks, I think." Christopher grinned weakly. Was she mocking him? "Maybe we should talk about Van Gogh."

"Ah . . ." Suvali reopened arts and entertainment. "I'm really sorry to miss this."

"I've always loved that chair," he said, gesturing.

"Which one, Gauguin's or Van Gogh's?" There were two paintings pictured in the article.

"The yellow one," Christopher said. "Didn't Van Gogh paint both?"

"He did, but the red one is Gauguin's, the yellow chair is his own. They were working together in Arles at the time."

"Is Van Gogh a particular favorite?"

"Of mine? I suppose. During his own time he turned art back toward its emotional core. Impressionism strikes me as superficial, all surfaces and light. Then Van Gogh came along and made painting urgent again. And sensual at the same time."

"You've studied art history."

"I'm a dabbler, really. But I don't respond well to sunny optimism, at least not among nineteenth century Europeans."

Christopher supposed she was talking about life on the short end of the colonial stick. "You don't strike me as a gloomy person," he said.

"British upbringing." Suvali shrugged. "Never wear one's heart on one's sleeve. And at all costs resist what you Americans call 'irrational exuberance.'"

"Bottom line, as a Yank I can't possibly have a clue."

"Exactly," she said, smiling.

Christopher let a few moments pass. "So can I ask what drew you to medicine?"

"That's a hard question to answer. Especially if cliché is off limits."

"I don't mean to press."

"No, no—it's just . . . there's more than I can sum up in a tidy little package. Seeing people suffer, admiring people who can relieve that. Making my family proud. Breaking into a professional class that's often closed to women of a certain background. See? It sounds so clichéd already."

"Not at all," Christopher said. "It sounds real and responsible. Admirable. I'm kind of partial to people who do the right thing."

"Well. You are very serious."

"People tell me that." They sat silently for a long minute. Christopher racked his brain for a segue into something lighter. "How often do you get back to England?" he asked, grasping at the first available straw.

"Twice in three years." She brightened a little at the question. "First Christmas and second summer."

"I suppose you miss it?"

In answer she pointed to her newspaper.

"I'd love to visit someday."

"Tell me about yourself, Chris. What do you do besides read science through a political lens and talk about art with strangers?"

"Actually, that pretty much covers it." Her ebullience buoyed him. "Born and raised across the bay," he said. "My dad's a professor at Berkeley."

"In what field?"

"Molecular biology."

"Ah, so the political interests are oppositional?"

That knocked Christopher back on his heels. "I suppose the town and time had an influence. My mom was a committed sign-waver, I guess you could say I grew up as mama's little activist. Dad's a dyed-in-the-wool liberal, but as far as genetic engineering goes he's too deeply immersed to see context."

"Fair enough," Suvali said. "I suppose that's true of specialists everywhere."

"Anyway."

"No, go on. I shouldn't be so sharp. You said when we met that you do layout for a living."

"Do you know the *Reporter*?"

"The weekly tabloid?"

"Right. I'm half of the production department."

"Why not write? You strike me as the type."

Christopher worried his glass, turning it slowly on the table's surface. "It's complicated," he said. "When you tally up pages, the *Reporter* is mostly ads and reviews. And I'm too involved as an activist to write political features. The publisher doesn't want the paper stained by partisan tendencies, other than his own. So the most I can hope for are short pieces. Producing the paper is steadier work. I write online news, agitprop, that sort of thing—on my own dime. For byline credit."

"What about other professional options?"

"Journalism or in general?"

"Either way."

"I suppose I'm not so interested in careers. I'm attached to the people I live with. We're a collective, people I've done political organizing with since college. A family of sorts."

"Do you live in a squat, then?"

"No," Christopher said, smiling. "Not exactly. The building is owned by a guy who likes to rent cheap to activists. We're the activists."

"How many are you?"

"Six," he said, consciously omitting Brendan. "Plus a rotating cast of four or five undergrads on the bottom floor—State, City College. We're closer to some than others."

"That's a sizable family. Any kids?"

"A teenage boy. His mom was a prominent lefty in our cohort at Berkeley, for whatever that's worth. The biological father blew us off years ago. Anyway, keeping all that together seems more important than a professional trajectory. I couldn't move for a job."

Suvali bit her lip. "I can't imagine."

"What?"

"I suppose it's just human variety," she said. "My family leapt to the UK, and I've jumped even farther to pursue medicine. I'd wager you're as capable as anyone in my program, but you'd forego a career rather than move two counties over."

Christopher shrugged. "Maybe it's just a generational phase. My dad's parents emigrated from Eastern Europe. My mom's family fled Ireland's potato famine. Ambition burned bright on both sides—look where my Dad got to. Then you fast-forward, and I'm born where I want to be."

"If you were lazy, it wouldn't be so striking," Suvali said, gesturing to the self-imposed curriculum piled on his side of the table.

She regarded him over her milky tea. He rested his gaze on the tabletop.

"I suppose I ought to move along," Christopher said. "Leave you to London."

"I hope I haven't scared you off with my brusque British manner."

"Absolutely not." Christopher wasn't as sure as he made himself sound. He began to pack his bag. If he didn't say something now . . . "I enjoy your company, Suvali, but we should quit meeting like this. How about a movie next week? Maybe Thursday?"

She hesitated, but only for a moment. "I've got exams next week, how about the Wednesday after?"

"A week from Wednesday?" Braced for rejection, Christopher had to conceal his shock. "A week from Wednesday is great. The seventh." They exchanged phone numbers. Christopher wrote out his e-mail address too. "I have to warn you, the number is a landline. I'm the last guy in town without a cell."

"Yes, you said when we met. The mad internet chatter is a Luddite!"

Christopher laughed away the allusion to his IRC with Chagall. "It's been a pleasure. Two for two."

"For me as well, Chris."

He picked his way through the tables, fighting an impulse to shout out loud.

NINE

Berkeley hadn't changed, Christopher thought as he ascended the escalator from the subway. The rotunda capping the BART station still squatted like a glossy brown cough drop spit onto the corner of Center Street. Runaway kids still mixed it up with junkies on Constitution Plaza, clean-cut Moonies hadn't stopped recruiting for mass marriages. At the moment nobody was circulating petitions to recall the governor or tax the rich, but that only meant the usual suspects had packed up and gone to meetings.

Stepping onto the bricked plaza, Christopher recalled the first vigil he ever attended, clutching his mother's hand in this very place, baffled by a crowd's surging passions.

He must have been about six, maybe 1975: the year the US evacuated Saigon. The year Weather Underground bombed the State Department. The shootout at Pine Ridge that killed three men and sent Leonard Peltier to prison for life. Whatever called their mother downtown that night, for him and Marshall the occasion was a weird sort of festival. A crowd of blue jeans and batik skirts, painted placards, candles in mason jars, one grown-up after another speaking incoherently into a bullhorn. Marshall, younger and smaller, had been frightened by the noise and the crush. He had demanded they go home immediately, and burst into tears when Christopher begged their mother to stay.

—

Christopher caught a bus most of the way up the hill. He was only the slightest bit winded when he turned off the familiar, buckled sidewalk. Behind the unlocked front door, the foyer was thick with the leafy scent of white chrysanthemums. A mass of flowers bobbed on spindly stems arcing out of a cut-glass vase that had been their mother's favorite. A wedding gift.

Squaring his shoulders, Christopher shook off dread of whatever mawkishness his brother might have dreamed up for the occasion. The key would be to keep expectations low.

If Betty were still alive, all four Kalmans would have marked the date with dinner at home. She would have conjured up a grand feast, combing cookbooks and magazines, shopping in farmers' markets and immigrant groceries, refusing all but token assistance in the kitchen even though the party was for her. Epicurean dinners receded into family history soon after she died. Yet Marshall insisted, over Christopher's weak protest and their father's distress, that the memory of Elizabeth O'Neill Kalman be honored on her birthday in the manner she would have orchestrated herself.

The house smelled like caramelizing onions, which didn't tell him much. Christopher supposed Marshall would serve something high on the food chain. Lamb chops or steaks. Foreboding settled like a fog as he shut the door noiselessly and skirted the kitchen. The study stood empty, weeping a faint scent of decomposing books. Christopher found his father tending a charcoal fire out back, in chinos and a bib apron.

"Chris, come look." The older man beckoned, pointing into the bowl of the barbecue. Christopher crossed the patio, sinking into fuzzy moss that grew unchecked between the bricks. The flowerbeds had gone to seed. Petals from the unpruned plum trees carpeted the yard. "Look how the heat circulates," his father was saying. "Like blood pumping through arteries and veins!"

The briquettes did have something of a pulse to them. Father and son stared into the coals. Christopher reflected that where the scientist deduced orderly patterns, he saw ebb and swell of ungraspable complexity. A plangent bell began to peal out the hour from the heart of the campus, a half mile to the south.

"No problems getting across the bay?"

Professor Kalman wore his departmental party face, cheeks tensed in a vacant smile. Christopher thought he looked thin. Seven bells, then silence. The sound of the Campanile made him nostalgic, and nostalgia made him feel like a sap.

"The trains ran on time," he said. "How've you been?"

"Not bad, not bad for an old guy. Did you see Marshall?"

"Not yet, Dad. How are your classes?"

"Fine, I suppose." Professor Kalman pushed at the coals with a poker, spreading them evenly across the grate. "It's my semester to teach introductory principles, but there's little to prepare once you've given the same course a dozen times. The computational biology seminar is quite lively."

"And the lab?"

"Good, very good actually. We're coming up with some promising analytical methods. The field is generating enormous data sets, you know, and it's easy to overlook meaningful results in the mass of information. Of data, I should say, as your brother has corrected me. The point is, this is now the fundamental problem in molecular biology." Professor Kalman made a last tender adjustment to the coals. "How to spot wheat among all the chaff."

Christopher studied the wispy white hair furring his father's forearms, his slack, dry skin. Was his wrist trembling? Or was that just heat rippling up from the grill? Christopher once suggested his father's field boiled down to a belief that scrying leaves at the bottom of billions of teacups gives more reliable results than sampling just a few. Tonight he was determined to be better behaved. "You'll be a pure computer scientist before long," he said.

"I don't think so."

"No?"

"Not at all." The elder Kalman spoke with studied neutrality. "My relationship to computers is no different from yours. You lay out a newspaper, I lay out the results of my experiments. Computers are equipment, not the focus of the exercise."

Christopher grunted noncommittally.

Professor Kalman fit the enameled lid of the barbecue to its bowl. "We'd better slow down," he said, "and see how your brother is coming along."

—

As they entered the kitchen Marshall slid a pan of fingerling potatoes back into the oven.

"Smells great," Christopher said.

Extricating himself from a pair of oven gloves, the cook embraced his brother awkwardly. "Glad you could come," he mumbled.

He'd put on weight. "You look good," Christopher said, curious where Marshall's growing bulk ranked in their father's catalog of worries. Avoiding his brother's doubled chin, his gaze wandered around the kitchen, settling on a print that had hung above the kitchen table for as long as he could remember. *Paris par la fenêtre.* He wondered idly whether the print had been pushing out of subconscious memory when he nicknamed his anonymous saboteur. Marc Chagall. The Eiffel Tower alongside an overturned train. It made a rough kind of sense, he supposed. "What can I do?" Christopher asked.

"Everything's about finished. The halibut can go on in ten minutes or so."

"Chris, can I get you something to drink?"

"Wine would be great. Whatever's open."

They tracked their father from the cabinet to the refrigerator to the butcher-block counter. Professor Kalman handed Christopher a glass of something white. "Cheers," he said. "Now where did I leave mine?"

Christopher gave the wine a swirl and a sniff. A sip confirmed his initial impression. "Nice," he said. "What are we drinking?"

"Rosenblum Cellars, a local outfit, in Alameda," Marshall said. "It's a Marsanne, a Rhône varietal."

"Alameda the naval base? Vineyards in Alameda?"

Marshall shook his head. "Vintners, not growers. The fruit comes from all over California, some from Australia. Zinfandel is the grape they're known for, but five or six years ago they started in on whites and Shiraz."

Christopher took another sip. "So what are you up to?"

"The usual," Marshall said. He turned to a cutting board piled with green beans. "Playing the markets, looking for an interesting gig."

"What's interesting these days?"

Professor Kalman stood in the kitchen doorway, listening.

"To borrow from the Supreme Court, I guess I'll know it when I see it."

Christopher ran a quick calculus in his head, and resisted temptation. Justice Stewart had been distinguishing hard-core from less offensive smut, but cracks about day traders agog over online pornography wouldn't help them get through dinner. "Then how about some investment advice for neophytes?" he asked, addressing Marshall's back. As near as he could tell, his brother was lining up green beans in parallel berms, fussing over nothing to avoid facing him.

Marshall sighed dramatically. "What's your stake?"

"A retirement account. I guess . . . oh, let's say enough to cover the down payment on a midsize sedan. A used sedan."

"Then I'd recommend a real job," Marshall said. "Or a spiritual cult that teaches fulfillment on brown rice and rainwater." He turned back to his father and brother, smirking. Professor Kalman looked away.

"Let's get that halibut going," Christopher said.

—

He kept trying when they sat down to eat. Christopher complimented the green beans, the Chardonnay Marshall poured with the meal, the papaya and chipotle salsa prepared for the fish. Neither his father nor brother had noticed the construction underway at the Harrington's. He wondered about the weedy flowerbeds out back. Christopher inquired after relatives he hadn't seen for years. Nothing generated conversational traction. The empty place laid at the end of the table kept catching his eye. It made his skin crawl.

After an endless interlude of flatware on china, a Mozart sonata drifting in from the kitchen, Professor Kalman spoke. "So I've been invited to give a paper in Prague."

"When?" Christopher asked, jumping at the chance to nurse any topic along.

"End of September, at the ISB meeting. The International Society for Bioinformatics."

"Why Prague? Somebody's cloning the golem?"

Marshall rolled his eyes. "Christopher, must you?"

"I'm sure it's much more prosaic than that," Professor Kalman said. "The right meeting space for a good price is how these things are usually decided."

"What will you present?" Marshall asked.

"I was starting to tell Chris. We've been working with students in the College of Engineering, applying signal-processing algorithms to filter out noisy microarray data. Like grooming a radio signal. A short article in *Nature* is not out of the question."

"Digital processing everywhere you look," Marshall said.

"Quite right, in any number of disciplines," Professor Kalman said. "Computational linguistics, astronomy, economics. The common thread is a corpus of data too big for a human mind to ingest. Molecular biology certainly fits the bill."

"I suppose," Marshall said after a moment, "there's the danger of conflating bits and pieces of useful analysis with a comprehensive model."

Christopher looked up, surprised his brother was engaging instead of lobbing the usual conversation-enders into their exchange. "How do you mean?" he asked.

"New methods always introduce the chance of false 'eureka' moments. One danger is to generalize too quickly from data that are less representative than they seem. Especially when the analysis is small in relation to the real world—say to the universe of DNA in biological organisms."

"That," Professor Kalman said, "is why biologists have always been careful to focus on simpler organisms before moving on to complex life-forms."

"A more interesting trap is the gulf between precise data at a small scale, and the properties of complex systems," Marshall said. "Whether the systems are biological, physical, or economic. The stock market, for example."

Christopher leaned forward. "Say more." Was it possible he might agree with Marshall? About anything?

"In physical science, large organizational principles emerge independently of microscopic properties. The rigidity of ice isn't a function of water's molecular structure, or ammonia's, or whatever happens to be frozen. Rigidity emerges out of how the molecules line up. Nothing to do with the state of particular atoms."

"Well, yes, Marshall," Professor Kalman said, "but that doesn't mean we can ignore atoms and molecules."

"No, it doesn't. But the point is that close study only goes so far. If the effect is what's interesting, the molecular-scale elements aren't necessarily the story."

Professor Kalman shook his head vigorously. "First one has to know which components are participating in any given event."

Christopher wasn't sure he followed, but plunged in anyway. "You can't just ignore that, Dad. If local mechanics don't predict the big picture, that's fundamental."

Marshall made a show of offering around the last of the wine before emptying the bottle into his own glass. "There's a guy at Princeton," he said, "doing this sort of thing with data that disparate schools of investing use to predict stock prices. Dividend yields, sector trends, currency trading patterns, housing starts—mashing it all together and using statistical algorithms to look for patterns over time."

"Is he beating the market?" Professor Kalman asked sardonically.

"This is important," Christopher said, heading off his father's dismissal. "It's the question of reductionism, isn't it? Whether you can describe a large system by dissecting it down to the smallest parts? Like the ocean. Waves washing up on the shore aren't determined by molecules of water either. And you can only apply a higher order of rules—fluid dynamics—if you idealize an ocean to the point that the mathematics don't describe the actual thing in the world."

"Science takes empirical measurements using the best tools we have," Professor Kalman said. "As the tools get better, our understanding deepens. Is that so complicated?"

"Not at all, Dad," Christopher said. "No rational person could have a problem with that. I object only when you take measurements at one scale and infer meaning at another. Where you see isolated qualities in an engineered bacterium, and leap to conclusions that you can improve agriculture by injecting your mutant into an evolved ecosystem—one that your experiments don't measure or model."

"That may be the most coherent set of statements I've heard you make since high school," Marshall said.

Christopher chuckled, because the alternative would be to throw something. "Don't ever lose that endearing arrogance, Marshall. Really, I mean it."

"By the way, the guy at Princeton is still an academic. If his analysis beat the market reliably, he'd be working for Wall Street."

"I hate to disagree when you boys are getting along," Professor Kalman said, "but let's examine the choices. Either we allow experts to build social and economic capacity based on considered, peer-reviewed analysis, or we throw such decisions to bands of self-appointed amateurs—driven by who knows what irrational agendas—and wind our way back down into the dark ages."

The silence that followed could have forked in any direction. Marshall looked at Christopher. Christopher looked at Marshall.

"Speaking of ivory towers," his brother said, "I believe I'll clear the table."

Their father shook his head dismissively. Christopher stood. "Let me." Rinsing plates and stacking them in the dishwasher, he heard Marshall rummaging around the dining room. "Should I start coffee?" he called.

"I'll get it," Marshall said, entering the kitchen.

"You already made dinner. I don't mind."

"I need to fix dessert. Go on, keep Dad company."

Professor Kalman was staring into his wineglass when Christopher returned to the dining room. "That's the most anyone has gotten out of Marshall in months," he said quietly.

"Seems lucid enough to me. Not especially likable, but—"

"Too isolated," his father said. "He never sees anyone."

"Do you?"

"I'm not a social butterfly, Chris. I never have been. But I leave the house every morning. I've got my students, my colleagues. Your brother sees no one. He hardly—"

Professor Kalman swallowed his words when Marshall appeared carrying a trifle dish. The tiramisu he prepared each year, soggy with rum and espresso, was Betty's recipe. Mercifully, there were no candles. The three fell over each other serving coffee, passing cream and sugar, dishing out dessert. Marshall poured generous measures of cognac all around, from a heavy, sapphire-blue decanter. He waited for the others to raise their snifters. "To Mom," he said.

From nowhere, Christopher felt a violent sob rising. He pulled hard at his brandy. For a long minute, breathing deeply, he struggled against showing himself.

Professor Kalman started in on the tiramisu. "This is awfully good."

Christopher cleared his throat and tasted a spoonful. "Better every year," he said, embracing banality.

Marshall poured himself another finger from the decanter. Something baroque slotted itself into the CD player.

"Your mother would have enjoyed this."

Christopher cringed. She would have, it was true, but enough already.

"If only." Marshall stared at the tablecloth, tracing its embroidered pattern with a spoon.

"Chris, tell us what you've been up to," his father said.

"The same as ever, work and politics." Christopher groped for something more concrete. "An old friend came back into town a couple weeks ago," he said, realizing as he spoke that Brendan's release from prison was too freighted a topic. "Someone I haven't seen for a while."

"Anybody we know?"

He shook his head, though either might remember Brendan from their time as undergraduates.

"Not an old girlfriend by any chance?"

Christopher glanced across the table. For years he and Marshall had been equally embarrassed by their father's yearning for grandchildren. "'Fraid not."

"So what's fermenting among the diehard Left?" Marshall asked after another awkward pause.

"Would I know?" Why go there, Christopher wondered, when they'd almost made it through the evening?

"Okay, try this. I heard there's a union that wants paid time off on the day Trotsky was elected to the Politburo. What's your call, Christopher?"

"Oh, *that* diehard Left. The Left that only exists on bitchy right-wing radio."

"Boys, stop it." Professor Kalman sighed. "Really, it's so old and worn out."

"What do you mean, Dad?" Marshall asked, grotesquely feigning innocence. "It's just our way of saying 'I love you.'"

"Leaving Trotsky aside," Christopher said, "the broad-based Left is opposing the president's push to eviscerate the Bill of Rights and conquer the Middle East."

"You could just say you're against the war in Iraq, like the rest of us," Marshall said. "This thing's going to come back to bite Bush, hard. Iraq and Afghanistan both. He'll have to steal the election again if he wants another term."

Christopher might have let it go, but his brother had tapped a deep resentment. Why was the stock market suitable dinner conversation, but political activism fit only for ridicule? "My own circle," he said, "is working to expose the world's largest genetic engineering convention as a forum for hubris and ruin."

"What's that?" Professor Kalman asked. "Is that GeneSynth you're talking about?"

"Sorry, Dad."

"If you were involved in that kind of protest I would be very disappointed."

"I suppose it won't be the first time."

"GeneSynth is a scientific conference," Professor Kalman said, "where researchers present the results of their efforts to discover what is true—"

"GeneSynth is a conclave," Christopher said, "where scientists offer their corporate sponsors a smorgasbord of opportunities to reap short-term profit at the expense of ecological equilibrium."

"That is pabulum!" Professor Kalman banged his fist on the table.

"StarLink corn leaked into the food supply is a direct consequence of supposedly innocent research—"

"And what harm did it do? Proven harm?"

"Disruption of its own ecosystem by killing butterfly larvae, for starters. The evidence is plain, but industry funded piles of specious studies to bury it."

"You should be ashamed to spout nonsense like that."

"Ashamed? Ashamed of having a perspective broader than the field of an electron microscope? Ashamed of worrying about scientists twiddling random knobs on the planet's most complex machinery? C'mon, Dad—"

"And so." Marshall was swirling his cognac in lazy circles and smiling like the *Mona Lisa*. "You'll stop the madness how? By sitting in the street with your adolescent minions, chanting to the news cameras?"

Christopher rounded on his brother. "Is political engagement beneath you, Marshall? You're going to smirk yourself to death if you don't suffocate under all that gold you're hoarding."

"Who do you imagine is going to suffocate first?" Marshall asked. "Me under the weight of my modest assets, or you under an insupportable burden of self-righteousness?"

"Stop!" Professor Kalman struck the table again. The dessert plates jumped, and the room went suddenly quiet.

Marshall set down his glass decisively. Christopher pushed away from the table, resolved to turn his back first. "I should go," he said.

"Not like this, Chris," their father said, pleading.

Marshall offered an alternate opinion. "Perhaps we should quit pretending," he said. "Perhaps the clock has run out on all this sort of . . . ceremony."

TEN

Buzz and Jonah rounded the corner. "It's backward, dude," Buzz said, running his fingers through a flaccid mohawk, the dyed hair twisted into bluish-black ropes. Buzz was first in his sixth grade class to pierce a lip, just the year before, to which he'd since added studs in his eyebrows and nose, and a thicket of steel hoops around the rims of both ears. A threadbare PiL t-shirt hung slack across his narrow chest, nearly lost under a bomber jacket cut for a far larger frame. "Ravi Shankar doesn't even have MySpace. Probably never even heard of the shit."

Jonah unlocked the front gate. "Ravi Shankar was famous before MySpace even happened. Same as the Sex Pistols. It's called history, dude."

"How come there's a gate on your house?" Buzz asked as it crashed shut behind them. "You guys get robbed?"

"Probably it was here when we moved in."

They clattered up the stairs. Partway up the second flight, Jonah grabbed Buzz by the elbow, braking them both to a halt. "Don't say anything," he whispered.

Buzz pulled out of the other boy's grasp. "You worry too much," he said, and continued climbing, now at a listless pace.

Jonah hesitated, then double-staired to catch up and lead the way back toward his room. They stopped at the refrigerator. Jonah yanked it open, rattling a clutter of canning jars perched on top. "Want anything?" he asked. Buzz pointed at a fresh six-pack of Anchor Steam. Jonah shook his head. "Better not," he said, just as Allison emerged from her room.

"How goes it, guys?" she asked. "Better not what?"

"Hey Miz Rayle."

"Hey Mom."

"What are you boys up to on a Saturday afternoon? Catching up on homework?"

"Not even." Jonah closed the refrigerator.

"Truth is, Miz Rayle, I'm all caught up."

Jonah rolled his eyes. "Dude . . ."

Zac bounced into the kitchen. "I heard that," he said. "How's my favorite Johnny Rotten wannabe? What's the capital of Uzbekistan?"

"Not on the test," Buzz said.

"You have to say John Lydon if he's wearing a PiL shirt," Jonah said. "Johnny Rotten was only before the Sex Pistols broke up."

"Picky, picky," Zac said, laughing.

Jonah opened the refrigerator again, more gently this time, and fished out a bottle of cranberry juice. He and Buzz disappeared into the pantry.

"I thought you were working," Allison said to Zac.

"Traded with Diego. I'm on my way now."

Brendan sauntered in. "Who's Diego?"

"Hey! Where'd you come from?" Zac asked.

"Dozed off in the front room. The *New York Times* isn't as gripping as it used to be. So who is he, some new boyfriend?"

Zac shook his head. "Another barista at the Royal. Cute, in a manly man kind of way. Not my type."

Jonah and Buzz stepped out of the pantry.

"Hey guys." Brendan held out a hand to Jonah's friend. "I'm Brendan."

Buzz nodded.

Brendan waited several beats, then withdrew his arm.

"Hey Mom, can me and Buzz go downtown?"

"'Buzz and I.' What's downtown?"

"Music stores and stuff—"

"So." Buzz cut in from where he stood leaning against the doorframe, still eyeing Brendan dubiously. "You don't look Mexican."

Nobody breathed. Jonah turned red as the juice in his glass. Brendan didn't move, but something inside him coiled. "On my stepmother's side," he said evenly.

The two faced off "like rotts in a dog park," the way Zac told it later.

"Skinny guy like you," Buzz said, "you'd have to figure, catcher. It's the same down south, right? You get butched in and shit?"

"Buzz . . ." Zac seemed about to step between the two, but Allison took his arm, gently holding him back.

"Stateside time is uglier. Except for the guys who get beaten to death. You wouldn't want to hear about it," Brendan said.

Buzz pushed off the wall, sneering. "I've heard plenty. Hey Jonah, let's catch a Muni."

Allison shook her head. "I don't think so."

"Mom . . ."

"Jonah, you and I need to have a talk. You can see Buzz to the door. Be in my room in five minutes."

"Mom—"

"In my room, in five minutes."

Back bowed, Jonah slipped into the hall. Buzz followed,

unflinching under Brendan's stare. The adults listened until the boys were out of earshot.

"What was that?" Zac asked. Neither of the others answered. He glanced at the clock above the stove. "I'll catch up with Buzz on my way to the café."

"I'll be in the front room," Brendan said. He turned, then turned back. "Maybe it's time for me to—"

"First things first," Allison said. "Let's figure out what kind of stories Jonah was telling."

He nodded. Zac followed him toward the front of the flat.

"Don't cut out on us," Zac said. "Shit happens. He's a teenager now."

"I'm not hiding," Brendan said. "But I'm not broadcasting that I'm here either. Rumors aren't helpful."

"It's kid stuff, don't make it into more than that. Let's see what we find out."

———

"Buzz!"

Already halfway up the block, Buzz didn't look back. "What?" he asked, deadpan, when Zac caught up.

"What yourself? What's with the hostility?"

"He's an asshole. Never met an ex-con who's not."

"He isn't . . ." Zac floundered. Actually, Brendan was an ex-con. And Zac couldn't very well compound Jonah's infraction by explaining how he'd landed in Tlaxitlán. "He's not an asshole. But . . . why all that business about prisons? Why provoke somebody like that? When you don't even know him?"

"Jonah doesn't need a fucking convict living in his house. If that—" Buzz cut himself short. "Fuck this, I don't owe you answers. I don't like him, deal with it."

Zac blanched at the boy's intensity but didn't back down.

"You're right," he said. "You don't owe me squat. But you're wrong about Brendan. I don't get it, but you're way off the mark. Brendan is family to Jonah, same as I am."

"Shit."

"Hear me out! I want Jonah's friends to be welcome in our house. If there's a problem you know about, speak up. Tell me, tell Allison. But there's no room at the Triangle for sneak attacks over secret grudges. That's not what we're about."

Buzz didn't respond. A low rumble from the tunnel under Buena Vista Park signaled the N-Judah's approach. He glanced toward the tracks.

"Jonah likes you, Johnny Rotten, and that earns points. Don't be a stranger to us."

Buzz walked away, crossing to the Muni stop. Zac watched until he climbed aboard and the train pulled away from the platform.

———

"I don't know why." Jonah sat on the worn quilt at the foot of Allison's bed. She leaned against the wall. He'd retreated behind a mask, his face closed tight as the fists clenched in his lap.

She studied him, this son of hers on the cusp between boyhood and sullen adolescence. "If you don't know why Buzz acted that way, tell me how he knows Brendan was in prison."

Silence.

"That wasn't a very interesting question," she said. "He knows because you told him. How about we put that on the table and go from there?"

Jonah didn't look up, but he nodded.

"Did you think it was okay to tell stories about Brendan?"

"No."

"Can you say why?"

A pause. "Because maybe the police'd put him back in jail even though Mexico let him go."

"Bull's eye," Allison said. "We don't quite know about Brendan's legal status. So we don't want to put him at risk."

"I didn't think Buzz'd be like that."

"I bet you asked him not to let on that he knew." Allison understood she was putting Jonah in an excruciating place. "Did you tell because you're angry at Brendan? Or at me?"

Now the tears. Jonah buried his face in his hands. He didn't want to cry in front of his mother; she was grateful he still could. Allison sat beside him, wrapping her son in a gentle embrace.

"I don't know," he ground out.

"It's okay . . . it's okay, sweetheart." She stroked his hair, losing herself in its golden river.

After a while Jonah straightened. "What should I do?"

"What do you think? Past, present, future?"

"It's a told secret," Jonah said, falling into the familiar drill. "It can't be undone."

"Okay."

"Future is, I won't do it again."

"I believe you," Allison said. What to do now, that was always the hardest for Jonah. She waited while he thought it through.

"I guess . . . the present is I have to apologize."

"To whom?"

"Brendan." He grimaced when he spoke the name.

"Are you still feeling weird around him?"

Jonah shrugged.

"Would you like me to be there with you?"

"I'm not scared, I told you. It's just . . ." Jonah swallowed. "Will Brendan have to go away now?"

"I hope not. Was that your intention?"

Jonah didn't answer. "I guess I'll go find him."

—

Edging just inside the doorway, Jonah stood with hands in his pockets. Brendan looked up from his book. "Hey."

"Hey," Jonah said back.

"I'm sorry about that thing with your friend."

Jonah shook his head. "I'm sorry I opened my big mouth." He glanced at the paperback Brendan was setting aside, a bright yellow cover against the dull blue of the sofa.

"It's better for me to lie low for a while."

"I know. I fucked up."

"We all fuck up," Brendan said. "Take me, for example. You spend a year in jail and all you can think about is that big, flashing 'I'm a Fuckup!' sign tied around your neck." He gestured toward the other sofa, its lumpy decrepitude masked by a blanket. Jonah collapsed onto a beanbag pillow instead, nearer to the door. "What do you know about Buzz?" Brendan asked.

Jonah shrugged. "He's a guy at my school."

"Political? Tough guy? Is he into music? Sports? Nuclear physics? Has he got a sense of humor?"

"He's my friend."

"Fair enough," Brendan said. "But he knows more about me than I'd like, so I was hoping to even things out a little."

Jonah picked at a loose thread in the pillow's seam. "He's a little bit tough. Not so political. No sports."

"Have you ever been to his house?"

"No."

"But he's been over here. A few times? Pretty often?"

"I didn't count," Jonah said. "I guess pretty often."

"Do you know what his parents do for work?"

"No."

"Any trouble with the police?"

"No way, we're in seventh grade!"

"What about somebody else in his family?"

"I don't like this conversation."

"Me neither." Brendan picked up his book and set it down again. "Look Jonah, it's not my place to make judgments about your friends. But I get a bad feeling off that kid."

"Because he acted like an asshole?"

"Lots of people act like assholes. That doesn't worry me."

"So?"

"I'm looking at two possibilities. One's paranoid, the other's treacherous."

"I don't get it."

Brendan stood and moved to the window. He looked out for a few moments, then turned back toward the room. "The paranoid possibility is that the police are watching me, and connected me to you because I'm staying here, then through you they drew a line to Buzz. And maybe they have some leverage, something you don't even suspect, that they used to get him to check me out. Or to stir me up. Whatever the cops are after."

Jonah stared. "I've seen 'freaked out' around this house," he said, "but that gets the lifetime achievement award."

"Shit." Brendan grinned. "Certified a lunatic by a thirteen-year-old shrink."

"What's the other possibility?" Jonah asked. "The so-called treacherous one?"

"Buzz knows more about prison than the fairy tales that pass for gangsta rap and gritty cop shows," Brendan replied. "I'm guessing he spent time around somebody who's been inside. That, and the fact he never invites you over to his house—the combination makes me nervous."

Jonah didn't say anything.

"I'm not your pops, okay? Neither one of us is confused on

that point. But I've known you since you were a worm in dia-pers. I care about you. About your whole family, everybody who's part of the Triangle." Brendan paused, choosing his words. "There are some hard-ass people out there, Jonah. I'd hate to see you get too close to people like that."

ELEVEN

November 2003

At twenty minutes to midnight, Romulus is wardriving through a quiet neighborhood some dozen miles east of his last access point, sampling airborne Ethernet. A few houses on each block show light through shaded windows. A laptop on the passenger seat chirps as his van approaches a small apartment building. He angles in to park beside a high-hedged yard.

Moving carefully to keep shocks and struts from creaking, Romulus squeezes his bulk between the front seats, setting the chirping laptop among a bank of its peers and muting its speaker. He pulls a thick, black curtain closed, hiding the glow of his screens from casual passersby. Data cascades down the LCD panels. He settles himself at the van's makeshift workbench, and rolls his head to stretch tight shoulders.

Only one of the networks in range of the vehicle's antennae is well encrypted. A weakly secured access point is carrying heavy traffic, downloading from a Grokster server at pipe-straining speed. Romulus won't be the only party committing illegal acts tonight.

Two accessible routers are transmitting cleartext, broadcasting identifier beacons that invite all comers.

—

Much attention has been paid to the conceit that destruction is the soil from which creation springs. *"Die Lust der Zerstörung ist zugleich eine schaffende Lust,"* wrote revolutionary anarchist Mikhail Bakunin in 1842. "The passion for destruction is a creative passion, too." Śiva the Destroyer has ruled the Hindu pantheon for thousands of years, in equipoise with Brahma the Creator and Vishnu the Preserver. The Nobel Peace Prize was founded by a Swedish arms manufacturer, the inventor of dynamite.

Collegiate wanking in this vein has no hold over Romulus. He sees no reason to dress up counterstrikes with weak rationalizations. Romulus came of age mucking through the backwash of sixties-era marches, rallies, sit-ins, and drop-outs, a tumult that convinced baby boomer malcontents of their own moral purity but gained precious little else. Nixon didn't nuke Hanoi. He'll give them that, and a few other tantrums of empire restrained by mass protest. But only a fool could deny that power remains fundamentally intact, whatever its guises.

Opposition opposes. It's a simple principle; Romulus holds it close. Symbolic mewling doesn't qualify. Neither does unfocused rage. Yet he knows too well that his own disruptive effect is pitifully narrow. He stalks Leviathan with blow darts. Meanwhile, the planet heats up, the ecosphere is brutalized, and strength accrues to the strong.

For years Romulus has acted where he can, navigating a digital ocean of packets and frames, setting in-memory hacks, laying Unix haiku like driftnet across gigabit currents and binary streams. He operates from plain commercial vans, bought and sold for cash, transformed by faux company logos silk-screened on magnetic stock. One day he drives a fleet vehicle for a sewer-cleaning firm, the next a flower shop, then a small-time caterer.

Inside an Econoline shell he's invisible as manhole covers. Any halfwit can siphon bandwidth from suburban neighborhoods, as easily as hooking up a garden hose.

Spectral existence has its advantages, but there's a flip side to the life he has chosen. No matter how cleverly Romulus cracks, hacks, spoofs, sniffs, decrypts, probes, hijacks, and munges, all he can touch are bits and bytes. And so, when he finally set out to find collaborators, he didn't look for a twin. He sought a skill set complementary to his own.

Combing through the internet's flood of constructed identities, lurking at the edges of chat rooms, filtering streams of e-mail tapped from poorly managed server farms, Romulus made tentative contact with dozens of candidates. His standards were exacting. At the first indiscretion, the slightest bluster, he dropped his discoveries. He unearthed and discarded hyperbolists whose polemic traced back to AOL accounts. He dismissed postings from anarcho-literati that led, through ineffective protection, to student co-ops in Madison, Berkeley, or Austin. Diehards on public terminals, advocating a socialist workers' commonwealth, same old, same old since Lenin stormed the Winter Palace? He couldn't be bothered.

Chagall was a different animal.

Romulus found him lurking on the edge of a moderately encrypted chat. Both of them were monitoring the exchange silently as other participants analyzed a recent spate of political arson against housing developments outside Boston. Chagall was scrambled by the same server used by an entity Romulus had seen picking through the website of a commercial demolition outfit several weeks before. He couldn't be sure this was the same cyberphantom, a point in the lurker's favor. Romulus adopted another identity, camouflaged through Vancouver, Buenos Aires, and Bangkok. He entered the discussion from a new terminal window.

"Who's looking for the *next* big bang?" Romulus typed into the chat, and the packets carrying his keystrokes bounced across three continents before arriving on a server in Kraków, where the chat had convened.

The lurker withdrew immediately. Romulus smiled approvingly in the thin radiance of his monitors, and set loose a host of sniffers to seek the anonymous avatar wherever he might surface next.

———

What's a responsible actor to do? When the world's going to hell and transformation is laughably unlikely, what direction is forward?

Romulus has tried turning a blind eye, cashing in on his natural talents. But he had a tough time choking down the corporate Kool-Aid.

Early in elementary school, his class took a field trip to Round Acre Ranch, a local organic dairy. He doesn't remember the bus ride out, or the tour of the grounds. He has no memory of how other seven-year-olds responded to the sickly sour smell that permeated the milking shed, or the dusty stink of the barnyard. What he can't forget is the narrowness of the lives they'd been ferried out to witness. Round Acre's sad-eyed bovines set an inchoate horror creeping through Romulus's emergent sense of self. "What do they do?" he asked Ms. Ferris. His teacher coughed up a distressingly short list. Eat grass. Give milk.

His dread was not allayed.

Fat salaries, burgeoning investments, bonuses, freebies, perks. For Romulus, material wealth adds up to eating and excreting. He has no more desire now to live like a dairy cow than he did in the second grade.

———

Direct contact with the lurking demolitionist came weeks later.

ROMULUS: Don't run, I can't see who you are and I'm not trying to find out. I can prove myself. I think we have common interests . . . philosophical discourse first. PGP encryption key below. Send secure contact info to 3046_29128@phrianom.net, account dies in 10 days. Learn why I thought I should contact you. If you're the type I'm looking for, you'll want to know. Pseudo-sender of this message no longer exists.

Chagall could not have been glad to draw notice, and wouldn't see how or why he'd been contacted under a freshly minted, well-cloaked identity. Romulus hoped uncertainty might keep him interested. With two and a half hours left on the clock, Chagall replied on a Saturday afternoon.

CHAGALL: Have we met? Are you a police officer or an agent of any government entity? Answer directly. Proof required. Public key attached. Post response to freediplomas4791033862@yahoo.com within 12 hours or don't contact me again.

Romulus approved. No one Chagall wanted to hear from took weekends off. An FBI hack idly trolling for terrorists might have missed the window while mowing a lawn in Reston, or firing up a barbecue in Silver Spring. Chagall would have figured it unlikely that anyone could rustle up a subpoena for a Yahoo account in twelve hours on a Saturday.

ROMULUS: Categorically no to both questions. Proof is on my agenda. Think of me as a white hat hacker for the other side. I seek a synergy of skills to further common goals.

Early on, Chagall sent Romulus a reading list. The presumption annoyed him. Perhaps he should have pushed back against his recruit's curt and controlling manner, but he cut Chagall a measure of slack. After all, he was asking the demolitionist to sublimate his gifts to the broader reach of a propaganda campaign. And Chagall's presumption seemed less egregious when he turned out to be pushing their collaboration even further. The saboteur saw the limits of his craft as clearly as Romulus viewed his own handicaps. Chagall insisted he put aside the fallacy that physical effect translates into political results, that explosions win a war. By way of example, Chagall referred him to the writings of a Latin American guerrilla, a man the Mexican government identified as a philosophy professor:

> We would like to make two things clear: one is our commitment to the Democratic National Convention; the other is our decision not to impose our point of view. We have also rejected any notion of chairing this Democratic National Convention. This convention represents a peaceful search for change; in no way should it be led by people who bear arms. We are grateful to you for giving us a place here, as one more among all of you, so that we may have our say.

Subcomandante Marcos is the rebel's nom de guerre. Romulus hadn't paid his movement much attention, but he understood the draw when he read the passages Chagall cited:

> If you want me to summarize it, I will say that just as we became soldiers so that one day soldiers would no longer

be necessary, we also remain poor so that one day poverty will be no more. This is why we use the weapon of resistance.

Chagall aims to trump their detractors with modesty and deference. If they act radically but yield to a moderate center, he argues, their attack might catch a wave that has buoyed the Zapatistas for ten years in the face of massive repression. Marcos often repeats a widely quoted slogan: *Para todos todo. Para nostros nada.* Everything for everyone. Nothing for ourselves. Chagall intends their own rhetoric, too, to be antithesis and paradox, powered by a militant shock to the media.

They fit the Chiapas insurgents' mold imperfectly. He and Chagall have no community, no political apparatus, will have nothing to show beyond their single dramatic act. But like the Zapatistas, they will explicitly set aside vengeful impulse. They will simply exact destruction and justify it, seeking to catalyze a movement that can never be theirs.

———

Cocooned among his screens, Romulus scans reports forwarded by a Trojan. He is looking for signs that security admins set traps to detect his return to the Facilities and Construction Office at the University of Nebraska. The department sprawls the length of a city block in the heart of Lincoln: cinderblock, flat roofs, double-glazed sliders with aluminum frames, lots and lots of parking spaces. Romulus has no interest in this bureaucracy's physical layout. He's visiting a world of IP addresses and ports.

A printer connected to Facilities and Construction's network segment provided an ideal niche for a logger bot. Romulus planted his mechanized spy during an earlier intrusion, and later returned to map the department's user names, IP addresses, and intercepted e-mail.

He soon gained access to drawings of a six-story structure rising out of flat, tilled prairie west of the campus. He installed automated fetch scripts, set to pull data from breached file-servers to compromised workstations, a trickle now, a dribble later. Over the course of a week, a complete set of engineering diagrams for the Randall P. Bailey Center for Agricultural Genomics has grown ripe for picking. Tonight's ectoplasmic visit to the University of Nebraska will be a harvest festival.

There is no sign that his intrusion was detected. Romulus marshals his bots.

As dawn breaks over Nebraska's state capitol, automated scripts will ready the digital spoils for beaming across the internet. Facilities and Construction may never realize they've been cracked. The path by which the diagrams are copied from Lincoln to obscure directories of a hobbyist's site in New South Wales will be wiped from the digital record long before the purpose of this theft is realized.

Romulus uses a phished password to log into a payroll administrator's workstation. He writes rogue executables to memory, then deletes the record of his login. Romulus adds the file-moving script to a queue and withdraws from the machine.

Twenty-six seconds.

In an hour, maybe two, he'll latch onto another network in a neighborhood miles distant, to confirm that all is unfolding according to plan.

TWELVE

Brendan woke late and groggy, as he had each morning since leaving Tlaxitlán. His insomnia fed on equal parts city noise and the absence of other men's breathing, gorged itself on dreams that locked him back inside. He lay haunted in the wakeful dark, night after night. The guard El Dentista and his roundhouse punch to Brendan's jaw, the whip-thin switchblade artist they called Culebra, the stench of scorched flesh in the House of Screams. Now Brendan groped for his jeans, squinting against sun pushing in around the edges of the window shade. He took a long, salty piss, and brushed smoke scum from teeth and tongue. Forgetting it was Sunday, that she wouldn't be at work, Brendan started when he found Allison in the second-floor kitchen.

"Hey," he croaked.

Allison looked up from the newspaper. "Kettle's loaded," she said. "Coffee's set up for a press pot."

Tongue-tied, Brendan thanked her with a slight, silent bow.

She returned to her article, head bending to the task. Allison led with an index finger, her concentration complete. Brendan might as well have been invisible. He lifted the kettle. Full, as advertised. Allison didn't look up as he bumbled his way toward caffeination. Not even a glance. When he brought mugs and milk to the table she nodded distractedly. He reached for a section of the paper. They read silently, but Brendan couldn't work up enthusiasm over a wife murderer who'd breached the tabloid-broadsheet barrier. Reopening the Statue of Liberty to tourists didn't hook him either. He tried to believe she wasn't ignoring him, that she was just allowing him space to wake up.

"Where's Jonah?" he asked.

Allison finger-marked her place in an account of Cambodian genocide. "Out with Zac," she said. "One of their Bollywood field trips."

"Any more fallout from yesterday?"

Allison shook her head. "Maybe tomorrow, he'll see Buzz at school. Zac said Buzz was angry when they talked right after . . . all that." She gave up her place in the article to gesture vaguely upstairs.

"Zac told me. But no clue what about."

"We'll just have to watch it unfold. I'm afraid it goes with the territory."

Brendan was sure that if he left a silence she'd return to her article. "I was thinking about Jonah's . . . what, his standoffishness? Not hostility. But there was an edge."

"Keep in mind how old he is."

"I know, Zac said the same thing. I'm not taking it personally." He set the paper aside. "But I was remembering the day I showed up. I disappointed him, I think."

She leaned forward. "How so?"

"Can't say exactly. He asked about prison, and I didn't say much. I wonder if he thought I didn't trust him, that I don't think he's old enough to know."

"Could be. That's a sore spot these days."

"But then he shifted gears. I don't remember how he put it, but he was struggling to see how people decide what to take a stand on, what political work to do. He didn't like my ambiguity about why I went south."

Allison sat back and poured another measure from the press pot. "First they trust. Then they question. Now he's getting to where he's convinced adults make no sense at all."

"And it's a rough ten or fifteen years 'til he figures out he won't make any either. That sense isn't a human trait."

"Do you really think that?" Allison asked.

"Yes and no." How had that happened? From making conversation to child-rearing to jostling for . . . for what? As if they were still juniors at Cal, still testing each other's mettle. Brendan felt the caffeine taking hold. He could play that game. "Why Chiapas and not Tibet?" he asked her back. "Why genetic engineering and not nuclear waste? Focus on a single issue and your politics are neurotic. Abstract your ideals to generalities like justice or equality, and there's too much, you're overwhelmed. If you pick issues that are ripe for making progress, you're reacting to somebody else's agenda, pragmatism over principle. Where's the sense in all that tangle?"

Allison sipped from her mug. "Making sense means seeing connections across a range of activity. Pragmatic means moving the levers you can reach." She held his gaze. "What's tough about explaining that to a thirteen-year-old is it's built on decades of experience."

Were they talking about raising children or political strategy? Maybe Allison didn't distinguish between the two. "Sense is muddied by complexity and disinformation," he said. "Pragmatism is surfing whatever crisis is bearing down on us right now. That's hard to explain to a teenager because it's scary to acknowledge how little we know and how much less we can do about it."

Allison laughed, breaking the tension. "Okay, enough abstract philosophy. Explain why you, Brendan James, dove into solidarity work for a revolution hatched thousands of miles south, and now you're pitching into a movement against mutant food grown in the States?"

"Opportunity knocked?"

"Seriously."

"When people build up wealth and power the result is usually widespread suffering. So a moral actor has to oppose greed, QED. Given multiple ways to do that, I want to choose the ones that are effective and that do the least damage."

"I think that makes sense."

"Of course you do. It follows from what you just laid out, connections and levers. 'Opportunity knocked' follows from what I said, the crisis right now. But guess what, Al? We're both resolving to the same chord, and either tune is plausible." Brendan leaned forward; his chair rapped sharply against the floor. "What do you say we take a walk? Maybe out along the water someplace?"

She looked into his eyes for long enough to worry him, then nodded assent. "Okay," she said. "The 22 gets us to the Marina in twenty minutes."

Brendan let a smile blossom for the first time in a week. "How 'bout let's ride," he said. "The Kawasaki's turning into grease spots and rust in that cave you guys call a garage."

—

Careening up Fillmore, he could tell Allison was trying not to hold on too tight, though it couldn't be easy with her arms wrapped around his waist. She followed his calibrated leans at the turns and did her best to maintain an illusion of distance. Allison tensed as they rounded a sharp corner. He pretended to take her touch in stride.

They parked in the Fort Mason lot and followed a path along the harbor's edge. Halyards chimed against aluminum masts, seagulls complained in gliding arcs along the waterfront, some-body's daysailer luffed around to the wind, jib riffling through the turn. After weeks in the city's interior, Brendan soaked up the space. Angel Island and Tiburon beckoned from across miles of open bay. The Golden Gate Bridge draped cat's cradle cables across a limitless Pacific. But once his gaze crossed Alcatraz, Brendan couldn't pull away from it. The decaying walls of San Francisco's retired penitentiary, a blur of weathered gray stone, sat like a grim cake topper set in steep sand and scrub. His focus narrowed until the prison island was the only thing visible in all that panoramic view.

"What are you seeing?" Allison asked, soft over the ping of a signal buoy.

"Nothing," he said, ripping away from possession.

They walked on. Alongside the docks he stopped to admire a teak-decked ketch jutting above the fiberglass crowd.

Allison followed his gaze. "Own a boat like that," she said, "you get really, really good at polishing brass."

Brendan nodded. "But think about it . . . that finely made thing and nothing else, out to every horizon. Just me at the helm. Is that right for a sailboat? At the helm?"

Allison sighed. "However much things change."

"What's that supposed to mean?"

Allison stood upright and relaxed, eyes on the harbor, as if she could never be harmed. Her invincibility made his blood boil.

"It means you can't stay still. You're already scouting for where you're off to next."

He stood for a few seconds, wavering, then stomped away at a furious clip. Fifty yards on Brendan halted abruptly, and waited. She took her time catching up. "I've been living in a god-damned kennel," he said, starting to walk again. "Is it such a goddamned surprise that I crave a little solitude?"

"It's no surprise. I can imagine wanting the same."

He tamped down his anger. "I'm sorry." He knew he didn't sound it. "Besides, I can't sail. Would you crew?"

"Don't know that I'm qualified."

"I thought you used to go out on Long Island Sound every summer with your uncle." He knew better, but couldn't keep from baiting her. "That uncle on the Baptist, cross-burning side of your family, right? Or was it the strikebreaking Pinkertons' side?"

She delivered a playful jab to his shoulder but it landed hard, catching Brendan by surprise. He tripped over his own sneakers, stumbling toward the harbor's edge.

Allison followed instinctively, sinking her weight into the ground as she caught his wrist. Brendan twisted like a top, spinning on a sneakered toe, and tripped back the other way—saved by the skin of his teeth from a saltwater dousing.

—

"I guess that black belt shit never leaves you," Brendan said, kneading his arm. They were sitting on the Marina Green, a safe distance from the water. He could have been grateful, could have been pissed off. He supposed he was both. His shoulder ached like she'd ripped the limb out of its socket.

"Look—"

"Forget it." Brendan lay back into the cool, groomed grass and stared at the sky. At least he'd learned something. She was still ashamed of her family's black sheep. Still penitent. Allison squinted northward, to where the Richmond Bridge disappeared behind Angel Island.

"Brendan . . ."

"Hmmmm?"

"Is it what happened in prison that's eating you up, or what landed you there?"

He mulled over her question. Closed his eyes. Opened them

again. "Both and neither," he said. "I can't shake Tlaxitlán out of my dreams. That's at night. In the mornings I obsess over what I'm going to ask the guys who set this thing in motion. Assuming I can convince them to meet. But I'll tell you, Al . . . the thing that's really killing me?"

"Yeah?" She turned back toward him.

"Is what didn't happen."

"How do you mean?"

"You get a lot of time to count in prison." Now Brendan measured what he ought to say. "You count everything. Bars on a cell window, spoonfuls of soup in a bowl, how many times the same *narcocorrido* track gets played on somebody's shitty boom box in a single afternoon. People who write in the course of four hundred twenty-six days. People who come to visit."

Allison looked away.

"Padre Raúl Jaime de la Cruz came calling, first thing," Brendan said. "Local priest, damned by a maudlin nature to visit any prisoner willing to suffer his company." He tallied up on his fingers. "My attorney, Jorge Vertiz, conniving bloodsucker at justice's bar. Doña Erlinda Cordella, paid by Vertiz to keep me fed. My beloved father, neoconservative diehard, steadfast despite his suspicions about the true nature of my road trip. And, last but furthest from least, Timothy Whalen James. You remember Tim, right? The most unremarkable ophthalmologist in the state of Maryland, long-suffering brother, gritted of tooth and rich in disappointments."

"Five," Allison said, acknowledging the obvious.

Brendan sat up. A catamaran was motoring by, its gray-and-blue sails furled. They watched it skim out of the harbor, then tack around toward the Marin Headlands. "It's not anybody's fault," he said. "I know that. I know what I wrote to everybody who offered—that the bastard warden wouldn't let gringos visit unless they were blood kin."

"That was true, wasn't it?"

"Hell yes, it was true. If I could've . . . had an honest conversation? Let's just say I wouldn't have been too proud to ask. This was the deepest shit I never imagined for myself, Allison. It taught me something I never wanted to learn."

She narrowed her eyes, almost imperceptibly. Bracing herself. "What was that?"

"It taught me that when you scrape off the lies we tell each other about solidarity—when it comes down to the raw real deal—either your family comes through or you're out on your own."

Allison exhaled a pent-up breath. "I don't want to believe that."

"Neither did I."

The catamaran disappeared behind a spit of landfill that sheltered the harbor.

"Do you really think we tell each other lies? Or is that poison that'll work its way out of your system?"

"I don't know yet. There's a lot we don't know 'til we're tested, and my test isn't finished."

"I believe the people I live with tell me the truth. And that our loyalties are proven."

"You believe it, but do you know it?" Brendan asked. "Maybe you can only know in retrospect."

Allison thought for a while before answering. "You can only act in the present. And belief isn't entirely blind. We have history as a guide. In fifteen years with Chris and Marty and Nora, and Zac for most of that time—history hasn't let me down."

"Maybe the tests haven't been severe enough."

"Severe enough for what? We've been living our lives. Should we creep around in fear of what-ifs? Should we seek out adversity?"

"No, of course not."

"Look at when Seth split. I had no idea how that was going to turn out, whether I'd have to give up everything to be a single mom. But everybody stepped up—Nora especially, but in the end, everybody. And now Jonah trusts his housecomrades as parents, because that's what they've been to him ever since he can remember. Another example: when Winton Collier got busted, during the first Gulf War. That was a situation where we *could* mount a political defense, and everybody we knew came through."

"Then Winton dropped out of politics, same as Seth."

"Come on, Brendan! Why are you so intent on finding weakness and fraud?"

"I didn't go looking, Al. They found me."

She sighed. "Maybe so. But where do you fit into all this?"

"All what?"

"The decision to go south. What happened. The support network watching your back."

"The support network? You tell me. Where do I figure in the Triangle's larger scheme?"

"Brendan . . ."

"What?"

"I think that's a question for you to answer."

He felt blood drain from his face; his heart beat loudly in his ears. "No, I don't think it is."

"Loyalty doesn't come into being spontaneously," she said. "It's a dividend paid out after long years of investment. Of constancy. Of being there for people."

Brendan leapt to his feet, fists clenched. "So it's my fault? I fucking—"

"Sit down."

He sat, trembling with fury.

"Everybody makes choices," she said. "Nobody is exempt from consequences, including me. Could I have written you more letters? Yes, but I let Chris carry that burden. *Mea culpa.* Could I have visited you? Not possible."

He shook his head. "It doesn't matter now."

"We all have regrets," she pressed, her voice taut, nearly breaking. "Every one of us does. The practical question is what to do today, in a world born of a past we can't change."

He couldn't look at her. "Yeah."

"What if you never learn what was really in the truck? What if you go the rest of your life never knowing whether the comrades you trusted broke their word, or if it was the Federales who set you up?"

She waited for him to speak. The silence between them grew.

"It could happen, Brendan. And if it does—so what? Either way you've got a life to put back together. A good, honest, generous life." Allison sighed heavily. "I don't know how to fix what hurt you. What I do know is it would be a terrible waste to reject everything you've done and been and believed just because a few people did you wrong. Even if it turns out they did you wrong in spades."

THIRTEEN

Christopher fed his ticket through the fare gate and descended into the BART station. His days had been crammed full. There was work, of course. Suvali. The family dustup. Planning for GeneSynth. When he tallied his waking hours, though, he'd spent a plurality on Chagall's manifesto. On his own writing project, strictly speaking.

He needed today's online meet-up to shed some decisive light. Could he trust the saboteur or not? Christopher had approached Balboa Park station after a roundabout walk through City College. Evasive maneuvers were becoming second nature, but running circles to mitigate Chagall's worries still left him feeling unclean.

Christopher boarded the first southbound train that rolled into the station and didn't bother to take a seat. The doors opened at Daly City, and he stepped onto the platform. Thirty-eight minutes from the Triangle. It felt a world apart.

"This is a Millbrae train," the operator's disembodied voice repeated. "Please stand clear of the doors."

The suburban expanse disoriented him. Even on a Sunday, acres of cars filled the asphalt moat surrounding the station. He tacked his way through the parked vehicles.

Christopher spotted Café Michelle easily. Its frilly awning looked like nothing else in the neighborhood of low-rent taquerias, appliance emporiums, and check cashing shops. Inside, the walls were hung with angular cityscapes painted by a local artist-of-the-month. A chalkboard menu featured Viennese specialties along with the usual espresso drinks. All in all, the place was trying way too hard to transcend its environment.

Ordering a café au lait, Christopher took a seat with his back to the room's far corner and ran quickly through the drill. Linux boot, a spoofed MAC address, encrypted IRC client. He was thinking through the points he wanted to hit when Chagall logged in.

CHAGALL: What you sent is a great start.

Christopher set down his coffee and typed.

CHRIS: Including the sample paragraphs? The regretful tone doesn't put you off?
CHAGALL: It's on the mark. "Destruction is a failure to mobilize and negotiate." We would like to see more on strategic selection of target.
CHRIS: That's difficult. I don't know what it is.
CHAGALL: And you can't know, for reasons we've covered. Strategy can be explained without reference to specifics.
CHRIS: Maybe this is something you'll need to tweak.
CHAGALL: Possible. But you could write generally. War against the biosphere is raging, our target is a weapon. Strategy is to reduce target's capacity for damage, even if our methods have only limited scope and temporary effect.
CHRIS: Okay, I see what you mean. Bearing in mind we're

still not certain I'm writing this for you, can I ask if target is research or manufacturing?

CHAGALL: No. No description beyond early communications.

CHRIS: So all I know is crops/agribusiness.

CHAGALL: Better not to repeat across dialog borders. How hard would it be to write two versions, for science and for industry? We could choose A or B.

CHRIS: I'll think about it.

CHAGALL: We'll want to say the scope of action is limited because we're targeting only one facility, this time. A regretful tone should not imply flagging resolution.

CHRIS: So you want a broad critique, one that will apply if extended to different facility types.

Christopher looked up from his screen. A hit of coffee, a glance around the room. No one seemed to be paying any attention to the guy in the corner with fast fingers. Chagall's reply popped into view.

CHAGALL: Exactly. Which fits your—what to call it? Your flexible model for composition. Imply this might be first of many actions, but don't say outright. At the same time, avoid argument that opposes scientific knowledge and development. Destruction of target should be acknowledged as a waste of resources that could have been used constructively. Science not the enemy, it's a tool, etc. Enemies are hubris, greed, shortsightedness.

CHRIS: Our positions are consistent. Does something in what I sent raise a flag on this?

CHAGALL: Section on what we don't know about biology. Humility is good. Attack on reason would not be helpful.

CHRIS: Understood. From my point of view, defrocking priests doesn't compel pulling down temples.

CHAGALL: Not sure about the metaphor.

CHRIS: Biologists understand micromechanics, at expense of the big picture. Genetic engineers attempt to break apart and reassemble a foundation without knowing what it supports. Scientists are moving too quickly because they're funded by profit-driven corporations. The funders have a free hand to impose risk on the rest of us because they also employ lobbyists, to thwart regulation.

CHAGALL: We'd want to keep it readable.

CHRIS: Sure. You mentioned Christian Right at one point. It's important to appeal to a religious audience. Can invoke humility again, preserving God's creation, without pandering to biblical literalism or to the ostrich mentality in vogue among reactionaries.

CHAGALL: If you can pull that off, appeal to religious might fit. But must not appeal only to one sector. Secular audience is key. Our natural "base."

CHRIS: I think it's important enough to try to make it work. You can judge when the draft is complete. Your take re: including critique of corporate-owned gov't, and consumer greed? As fundamental issues to civil society retaking reins?

CHAGALL: Fundamental, yes. But people glaze over at theory. Use accessible examples. Pension funds going broke, top salaries at 500x ordinary workers'—those are easy to understand. Not Marx, no references to commodity fetishism.

CHRIS: That's fair. But the argument must address wealth directly. Planet can't sustain excessive consumer demand. This is a major part of logic behind agribusiness and other environmentally destructive industry: "if the world won't support manufactured cravings, change the world." While profit-controlled government aids and abets.

CHAGALL: Again, can't read like a dissertation. On a different note, you include a prominent argument re: no harm to humans. Of course we remain fully committed to this intention. But circumstances are never under complete control.

Christopher stared at his screen. Then he typed, a flurry of keystrokes.

CHRIS: No. A thousand times no. I am writing a defense of no-harm activity, period. Require ironclad guarantee before giving you permission to use. Anything is *theoretically* possible. But I'm out unless there's strong assertion re: zero harm.

CHAGALL: Slow down.

CHRIS: There's nothing to negotiate here.

A tall, strikingly handsome guy in skinny jeans and a narrow-shouldered trench coat smiled at him from across the café. It was a piss-poor moment to be distracted. Male attention didn't bother him, but the guy was barely half his age. What was it about IRC in public venues that incited flirtation? Christopher pretended not to notice.

CHAGALL: Point conceded. Understand that we have 100% commitment to harming no one, only property. You're right, and we won't compromise written material. Care and planning are thorough and safe as possible.

CHRIS: Line in the sand: even if I do eventually permit use of something I'm writing, I revoke permission if catastrophe happens. What I have to say will make political sense *only* in the event of success & no harm. Otherwise your group must write its own apology and self-criticism. I do *not* and will *never* agree to justify an action in which people are injured, regardless of intent. These are not negotiable requirements. I need unconditional agreement.

Christopher had no reason to believe his demand would be honored if Chagall fucked up, no matter how fiercely he declared it. His ultimatum amounted to rhetorical bluster. But why had Chagall raised the question in the first place?

CHAGALL: Agreed and accepted. I did not mean to complicate your contribution. Your work is top quality, we'd like to see this through. Can you estimate a finish date for a complete draft?

Christopher typed a reluctant reply.

CHRIS: Maybe a week. Not polished, but fleshed out.
CHAGALL: Awaiting next e-mail. Appreciate your careful thinking. Anything else needed from our end?
CHRIS: Will need to consider today's exchange.
CHAGALL: Didn't mean to rile you up. Would rewind if I could. Our commitment to no-harm is absolute. Until next time.
CHRIS: Until next time.

Christopher disconnected from the café's wireless. He took a few moments to collect himself, then dove into housekeeping. First, a set of shorthand notes. A sip of his cooling coffee. Then he encoded the chat transcript. Chagall would blow a gasket if he knew, though Christopher did wipe the original with software that conformed to a formal specification the saboteur insisted he use. A MilSpec. Even NSA types wouldn't be able to excavate those bits from the disk. It took a few minutes to replace the cleartext file with randomized zeros and ones, overwriting the data multiple times to scrub the drive irreversibly. A green progress bar flashed completion. Christopher confirmed his notes looked like gibberish in the absence of a password, then shut down the laptop.

The guy who'd been glancing Christopher's way was chatting up a glum neo-punk, showing her pages in a bulky paperback. She nodded her spikey-haired head indifferently. Christopher recognized an edition of Neruda poems that Brendan had been reading a few nights before. He blushed at his own presumption. The guy had been looking to strike up a conversation. About poetry. He hadn't been cruising at all.

Christopher exchanged the laptop for a sheaf of articles out of his bag, but couldn't make himself concentrate on yet another analysis of genetically modified corn. Not with Chagall's hedge looping in his head: "circumstances are never under complete control."

Neither was his own certainty. With the exception of this morning's lapse, Chagall didn't come off as reckless. But what was he planning? If things went wrong, it would endanger life and limb, his recruiter had now given that much away.

Brendan's return made it hard to avoid the obvious comparison. His friend's handlers had signed him up to do one thing. Then, in the reading Christopher found most plausible, they tricked him into doing something different. Chagall could be planning to fly a plane into a building. An empty building, after parachuting out if his professed intentions were genuine—but how the hell could Christopher know?

If he was in, he had to assume a huge target. That's what

Chagall claimed, that's what would generate an audience, that's why taking on his manifesto made sense. It wouldn't be worth the effort if the saboteur was blowing smoke.

Seeing Chagall waver on the question of zero harm forced Christopher to acknowledge how close he'd already crept to the cliff. What if people got hurt, or even killed? That eco-saboteurs had a lucky history didn't guarantee anything about future exploits.

He couldn't know.

That was the bottom line, and it came out the same every time he weighed the risks. Whatever promises Chagall offered, Christopher wouldn't know what he had up his sleeve until after the fact. All he had to protect himself were ignorance of the plan, the barely provable fact that he hadn't agreed Chagall could use his work, and whatever cover the First Amendment offered. It amounted to thin ice.

He could take more rigorous precautions. He could weave commitment not to harm any living thing deeper into the text. Or—it occurred to him suddenly—he could submit the manifesto to some obscure public discussion forum where it would languish until Chagall "found" and "cribbed" it. Maybe that was the answer. Prior publication would insulate him from any connection with whatever Chagall and his cadre had planned. He wondered whether the saboteur could live with something along those lines.

But Christopher had to acknowledge the larger picture too. Not just what he could do to protect himself, but why he wanted to write Chagall's manifesto in the first place.

If he was an activist, he had to assume responsibility first and foremost. Years before he'd resolved never to be cowed by theoretical threat, whether from the government or anyone else. It wasn't even a matter of resolve anymore. It was personality.

Activists act.

If he ran scared, who would hold the line?

Christopher knew the world was running off its rails. He knew that if he knew anything. If people like him—people willing to take risks—failed to force change, then change wasn't going to happen.

The options didn't leave much wiggle room.

FOURTEEN

Passing a shop next door to the Bombay Bijou, Zac bent like a kurta-clad reed, ducking away from a breeze-blown flutter of orange, saffron, and sky-blue saris.

Jonah laughed at his narrow escape and inhaled deeply. "This street smells awesome!"

"Doesn't it?"

Scents of cinnamon and cardamom wafted from markets packed so full their wares spilled onto the sidewalks. Restaurants breathed warm curry into the sunny afternoon. Zac and Jonah had crossed the bay to see a Raj Kapoor classic at a storefront cinema in Berkeley's Little India.

"So what did you think of *Awāra?*" Zac asked.

"Pretty good. I liked how everybody's lives got mixed up. But *Karan Arjun* was better. Not so drippy."

"Drippy?"

"All that love stuff."

Zac rolled his eyes. "You'd rather muck around in all that blood and swords stuff."

"Heck yeah!" They came to a shop window brimming with

wicker baskets of snacks. The air was rich with asafetida and cumin. "Let's go in," Jonah said.

He picked out spiral crackers studded with sesame seeds, and plantain chips. Zac chose spice-dusted nuts. A stout, dark-skinned man weighed out *chakli, masala badam kaju,* and *vazhak-kai varuval* into waxed paper bags, and figured the bill on an adding machine that could have predated India's independence. They found a place to sit on the stairs of a church around the corner.

"You know what's weird?" Jonah asked.

"I've got a few ideas," Zac said. "What are you thinking?"

"I don't know anybody else who's into Indian movies."

"Nobody at school?"

"I tried to tell this guy Deepak about that one by Satyajit Ray, but he acted all embarrassed."

"Why is that, do you think?"

"Deepak wants everybody to forget he's from Delhi." Jonah said. He continued to pop plantain chips into his mouth, one at a time.

"How about you?"

"I'm from here."

"Duh! I mean, do you want to fit in like that?"

"Well . . . not exactly. It's kind of like, if you refuse to fit in that can be just as cool."

"I like that angle. Is that Buzz's strategy too?" Zac leaned back into the weathered wooden steps, as if the dull pressure against his spine might ground him as their conversation edged into volatile territory.

"Yeah. I guess." Jonah squirmed, just enough to notice.

"So is watching 1950s Bollywood musicals cool or not cool?"

"It depends on your attitude."

"How so?" Zac asked.

"It's like . . . if I talk about *Awāra*, and some kid says, 'Oh, Jonah's obsessing about stupid India again'—then it's up to how I react. If I'm all embarrassed, the other kid wins. If I act like he's totally ignorant, then I turn uncool into cool."

"By force of personality."

"Yup." Jonah reached for a handful of the spicy nuts. "Buzz has more force than me, though. If he talked about *Awāra* it'd for sure be cool."

"But it's not just self-confidence, is it?" Zac asked, helping himself to a sesame cracker. "I mean, someone can be cocky and still not be cool."

"You know who Buzz reminds me of?"

"Who?"

"Brendan. Not exactly, but they both do what they want."

"Touché," Zac said, nodding thoughtfully. "Maybe that's why they both got their backs up yesterday. Two tomcats scrapping over territory."

"Um . . . yeah, maybe."

A few moments passed. "So are you cool with having Brendan around?"

"It's a little weird."

"He's not the easiest person," Zac said. He idly fingered the sharp spines of a live oak leaf, fallen from a tree in the next lot over.

"Do you remember him being all moody before?"

"I never knew him as well as you guys. You know, from living on Carleton Street? I've only got his visits to the Triangle to go on. But he does have that brooding side."

"Hmmm . . ." Jonah leaned back and looked up into the eaves. "That's what I mean about Buzz," he said. "It's like both of them have some kind of mystery. With Brendan it's coming back from jail."

Zac looked up too. Swallows' nests clung to the church's siding. "Buzz sounded like he knew a thing or two about prison."

"That was weird."

"Does Buzz talk a lot about stuff like that?"

"Not really. One time he told this guy Dennis that a baby like him wouldn't last ten minutes in a holding cell."

Zac frowned. "What was Dennis doing?"

"I don't—oh, yeah, Buzz was smoking a cigarette and Dennis acted all shocked."

"Buzz smokes?"

"Hey, I didn't say I do!"

"I'm glad," Zac said. "But why would Buzz come back with a put-down about jail?"

Jonah shrugged.

"Do you think Buzz's mystery is about his family?"

"I never even went to his house."

"That's kind of curious."

"With Brendan," Jonah said, "I think my mom is deciding whether to let him be one of her projects."

"Her 'projects'?"

"Somebody she helps out."

Zac stood, firmly setting aside a can of worms that wasn't his to open. They still had an errand to run. "How 'bout we haul over to Cal Surplus before it closes?" he said.

———

The shop's owner, a fit man with a salt-and-pepper brush cut, stood behind a display case bristling with knives, compasses, and binoculars. The store was otherwise empty when they walked in. Looking up over his reading glasses, the man reached to turn down a radio talk show. Zac nodded a greeting. "Just holler if you can't find what you need," the proprietor called after them.

Climbing equipment lay piled onto shelves in a back alcove. The banner team needed static rappelling rope, though Marty had instructed Zac to buy only if the rope was new and cost less than fifty cents a foot. The Cal Surplus price was twice that. Jonah whistled. "Sticker shock, huh?"

Zac spoke quietly, so the man up front wouldn't hear. "Marty didn't think we'd find a deal on rope today. We're mainly shopping for hardware."

"Who else is doing the action?"

"Need-to-know. And not here." Zac picked out a silver, D-shaped carabiner. "We want eight of these."

"What are they?"

"For attaching rope to something else, like a tree."

"Or a hotel."

Zac shot him a look. Jonah hadn't been told about the bridge. As far as he knew—as far as he needed to know—the collective was planning to hang a banner off the roof of a building beside the Moscone Center. Zac flexed the carabiner's spring-loaded gate. "Help me out Jonah," he said. "See how this one goes back and forth? The way it feels really smooth?"

Jonah gave it a try. "Yeah, okay."

"Find seven more just like that. Watch out for ones that feel stiff, or that don't click shut just perfectly."

While Jonah vetted the asymmetrical Ds, Zac picked out four similar devices with locking gates, four figure-eight descenders, and two pairs of belay gloves, one that just fit his hands, and one in the next larger size. Summing up in his head, Zac estimated they were on target. "Remember the story," he said under his breath.

They dumped their haul onto a rubber mat atop the display case. "Doing some climbing?" the storekeeper asked, looking down a long, Grecian nose as he sorted and counted.

Zac nodded. "Scouts."

"What troop?"

"Four-one-five," Jonah said, improvising. "It's in San Francisco."

"Don't know that one. I mostly get East Bay troops."

The damage came to just under a hundred dollars. Zac paid cash, five crisp twenties.

"Just printed this morning," the storekeeper said, inspecting the Jacksons closely before handing over a paper bag and change. He came around the counter to lock up behind them. "Had a gang of animal rights fanatics come in a few years ago," he said as he took hold of the doorknob. "Bought my gear to do a protest up on the campus." He stood blocking the door, staring Zac down with blunt suspicion.

Zac swallowed.

"Animal rights?" Jonah said. "I don't think they have a merit badge for that."

The storekeeper sneered, keeping his eyes fixed on Zac. After a long moment he pulled the door open halfway, and allowed them to sidle out.

Jonah gave an attenuated wave as the man flipped his window sign from open to closed. "Creepy," he said.

"Yes," Zac said, exhaling. "Something about places like that." As they waited for a break in traffic Zac traced an arc with his free hand, framing his narrow build, his long straight hair, his flowing kurta. "I guess it's not too hard for guys like that to peg me as the enemy."

They scurried across San Pablo Avenue, then slowed as they stepped into a neighborhood of single-story, stuccoed Craftsman houses.

"Hey, Zac?"

"Hmmmm?"

"Where does the money come from?" Jonah asked.

"What money?" Zac looked around. No one was following them.

"For ropes and stuff," Jonah said. "I mean, it's like we dumpster dive and shop at Thrift Town so we can buy stuff to hang banners. Isn't that kind of weird?"

"I wouldn't put it quite like that."

"How would you put it?"

Zac thought for a while before answering. "A few things," he said. "First of all, you know our rent is cheap because Eddie doesn't make money from the building."

"Yeah. Because he likes having a political collective that he kinda-sorta belongs to."

"Right. Like your mom says, we're the penance he pays for living like a satyr."

"And cheap rent lets everybody have jobs that pay squat."

"More or less," Zac said. "But it's also the reason we can afford to tithe."

"Oh yeah. Politics tax."

Zac laughed, shaking off the storekeeper's provocation. "Who calls it that?"

"Marty. Is that enough for all the protests?"

"Not always. But other people chip in."

"Does my dad chip in?"

"Seth?" Zac reached to brush his fingertips across the intensely yellow blooms of a flannelbush growing in someone's front yard. "I'm not sure," he said.

They were nearing the BART station. "Anyway, does it make a difference?" Jonah asked.

"Does what make a difference?"

"Our politics and stuff. Is it making peace and justice?" Jonah kicked a spiky fruit, fallen from a sweetgum tree, off the sidewalk and into the gutter.

"That's a hard question."

"Yeah, but you must have thought about it."

"I think about it all the time," Zac said.

"So what's the answer?"

Zac put his arm over the boy's shoulder. "I don't know the answer," he said. "Most times I'm pretty sure that we're fighting for lost causes."

"Then why bother?"

"Because it's the right thing to do. Because compassion is the path to the end of suffering. Because standing up for justice is a way to remain human. I think everybody at the Triangle believes something along those lines."

"But nobody thinks we're actually going to win?"

They were at the fare gates. Zac pulled Jonah's ticket from his wallet and handed it to him. "Do you remember Krishna's instruction on the field of Kurukshetra? About detachment from the fruits of action?"

"Um, I don't think so."

"I read it to you, from the *Bhagavad Gita*—but never mind. Your mom has faith that we're going to win. Eventually." They made their way to the escalator.

"My mom?"

"She's our true believer," Zac said. "In some ways it's her certainty that keeps us together." The noise of an approaching train rose steadily, its headlights glowing in the underground bore. "What makes you ask all that stuff?"

"I don't know," Jonah said. "I'm just thinking."

FIFTEEN

Eddie Bourgeaut held title to the Triangle's San Francisco quarters, but he lived in the remote heart of Northern California's Mendocino Range, on acres owned by a commune he helped to found some twenty years before. Christopher kept one eye on a topo map, but was pretty sure the gravel-patched road beside Kitchen Creek looked familiar. He'd visited once before. As Brendan watched for potholes, he took in Douglas fir, leafy black oak, the occasional stand of second-growth redwood. Wide clearings opened into the woods where trees hadn't begun to come back yet. The land would be recovering for decades to come from a century's logging. "There," he said, as Brendan steered the borrowed pickup around another hairpin turn. A plank hanging from the trunk of an old madrone marked the turn they were looking for: "Sleepy Hollow," Eddie called his place. The painted figure of a pumpkin-headed horseman had all but faded from his weathered sign.

Up a steep dirt incline and a quarter mile farther into the woods, they came to his yurt. As Brendan cut the ignition, Eddie emerged from the structure's wooden door, round-bellied in soft, deerskin boots and bulky overalls. "Not bad, boys," he called out, gesturing with a carved elkhorn pipe as he exhaled a cloud of smoke. "You found the place before the Yeti found you."

"I don't know how you can stand it, Eddie," Christopher said, hauling himself stiffly out of the truck. "No neon, no dirty needles, no espresso machines."

"I can get all that! Quarter tank of gas and I'm in Fort Bragg. Brendan, it's been a hell of a long time."

"It has, Eddie, good to see you." Brendan deflected Eddie's embrace with a handshake.

"That was a crap deal you got handed in Mexico."

"It was. I don't expect to go back anytime soon."

"But it's done now?"

Brendan shook his head, declining Eddie's proffered pipe. "If anybody wanted to ask questions I'm pretty sure they'd have picked me up already," he said.

Christopher wandered over to Eddie's makeshift garage, several thick blue tarps laced together and stretched between trees. A cluster of haphazardly dented vehicles crowded together beneath them.

"Chris, can I interest you in a hit of the county's finest bud?"

"Not for me, thanks," Christopher called back. "These are brilliant! Brendan, come look at these beauties."

Eddie laughed. "You have a discerning eye."

"Form follows function, right?"

Brendan ambled over to survey the cars, gauging the bounce in a station wagon's strut, peering through a sedan's grimy window. "Twenty-six, twenty-eight people?" he asked.

"Something like that."

"That's almost enough," Christopher said. "Depending how the vans load up, some can ride with the tower crew."

"We've got a few weeks yet," Eddie said. "I've got my eye on one or two more of these lovely wrecks."

"What's the story on registrations?" Brendan was crouched down behind a wide-bodied Ford wagon, inspecting its banged up, black-and-gold plate.

"I've got people who can't be on the bridge," Eddie said, "but agreed to take their time noticing when a front plate goes missing off their car. We'll swap just before the action, and look legal unless somebody actually gets stopped."

"Nice." Brendan popped the hood of a blue Monte Carlo. "This the one needs an alternator?"

"Yes, indeed. You found the part?"

"At a shop out in the Avenues," Christopher said.

Eddie showed them around—the yurt, the well, the composting outhouse. Brendan smoked a cigarette while Eddie fussed with his pipe. They retrieved tools from the truck, and Brendan started to dig past the Monte Carlo's bolts, belts, and brackets. Eddie lent a hand when Brendan needed one; Christopher took charge of fetching cold beers up from the creek.

For lunch they had picked up sandwiches in Hopland. The temperature was dropping by the time Brendan began to put the car back together, in midafternoon. Eddie started the engine, the alternator light on the dashboard blinked off, and they pronounced the transplant a success. Brendan and Christopher hoped to get back to paved road before nightfall, so they passed on Eddie's dinner invitation.

"What do you hear about numbers for the public protests?" Eddie asked as Brendan poked around the rest of the vehicles.

"Not a lot," Christopher said. "It's mostly Nora and Zac going to the meetings. Leona Kim told me Meg is shooting for thirty thousand, but she thinks that's high."

"Thirty thousand is high? How come?"

"It's not an antiwar march. Peace is easy to understand, transgenic agriculture is complex. Leona says unions and churches are all about Iraq. It's been hard to get traction."

"Well, you can't ignore twenty thousand. Or even ten, not when we take over the damn bridge."

"GeneSynth won't decide anything," Brendan said. "But it'll sure as hell add to the noise."

He slid into a Volkswagen Vanagon, its rear bumper held in place with baling wire. The engine caught easily, and Brendan circled around to listen. After a couple of minutes he killed the ignition. "All serviceable, I'd say. The van's running a little rough, probably could use a timing adjustment."

"They're all going to Sebastopol next week," Eddie said. "I know a mechanic down there, I'll have him take a look."

———

On the way up Christopher had asked more about Brendan's time in prison. "It was animal," was all he would say. "Eat or be eaten. That was the world for ninety percent of the guys." Brendan insisted that talking about it wouldn't help, that the road through Tlaxitlán dead-ended in despair. "If I can't back my way out," he said, "I'm done for."

How the trip to Chiapas had come about, and how the bust went down, were easier terrain. Brendan explained that there was a principal contact and a guy who produced the loaded truck in Tucson. There had been a third fellow early on, he said, who had been yanked out of the picture without explanation. In hindsight Brendan wondered about that. Internal politics, he speculated, and still wasn't sure whether some organizational rift he knew nothing about might have heightened his risk. They'd told him the hollow spaces behind the pickup's body panels would be packed with military-grade satellite phones necessary to coordinate between Zapatista bases, across miles of dense rain forest. Brendan had said it before, and repeated it to Christopher on the drive that morning: his contacts had assured him there would be no weapons whatsoever.

As they wound back toward the highway, Christopher tried to imagine his friend's long, skittish trek south. It must have seemed so abstract and unlikely to conceive an outcome as catastrophic as Tlaxitlán. Was Chagall leading him into the kind of trap that had snared Brendan? Or was that sort of worry a melodramatic conceit? "I've been thinking about when the Federales stopped you on the road through Oaxaca," he said as Brendan turned off the last of the gnarled logging roads, onto smooth tarmac.

"I remember it well."

"So you didn't see anything when they opened up the truck?" Christopher asked. "What you were carrying?"

"They hustled me into an SUV with blacked out windows," Brendan said. "Like a kidnapping. By the time they broke down the truck I was jammed in a cell with twenty other guys, sweating bullets over the screaming down the hall. Every few hours the Federales started in on somebody new."

Christopher didn't dare interrupt.

"Did the newspapers lie?" Brendan shrugged. "They exaggerated, at least. Listed more firepower than a one-ton truck could hide. More than I could possibly have carried. But I won't know if the weapons charges were invented wholesale until my contact agrees to talk."

"A couple weeks ago you said the quantities in the indictment were closer to possible. Closer than what the press first reported."

"Yeah, the indictment seemed plausible. Enough to make me wonder. It's hard to be sure looking back, but the F350 might have been driving stiff. It's possible the guys beefed up the suspension to support a heavier load."

"Jesus."

"What?"

Christopher watched Brendan's profile out of the corner of his eye. That kind of thing, a beefed-up suspension, was exactly what he had meant when he asked whether Brendan's handlers might have played him for a patsy. "I'm thinking," he said, treading carefully, "if they set up the truck like that beforehand . . . wouldn't that mean they were lying to you from the start?"

"Look, Chris, the Mexican government could have been as pissed off about telecom gear as they would have been by AK-47s. Maybe they're the ones who lied, because a judge'll hand a gringo five years for carrying a single round of ammunition across the border."

"Seriously?"

Brendan nodded. "Special rules for *norteamericanos.* And the Federales are pragmatic. If that's what would keep my ass locked up, why not play the case that way?"

"But—"

Brendan cut him off. "I really don't want to go there. I'm already tied up in knots, it doesn't help to pull the knots tighter." Keeping his eyes on the road, Brendan slotted a CD into the pickup's player. Percussion in staccato rhythms, dramatic sweeps of orchestral strings, and Kazem Al Saher's mournful tenor filled the cab. Christopher watched out the window as they accelerated onto Highway 101 and sped south, following a steady march of telephone wires strung atop pocked wooden poles. He tried to visualize the surrounding acres as wetland, teeming with wildlife in the centuries before the state was logged, drained, burned, and given over to cattle and monocropping. At least the farms were smaller here, he thought. And a lot more of them grew organic than in the Central Valley. It was a start.

Some miles farther, a group of farmworkers were picking weeds out of a leafy field west of the road. To Christopher's poorly tutored eye, nothing signaled whether they labored over sprayed or clean acres, whether the crop was heirloom, hybrid, or mutant. You'd be hard-pressed to make a documentary, he thought. Let alone a single, dramatically compelling photo. Nora's time to find a banner image was just about up, and so far she had nothing to show. Not that he was surprised. There was no easy agribusiness corollary to dolphins getting caught in tuna nets, or poultry processing, or cookie cutter meals being assembled by lumpen proles. Away to the left, green down fuzzed the earth. A wheel-line irrigator stretched across the broad, furrowed expanse.

"Penny for your thoughts?" Brendan turned the stereo's volume down a few notches.

"The fields look idyllic." Christopher raised his arms in a stretch, touching elbows to the cab's roof. "But you can't tell by looking what's been sprayed and plowed into the soil, or whether the crops come from laboratories."

"Most of these farms are clean, I'd say."

"I know that. But only because I follow food politics. There's not a visual, it's almost impossible to make genetic engineering tangible. No clear-cut, Michael Moore moments."

A biplane flew low to the ground on the far side of the highway. "There's the opening shot to your infomercial," Brendan said. "Crop dusters. How would Michael Moore frame it? Like the opening to *Apocalypse Now?*"

Christopher laughed. "Sure. A quote and a slow fade. From napalm wasting Vietnamese jungle to crop dusters over California farmland."

"Maybe a Poison soundtrack. 'Life Loves a Tragedy.'"

The light trickled away as the miles rolled behind them. "So what's with you and Allison?" Christopher asked after a long silence.

Brendan didn't respond.

"Maybe I shouldn't—"

"No, Chris," Brendan said. "It's fair to ask. "

He was glad for the dusk. What Christopher really wondered was what would change for him if Brendan and Allison got back together after all this time, not that Brendan showed any signs of actually settling down. There were days Christopher welcomed the thought of an excuse to set aside his still-smoldering interest. There was something unseemly about holding a torch for as long as he had, however dim and well concealed.

"The funny thing is you spend months in prison starved for women," Brendan said, as if reading Christopher's thoughts. "For women's company, for relief from bluffing machismo. For sex too, but that's only part of it. So here I am, free as a soup kitchen. But love? Relationships? Not on my front burner. I've got months of suppressed rage clambering for attention before I can step into the present." He glanced over to the passenger seat. "I'm a goddamned basket case."

They let Kazem carry them along for a couple of exits.

"I met somebody a few weeks back," Christopher said in a lull between tracks. He regretted the words almost before he'd spoken them.

"Who? Where? Why haven't I heard about this?"

Christopher shook his head. "Because nothing actually happened. She's a med student at UCSF. We met by chance a couple times in a café."

"Has she got a name?"

"Suvali. Anglo-Indian. She grew up in Brighton and came here for school."

"So what's the story?"

"Don't say anything, Brendan."

"To the rest of the gang? My lips are sealed."

"We're supposed to see a movie later this week."

He nodded judiciously. "British accent?"

"Yup."

"I'm a sucker for that."

They were coming up on the far edge of the Bay Area. Christopher leaned over to check the dashboard. "Gas up in Healdsburg?" he asked.

"Yeah, let's," Brendan said. "I could use a coffee too."

SIXTEEN

Marshall had a hell of a time parking in his brother's neighborhood. He orbited Christopher's block twice, turned his silver roadster down Sanchez, circled up Noe to its dead end, then crawled along the narrow streets surrounding the Triangle, ready to pounce at the first flash of brake lights.

Germania and Hermann.

Belcher, Walter, Laussat.

Nothing.

Maybe Christopher could be coaxed to have a drink someplace else. Marshall had planned to show up unannounced, for dramatic impact. Shock and awe writ small. So it goes, he thought, digging in a pocket for his cell phone, but just as Marshall flipped open to call, a green Expedition switched on its headlights. He tapped the gas, whipping into position.

Then he waited.

The lumbering vehicle sawed back and forth. And again. And a third time, forward and reverse.

Drumming impatiently on the M Coupe's steering wheel, Marshall considered the miracle that human beings, equipped with opposed thumbs and the biggest share of cerebral cortex on the planet, nonetheless drive SUVs into congested city centers. At last the chunky Ford swung into the street. His BMW slipped easily into the space.

Cutting the ignition, Marshall sat for a moment, making up his mind one last time. No one would ever know if he bailed. "Can't," he muttered aloud. Then, popping open the door, he nearly took out a brightly flex-laminated bicyclist.

"Asshole!" she shouted over her shoulder.

Marshall lurched out of his car, reflexively setting the vehicle's alarm. As if anyone would care if it were triggered. He wouldn't dare park the roadster in Christopher's neighborhood overnight.

Where transit lines converged half a block down Church Street, people scurried in packs. Burberry suits mixed with polyester fishnet and torn denim. Swish, grunge, goth. Preppy, matron, mod. Marshall approached the human stew uneasily. He rounded the corner and nearly ran down a wild-haired old man, who got right up in his face to sputter a rotten-toothed demand for spare change. Marshall reared back, holding his breath. Hugging an apartment building's brick façade, he edged past a crowd waiting shoulder to shoulder for the N-Judah train.

How in hell, he wondered, can people stand to live like this?

—

No one answered the bell. Marshall peered through the metal gate. There were two glass-paneled doors on the other side of the building's shallow front stoop, and a blank space of exterior wall where a third used to be. Odd, he thought, turning to look up and down Duboce Avenue, trying to see the neighborhood as his brother might. He rang the bell a second time. Christopher lived with a hive of others. How could no one be home on Tuesday night?

A Muni train screeched by, then a tumble of sneakered feet

came clattering down the building's stairs. An angular man's shadow sharpened through the right-side door's glass panel. He appeared, backlit, and emerged onto the stoop. Cropped red hair, boot-cut jeans, a faded Palestinian flag printed on his t-shirt. Marshall suppressed an instant aversion. "Is Christopher in?" he asked.

The man on the other side of the gate stared quizzically. "You're Chris's brother," he said.

"Uh—yeah." That wasn't in the game plan either. Why would Christopher's people know him? "I'm sorry, I—"

"Brendan James," he said, and unlatched the gate. "I lived on Carleton Street when your brother was in school."

"Right. Right, I didn't recognize you. I'm Marshall."

"No reason you'd remember. Come on in, Chris just called. He's on his way from work."

"I—no, really. I could come back later."

"Please." Brendan held the gate wide. "Come up and have a beer. He's getting a couple things from the store—he'll be home in minutes."

Marshall followed reluctantly. He accepted a bottle after Brendan coaxed him past a ceremonial refusal. Russian River Stout. The label was well done, depicting the estuary at Jenner. Fruity nose, the color of brazil nuts, a burnt-cork finish. "That's excellent brew," he said.

"Sonoma County's best." Brendan retrieved his own bottle from the kitchen counter. "Pull up a chair."

"Have you lived with Christopher all this time?" Marshall saw that the refrigerator had to be forty years old. The stove was an unrestored Wedgewood that no one had bothered to move for ages; the linoleum underneath was greasy and black past a sponge mop's easy reach.

"Not even close," Brendan was saying. "I wander in and out. A glorified houseguest, in a repeat offender sort of way."

"Ah. So where's home?"

"Santa Cruz most recently, not sure what's next. How about you? Are you local?"

"I live in the house Christopher and I grew up in."

"Keeping the good professor company?"

"I suppose," Marshall said. "Something like that."

The two sipped at their beers.

"So nobody else is home?" Marshall asked.

"Work, meetings, classes . . . everybody scatters."

"I had the idea Christopher lived in a constant frenzy."

"There've been periods like that, not so much anymore," Brendan said. "Some of the crowd moved on. Everybody left is older and more responsible. 'Cept for me, maybe. I'm just older."

"The one trend you can count on. But tell me, what made you decide to go your own way while Christopher and the others are still . . . here?"

"You're not the first to ask that question."

"I suppose I've never understood it. What Christopher gets from the arrangement."

Brendan looked surprised. "People are social animals. The people who are part of the Triangle are social and political animals. I don't think it's much more complicated than that."

"I see."

Brendan took a swig from his bottle. "So you were part of the dot-com boom, do I remember right?"

"I guess you could put it that way."

"Programmer?"

"Closer to product development. The business was mostly vaporware. Some good ideas, but nothing went to market."

"I hear there was a lot of that. And nowadays?" Just then the front door shut with a rattle, and someone started up the stairs. "Your bro," Brendan said.

Marshall stood.

"Hey Chris!" Brendan called. "Surprise in the kitchen."

"I hate surprises." Christopher rounded the corner, biting back whatever he'd been planning to say next.

"Hey," Marshall said into the sudden vacuum. Raising the stout, he saluted with what he hoped would pass for mild irony.

Apprehension flashed across Christopher's face. "What's wrong?" he demanded.

"I just—nothing's wrong."

"Let me put those away." Brendan reached for Christopher's grocery bags. "Nobody's upstairs. You guys can hang out in the front room."

———

Marshall took in the worn furniture, the Che icon in its crappy frame, speaker wire running along the moldings from pocket doors opposite the windows. "What's with the technology?" he asked. "Is the room bugged?"

"Hardly." Christopher wedged himself into a corner of one broken sofa and gestured toward the other.

"But those are speakers on the windows, am I right?"

"They scramble attempts to monitor meetings. Some groups that use this room have been surveilled by the police."

Marshall guffawed at the explanation, unable to help himself. "That's a little paranoid, don't you think?"

"No, based on documentary evidence, I don't. There was a lawsuit in the nineties, discovery unearthed some damning police dossiers. But is that the reason you dropped in? To throw darts?"

"Sorry. It's just the opposite, actually. I came because I think we need to call a truce."

"Are we at war?"

Marshall sat, sinking deep into the slack cushions. He sipped from his bottle. "I'd offer you one, but it's not my house." His attempt at an icebreaker ran aground. "I don't know, Christopher. Seems that way to Dad."

His brother sighed. "I see. I'm not holding up my end of the pretense."

"What pretense?"

"That we're one big, happy family."

"You're not the only villain. I provoked you the other night. Not for the first time, either."

"And not for any discernible reason. So Dad's upset."

"He won't stop harping on how you stormed off." This was the most intrusive downside to living at home, Marshall recognized. To living with anyone else, for that matter. The scrutiny. "And he's not going to let up until I tell him we worked something out."

Two people, speaking in low voices, were climbing the stairs. Marshall looked back to the hall but his brother paid no mind. More housemates, he supposed.

"So what would a truce look like?" Christopher asked. "Different, I mean, from business as usual. Staying on our respective sides of the bay?"

Marshall grimaced. "Look, I don't know exactly. Maybe you could call Dad more often? Maybe you and I need to be in touch. Superficially . . . whatever. Enough that I can say to him, 'Oh, I got an e-mail from Christopher.' Nothing elaborate."

Christopher stood and stepped over to the window. "Did you drive in?"

"Yeah. Hell of a neighborhood for parking."

"What makes this flare-up special?" Christopher asked. "All the time I've lived here you never came by. Why the sudden crisis?"

Marshall joined his brother. Together, they looked down into the street. "He's not getting any younger, you know."

"That wasn't the question."

"Okay, maybe I'm not getting any younger either. We haven't been best pals for a long time, Christopher, but Dad doesn't have to carry that."

"Why have things gone that way?"

"What way?"

"Why do we antagonize each other?"

"I don't know," Marshall said, aware that this would be the exact wrong moment to advance his theories. "We take different approaches, I suppose."

"Different approaches to what?"

"Life, work, politics." Marshall shrugged. "You name it."

"I'm damned if I can imagine what we'd e-mail about."

"The substance doesn't matter. Need stock advice?"

"Yeah, right. Wanna read meeting minutes from Direct Action to Stop the War?"

Marshall stared out the window, acutely conscious of the gulf estranging him from Christopher. Was there any chance of having a real conversation? "Tell me about this protest that got Dad so worked up," he said.

"There's nothing to tell."

"You plan all these . . . things in big groups, right?" With a fingernail Marshall tapped one of the speakers glued to the windowpane. "With labor unions? Churches?"

"Big groups, small groups. Sometimes with unions, sometimes with progressive churches. It depends."

"How do you know there aren't police infiltrators?"

"You get a sense. Most of what we do isn't important enough for the cops to bother, as you often remind me."

Marshall sighed. "I didn't mean it that way."

Christopher scratched his head. Marshall looked around for a place to set his empty bottle. They returned to their respective sofas, but neither one sat.

"So," Christopher said.

"So what should I tell Dad?"

"I'm not sure I know."

"Christopher, I'm sorry I pissed you off over dinner."

"I'll call next week."

"That'd help. And I'll send hot tips on penny stocks?"

"Don't expect me to buy any."

"Wouldn't dream of it." Marshall supposed that would have to do. His brother was too well defended. They had too much history between them. "Look, I'm sorry to burst in."

"Not a problem."

"I just want to keep things at a lower temperature."

"Okay. I'm in," Christopher said. "Walk you to your car?"

Marshall shook his head. "No need, I'm just around the corner."

SEVENTEEN

Zac and Allison strolled through a slowly falling mist, but neither seemed to notice the chill. "There are so many bodhisattvas," Zac explained. "And within those, so many variants of Avalokiteśvara. Every tradition, every sect meditates around its own."

"Do they all have four hands?"

"In some sects you see eight arms. In most of Asia the bodhisattva of compassion takes female form. Guan Yin has eleven heads and a thousand arms so she can hear all the suffering beings and attend to them. In our Vajrayāna tradition, though, his four arms hold a jewel, a lotus representing freedom from obstacles to enlightenment, and a mala—"

"The prayer beads," Allison interjected. "What does the mala mean?"

"Devotion to rescuing all sentient beings from suffering."

"How do you keep all that in your head, Zac?"

"Oh, I don't know. Early fascination with Catholic ritual filtered through a queer-pagan-multicultural prism? Or maybe obsessive-compulsive disorder?"

"Must be the Catholic upbringing. We Lutherans miss out on that riot of saints and symbols."

Zac stopped in his tracks.

"What is it?"

He put a hand to his mouth. Half a block ahead, Brendan was leaning into a pay phone. Allison covered her ears as Zac blew a piercing wolf whistle, but Brendan didn't look up.

"That is him, isn't it?"

"Looks like," she said.

"What's he doing, calling his NSA handler?"

Allison gave Zac a look and they continued up the block. Brendan turned when they were almost upon him. Eyes widening, he stepped backward and mashed against the phone. "Damn!" he exclaimed sheepishly, fumbling to put the receiver back on the hook. "You guys startled me."

"Didn't mean to," Allison said. "Aren't we emanating pure peace and tranquility? Zac and I just finished meditating at the Padmasambhava Temple. My first time, and I can already pronounce it, see?"

Brendan rolled his eyes. "Auras scrubbed squeaky clean?"

"Ye of little faith." Allison placed a hand on Brendan's shoulder. "Where are you headed, my little lost grasshopper?"

"Back to the Triangle," Brendan said. "If I can find my little lost way."

"Nobody takes me seriously," Zac sighed. "This is my spiritual practice, people. Can we have a little respect?"

Brendan threw him a wink. "Life is suffering, man, buck up."

They crossed the intersection three abreast. "I heard Chris's brother came by," Zac said. "What was he like?"

"Marshall? When was that?"

"Last night," Zac said. "I forgot to tell you, Al."

"That's what happens when you empty your mind," Brendan said. He turned to Allison. "But, yeah—I thought I heard you and Jonah come in when they were upstairs. Figured you ran into them."

She shook her head. "Marshall just showed up?"

"It was weird to see him. After all Chris's complaints."

"So what was the takeaway?"

"I don't know how good an impression I got. Ten minutes, a couple of cranky hermits drinking beers and grasping for something to say. Then Chris came home."

"Please," Allison said, "you used to denounce classmates on the strength of thirty-second comments in a lecture hall."

"Oh, hell," Brendan sighed. "He's built a bit like a pear, forms coherent sentences, recognizes a good stout—"

"C'mon, cut to the chase. Has he really turned into the Wicked Brother of the East Bay?"

"I suppose he was on good behavior."

"What brought him over to the city?" Zac asked.

"Chris said his dad was up in arms about them scrapping last week, when he went over for dinner."

"Was he worried?"

"Nah. Chris thought it was weird to make such a big deal."

They stopped for the light at Market Street.

"Walk up Noe?" Brendan asked. "I need to duck into the corner store."

"Sure," Zac said.

"So, Brendan?" Allison asked.

"Hmmmm?"

"Was that . . ." The light turned and they stepped into the intersection. "Were you calling the guys you've been trying to get in touch with?"

"Yup," he said. "Didn't want to use the house phone."

"You'll be able to meet up?"

"Still ironing out details. Everybody's being careful."

Allison nodded. "Careful is good."

They came to the mom-and-pop on the corner of Henry. "Smokes," Brendan said, as though the others hadn't figured.

Zac and Allison waited under the store's shallow awning. "It's strange," she said. "Marshall coming by."

"I wonder if there's more to it. He never came over before, right?"

"I'm pretty sure it's a first. I don't even remember him at Carleton Street."

Brendan emerged from the shop and lit up. "So what's with this weather? Is it going to rain or what?"

"Wardrobe uncertainty, huh?" Zac asked. "It's a killer deciding between the fake fox fur and a flowered raincoat."

Allison and Brendan laughed; Zac blinked coquettishly.

He put on a serious mien as they neared home. "What's it been like with Jonah?"

Brendan shrugged. "We haven't crossed paths since Saturday. I figure he's steering clear of me."

"He won't talk about Buzz," Allison said. "They saw each other, that's all he's saying."

"I guess we'll want to tread lightly," Zac said.

"Agreed."

Zac pulled his hands from the pockets of his baja pullover. "Jonah told me after the movie on Sunday that Buzz talked tough about jail one other time. He doesn't know where that comes from, though." Duboce Park was eerily empty. At Sanchez, Zac stopped. "I'm heading to the café," he said. "Noon to six today."

Brendan took a last hit off his cigarette, and flicked it into the gutter. "Thing is," he said, "I've got a bad feeling about Buzz."

Allison followed the butt's arc, but withheld comment. "Meaning?"

"Not sure yet. Something's off-kilter."

"I think he might be in trouble," Zac said.

"Could be," Brendan said. "But hard to say how. Or how to come in."

"Jonah's friends are our godchildren," Zac said, not missing a beat. "That's how we'd come in."

"I don't know. I'd rather have a sense how hot a fire's burning before I mess with it."

"That's not real, Brendan," Allison said. "They're already tight. We can't just turn our heads."

"I gotta move," Zac said after a pause. "Kai's got something going after his shift. I promised I wouldn't be late."

"Thanks for the meditation."

"Thanks for scaring the shit out of me back there at the pay phone."

Zac put his palms together and gave a slight bow. "Namasté," he said, then turned up the street.

EIGHTEEN

December 2003

Steel bars lattice the skylight, casting a shadow-grid across Chagall's plank table. He shifts, turning his laptop a few degrees to the right. In an hour the watery sun will sink behind conifers surrounding the upper meadow. As the days ebb toward solstice, these acres get a grudging few hours of direct light.

An LED matrix simmers on the east wall, registering signal filtered from microphones arrayed around the perimeter of his land. When a vertical trill emerges from the background, Chagall senses the anomaly out of the corner of his eye. He lifts his gaze to watch traces spike across an oscilloscope's screen. After a few seconds the peaks die back into baseline chatter. A family of deer, Chagall figures, crossing the road that twists through heavily forested hills. Humans wouldn't move out of range so quickly.

He doesn't welcome visitors. Chagall lives in a remote stretch of the mountainous west, surrounded by a scatter of like-minded recluses, libertarians, and methamphetamine cooks. Everybody in the county guards against intrusion. Methods vary, from smart fences and electronic sensors, to mechanical traps, canine patrols, and armed ex-cons. One eccentric, on land several valleys north, was said to employ jackals until the climate did them in. Chagall's Remington bolt action and 10/22 autoloader wouldn't raise a local lawman's eyebrow. Neither would the 12 gauge clipped to the underframe of his bed, or the Glock holstered at his hip. Like millions of his armed American fellows, Chagall relies on ample and obvious capacity to preclude any need to shoot another human being.

Except for engineering diagrams on his laptop's encrypted hard drive, there's nothing indictable on the property. Chagall conducts business elsewhere, never risking a domestic inventory of the custom intrusion sensors, spycams, and covert listening devices he crafts in rented warehouses, here and there, for parties willing to pay top dollar. Incendiaries and explosives that advance his political goals are kept even farther from where he lives.

Chagall turns away from the warning system and returns to his laptop.

Public documents on the University of Nebraska website show the institution's AgBio complex-to-be anchored by a rectangular, six-story structure. Two hundred feet wide by a hundred fifty deep, the building is rising on the outskirts of Lincoln, surrounded by greenhouses, ample paved parking, and broad, flat fields.

Architectural plans procured by Romulus lay out the upper floors as laboratories. The main entrance will open onto a two-story lobby faced in plate glass, ten yards deep and stretching across the building's width. Profitable advances in agro-engineering will be presented in a grandly proportioned, ground-level auditorium that sinks gently into greater Lincoln's silty earth. Beyond the auditorium, library patrons will look out over acres of genetically modified crops.

As Chagall studies its plan views and elevations half a continent away, the building's bones have already been erected. He stares at the drawings until he can see, until he can all but feel the vertical steel that bears deep transfer beams spanning the auditorium and the library. Until he can sense how columns will be stabilized by spandrel walls. Until he can fully imagine the labs that will soon float on concrete slabs bonded to ribbed steel decking.

Plumbing, ductwork, electrical cable, and the facility's data backbone will ascend through risers on either side of the auditorium. Each of the upper stories is set to be hatched with thick concrete pads for lab benches and heavy equipment. Between these masses, the diagrams show wide underfloor channels for ventilation, through which utilities will fan across the building's working space. The channels are just deep enough for a lean man to army crawl. He would need to train, but that's the least of his worries.

Construction on this scale lies outside Chagall's experience. Dynamiting electrical towers, torching tract homes, blasting the innards out of heavy equipment: his credentials for wreckage and ruin in these veins are in order. He cut his teeth taking down abandoned miners' cabins for sport, in secluded wilderness near his boyhood home. Roughly framed, saddle-notched log shacks, however, bear only distant resemblance to engineered structures of concrete and steel.

There are common threads. Columns joined to beams, compression and shear, gravity. As Chagall pores over the diagrams, he is looking for gravity and shear: vulnerable junctions of vertical and horizontal where the structure can be knocked off its frame.

—

Terabytes have been posted to the internet on the structural failures that felled the twin towers in 2001. For Chagall the attack on New York is neither a tactical model nor a strategic ideal. Morally, it's a cesspool. Still, September 11th is a rich lesson in the physics of demolition.

Published analysis of Al Qaeda's attack reduces to a simple narrative. Burning jet fuel weakened load-bearing structures already compromised by impact. Beams and connections failed at each of the towers' crash points, collapsing stories directly hit by two hundred tons of Boeing 767. Once a single floor buckled, the downward-cascading mass pancaked one story after the next like vertical dominos, all the way to bedrock.

Six stories, of course, are not a hundred and ten. Chagall is neither a pilot nor suicidal, and a single lost life, with the possible exception of his own, would render his mission a failure. Lessons to be drawn from the World Trade Center, then, are more general than specific. Heat can weaken structural steel to the point of failure. The collapse of long beams—over an open auditorium, for example—releases potential energy locked in a building's upper stories.

Timothy McVeigh, no less a mass murderer than the Al Qaeda hijackers, destroyed an Oklahoma City office block with a fertilizer bomb in 1995. The scale of Nebraska's AgBio complex is on a par with McVeigh's target; though, unlike Oklahoma City's federal building, the AgBio complex will be empty when Chagall strikes. The Nebraska structure is about as wide, twice as deep, and is supported by a column grid on thirty-foot centers, versus the Oklahoma City building's twenty. Chagall would have no trouble driving a truck packed with ammonium nitrate into Lincoln. An airplane is out of the question. The essential physics are the same.

Chagall intends to inflict enough damage that the AgBio building will have to be scrapped. Enough to pierce the nation's indifference for long enough to achieve an immediate purpose. In the hush that will precede an unbridled media scrum—Terrorism in the Heartland!—he and Romulus will offer Americans a challenge: either render ecotage obsolete by bending politics to constrain industry, or suffer an escalating cascade of bombings and burnings committed by those who refuse to stand by while the planet is sacked.

In the time left to pull Earth out of its nosedive—manufactured heat roiling weather into peril, monoculture wringing out the planet's arable land, radiation concentrated to poison vast landscapes in the wake of inevitable nuclear meltdowns— no one can credibly argue that scattered cells of eco-saboteurs will save a biosphere. Yet paralysis is a coward's response. Hope dwindles, but Chagall's world is dying and he'll fight for it, as long as he lives.

The chances they'll succeed, in the long run, are vanishingly small. But despair confers no exemption from responsibility.

Chagall is equally certain that despair makes poor argument. He will do what he does best, but crafting a credible justification requires belief in a future, and faith that disparate and self-interested communities might join together to confront crisis, might act for a common good. His own outlook is too dark to rally others. As he argued to Romulus, there is tactical advantage to cloaking their message in a voice insulated from operational planning. But hope is the key reason to bring a third party into their circle.

Four months and change are all that remain before their window of opportunity closes. He has identified candidates: an academic in Ann Arbor, a journalist in Chapel Hill, and two activist types nominated by Romulus, both on the West Coast. After the turn of the year Chagall will initiate contact. By the time he selects their propagandist-to-be, logistical planning will be largely complete. He'll be free to focus on implementation. With messaging and broadcast outsourced, his part will be to bring the building down.

—

Chagall slides a fresh split of oak into his woodstove.

The structural drawings suggest two options.

The first involves compact caches of Thermate-TH3 planted where transfer beams meet supporting columns along the auditorium's perimeter. Ignited remotely or on a timer, underfloor charges would vaporize steel in a half-meter radius, severing the building's key joints and deforming its upper stories. If the library were already furnished, fire and smoke might spread, damaging costly equipment in the labs.

The second borrows from the Oklahoma City attack. Fertilizer is plentiful in the farmland surrounding Lincoln, as is gasoline and propane. It doesn't take a rocket scientist to turn a truck into a missile. As McVeigh himself proved, any moderately trained tweaker can manage. The trick would be to send a vehicle hurtling on autopilot into the heart of the building. It won't be enough to simply park outside and amble away, as McVeigh did. The site is too isolated, and to get that close would risk capture. Just as crucially, an explosion on the perimeter might fail to dislodge interior transfer beams. Chagall has sketched extensions to adaptive driving equipment that could steer a truck its final quarter mile under mechanical guidance, enough to open a plausible chance of escape. The execution would be risky, but the effect vastly more dramatic than a remotely triggered burn.

As he calculates angles and payloads and margins of error, Chagall sees that a third tactic might combine the two modes of attack. Looser tolerances in each element would be possible if he employed both. Smaller charges could weaken critical welds, and they'd be easier to place solo. A lesser blast in the lobby, even if it struck some yards off an ideal center, would still fracture shear connections if they were already compromised.

The laptop's hard drive spins in the cabin's silence. Chagall stares through his mullioned window, past a fenced, December-spare garden to the meadow beyond. He is thinking of Nebraska, blanketed in snow, a kilometer lower in altitude but thousands distant from the moderating Pacific.

There won't be time to wait for kinder weather before paying a visit. Groundwork needs to be laid before spring, and he'll have to take care not to cut a memorable figure. Sensible men don't loiter in the icy plains. He'll want to be passing through, on business set to ripen later in the year.

A clipped motion on the far side of the vegetable plot catches his eye, some small mammal rustling through the sedge. Now stillness. After a few moments he makes out the dark, pointy tips of elongated ears among the thingrass and spikerush. It's the jackrabbit he spotted a week or so before, looking for a way past his chicken wire.

Chagall rises stealthily, careful to avoid a sudden step or scrape that might carry through the floorboards. He slips the Ruger 10/22 from its rack and glides toward the door. Outside, by the cabin's southeast corner, breathing soft clouds of steam into the chill, he scans the near quarter of the meadow.

Nothing.

Perhaps he's missed his chance.

Minutes pass and damp penetrates Chagall's woolen shirt. Then, a telltale movement beyond a patch of curly leaf kale. The only shot he'll get is through the fence. Not ideal. Still, even if he fails to bag stew meat, the attempt will scare the varmint off his cabbage and carrots for a while. Chagall raises the Ruger and steadies his aim.

A thin wedge of gray-brown face pokes into the cleared gap around his garden. Ears folded back, the jackrabbit sniffs for trouble. Chagall trains the rifle on a spot just his side of the uncut wild, waiting for the critter to inch into the open. The hare, three kilos if it weighs a pound, emerges warily, whiskers aquiver. Chagall presses the trigger.

His shot scuffs short, raising a spray of gravely loam. The twanging fence tells how the bullet went off its mark.

In long, arcing leaps, the jackrabbit flees to the near tree line.

NINETEEN

Christopher held the door for Suvali as they left the theater, a low-slung building on Irving Street, not far from the medical center where she interned. A woman of a certain age followed, and he held the door for her as well. Red cashmere sweater, a necklace of squarish, wooden beads. Associate professor, he guessed. The woman nodded thanks, and Christopher caught up with Suvali.

"So what did you think?" he asked. "I'm curious how that period looks to someone who didn't grow up on the Weather Underground's legend."

"As a documentary?" Suvali turned up the collar of her coat. "The issues around militancy were universal, I think. The tension between retrospective justification and horrified regret. But the group's politics were hard for an outsider to follow."

Christopher assumed she was horrified, justifiably, that three members of the group's New York collective had blown themselves up in 1970, as they prepared explosives to inflict Vietnam-scale carnage on an Army dance at Fort Dix. He suppressed an involuntary shiver. "I was in preschool myself when those guys were active," he said. "Nobody admires them for that Greenwich Village bomb lab, and thank God they failed. It's how they responded afterward. The collective's complete disavowal of violence against people, their commitment to avoid injury in all their subsequent actions—without backing down from attacking and exposing the death and destruction for which we all were responsible. Every person in the United States. Our government was murdering millions in Vietnam, in our names."

"It's a very fine line, Chris."

"I agree, it is. But for all the bombs they planted after those three of their own died, not a single person was hurt. And then, for me at least, it's sobering to think how few degrees of separation there are between the long-time activists in my circle now, and Mark Rudd, or Bernardine Dohrn. How close that history is. How their influence echoes."

"Really? You know these people?"

"I don't know anybody who went underground," he said hastily. "And nobody who was in the film. But everybody was in college or at a demonstration with everybody else. And there's a core of old timers still turning out for protests."

"Will I be deported if I'm seen with you?"

Christopher couldn't tell if she was teasing. "My crowd has nothing to do with dynamite or prison breaks," he said. "But the issues those guys were talking about aren't ancient history. Every place you turn there are people aggrieved enough to blow up a bus or a train station."

"Or four airplanes and the tallest office towers in New York." She glanced over, a deep sadness in her eyes. "It's remarkable that these Weather people acted on account of somebody else's struggles. The war in Vietnam as you said, and Black nationalism at home."

"True," he said. Her disclaimer about following the politics was too modest. "But it was Weather's war too. Fifty-five thousand US soldiers killed in Vietnam by the time we evacuated Saigon." They stepped around a foursome saying goodbyes outside an Eritrean restaurant. "So . . . can I buy you a drink?" Christopher asked. He had something bracing in mind. A scotch, maybe a cognac. The fog had come in and his hands felt like icicles.

"Depends what you mean by a drink. Maybe some tea?"

Ouch. Her family was Sikh, she'd already told him. No booze.

"There's a café the next street over," he said. "Kind of a combination café and art gallery."

"I hope you don't mind?"

"Of course not."

—

Suvali found a table by the windows along Lincoln Avenue, across from the eucalyptus trees edging Golden Gate Park. Christopher waited for their order, watching the lazy spin of a mobile hung above the Paint & Palette's cash register. When their drinks came up he crossed to the table. "Did you want milk?" he asked, slipping into a wooden chair.

"No," Suvali said, smiling that enigmatic smile again. "Not with mint tea."

She was beyond beautiful. Christopher looked away, taking in the art on nearby walls. A leering figure with the president's face caught his eye. The painting depicted a man standing in a fiery landscape strewn with bones, dressed in a monk's robe and shouldering a pennant decorated with a blood-red cross. St. George, he realized as his gaze returned to Suvali. She was staring into her tea. "What are you thinking?" he asked.

"About the movie."

Christopher waited for her to say more.

"Something that dark-haired woman talked about—the one sitting at the picnic table. That doing nothing when the world is in a period of violence is itself a form of violence."

"Yes, I remember that. Naomi Jaffe. A pivotal abstraction."

"I'm not sure I agree with it." Suvali looked up, as if challenging him.

"There's a whiff of original sin in her idea," Christopher said carefully. "That a person is stained from the get-go."

"I wasn't thinking in religious terms. Or perhaps I was, but using karma as a frame." Suvali blew gently across her mug. "I'd say that exchanging one violence for another only digs a person in more deeply. The way to end the cycle is to step away from it."

"But Jaffe didn't say 'doing anything other than violence'—she said 'doing nothing.' She was talking about collective responsibility."

"She was defending the group's decisions, Chris. The bombings they did commit, which were terribly dangerous even if they did take measures to keep from hurting anyone."

Christopher nodded. "The thing is, their group grew out of total impotence. The government kept escalating in Vietnam no matter how many people came to peaceful protests. Nixon didn't care. It's not a whole lot different from all those millions on the streets last February, then in March the US invades Iraq."

"But look what it came to. In the seventies, I mean. What that man who was critical of the Weather people said—"

"Todd Gitlin?"

"The one with the round glasses. He said that this kind of thinking, that you know what's best for people, is what allowed all the Hitlers and Stalins in history to justify their programs of mass murder."

"He's right."

"So how do you reconcile those ideas?"

Christopher swirled milky coffee in his glass. "Gitlin is still angry that Weather hijacked SDS—Students for a Democratic Society—which . . . well, never mind all that. But what he didn't acknowledge in the film is that the logic that drove Stalin and Hitler and Mao to lunatic ends was the same logic that brought

Moses to the Red Sea and Washington to the Delaware River. And Gandhi to Delhi, for that matter."

"I'm not sure I see what you mean."

"I mean that leaders lead. And things contain their opposites. Mao's horrific rule lifted tens of millions of Chinese peasants out of poverty and illiteracy. Washington's 'free' government institutionalized slavery." Christopher was starting to wish he had suggested a lighter movie. "There are inevitable failures and contradictions when theory confronts practice. Still, you have to find the border between standing up for what's right, versus acts that are dictatorial or violent. Or worse."

She sipped from her mug. "Do you think the Weather Underground found that border?"

"If it weren't for the comrades who died making their first explosives they would have become murderers. But it didn't happen that way. They started to step off the precipice, then scrabbled their way back to solid ground. I think you've got to give them credit for that."

Suvali didn't answer right away. A fire truck hurtled by, lights blazing. She watched it pass. "Perhaps this is too direct a question," she said, then raised her eyes to his. "Do people you know do this kind of thing?"

"Planting bombs?" Christopher sat back and lifted his hands, showing empty palms. "Not a chance. I'm firmly grounded in the impotent, sign-waving camp." He wondered whether that would still be true if he let Chagall use his manifesto. And where did Brendan fit in, attempting to ferry material aid to the Zapatistas?

"Then why do anything?" Suvali asked. "Why pour your time and talent into something you think is hopeless?"

"Because I'm dense?"

"Seriously."

"Seriously?" She was pushing him to show himself. "Because it's the only morally coherent place I can find," he said, leaning forward. "It's what Laura Whitehorn said at the end of the movie: people never stop struggling to change things that make life unlivable. Everybody looks for a way to make a difference. For some that means trying to give their kids a good life. For others it's something . . . more general. Waving signs may seem pointless, but it holds open a space. Someday people are going to jump into that space, when the moment comes around again."

Christopher lifted his latte, and sipped. She probably thought he was an imbecile.

"You're a good man," Suvali murmured.

He set the drink down, embarrassed. "You don't know me well enough to say that."

"What I mean is, I think it's awfully difficult to stake so much on a hope that slim. It's much easier to make one's world smaller, to draw a little circle and say, 'This is what I can affect.' If you don't, it's so easy to overreach. That's what happened to the people in the film."

"Maybe," Christopher said. He watched her hands. Doctor's hands, long fingers, nails short and scrubbed. Hands that would probably do more concrete good in the world than his. Good that would be far easier to see.

"My uncle says that no matter where a person is in the cycles of history, the tangents leading toward tragedy are easier to follow than the paths that lead to balance."

"This is the uncle you told me about? The professor?"

Suvali nodded.

"Where does he teach?"

"At a university in the Punjab. Do you know about the separatists there? The Golden Temple, Indira Gandhi?"

"Not very much," he said. "I know she was assassinated after an awful massacre. I was in high school, I think."

"It happened in 1984. My uncle was badly injured in the fighting then."

"I'm feeling extremely ignorant right now."

"It doesn't matter. I don't know your Weather Underground, you don't know Shiromani Akali Dal. It's a big world."

"Humbling."

A silence fell.

"What field is your uncle in?"

"Mathematics." Suvali smiled. "I'd be hard-pressed to say anything more exact than that. If doctors had to calculate anything more complex than long division, I'd be in Brighton dishing out fish and chips at the Palace Pier."

Christopher laughed. "I don't think so," he said. "Was Brighton a place you wanted to escape?"

"I suppose I did." Suvali looked at Christopher, then lowered her eyes again. "Perhaps London was far enough, really. But then I kept going. Westward ho."

"And once you finish your program?"

"That's hard to say. Licensure is a bit complicated."

Christopher watched as a resolution settled over her, a determination she breathed into her posture, the slightest tightening of her expression. How did she see the trajectory of her life?

"What does your father think of you working in newspapers?" she asked. "Doesn't he want you to be a professor?"

"Oh, sure, he thinks I'm wasting my genetic inheritance." Christopher smiled, he hoped not too bitterly. "At this point he'd settle for law school."

"Would you go that route?"

"Not likely. Though it's hard to say how much longer I can stick with this electronic paste-up gig."

She nodded. "Did you tell me already whether you have siblings?"

"A brother, Marshall. Struck it rich in the dot-com years, and now he shifts money around the stock market. Another loser in Dad's book. Money doesn't count for much in my family."

"A loser in your book too, if I'm catching your drift."

Christopher shrugged. He'd aired enough dirty laundry for a first date. "It's an old story," he said. "Cain and Abel, Jacob and Esau."

"Vali and Sugriva."

"I am so out of my depth."

The crowd in the café had begun to thin. Christopher looked up into a cloud of vellum wings, strung on nylon lines suspended from the ceiling. "Like a kelp forest from below," he observed. "I wonder if that's what the artist had in mind."

Suvali followed his gaze. "It reminds me of the aquarium in Monterey."

"I haven't been there for years," he said. "Do they still have that cylindrical tank, the one full of sardines? Or anchovies, maybe? Flashing around and around, like silver bracelets."

"They do. It's hypnotic, isn't it?"

He watched her stare into the slowly spinning artwork. "I don't want to keep you too late."

"Thank you, Chris. I do have to be at the hospital tomorrow."

———

He flagged down a taxi on the corner. It was a short distance to where she lived, but buses were infrequent at that hour. As the yellow Impala pulled over he leaned in a few uncertain degrees. She pulled away, just enough to rebuff his hope.

"It means more in my world," she said, placing a hand on his arm. "But I would like to see you again. I . . . I like talking with you. Will you call me?"

He nodded dumbly. The driver was waiting; Christopher opened the taxi's door.

"I mean it, Chris. Maybe next week?"

"I'll call," he said, and tried to smile as if her refusal hadn't mattered.

TWENTY

Christopher slipped out of his room and tiptoed toward the stairs, doing his best to preserve the Triangle's early afternoon silence. His messenger bag pulled him into a starboard list. When someone stepped into the hall he started, failing for an instant to recognize Brendan behind Ray-Bans and a leather jacket. "Christ," he exclaimed. "You look like undercover FBI in those shades."

Brendan put on a noirish air, reached for his wallet, and let it fall open to reveal a limp accordion of tattered plastic pockets. "Not too convincing, is it?"

Christopher laughed. "Not too."

"It's spooky that the Triangle's so empty now."

"Fewer and fewer." Christopher hiked up his bag. "When are you going to give up couch surfing and come back in for real?"

"Too soon to make a plan, Chris. You heading out?"

"Um, yeah. Meeting a friend."

"Oh?" Brendan asked. "The woman from the café?"

Christopher felt himself color. He hadn't phoned since Suvali sped off in her cab the week before, and neither had she. "No," he said. "Someone else."

Brendan followed him down the stairs. On the sidewalk they hesitated, each as if on cue.

"So," Christopher said. He made a birdlike gesture toward Church Street. "I'm heading this way."

Brendan thumbed over his shoulder in the opposite direction, and gave an exaggerated wink.

Another call to the Zapatista contacts, Christopher guessed. Or maybe just buying cigarettes. Asking would have invited more questions. "See you tonight," he said, and turned toward the Muni stop.

—

Coming up into UN Plaza Christopher hurried around to the main library's entrance, barely watching for anybody who might have followed him off the train. Still, he pretended deep preoccupation as he approached the security station. It was all he could do to keep a straight face. To imagine the library guards would be interested in his business, let alone that any of the patrons cared. Who would be watching him? The mohawked skateboy waiting in line at the checkout counter? That horse-faced guy wearing a straw Stetson?

The uniformed guards by the Tattle-Tape sensors ignored him, as expected. He stepped aside for a toothless grandmother shambling by with a pair of fully loaded shopping bags.

Christopher hadn't run on so little shut-eye since college. The only way to deliver Chagall's manifesto, he had realized, was to write and rewrite 'til his fingers bled. A stretch of late nights and several quick round-trips with Chagall in e-mail had leapfrogged the project to its last act. Today's IRC would be all about the fine points, including delivery.

Christopher crossed the lobby and climbed a flight of marble steps, then ascended a staircase that wound up the atrium. From the third floor he took an elevator to five, where the periodical room was jammed, two or three neatly groomed older men at every table. Christopher hadn't accounted for weekday news fiends. None seemed a threat, particularly. But Christopher needed a seat without an over-the-shoulder view.

He took the stairs back down a level, and found the Patent and Trademark Center vacant.

The usual rites ensued. By the time he got to the chat prompt Chagall was signed on.

CHAGALL: Sorry I missed our rendezvous a few days back.
CHRIS: Shit happens, no apology needed.
CHAGALL: My partners and I think your changes are excellent.
CHRIS: Glad to hear it. You still think generic on strategy works? Without reference to target?
CHAGALL: Yes, powerful as is. Especially latest analogy to cancer. Waiting idly for lumps & fatigue vs. active treatment. Could have been morbid but you made it work.
CHRIS: Thanks. Critique of reductionist science?
CHAGALL: Digestible now. Comparison of scientific complexity to relationships in one-child family vs. multiple is easy way into hard topic. We also like comparison of average weather patterns to what's it like outside today, that science is less certain than it seems. Prior draft was sound, but couldn't have reached a broad audience.

Somebody's car alarm began to wail on Hyde Street. He typed out his reply, ducking Chagall's uncharacteristic praise.

CHRIS: Your comments were helpful. What about call to Civil Society?
CHAGALL: What we liked this time was tight bond between

democratic engagement and 'withering away of the vanguard.'

CHRIS: Nicely put. Too clever a phrase to include though, right? Only parties slated for the dustbin of history would get it. The critical leap is from agreement with moral argument to actual, effective behavior.

CHAGALL: Yes. As in description of nodding while the pastor preaches, then acting badly after church.

CHRIS: So what are next steps?

CHAGALL: What you've done is more than satisfactory. Now we dissolve our ties. Essential to destroy all contact info, encryption keys, notes, drafts, etc. To protect all of us.

Chagall's garrulousness suddenly made sense. This was his shadow-comrade's last chance to assure the proper steps would be taken.

CHRIS: I didn't think we were quite finished.

CHAGALL: We can take it from here. Assume you are using win/linux dual boot, as discussed? All relevant data, software, logs on linux partition?

CHRIS: Correct.

CHAGALL: Necessary to completely and repeatedly wipe that partition. Multiple methods—Gutmann, DoD spec, pseudorandom writes. Are these techniques known to you?

CHRIS: Yes. I have open-source software that does all that. So . . . if we're done, I wonder if it would pay to ask when I might see this document distributed.

CHAGALL: Not a dime.

CHRIS: I'll assume, however, if not used within—what, six months?—that you have aborted and I am free to recreate for other purposes.

CHAGALL: Do not keep a copy. You'll see it on the wire soon enough.

CHRIS: Several cycles back I proposed a public mode of handoff. Safer for me. Post in an obscure public venue, you "find it" and republish. Weakens any possible inference that we had contact.

CHAGALL: We discussed on our side. Though we recognize this would be safer for you, we need a fresh communiqué to put action on media map with proper gravitas. Your work is very strong. We do not want to dilute it.

CHRIS: Did not expect to have to make this decision today. Give me a week to consider?

CHAGALL: Three days? Gives time for e-mail exchange within one week frame.

CHRIS: I can live with that. I'll mail to next address in cycle.

CHAGALL: We ask you to consider contact to-date. The care with which we have conducted all communication. On completion of this last exchange, we will purge all evidence.

CHRIS: Understood. Your competence is not an issue.

CHAGALL: Unless you insist on posting early, I will not respond to your final e-mail.

CHRIS: I'll try not to feel jilted.

CHAGALL: Nothing personal, just the nature of the game. Many thanks. You will see your work put to good use. Over and out.

That was it.

Christopher sat alone in chatspace. Oddly enough, despite his intended sarcasm, the exchange did feel a bit like being unceremoniously dumped. Twice in ten days if Suvali's actions spoke more truthfully than her words.

He contemplated the possibility that Chagall's plans might

be thwarted. It would be impossible to reconstitute the manifesto from memory. And it was good, perhaps the best argument he'd ever written. He didn't want to lose it.

Christopher hugged the perimeter walls as he scuttled to the opposite corner of the building. Like a rat, he thought, striking out for the stairway.

If his screed was disseminated as Chagall promised, he could easily destroy a secretly saved copy. And until Chagall and his comrades broadcast it, possession of the text tied Christopher to nothing and no one. Industrial-strength security had been enough to protect the document as they shot it back and forth over the internet. What harm, he reasoned, could come of holding an encrypted draft in reserve?

Whether to post early—that was a harder question.

Christopher didn't feel confident about setting up anonymous publication on his own. He needed Chagall's advice to be sure the plant would be truly untraceable. And if the saboteur's action was imminent, posting in advance could look to police like a coordinated handoff. That would draw more scrutiny his way, not less.

He resolved to sleep on it. There were still a few days to decide.

TWENTY-ONE

The apple-cheeked cashier snickered through a tangle of piercings. "On Aleister Crowley's warts, I swear: meek little Lady Nodsalot in a balls-out pillow fight."

Buzz shook his head knowingly as Casey pushed off the record store counter and crouched to adjust the sound system's equalizer. When he stood again, stretching, Buzz looked away from the androgynous boi's pectoral swell. "Must have been a fucking scene," he said.

"Puppy fucker!" Casey squealed, lunging with a phantom pillow. "You're a dirty goddamn puppy fucker!" The CD player paused to shuffle discs. "I feel sorry for her. She's what, fifteen? She ain't tough enough to be on her own out there."

"It's the shits," Buzz said, but his voice conveyed little sympathy. He craned around to check on Jonah, still tapping rhythms on the edge of a listening station. His eyes were closed, his face innocent and rapt.

"Your pal likes those Indian tunes."

"Yeah. Go figure." Buzz made a bevel of his thumb and index finger and gave a shattering whistle. Jonah looked up and Buzz gestured impatiently.

"At least he's not a Deadhead."

"It's like—what do they call that shit? Like when spliff leads to smack?"

Casey snickered. "Yeah, ain't it? A gateway drug."

Jonah shed his headphones. "What are you guys talking about?"

"How fucked up it'd be if you turned into a Deadhead."

"No way, dude." Jonah sauntered over and set a Chatur Lal CD on the counter. "Can you guys hold this?"

"Two bucks deposit, I can hold up to five days," Casey said, tapping a painted fingernail on a sign stuck to the register. "Store policy. You miss the deadline, Fungible Beats keeps the deuce."

Jonah frowned. "Nah," he said, reaching for the disc. "Guess I better put it back."

"Give it here," Casey said, relenting. "I'll put it in the play pile. If I'm not around when you come back, say you heard it on the sound system."

"Thanks, man."

"S'cool."

The boys slouched toward Haight Street. "Hey," Casey called as they pushed through the door. "Look out for them puppy fuckers."

Buzz threw him a sign from the other side of the glass.

"What's Puppy Fuckers?" Jonah asked. "Some new band?"

"Some band," Buzz guffawed. "That's good, man."

"So what was he talking about?"

"Dude dumped this homeless chick and got a dog, so she lost it. Started beatin' him with a pillow and calling him a puppy fucker."

Jonah snorted. "Bad visual."

"That's no lie."

A sleepy-looking teenager stirred in his bedroll on the sidewalk. "Dude," he called out as they passed. "Yo, Buzz!"

Both of them wheeled around. "Yo, Jaggery." Buzz bumped fists with the fuzz-bearded street dweller. "Didn't see you under all that shit."

"Cops kicked everybody off the sidewalks last night, man."

"That sucks."

Jaggery squirmed his way into a sitting position. "Got a smoke, dude?"

Buzz produced a cyan packet from the depths of his trench coat and sat cross-legged next to Jaggery's backpack. The two busied themselves rolling cigarettes. "This here's Jonah," Buzz said, without looking up.

"Hey."

"Hey." Jonah propped himself against a parking meter.

"Got fire?" Jaggery asked. He licked his rollie and twisted the ends. Buzz handed him a book of matches, then leaned in for a light off the one Jaggery struck.

"Thanks, dude."

"S'cool." Buzz stood. "You be around?"

"Yeah, pretty much. Free meal at the church. But after that."

"Maybe I'll catch you."

Jonah fell into step with Buzz. Turning onto Clayton they were hailed again, this time from the opposite corner.

"Heeeeey, fellas, whassup?"

Tyler Cole. Jonah didn't need to look to recognize his treacly, TV-host voice. Tyler crossed over, flanked by two more of their schoolmates.

Buzz leaned against the side of a building and embodied boredom.

"Hey guys." Jonah pitched his tone neutrally. He wasn't friends with any of the three, especially. Nate Williams was in his science class. Everybody knew about Ethan Walrick's ambition to make it on *American Idol*.

"Whassup," Ethan said, turning on his winningest smile.

"Hey," echoed Nate in a baritone deeper than his years. He cast his eyes downward.

"Is that a joint?" Tyler asked.

Buzz ignored him.

"Cigarette," Jonah said.

"What a tragic shame."

"You guys want to smoke some weed?" Ethan asked. "We're on our way over to the park."

Tyler shot him a withering look.

"Whatever," Buzz said, glancing in Jonah's direction.

Jonah shrugged.

The boys scuffed their way across Oak Street and into Golden Gate Park's narrow Panhandle, then screened themselves behind a cluster of trees. Nate and Jonah both hung back as Tyler lit up, toked deeply, and passed his spliff to Ethan. When his turn came, Buzz wolfed down the thick sweet smoke. After inhaling his fill he offered the twist to Nate, who refused it; then, for appearance's sake, to Jonah; and finally back to Tyler. Tyler inspected the joint from all angles, as if mystified to see how far down it had burned.

"What do you think of Ms. Sepko?" Jonah asked Nate in a low voice.

"She's pretty smart." Nate shoved his hands deep into his pockets. "Not so much in physics, but okay in bio and chem."

"Like when you asked how gravity works in space and she didn't know?"

"Uh-huh." Nate might have been blushing but dark skin masked his embarrassment. "It's Einstein," he said. "Space is curved by large masses, like planets and stars, so Newton's equations can't explain stuff."

"Dude," Tyler said, "space is curved by excellent weed. You should try the shit."

Ethan laughed compliantly. Nate just clammed up.

"Hey," Tyler said, gesturing in Jonah's direction. "How come you don't get high? You straight edge or something?"

"Just not into it," Jonah mumbled.

"Weird. Both you guys."

"Fuck off, Tyler," Buzz said jovially as he passed the joint. "They ain't weird, just different from you."

"Damn," Tyler exclaimed. "Little Arjuna's grown up to be a diversity consultant." He spoke Buzz's birth name in three disdainful syllables.

A silence like slow motion fell over the group. Tyler took his hit and passed the dwindling roach to Ethan. Jonah looked at the ground.

Buzz cleared his throat loudly, and hocked a slimy mass inches from Tyler's Air Jordans. "Watch yourself, bitch."

"Speaking of bitches," Tyler said, exhaling, "how's your mom? Still shacked up with that ex-con—what's his name?"

"Shut up, Tyler."

"Vince. That's it, big ol' Vince, the brooding bully. What's it like living with an ex-con, Arjuna? Ya' think Vince is a booty bandit? He ever get all tripped out like he's back in Soledad, come looking for your tender ass in the shower?"

Jonah didn't see Buzz move until Tyler was bent over double, gasping and retching into the mangy lawn. Then Buzz faced each of them in turn, staring down any inkling of challenge before it could form. He slipped something short and cylindrical into his coat. A siren sounded north of Fell Street.

"We're out of here," Buzz said to Jonah. Tyler was struggling for breath. Everyone else stood frozen in place. "Now," Buzz commanded.

Jonah had to run to catch up. "Where are we going?"

"Away."

"What the fuck happened?"

"What the fuck happened is Tyler thought he had a free pass to play biggest-asshole-on-the-street."

"But—"

"He was wrong." Buzz looked over his shoulder and cut over to the north side of the park. Jonah scurried after. "It's a long, boring story," Buzz said finally, as they headed up Lyon. "Me and Tyler."

"That stuff he said . . . ?"

"He don't know shit. Me and him haven't spoke three words at a time since fourth grade."

"That thing in your pocket—"

"You didn't see it."

Jonah took a moment to digest this. "Tyler's not really hurt, right?"

"Nah. Not this time." When they came to Hayes, Buzz looked impatiently up and down the street. There wasn't a bus in sight. "Up a couple more," he said, half to himself. They kept walking north. "We can chill over on Polk Street."

Jonah followed uneasily. If Tyler were hurt . . . He thought better of asking anything more. If they were lucky, the 5-Fulton would come bearing down on the corner just as they did.

TWENTY-TWO

April 2004

Romulus parks his van on a side street at the border of a modest commercial district. The night is dim and drizzly, ideal conditions for piggybacking off open networks: no one is watching what little there is to see.

He is not looking forward to a chat with Chagall. Romulus has grown uneasy about how little the demolitionist explains. Need-to-know is a powerful argument under the circumstances, but at the same time it's surreal to engage in only half of a project week after week. From early in the year they have prepared independently, overlapping solely to develop a political line that is now, in the eleventh hour, being drafted as a communiqué that neither of them controls. Their target date is three weeks away. Chagall continues to demand that Romulus deliver a brick-and-mortar contribution to their conspiracy, and time for hedging has run out. If he admits his physical bulk, his lack of stamina, his dread of capture, Romulus is certain he'll lose the little influence Chagall still concedes.

He smooths rough edges in the hoard of e-mail addresses amassed since midautumn. Like straightening a deck of cards, the simple, repetitive task calms him. Romulus has gathered tens of millions of addresses from spybots and crawlers and worms, from list merchants, from internet forums and social networking sites. At this stage he is winnowing out malformed data and expired domains, scrubbing administrative accounts, eliminating duplicates.

As he scans console logs, a dialog pops up on the third monitor in the van's array, silently blinking for attention.

CHAGALL: Site visit successful. Documents you provided were accurate and useful.

He reads, switches keyboards, and types.

ROMULUS: Target is attainable?

Only after he encrypts and sends does Romulus recognize he has fallen immediately into the tone his building slayer sets, terse and challenging. Chagall is a far more domineering partner than he sought or expected. A bully, almost. His skin crawls as Romulus anticipates his marching orders.

CHAGALL: Its vulnerabilities can be exploited. What's your status?
ROMULUS: Distribution channel is on track. I've harvested 40M unique addresses so far. 50M possible by the time we send.
CHAGALL: News sites?
ROMULUS: Confident of only one on A-list, the domains are well protected. Success with two or three top targets would be a coup, as discussed. Splash and secondary coverage is the real goal. Hacked pages won't last.
CHAGALL: Right. Am ready to coordinate on-location task.

Romulus bites his lip. Someone is approaching up the sidewalk. He can hear voices, male and female, and just ahead of them, the aluminum jangle of dog tags. They come to a halt beside the van.

"C'mon, Tuxedo," a man's voice urges.

"What's he doing?"

A female voice, younger, petulant, perhaps a teenage daughter. The dog growls, then erupts in a curt, menacing bark.

"Enough, Tuxedo."

"Quiet, Tux!" the daughter commands. "I bet it's a cat."

He doesn't dare type. The dog sounds like a barrel-chested brute. Romulus imagines the animal's jaws, and notices he is sweating copiously. It's a matter of time until the beast smells his fear leaking from the van.

CHAGALL: Problem?

Finally the trio moves away down the sidewalk. The dog growls malicious regret. Romulus types.

ROMULUS: Slight disturbance. All clear now.
CHAGALL: Certain?
ROMULUS: Yes. Let's discuss manifesto next. Location task after.

Romulus reaches for a roll of paper towels. He mops sweat from his forehead.

CHAGALL: If you insist.
ROMULUS: Again I question the wisdom of bringing in a third party. Religious undertone distracts from core message.
CHAGALL: Writer has demonstrated openness to guidance. Draft is strong. Some religiosity meets intended audience on their own ground.

ROMULUS: I need to know more about this invisible partner. To evaluate risk. I have concluded our writer is not one of the individuals I put forward. My suggestions would not have presented this "religiosity" problem.

CHAGALL: I do not see it as a problem. I will not respond to speculation about writer identity. As before, if there are concerns we agree on, I will communicate direction. Risk is nil. Once text is acceptable the author is irrelevant. It is you who retains power to betray our agreement and send a message I have never seen. We've been over this ground endlessly. Let's return to location task.

Romulus shakes his head in the dim solitude of his van. Chagall thinks he's stalling. Yet everything depends on the trustworthiness of each actor, on rigorous care to remain undetected. Romulus has a handle on the nature of the demolitionist he recruited himself. He has no clue whether or how the unknown writer might botch up their operation. Maybe it's just as well that Chagall didn't recruit his candidates. The risk—to all of them—is now on the saboteur alone. In any case, Romulus can't turn Chagall a degree off course.

ROMULUS: Go on.

CHAGALL: Good. Overview first. Closed-circuit cameras monitor building entrances. UTP cables route to multiplexer in a basement utility room, from there to security desk in lobby. From security, repeater links to kiosk at periphery of construction site, where guard is currently stationed. Picture that?

ROMULUS: Yes. Assume you need to divert signals?

CHAGALL: Correct, on a single door. A device spliced into the circuit will record camera signal for a defined period.

Device plays back recorded loop when remotely commanded.

ROMULUS: I could produce such a device.

CHAGALL: Producing such a device is not an on-site task. And it already exists. It only needs to be placed.

Romulus feels a sudden urge to move his bowels. He clenches and types.

ROMULUS: I've said before, I'm not a cat burglar.

CHAGALL: Guard walks building perimeter, then through the facility itself several times per shift. When guard leaves the kiosk, intruder can approach unobserved. Intruder is off camera when flat against building. As guard returns to kiosk, intruder enters. Waits for next walk-through to withdraw.

ROMULUS: Are cameras recording?

CHAGALL: Probably. But security staff is unlikely to review unless planted equipment is discovered in building. Device will be well disguised. You'll wear ski mask, common brand dark clothing, latex gloves. A recording leads nowhere.

ROMULUS: What if I'm tall as a basketball center? Or paraplegic?

CHAGALL: If you're tall, crouch. If you're a cripple, or a liar, or a coward, you should have pulled the plug months ago.

ROMULUS: I'm not pulling any plugs.

CHAGALL: Proceed to basement. Identify cable in utility room, I will specify how in written instructions. Perform splice using procedure that won't interrupt signal—again, detail to be provided. Sufficient for now to know that procedure requires minimal tools, minimal expertise.

ROMULUS: Requires travel.

CHAGALL: You'll drive. If you're not in US enter from Canada or Mexico. Pay cash for everything.

ROMULUS: Okay, never mind. That's my problem. How to enter building? I can't pick locks either.

CHAGALL: Doors are electronically and manually keyed. I'll provide a master for the outer door, also for utility room.

ROMULUS: You're a fountain of resources.

CHAGALL: Open doors are indicated on security desk console, but signaling is not extended to kiosk.

ROMULUS: Sounds as if you could have finished the job yourself.

CHAGALL: I prefer to share.

Romulus is certain he would hate Chagall's guts if they met in the flesh. Humorless, unflappable bastard.

ROMULUS: Need more detailed plan, diagrams, tool list. In advance, for study. This may be a regular day's work for you but it's out of my league.

CHAGALL: I'll provide a complete kit 48 hours in advance. Need to set date.

Romulus swallows. He is acutely conscious of his uncoordinated body. Chagall, he imagines, is a flat-muscled Special Forces type. His fellow conspirator is toying with him. How much more clearly does he have to say "I can't do this"?

And yet. If the demolitionist were any less cagey, Romulus would doubt his ability to execute. In Chagall's place he'd insist just as hard. And therefore: one step at a time.

ROMULUS: What range?

CHAGALL: Best five to seven days before our target.

ROMULUS: How to hand off tools, etc.?

CHAGALL: Will conceal at a location within 100 miles of
site. Suggest you read up on CCTV installation, splicing
UTP cable using EMI-detect/decode bypass.

ROMULUS: Say I accomplish the splice. How will I test?

CHAGALL: Wireless LAN is running in building, currently
unsecured. There's signal at top of stairs leading to basement. Will provide device to test communication.

ROMULUS: What if test fails?

CHAGALL: I will retest prior to start of operation. If your
part is not completed fully and successfully, I will not proceed.

ROMULUS: We're heavily invested. There has to be a fallback
plan.

CHAGALL: Not negotiable, as previously discussed.

ROMULUS: You're necessarily providing material resources.
I assume there's significant cost. What's the financing?

CHAGALL: Thought you'd never wonder.

ROMULUS: So?

CHAGALL: It would compromise my anonymity to tell.

ROMULUS: Is that a hint?

CHAGALL: I intend it as misdirection. There is no shadow
organization. Cash is mine, unencumbered.

His leftmost laptop begins to log new traffic on the hacked
network. Romulus studies the packets for a few moments. It's an
FTP connection, to a security software vendor. Somebody's
machine is updating antivirus definitions.

ROMULUS: Still. Has to be a lot. Would assist in form of
financing satisfy requirement for non-virtual participation?

CHAGALL: Negative. A desperate offer, but I am willing to

suspend judgment. The equipment you work with is not free either.

ROMULUS: If I was some kind of cop I'd be pretty g.d. frustrated.

CHAGALL: Without prejudice as to what you might or might not be, it's not my job to help cops do theirs. Can you commit to a specific date?

ROMULUS: I can commit to the week.

CHAGALL: I need to know soon. By Friday, say.

ROMULUS: Why the rush?

CHAGALL: You deferred this for months.

ROMULUS: I'm squeamish, that's no secret. As I've said. Not my strong suit.

CHAGALL: We're both operating in unfamiliar territory.

ROMULUS: I'll withdraw if plan fails to convince I can get in and out.

CHAGALL: Plan will be airtight. I do not intend to see our interest in target unmasked, or to sacrifice essential propaganda element.

ROMULUS: Neither do I.

CHAGALL: Expecting contact in 48 hours, then, drop 29b.

ROMULUS: Yes. O&O.

Romulus shuts down the chat link and rips another length of paper toweling to dab his forehead dry, and the back of his neck.

Splicing and crimping is simple enough—he can handle wire. But the set up. Burglarizing a secured construction facility, with two days to prepare, in a state he's only flown over. There are so many ways he could fuck it all up.

He imagines himself groping down a dimly lit stairwell, missing a step, taking a hard tumble. He visualizes the fall so vividly that he starts, setting the van rocking on its struts. Romulus holds his breath, listening to the neighborhood.

What then?

His body splayed across a landing like a beached whale, knocked out, maybe paralyzed. In the morning, thick-muscled men in jeans and tool belts haul him up into glaring Midwestern light. Then the Homeland Security goons. Truth serums, stress positions, splints under his fingernails.

He shakes off morbid conjecture and pushes away from the bank of keyboards and screens. Romulus ducks through the heavyweight curtain installed to conceal his laptops' ghostly light, and settles himself in the driver's seat. Caving in to fear will return him to the same dead end that sent him looking for Chagall in the first place. Firing up the engine, he eases away from the curb.

A hell of a lot of people are going to read that communiqué.

Their exhortation won't flip everybody's switch. How could it? But they might move a million, or two, or ten. Chagall could be right about what will draw their audience in. It's not that the writer is doing a bad job; he's clearly done his homework. They stand a chance of forcing realization that the time is now or never. That another decade spent mortgaging the biosphere could prove ten years too many.

And doing his part means he's got to walk into that goddamned construction site on the outskirts of Lincoln.

He has little choice but to double down. Romulus has spent years taking virtual potshots at industry. Either he's serious about his enmities or he's a loser and a fool. He can't bear to go back to impotent bit-twiddling.

At a stop sign a few blocks from the freeway, no traffic behind or before him, Romulus drills down into an off-market MP3 player and queues up a track from *Il Trovatore*. A scene from Verdi's opera has popped unbidden into his mind's ear.

Romulus taps an icon on the device's screen, and a smoky soprano fills the vehicle.

> *Ora il mio fine impavida,*
> *Piena di gioia attendo ...*
> *Potrò dirgli morendo:*
> *Salvo tu sei per me!*

Leontyne Price is singing Leonora, her tragic ecstasy blooming like a peaty single malt across his aural palate. She has bartered her life for her lover's. And now the smitten Count di Luna edges in with his doubting counterpoint, bitter, incredulous that Leonora would offer herself on the terms he's been led to misunderstand.

A thin rain sweeps across the roof as the voices duel and Zubin Mehta coaxes the strings forward. His windshield is misting up. Romulus cranks the defrost fan as he accelerates toward an on-ramp, singing along in imperfect tune and octaves below the heroine, willing himself to desperate resolve.

TWENTY-THREE

Christopher stood a few hundred yards from the cliff, by a fast-flowing fork of the American River, watching the climbers through a pair of binoculars.

Today marked their last practice. Duncan Caselli crouched atop a boulder a short distance from the cliff's base, coaching over a walkie-talkie. The ground crew, Becca and Mickey, would soon send weighted backpacks skyward in lieu of the banner. Christopher followed Duncan's instruction with a neophyte's uncertainty while Marty and Phil cavorted up the rock face. Their seconds, Laura and Keith, followed steadily behind. Christopher's role would kick in with the ersatz banner hoist.

"Phil, don't skimp on the gear," Duncan said. "You're training for solid protection every few feet."

"Sorry, Dunc." Phil's voice sounded strained through the walkie-talkie's static. "I hope you're right about this wall being harder than the real thing."

"No question. But don't think about that. Be right here. Care before speed—remember the stakes."

"Right."

"You're cool, Phil," Marty radioed from across the cliff face. Christopher swung his binoculars over. Marty hugged the mottled gray stone, feeling his way onto a foothold Christopher could barely make out. Two ropes hung from his harness, as from Phil's: a kernmantle weaving its way through carabiners and quickdraws to the belayer lower on the cliff, and a static line running all the way down to the ground crew, who would clip it to the mock banner once the climbers reached their marks. "Run Duncan's rack dry," Marty was saying. "Leave the bully's hardware tacked to the wall."

"As for you, Martin," Duncan said, "come down one nut short and it's back up you go."

"Nora says he doesn't even pick up his socks," Laura chimed in. "You better count 'em real careful."

"Will do," Duncan said. "Keep your focus, climbers."

Christopher seconded that, if only to himself. Duncan had put the crew through a grueling regimen, from specialty gyms to parks radiating out from the Bay Area in every direction but west. They'd been bouldering at Castle Rock, Jenner, and the Pinnacles, and climbing at Oroville, Phantom Spires, and here, at Lovers Leap. From what Christopher could tell they'd learned plenty. Still, you had to figure that scrambling like geckos over unforgiving rock wouldn't mix well with casual banter. The bridge might be an easier climb, what with ladders running up the tower, but factor in the pressure of traffic backed up six miles into Oakland, and the cops rushing their blockade? It wasn't going to be a romp in the park.

He let the binoculars hang against his chest and rested his eyes on the foaming river. A fallen cedar and a length of sisal bridged the torrent around an upstream bend. Christopher figured climbing enthusiasts had strung the rope, to cross over more easily from the summer cabins behind him. The ground, carpeted with needles shed by Jeffrey pines, felt soft as a persian rug shop's floor. River noise masked the rumble from Highway 50, and the air smelled clean and new, faintly like vanilla. His position approximated the distance between their planned blockade line and the bridge tower. Christopher had set up a tripod and camera, to explain himself should anyone come along.

The climbers were still ascending. Christopher settled himself on a low shelf of veined white stone, and wondered what Suvali was doing. Sitting in a seminar? Following a preceptor on rounds? Their parting outside the Paint & Palette baffled him. Despite what she'd said, he couldn't convince himself to pick up the phone. She had no romantic interest in him, or she abhorred his politics, or both. He would look like a fool if he failed to take her hints. On the other hand, she'd urged him to call, flat-out. So was he a fool if he didn't?

Unusually, he was carrying a cell phone, one they'd rented so he could be in touch with the action's command post on the day of the blockade. Jammed into the front pocket of his jeans, the flip phone dug into Christopher's thigh. His stone seat was bleeding warmth from his body. He stood, stamping his feet.

The phone took a few seconds to boot. Christopher was surprised it registered a strong signal, even in the middle of the mountains. He remembered Suvali's number, but hesitated. Maybe calling wouldn't be so smart after all. Maybe it had been too long already. She could have called him, but she hadn't; he had to factor that in. On impulse, Christopher punched in his father's campus number instead. The phone rang. Twice. Three times. Then Professor Kalman picked up.

"Hello?"

"Hi, Dad."

"Chris? I didn't recognize your number."

"Sorry," Christopher said. "I'm borrowing a cell phone."

"Is something the matter?"

"No, no, just had a moment, and I thought I'd check in. Is this a bad time?"

"I'm happy to hear from you. What's new?"

"Not a lot. Busy at the paper, the usual at home. How are you? I heard from Marshall that you might visit Paris on the way back from Prague."

"Yes," Professor Kalman said, his voice brightening. "I'm thinking about it. It's a good time of year, and a colleague from Tufts keeps a pied-à-terre near the Panthéon."

"That's excellent." Christopher stepped back and leaned against a tree, sheltering from the noisy river. "Are things okay between you and Marshall?"

"I suppose." His father sighed. "It's good that you and he are in touch. I hear him up at all hours, in and out of the house. I have no idea what he's up to. Your brother has turned out to be quite the introvert, Chris."

"Maybe that wouldn't be so bothersome if you lived separately. Do you think?"

Professor Kalman hesitated. "I don't know," he said. "I don't know whether Marshall wants that."

"If you wanted it, could you ask him to find another place?"

"I don't know about that either. It would be awkward."

"Maybe you could drop a few hints. About the different hours you keep, something like that."

"I'll think about it."

"Well, listen," Christopher said after a silence. "I know you're working, I only wanted to say hello. I won't keep you."

"I'm glad you called, Chris. Let's talk again soon."

"Sure thing."

"Goodbye, then."

Christopher pocketed the phone. His father wasn't going to do anything about the secret lives of day-trading offspring. Not that he should, necessarily. But spinning around in circles while their father wrung his hands—how was that supposed to help? Why did Marshall want him involved?

The sun lit up the snowmelt tumbling by between Christopher and the cliff. Marty and Phil were approaching their targets, shallow ledges at roughly equal heights, from which they'd haul the stand-in for the banner. Laura and Keith were already set on their respective niches lower on the rock face, resting spots and solid perches from which they could belay the lead climbers—though Christopher had a hard time reconciling "rest" with a vertical rock face.

He raised his binoculars and zoomed in on Marty, just a few feet shy of his ledge.

Duncan's voice crackled out of the walkie-talkie. "Steady," he said. "Stay focused as you approach your goal. Marty, that means you. We're looking for excellent anchorage here. Nuke-proof."

With fingers of one hand wedged into a crack, Marty pulled a small metal nut from his rack. From Christopher's distance, he seemed to push it into solid rock. Marty pulled on the nut's dangling cable to set it, then yanked to test the hold.

"Marty, tie in with opposed carabiners here," Duncan said. "Phil, same thing. You each want two secure anchors just below your ledge. Ideally, you'll stand between them."

"Got it, Dunc."

"Roger that, coach."

Christopher lowered the binoculars and watched the climbers in a less nerve-racking miniature. Becca waved from where she stood amid the sagebrush and scree at the foot of the cliff, below Phil and Keith. Christopher waved back.

"Keith, look sharp!"

Christopher lifted his gaze to the south-team belayer, then higher to find Phil pumping his legs in thin air, tenuously gripping the cliff face.

"Phil, relax," Duncan was saying. "Stay deliberate, the rope's your safety. Smear your shoe on the wall, don't kick . . . good. Yes, push up with the ankle, give your arm some relief."

Christopher couldn't take his eyes off a thin stone shower flaking off the cliff, a fine cascade arcing into the void. He missed the moment Phil slipped. One instant it looked like he'd gotten back onto the wall, the next he was plummeting earthward.

Duncan's voice remained steady over the walkie-talkie. "Joints relaxed," he said. "Face the cliff." Rooted in place, unable to grasp what he saw, Christopher went blind to the sun and trees, deaf to the river-roar. There was only Phil, a mere speck of Phil, falling soundlessly through the vast tableau.

It was over in seconds. Maybe tenths of seconds. The rope was already tightening as Christopher's knees began to buckle. The kernmantle stretched, then held. Phil swung like a trapeze artist. Christopher grabbed for his decoy tripod, saving himself from a near faint. Keith, steady as a statue, crouched against the belay line's pull.

"Everybody breathe," Duncan said. "Phil—yes, knees bent. You want to muscle yourself to a gentle stop."

Christopher lifted the binoculars to the cliff, but had to lower them immediately. He couldn't watch. His shirt clung to his torso, sweat-soaked. Marty lay against the stone, still as sleep, turned away lest the other climber's panic infect him too.

—

"Falls go with the territory," Duncan said, talking the team down from averted disaster. The leads had gained their ledges, and were taking a few minutes to settle. "It's like boxing," he continued. "You can't believe it's no big deal to get hit until you're past the first few hooks and jabs and bloody noses. All of a sudden you get it—you survived!"

Christopher had stopped trembling, but at that moment he hated sport, and coaches, and reckless machismo. He held himself in check. Falling was why they used ropes, he knew that. Wimps and acrophobics need not apply. Christopher had no illusions about why he'd be sitting in a decoy car while the climbers risked their necks hundreds of feet above the bay.

Keith's voice came squawking over the walkie-talkie. "So would you call that a safer accident than, um, one next week?"

"Safer, yes. Relatively speaking," Duncan said. "Nobody enjoys slipping off a wall—but think about it, Keith. The face you're climbing today is relatively smooth, there's not much on it to catch an arm or a leg. Not so next week. That's why I talk about keeping your lead short. You don't want to fall more than a few feet off that climb."

"Let's haul if you're ready, Phil," Marty radioed.

"Right, I'm okay now."

"Ground team south is ready to go."

"Ground team north ready."

"Chris, are you on?"

Christopher fumbled for the instrument's talk button. "Ready," he said. To himself, at least, his voice sounded shaky. There was something out-of-body about standing in clear sight of the others but being entirely alone.

The women on the ground had quit paying out static line to the climbers once they attained elevation, and tied off slack before they clipped in the weighted bags. On Christopher's signal, Marty and Phil started reeling in, and the lower climbers coiled cords that they'd been trailing up the cliff, the other ends tied to the bottom of the mock banner. Marty was pulling in line a little faster than Phil, causing the two ends of the payload to drift apart.

"Spotter to north, slow it down just a little," Christopher said into the microphone. On the day of the action he would keep an eye on the furled banner's position and tilt, helping the teams to keep the weight balanced.

"Marty, watch your lean," Duncan said. The leads were supposed to push into the wall while they hauled rope in overhand.

"Thanks, Dunc, roger that."

"Both sides slow," Christopher said, "we're passing the lower climbers."

Laura and Keith, on either side of the mock banner, guided the loaded sacs past their positions, pushing them away from the cliff face as the upper climbers inched the payload higher.

"Yo ho, yo ho, a pirate's life for me," Marty sang out into the on-air silence.

"Banner is past the lower team. Laura and Keith, confirm you've got bottomside cords in hand."

"North lower, paying out bottomside cord."

"South lower, ditto."

"Okay, fellas, you can pick up the pace again."

"Aye, he's a hard master," Phil grumbled.

"Sure, it ain't a job for shirkers."

"You guys can file grievances," Christopher said. "After next week."

Once they got the load all the way up, Marty and Phil tied it to topside anchors. Then they rehearsed the unfurling, paying out line that in the actual event would weave through grommeted eyelets spaced so the banner could open in folds, like a roman shade. Keith and Laura would tie the bottom of the banner to the bridge, stretching the synthetic fabric as flat as they could without risking a tear. Even with wind holes, the banner would pull at the ropes like an enormous sail.

Nora's whistleblower hadn't come through after all. Or, to be precise, he had, but his photos of a failed breed of GMO tomato were visually indistinguishable from strangely shaped organic heirlooms. For the banner they were falling back on Photoshopped caricatures of mutant produce. Obvious fakes, rhetoric that they intended to read like cartoons—not evidence. As he watched his comrades rehearse, and imagined their action on the bridge a week from that morning, Christopher could practically hear Marshall's sneer. *Stack your tatty little banner against a single week's output of the biotech lobby,* his brother might say. *Every venture you and your bleeding-heart friends pull off amounts to chickenshit and chump change.*

"South, you're getting ahead now. Both sides slow down, the lower team's falling behind." A breeze soughed through the treetops above him, and Christopher shivered at the thought of the wind up on the cliff face.

He didn't need Marshall's arguments. He had plenty of his own. Political slush funds and planted news, slanted science, highly paid professionals convincing shoppers that GMOs are perfectly safe. That was biotech's side of the scale. On the other pan, a raggedy band of activists, a traffic jam, and a few visual metaphors.

"Better," he radioed once Laura and Keith caught up, the bottom lines no longer sagging.

—

They ran the ersatz banner up and down the cliff several times, to take full advantage of the climb. Christopher felt low. Nothing had gone awry since Phil regained the cliff face, but he couldn't see past the mess of contingencies they had to cover on the day of the action, contingencies that precision rehearsals and quality equipment couldn't prevent. If the fog came in, or the banner got hung up, or wind ripped the Tyvek sheet away from its ropes and grommets—would they be able to spin the press coverage anyway? What if one of the cars broke down, or if highway patrol merged into their ranks?

And if everything went right there was still the big picture. How likely was it that even Chagall could advance the issues at a scale that would matter? Even if he made good on his promise, even if he delivered an action that soared past banners hung on bridge towers. Even if Christopher's own polemic were successfully hacked into a hundred thousand e-mailboxes, onto dozens of newspaper sites. Then what?

Novartis would chuck a million more into campaign coffers.

Monsanto could double the size of its PR budget.

DuPont? They'd sponsor a score of studies to shore up claims that mutant corn syrup and cloned burgers yield longer, happier lives.

Christopher had to force his attention to the job at hand. There was no going back now. He'd written to the saboteur, accepting that his work should be kept under wraps until Chagall released it. Taking in the landscape, the soaring granite, the undergrowth budding into springtime, he recalled words he'd written into the manifesto:

> It's a pitched battle, and we're all losing. Even those who profit from genetic engineering are going down to crushing defeat.
>
> Perhaps that doesn't matter in the grandest of schemes. Relative to the age and vastness of the universe, perhaps poisoning our own little planet doesn't count for much. But morally, if we allow life on Earth to be destroyed by human negligence?
>
> Morally the human race will have failed.

The sun shone bright into the sparkle and white of the river, glinting off enduring stone, warming the brittle duff.

"Payload's on the ground, north and south," he said into the walkie-talkie. "Climbers, you're cleared to descend."

What else could they do? Give up?

The bridge blockade would work or it wouldn't. Ditto for whatever Chagall had in the pipeline.

They would take all the risk they could tolerate, and resist the unbearable for a little while longer.

TWENTY-FOUR

Brendan descended the back stairs stealthily, though no one was home to notice: Chris and Marty were drilling the banner action on a cliff face near Placerville; Jonah was still in school at two-thirty on a Tuesday; the others were at work. He hopped the fence, squeezed through a gap between adjacent buildings on Sanchez Street, then circled and backtracked his way up to Waller. He owed it to Adolfo to take precautions. Brendan stopped in a doorway to watch the street, busying himself with a cigarette. A few minutes later the 24-Divisadero rounded a curve and coasted toward the intersection. He jogged over to the opposite corner and boarded the bus.

When he reached the address given over the phone, the Prince Albatross didn't look like much. The pub's windows were shuttered and flyspecked, a weatherworn sign hung from a bent, wrought-iron scroll. Inside, the single room was deep and inscrutably dim. As his eyes adjusted Brendan took in an old fellow at the near end of the bar wearing dentures and a watch cap, nursing a watery draft. The short, round barman leaned against his cash register, staring at a television.

The walls had been papered over with book jackets, tacked in overlapping layers and no apparent order. Brendan hadn't expected the whiff of literary North Beach from a bar at the western edge of the city. A lot of poetry, he saw, and only about half in English. Brendan recognized a García Lorca volume that he'd once owned himself. Goethe and Rilke and Hegel in German; a strong representation in French.

He distracted the bartender from his soccer match for long enough to draw a pint of pilsner. Brendan could see into the room now. Adolfo had already arrived. Even in shadow, his hatchet-faced profile was unmistakable. At an alcove table next to a sorry little bank of pinball machines he was sitting with somebody else, a stranger.

That hadn't been the plan.

Heat pulsed through Brendan's body, and receded. He stared at the two men, feeling a knot in his belly grow heavy and hard.

The man who'd sent him into Mexico looked over and gave a subtle nod. Brendan approached, taking slow, deliberate steps, and sat opposite Adolfo's companion, his back to the bar. "I didn't realize our discussion would be so well attended," he said in an undertone.

"This is . . . José," Adolfo said. The other man was small and stocky, with a broad nose and dark, sad eyes. A Mayan, Brendan assumed. The stranger's expression didn't change when he nodded a greeting; he could have been wearing a mask. "José is part of my organization. I vouch for him."

"I mean no disrespect, José," Brendan said across the worn wooden table. He wasn't certain the Mayan understood, but the arrangement was to speak in English. Brendan turned to his right. "I thought we agreed to a frank discussion. That's only possible between old friends."

"Of course." Adolfo scrutinized him carefully. "In a few minutes, José will step away for a smoke, maybe a little walk. Then we can have a talk between old friends. I can explain why we are three instead of two."

Brendan didn't reply, and José kept silent.

"You look thin," Adolfo said.

"I've been in a place where there was little to eat."

"You made a great sacrifice. Only a man of great honor would endure such a sacrifice silently."

"I was sorry to lose touch with my friends."

"Your friends were sorry, too. Their attempts to establish contact were refused."

Brendan sipped from his pilsner and set the glass back on the table, taking his time. "After no word for many long and difficult weeks, one loses confidence that old friends can be trusted."

"And yet a man of honor keeps his secrets."

"He does, yes."

"These secrets are kept even from a man of honor's attorney, would you agree?"

"Of course," Brendan said, permitting himself a bitter smile. "Especially from such a man's attorney. One wonders whether an attorney is a man of honor himself."

The Mayan appeared to answer Brendan with the barest flicker of amusement in his eyes. Lawyer jokes were the same all over. José placed both hands on the table—blunt peasant hands with rough-edged nails—and gestured toward the street. He hadn't uttered a word. If Adolfo had given a signal, Brendan missed it. José walked slowly away from their table, pulling a crumpled pack of cigarettes from his shirt pocket as he neared the door.

"He will give us a few minutes," Adolfo said. "Perhaps—"

"I'd like to start with some questions," Brendan interrupted.

Adolfo watched while José pulled the door shut behind him, then nodded.

"Why was I stopped in . . . that particular place, so far past the border?"

Adolfo answered carefully. "There was no tip-off," he said. "Just bad luck. The Federale *chingadero* who stopped you, we found out he has a reputation, very rough, very suspicious of *norteamericanos*."

"No tip-off you know about. What happened to the escort?" "Did you see him?"

"I saw a white truck, a Dodge. Picked me up just outside Puebla. He was keeping pretty close, but I didn't see him in the mirror when the Federales pulled me over."

Adolfo frowned. "A Dodge? Are you sure it wasn't a Chevy?"

"Yes, right—a Chevy," Brendan deadpanned.

Adolfo let a few seconds pass, acknowledging Brendan's distrust. "*Sí*, that was him. He saw you with the Federales, and kept driving until he could get off the road, to hide. When you didn't drive past, he went back. You were gone, and the truck was guarded by police."

"I didn't see him pass."

"I don't know why," Adolfo said. "Maybe the police made you face a different way?"

"How long did he wait before turning around?"

"Twenty or thirty minutes. That is what he told us."

"How do you know he wasn't working with the police?"

"This *compañero* was checked very carefully, before and after. He did not betray us."

Brendan saw that Adolfo would continue to act as if he and his organization were above suspicion. "Okay, let's put that aside. What was I carrying?"

Adolfo leaned in to speak more softly. "There were only the things we discussed."

"How do you know?"

"You paid a very great price for what happened, my friend,

but this was difficult for us too." He scanned the room nervously. "There was an investigation. We found out everything. The contents of the truck, we went over it many times. There was not one weapon. Everyone knows how it is when a *norteamericano* brings even ammunition across the border. We would not risk it. If someone wanted to move this kind of cargo, there are *Mexicanos* who could drive."

"Then the government made up evidence?"

"*Sí.*"

"*Porqué?*"

Adolfo gave an unhappy shrug. "We don't know why. Maybe the Federales stole those things, from a drug gangster or some other police. They need to keep it secret, so they pretend the guns are from you. Now they can do what they want. Sell them, use them, give them to *grupos paramilitares*. Or maybe they don't want to admit they stop medical supplies and radios, that even these simple things must be smuggled to the *comunidades*. Any of these could be true."

"So why did it take so goddamned long to attempt contact?"

Adolfo looked down at the table. "We were not ready for trouble in Oaxaca. Chiapas, yes. At the border, of course. This was a place we failed you. My friends and I feel very bad for this."

Brendan stared fixedly at the other man. Adolfo looked up only when the bar's door opened. The Mayan had returned. "José has come from very high up," Adolfo said, explaining quickly. "He is here to thank you for helping our effort in this very hard circumstance."

Brendan didn't bother to reply. So José was an emissary. Did that matter to him? He didn't know much more than he had when he walked into the place. Bad luck, Adolfo said. What would José add? Whatever the Mayan acknowledged implicated him in a smuggling ring. José hadn't come to explain why they'd left him to shit fourteen months down the pit latrines at Tlaxitlán. They'd shown up to make sure he hadn't squealed.

José resumed his seat across the table from Brendan. He looked to Adolfo. Adolfo nodded. "We do not exist without our friends," José began, speaking through a thick accent. His voice was pitched low but seemed somehow reedy, projected from high in his throat. "You are our very great friend. *El Comité* is knowing your sacrifice and your—*lealtad*—"

"Loyalty," Adolfo prompted.

The envoy had abridged the full name of the Zapatistas' central command. The Committee. Brendan shifted in his chair.

"—is knowing your loyalty," José continued. "We are struggle to make better life for poor *indígenas*. But we cannot same time make hard life for our friend. Our struggle, your struggle. We are same."

José looked to Adolfo, who reached inside his jacket and pulled out a thick manila envelope. Adolfo set the envelope down on the table. Brendan broke out in a mortified sweat.

"You must make life here in *Estados Unidos*," José said. "Is hard after long time away. This is for help you, very small, and show our thanking."

Brendan's mouth felt as if it were filled with paste. "I am honored that our friends in the South are concerned about my small, unimportant life." While Adolfo murmured a translation, Brendan took a long pull of pilsner. Adolfo turned back to him. Brendan set his pint back on the table. The knock of glass on wood rippled out over the television's shapeless murmur. "The envelope is . . . ?"

"Three thousand," Adolfo said softly. "A small token—"

Brendan held up his hand. "I do not want anything—not anything—taken from the hands and mouths of my friends in the

South," he said, addressing both men. "That is not the reason I asked to speak with you."

Again, Adolfo whispered a translation, though the Mayan seemed to have caught the gist. José nodded. "We know you are not asking this. We see you are very loyalty to our struggle."

Adolfo picked up the thread for his comrade. "Our friends know you helped us from political commitment. But also they see you must build a life here, from many broken pieces. This is respect for your part in our work. *El Comité* does not abandon its friends."

José nodded approval. "You must take."

"We have great sorrow that this must be our last meeting," Adolfo continued formally. "So we can continue forward without each one putting the other in danger."

Brendan raised an eyebrow, astonished. "The purpose of meeting should be to discover why this happened—why our work last year put us at risk. If we don't figure that out we'll repeat the same failure, again and again."

Adolfo looked to José, who remained silent. "Our investigation was complete," he said.

They were shutting him out. The money wasn't a gesture of respect. José was handing him severance pay. By taking this envelope you agree to vacate the premises. Don't call us, we won't call you back.

The other men watched him realize what was happening. Brendan examined the stranger with open suspicion. Maybe José wasn't with the Zapatistas at all. Maybe there *had* been guns in the truck. Maybe Adolfo had known ahead of time and maybe he hadn't. How had the other contact fit in, the chunky, hard-faced Central American who had been with Adolfo when they first proposed the run to Chiapas? "Tell me," Brendan said, his voice now rimed with icy control. "What ever happened to César?"

It would prove to be his last unanswered question. José's eyes flashed, but only for an instant.

"I am sorry, *compañero*," Adolfo said, pushing back his chair. José stood when he did. The envelope lay inert, sealed and smug on the scarred tabletop.

"*Viva la lucha*," Adolfo said. Long live the struggle. The two men walked away.

TWENTY-FIVE

The dark is raucous with crickets and frogs. On his way in from the coast Romulus imagined eerie silence here, in the middle of Nebraskan noplace. Monotonous rows of soybean and corn mock any notion of wildlife, however prosaic. The landscape's motif is control. Yet the insects and amphibians defy expectation, thousands of them, judging from the sound. Tens of thousands. Their noise is welcome cover. Rough buzz and throaty croak rise out of the fields loudly enough, almost, to mask the thumping of his heart.

Romulus parked a mile north of the construction site, on the alley side of a strip mall. Following a crudely paved road, then striking out along a dirt rampart between adjacent fields, he crept up on the AgBio complex and now crouches at its border. He surveys the object of these last months' focus, and the security kiosk that guards it at a distant edge of the lot. He feels colder than he ought to. The land has a dry, sandy smell: spent, almost sterile. In the vast agricultural plain, the research building's six stories seem puny. Though he knows he should know better, disappointment gnaws at his sense of mission.

Romulus reminds himself that their target's value is better measured by millions in grant proposals, dozens of corporate press advisories, trillions of seeds to be mutated in this klieg-lit island of concrete and glass. The building's physical scale belies its significance. The facility has taken years and acts of Congress to be realized. Equipment for its labs is being trucked in daily, at staggering cost.

Lifting a pair of night-vision binoculars, Romulus looks to the surveillance camera he staked in a furrow some hundred yards to his right. He knows where he planted the gadget, but it takes a few moments to make out the dark-on-dark profile. When he turns back to the security kiosk, the lone guard is rising from his chair at its plate glass window. The uniformed man steps outside, and paces toward the facility proper.

It's time.

Blood pounds in his temples. Romulus glances at the smartphone Chagall supplied. The screen shows a clear, yellowish field where the guard's dark-uniformed blotch registered several frames before. Remote imaging isn't rocket science, but it isn't explosives either. As the device continues to download three still frames per minute from the planted camera, Romulus reflects that his coconspirator is a man of unexpected talents. He pushes aside the question of what he's adding to their combined skill set. What matters is how he'll recognize the guard's position from the grainy screen image.

The guard appears to enter the building. Not what Chagall advised him to expect. The guard's habit, wrote the saboteur, is to circle the perimeter first. Evidence that Chagall is not omniscient is oddly calming, even in this hour of extreme dependence. Romulus adjusts his ski mask.

By some quirk of the site's acoustics, he hears the glass door snick shut. Romulus rises to his feet. Shouldering a heavy pack, stepping from clodded earth to the edge of the parking lot, he closes the distance to a utility entrance at the facility's northeast corner. Romulus flattens himself against the building to wait for the guard to emerge. He sweats inside the mask. After a quarter of an hour the cell phone screen shows a shadowy figure several yards from the main entrance. Twenty seconds later the shadow is positioned halfway between building and kiosk.

Fitting the master Chagall provided into the door's keyway, he torques counterclockwise. The key fails to turn. Romulus jiggles it in the lock to no effect.

Twisting it this way and that, he jams the key into the lock plate. Nothing. Beginning to panic, Romulus pulls it halfway free before jamming the key forward again.

It slips a millimeter farther in.

He stops, listens, lets himself sink back into sonic invisibility beneath the frog and cricket chorus.

Fully engaged, the key turns easily. He slips inside. The door pulls closed behind him, and Romulus sees the hallways are dimly lit, as Chagall foretold. The night noise is silenced. The only sound is a soothing electronic hum. The lights would come on now, the corridor would fill with uniformed SWAT goons, if Chagall had been luring him into a trap. The stillness remains unbroken.

Romulus pulls out the cell and checks on the guard. He now stands beside the kiosk, a blurry bulge at chest level suggesting a hand held to mouth. In the next frame the arm is positioned by his side. There's a barely visible haze to the left of his head. The man is smoking, standing outside the kiosk, paying no attention to the monitors at his station.

Switching off the phone to conserve power, Romulus removes the stifling mask. He's suddenly thirsty, longing for icy cold water burbling over stone. It has been an eternity since he last hiked an alpine trail. This brutally tamed place makes him crave wildness that tonight is echoed only in a menacing aspect, by this ridiculous burglary Chagall has imposed on him. He is watching himself act out a scene from a spy movie. The scene is surreal, yet it's happening. If he were asked at this moment to explain what brought him here, Romulus would draw a blank.

He closes his eyes, collecting himself.

—

The utility room is suffused with a familiar glow. Romulus cracks a light stick and adjusts to its sickly blue gleam. He is relieved to be in this narrow space, surrounded by routers, blinking LEDs, the electromagnetic aura of signal surging through copper and glass. Bundles of gray Ethernet cable converge on racked patch panels. To his right, a bank of punch blocks connects thick fiber-optic coming in from the local phone company with sister cables that climb the risers. Blue coaxial cable transmits TV signal through the same conduit as the telephone lines, to jacks in the offices and labs. To the left of the television blocks, UTP cables feed signal from security cameras into a trio of multiplexers.

Donning a headlamp, Romulus examines the video routers closely. Cables and their corresponding ports are cryptically marked, but Chagall has instructed that connection OD6 is his man. "Outside door," Romulus supposes.

The intercepting device is the size and shape of a laptop's power brick. A metal box painted matte black, Chagall either made it himself or has friends in the espionage business. The box is soldered shut, and Romulus has been warned not to risk a self-wipe by poking or prying. The apparatus is necked and tailed with cable sheathed in the same bright yellow as the UTP coming in from the facility's cameras. Chagall has also supplied a bypass line, its ends terminated by knobby, wraparound clips that decode magnetic pulse into underlying signal, then transform it back again.

He has rehearsed the splice on lengths of dummy cable to get a feel for the tools. Chagall suggested several possible placements. With gloved hands, Romulus explores the likeliest, behind two adjacent bundles of Cat 5 that run down the corner of the room. At chest level the bundles split toward their respective routers, but it looks like a spot near the ceiling is sufficiently shielded, out of an idle eye's way. He stands in turn by the door, the phone box, the router bank, and the multiplexers to check the view. The overhead fluorescents won't cast telling shadows that high on the wall.

Romulus prepares the leads for splicing. Stepping onto a stool meant for legitimate technicians, he carefully follows his cable toward the mouth of the west-wall conduit. He attaches the bypass, bracketing a stretch that passes behind a cluster of telephone wires. Flashing diodes confirm that the terminals are translating signal. He wiggles the bypassed strand to check one last time that he's holding the right line, then severs it with a pair of diagonal cutters.

His hands tremble as he positions wires the thickness of pencil lead in the splicing tool's maw. It's touchier here than it was on the surface of a motel desk. Romulus is fully focused on the task. Place, set, squeeze. And again. He wraps the joins with electrical tape. Cable ties secure the device in position. He unclips the bypass. Stepping down from the stool, Romulus repeats his walk-around. He can't see the interceptor, not even when he looks straight at it.

Placing a cell phone antenna is a simpler proposition. The device is a commodity, so common that its manufacturer doesn't bother with serial numbers. Chagall has wired in a filter that leaves it network-visible only to the interceptor and Chagall's smartphone. He shoves the device under a shelving unit, in a corner where rat poison would one day molder if the AgBio complex were fated to last. The antenna's cable runs inconspicuously up the back of the shelves and plugs into a spare coverage-extension port.

Again, a visual inspection.

He gathers up his tools, the bypass device, clipped ends of cable ties, the still glowing chem light, and packs them all away. A last look around, methodically beaming his headlamp across the floor, along every horizontal surface. The electrical tape startles him when the light catches it, forgotten where he set the roll down on a shelf. He pockets the tape and steals out of the utility room, tiptoeing up to ground level.

From the stairwell, Romulus checks on his pal in the kiosk. The blurry blotch sits inert at his station. On the smartphone's screen he taps a biohazard icon to launch Chagall's diagnostic. A spew of log output rolls by, ending in an almost conversational message:

DEVICE TEST PASSED.
CONGRATS.
BE ON YOUR MERRY WAY.

Romulus is not out of the woods yet. More exactly, the bright clearing of the parking lot still separates him from the fields' concealing gloom. There are no woods here.

Flipping back, he again checks the kiosk. Romulus has been inside the building for fifty-eight minutes. Hours remain before dawn rises over fields of genetically modified soybean. It could be an eternity before the guard's next walkabout.

Romulus isn't eager to wait. He wants out. He wants to haul his ass over the state line, to crack a bottle of jammy Zinfandel in his Podunk, Missouri motel room.

Staring up at the ceiling, he visualizes an overhead plan of the construction site. If he strikes out at a slant, bearing right, the building will stand between his line of retreat and the kiosk.

Once the guard steps away from his monitors there's no need to wait. Romulus can flee at the next nicotine break.

He slips into the ground-floor corridor and finds an alcove sheltered from the hallway's sight lines. Three bars of cell signal. Leaning heavily against the concrete wall, he stares into the screen and thinks cigarette commercials toward the kiosk outside.

TWENTY-SIX

The late-afternoon sun streamed into the front room, silhouetting Brendan against the bay window. "Sure, I could be angry," he said, pressing against the window's frame hard enough to dent his forehead. "Or demoralized, or mystified. One way or another they demoted me from comrade to mercenary. Then they left me wondering who I was working for in the first place."

He heard Allison set her coffee mug onto the table behind him. "Let's not say more than we ought to," she said.

"Yeah, I know. The walls have ears, or so we imagine. But what the fuck, Al? Either they're criminals, and they insulted me with a bribe that works out to thirty cents for every hour I kept my mouth shut. Or they are who they claim, and they excommunicated me, no questions answered."

"It's yours to decide," she said.

He turned to face her. "What is?"

"If they're thugs, you risk their violence," she said. "If they're part of a movement you believe in, you risk damage to that movement, and prosecution for whatever charge the government dreams up once you goad them into paying attention. So. Pick a story that gives you peace of mind, and move on."

Brendan massaged his temples. He couldn't look at it that way. Not until he'd blown off some steam. Maybe a lot of steam.

The telephone rang. Zac crossed the hall downstairs to answer.

"Marty already?" Brendan asked.

"Doubt it. We're not due at Turnabout 'til six."

"I can't say I'm excited about spending the evening setting grommets and folding Tyvek."

"You don't have to," Allison said. "Zac and Marty and me, plus three or four from Turnabout—we can handle the banner."

"Allison?!" Zac was shouting up from the second floor, voice pinched and panicky. "Come quick!" She was running for the stairwell before the echo died away. Brendan followed, flashing on car wrecks, on Christopher and Nora busted in a raid on the spokescouncil meeting, on a bullied goth with a hunting rifle in Jonah's schoolyard. He stumbled into the dining room on Allison's heels.

"It's Jonah," Zac said in a whisper.

Allison took the phone from him. "Jonah?"

"What happened?" Brendan asked.

"Buzz," Zac said, leaning against the wall and slowly sinking to the floor. "I think he OD'd."

"Take a deep breath," Allison was saying. "Yes. Yes, that's right. Now tell me exactly, did you take any kind of drugs? . . . Any at all? . . . It's not about good or bad, Jonah, I need to know so I can help you. . . . Okay. . . . Okay, just Buzz . . . Buzz and Luke. . . . Luke just smoked pot. . . . Wait—heroin? Are you sure?"

"Jesus Christ." Brendan struck the wall with his fist. "Who the hell's Luke?"

"School friend," Zac said softly.

"Is he sitting up? . . . Can Luke help him to walk around?" Allison covered the phone's mouthpiece. "We need to get over there, pronto."

"Where are they?" Brendan asked. "The bike'll be quick."

"They need to keep him awake," Zac said to Allison. "If he lies down make sure he's on his side"—he mimed to illustrate—"not on his back, or he might choke."

Allison waved him silent. "Jonah . . . Jonah? Listen, I need you to tell me where you are. What's the address?"

"If he's sitting up and breathing he'll be okay."

"Jonah says he's up and down," Allison whispered. "Heavy nodding, sounds like."

"Do you still do needle exchange?" Brendan asked Zac.

"Not for years," Zac said. "No naloxone buried in the sock drawer."

"Fucking heroin?"

Zac shook his head. "That kid's got a backstory."

"Jonah . . . Jonah, listen. Look around where you're standing. See if you can find an envelope with an address on it . . . or a magazine—yes! Belvedere? Sixty-three Belvedere. Excellent work. I'm going to give the phone to Zac now, okay?" She covered up the mouthpiece. "I'll ride with Brendan. See if Jonah can hang something out a window to help us find the place. But first you and he both need to call 9-1-1."

Zac took the phone. "Jonah? Your mom and Brendan are on their way—but stay on the call for a couple more minutes, okay?" His face was ashen, but his voice held steady.

"Get the bike," Allison said to Brendan. "I'll find one of the downstairs kids to help Zac. Sixty-three Belvedere, last name is Conners."

Brendan bolted for the stairs.

———

They blew the last stop sign and took the corner onto Belvedere at a sharp angle. Allison scooted off the Kawasaki as Brendan cut its engine.

"Say again?" she shouted into her cell.

Number sixty-three was the middle flat of a peeling, Italianate Victorian. Barred basement windows stood sentry along the sidewalk; a round turret rose skyward in decorated bands. Limp in the still air, a batik spread hung from a sill on the second floor.

"We see the blanket," she said to Zac.

Brendan sprinted up the steps and rattled the door in its frame. "Locked!"

Allison grabbed Brendan's leather jacket, pulling him away from the doorbell. "Wait," she commanded. "Again?" she said into the phone, then relayed Zac's report. "Luke went postal over calling 9-1-1. Zac heard something about a knife then the phone cut off."

Brendan turned and stared into Allison's eyes. "We gotta go in," he said. She nodded. He stepped back to the edge of the stoop. When his sneaker sole struck at deadbolt height, the doorframe splintered. Hurtling up the stairs, he bellowed Jonah's name.

"No cops," somebody was shouting from the front of the flat. Jonah cried out, "He's got a knife!"

"There's no cops, no cops," Brendan shouted as he gained the landing. He held his hands out as he approached the front room. "No cops," he said. "We're here to help Buzz."

Brendan took the place in. Jimi Hendrix sang mutely into the room from a poster of the *Electric Ladyland* cover, hung beside a boarded-over fireplace. A glass bong poked up from a litter of chip bags and soda cans on a low table.

"I've got a knife," Luke said. A curtain of frizzy brown hair obscured his face. With a sturdy left arm circling Jonah's chest, he stood in front of the fireplace waving a *santoku* blade. Jonah shrank from the wicked-looking weapon, but Luke held him immobile. Buzz lay beside the far end of the coffee table, sprawled against a heavy sofa by the bay windows. He'd been mumbling inarticulately as Brendan entered the room, but now was still, head lolling back.

"Yes, you do," Brendan said. On the other side of the chimney, another poster depicted a crowd of Sandanista peasants carrying a banner and flag. *No la deseamos pero no la tememos.* We did not wish it but we do not fear it. He turned his full attention to the boys across the room. Luke's right arm extended at an uncertain angle: he was as terrified of the blade as Jonah. "I see the knife. And I get what you want."

"No cops is what I want!"

"So here's what we need to do. Jonah's mom is here. She needs to make sure Buzz is okay, and she needs to do that now. Right now. Then we can take him outside. When the ambulance comes, they don't have to know what house he was in when he shot up. You see where I'm going here?"

Luke lowered the blade a few degrees. Brendan could hear Allison breathing through her teeth, directly behind him.

"I need you to let go of Jonah. I need him to help with Buzz. If you want to hang onto the knife, that's your business. But we could get out of here faster if you help us."

Allison edged past Brendan, into the room. "I'm going over to Buzz now," she said.

"Mom?"

"Okay." Luke relaxed his hold on Jonah, but only slightly. "Okay. No 9-1-1 from my phone. They'll trace it."

"Buzz. Buzz!" Allison knelt next to the boy's limp body, listening for breath without taking her eyes off Luke and Jonah.

"Let him go," Brendan repeated. "No calls from your phone."

"Jonah, I need you to help," Allison said firmly.

Brendan nodded. Tentatively at first, Jonah withdrew, sidling toward an elaborate stereo setup opposite the windows. Brendan took a careful step into the room, allowing Jonah to circle behind him. Not for a second did he look away from Luke.

"Other side," Allison said as Jonah approached the sofa. "Help me move him, flat on his back."

"Like this?"

A siren's wail floated in through the open window.

"Lift . . . yes . . . ease him away from the sofa."

As Allison began rescue breathing the siren drew closer, ratcheting up from distant city noise to a piercing blast. The ambulance turned into Belvedere Street and sounded a deep, window-rattling horn. Allison knelt, breathing and counting, breathing again.

"Shit!" Luke cried out as the ambulance went quiet. He lurched toward the three by the sofa.

Brendan stepped in to intercept the boy, grabbing Luke's left arm and yanking him off course. Luke's sneaker caught the edge of the table and he was suddenly airborne. Brendan brought his free hand up the hefty kid's side, aiming to control his knife arm, and struck hard between elbow and shoulder. Luke released the *santoku.*

"Duck!" Brendan yelled, but everything happened way too fast. Stainless steel bit into painted wooden wainscoting. Luke hit the wall and fell heavily onto his side.

Nobody moved. Then the knife, jarred loose by the boy's impact, clattered to the floor between Buzz's high tops and Luke's green velour Vans. Luke struggled to sit up.

"Steady . . ." Brendan scooped up the weapon and sent it sliding across the floorboards, under the sofa and out of Luke's reach. Heart slamming in his rib cage, he checked his arms for blood. There was a fresh slit in the sleeve of his jacket, and he was suddenly aware of a warm, wet sting. He wiggled the fingers of his left hand, then pressed his right against the cut, not prepared yet to look. "That's an ambulance, not police," he said, giving Luke a once-over. "Jonah, run downstairs, bring 'em up here quick as you can."

Jonah hugged the wall, keeping away from Luke and Brendan. Allison returned to keeping Buzz in oxygen. Luke was trying to stand. "But you said—"

"Listen to me." Brendan leaned right up in the boy's face. "It's too late for that. I got rid of the knife. But if there's anything else you need to hide, pull yourself together now."

A cadence of heavy boots came clomping up the stairs.

"We're here," Brendan called out. "In the front."

Luke staggered over to the table and scooped up the bong and a sandwich bag. He was jamming them behind the stereo cabinet when the first paramedic stepped into the room. Allison scooted aside as the professionals took charge.

———

Hovering over Buzz, one of the paramedics adjusted an oxygen tank while the second radioed med-speak back to their dispatcher. Brendan stood with Luke and Jonah in the hallway. "You can hate my guts if you like," he said, noting a bruise blooming under Luke's skewed t-shirt. "But the cops are going to show up any minute. If you need to keep them out of here, there's things we can do. Are you up for it?"

"Up for what?"

"Stalling. Keeping them from coming upstairs while the paramedics are here."

"You can't stall the cops," Luke said.

"Yeah, you can. You tell them what happened, and you tell it all mixed-up and slow so they have to keep going over your story. First thing, though, I need a clean cloth to wrap around my arm." Brendan shrugged out of his jacket. His shirtsleeve was soaked red. Both boys paled. Brendan stepped into a bathroom off the hall and ran water into the tub. "Hurry it up, Luke, no time to waste." Brendan winced as the cold stream sluiced over his forearm.

Jonah stood at the bathroom door. "Is it—"

"Just a flesh wound," he said, not that he really knew.

When Luke returned with an old shirt and a pair of scissors, Brendan talked him through cutting a makeshift bandage.

"What about me?" Jonah asked as Brendan bound his wound.

"Stay here with your mom," Brendan said. "When they bring Buzz down, grab any medical stuff they leave behind. Bring it out to the ambulance. Luke's going to lock himself inside, and your job is to make sure there's no reason for the paramedics to come back."

Brendan worked back into his jacket as he and Luke descended the stairs. "Once Buzz is out, you slip back in and shut the door," Brendan said. "You're going to have to block it with a chair or a piece of wood." He showed Luke where he'd busted the deadbolt on the way in. "Don't open when they knock. Say your dad doesn't allow you to open the door for strangers. If they hassle you, say you have to call your parents first."

Clusters of neighbors had gathered to see what was up. Brendan and Luke huddled at the foot of the stairs and refined their plan.

"What's going on?" a jowly man in sweats called over.

"Medical problem," Brendan said. "Nothing serious."

It didn't take long for a police cruiser to pull up and double-park behind the ambulance. "Remember," Brendan said quietly. "Make him ask twice."

Luke grunted. A burly, clean-shaven cop stepped out of the car and spoke into a microphone strapped to his epaulet. Ebony-skinned and stern, he approached.

"The problem's here," Brendan said, stepping up to meet him. "A kid passed out."

"Is this your residence, sir?" the policeman asked. His name tag identified him as T. R. Williams.

"No, Officer. If I got the story right, the kid showed up at this young man's door, drunk or high or whatever. Showed up with his friend, who lives in the house I'm staying at—over by Market Street? I'm just visiting. Anyway, the kids know each other from school. What school is it again, Luke?"

"Dorothy Day."

"Right. Dorothy Day Middle School. So anyway, the one kid started to pass out, and they called the house I'm staying at? They didn't know what to do. The parents weren't home and we didn't want to take any chances. So we called 9-1-1 and rushed over."

"Where's the kid now? The one who passed out."

"Oh, he's with the paramedics," Brendan said. "They had it under control, so we just got out of the way."

"They radioed in a heroin overdose, white male adolescent."

"Heroin?" Brendan echoed, giving surprised-and-distressed his best shot. "Luke, does Buzz do that shit?"

"I don't know."

Brendan winked encouragement, then turned back to the cop. "Heroin, jeez. These kids are thirteen years old, Officer."

"What happened to your arm?" The officer gestured to the bloodied rip in Brendan's sleeve.

"Oh, Christ—yeah—I nicked that moving furniture aside, getting to where Buzz passed out."

"I need some names," Williams said, pulling out a notebook. "Who's Buzz?"

The two talked over each other, backtracked, answered vaguely, and otherwise occupied SFPD's finest. Another police cruiser pulled up. Luke elbowed Brendan; Brendan held the boy's shoulder lightly to keep him from bolting too soon. Gently, he steered Luke into position, putting himself between Officer Williams and the Conners' front door. When the ambulance crew emerged with Buzz, Luke slipped inside. Allison followed the paramedics; then Jonah, lugging the oxygen tank.

"Where are they taking him?" Brendan asked.

"SF General," Allison said. "We'll ride along. I called Zac, he'll meet us there."

Brendan gestured in the police officer's direction. "I'll come after I finish with Officer Williams."

"Can I get your name, ma'am?" Williams asked.

"Allison Rayle."

"Are you the boy's mother?"

"I am this young man's mother," she said, holding Jonah close. "The boy they're putting in the ambulance is a school friend and a friend of our family. I was breathing for him until the paramedics got here."

Brendan stole a backward glance. Luke's door was shut tight. The kid must have thought through his moves while they were running circles around the cop.

"How did you—"

"Officer, we're the closest thing Buzz has to family here. We haven't reached his mom yet. He's in the seventh grade, and he needs somebody to stay with him. I'm happy to answer questions after we get Buzz to the hospital. Is that okay?"

"Yeah, sure. Now where did Luke get to?"

"You guys better climb on," Brendan said, shepherding Allison and Jonah toward the ambulance.

"Right," she said. "C'mon, Jonah, let's go."

TWENTY-SEVEN

The spokescouncil's last meeting before the GeneSynth protest was about to begin. Christopher and Leona huddled with two out-of-town activists in a corridor of the Women's Building, a community center in the heart of the Mission. "It's late in the game to pull that kind of shit," said the woman who had just arrived from Seattle.

The dreadlocked white kid, up from Santa Cruz to represent a cluster of environmentalist affinity groups, agreed. "Bummer to have this crap to deal with."

"So what's her angle?"

Christopher sighed. "It's Celia, right?"

The woman nodded.

"Look," he said, "I have my theories about Meg Wyneken, but venting isn't going to get us through tonight's agenda. She favors strong central organization. Let's leave it at that."

"She ain't the ogre Chris thinks," Leona said. "She's hella good at spinning media, and free-for-alls bring on a lot of bad press, not just in San Francisco."

"Yeah, we seen that up north, for sure," Celia said, slouching against a mural commemorating the Greensboro sit-ins. "Look at WTO. Media slaughtered us."

"That would have happened no matter what we did in '99." The kid from Santa Cruz brushed back his dreads. "The press wrote those stories before anybody even showed up."

"Let's focus on here and now." Christopher bit back his impatience, wishing Allison had pulled spokescouncil duty, and that he was at the Turnabout Collective helping with the banner. "When Meg pushes the Triangle on its action, I'm going to say flat-out that the plan is nonviolent. We're not going to destroy property, and we intend to abide by the coalition's principles of unity. We're going to handle any reporters who talk to us in full alignment with the media committee's talking points. There's zero strategic divergence. If there were we would expect leadership to disavow us. But only if we screw up, and only on principle. End of story."

"Meg's heard all that?" Celia asked.

"She heard it," Leona said.

"And she still needs to thrash it out tonight?"

"I tried to chill her. No dice."

"So what do y'all want from us?" Celia looked through the double doors at the crowd of activists milling around the meeting room. "This thing's going to start any minute."

"I'm hoping you'll speak up if there's a problem," Christopher said. "Advocate for trust in a group of well-known activists. Encourage the spokescouncil to move on."

"So the goal is to table the issue."

Christopher shook his head decisively. "The goal is to table the *question*. It's not an issue unless the spokes accept that every affinity-group action has to be micromanaged."

"Right," Celia said. "And that can't happen."

"Tactical leadership stays at a high level," Leona said. "If we know in advance, we do better at coordinating. What we don't know happens fresh, and that's cool."

"That's it," Christopher said, grateful for the quasi-official support.

"One more thing," Leona said. "The Triangle don't have a license to hijack coalition plans. If people put out the trust and it ain't put back, we're talkin' cold shoulders, way past next week. We're talkin' ice age."

"Fair enough. And nobody's going to hijack anything."

The guy from Santa Cruz had beads in his hair that clicked and clacked when he bobbed his head affirmatively. "I'm in," he said.

Celia pushed off the wall. "So's Seattle."

———

Nora flashed a high sign as Christopher worked his way through the room. While he rounded up support, she'd been fomenting a movement to rearrange the chairs. Meg had corralled tactical leadership into kicking off with a formal presentation, and used that as an excuse to set the room up like a student council meeting: rank and file in docile formation, facing their leaders. "All she's missing is a throne," Nora said when they saw the layout, and immediately launched her subversive campaign.

Activists had come to represent all corners of the greater Bay Area, and beyond. Spokespeople had been sent from groups in Davis, Santa Cruz, Watsonville, and up and down the North Coast—from Bolinas to Fort Bragg, from Eureka and Eugene all the way to the Canadian border. Christopher hadn't seen Eddie Bourgeaut slip in. "I had no idea you'd be here!" he said once Eddie released him from a bear hug.

"Me neither. I was in Sebastopol on election business." Eddie chortled from behind his shaggy beard. "I swear, Chris, the whole northern coast is done with genetically modified organisms. Anyway, I was close enough to show up."

"So what's the latest tally from up your way?"

"Hundreds," Eddie said. "There's four buses booked as of last night, plus people carpooling down on their own."

Christopher whistled. "All built off the GMO campaigns?"

"In Mendocino County, hell yes. Marin, Napa, Humboldt, there's all kinds of ferment around the November ballot now. Did you hear Sonoma's organizing a ban?"

"Just the other day. If I were an optimist I'd call it a movement."

Eddie clapped him on the back and laughed from deep in his belly. "It's a movement whether or not you're an optimist!" he said, then leaned to whisper in Christopher's ear. "We got another vehicle—"

"Not here," Christopher said. "Outside, afterwards?"

Eddie nodded.

"Will you stay over at the Triangle?"

"I'll head up to Fairfax," Eddie said. "Got an old friend to visit, and I can use the head start tomorrow morning."

The room settled and Meg took the microphone, slight and sharp-chinned in jeans and a Jamawar shawl. She introduced tactical leadership and quickly laid out the agenda. "So let's get started with the orientation," she said brightly. "This is especially for groups who are coming from out of town, but all of us here at the front learned a lot as we prepared it."

She fiddled with a laptop and projector. Christopher jostled Nora when Meg's slide deck came up on the screen. "I know," Nora whispered. "It's like she's running a shareholder meeting."

Meg flipped through the Moscone Center layout and maps of downtown, using a laser pointer to show where conference events would take place, where the attendees would be staying, and choke points where police were likely to set up barricades. She identified staging points for marches, and described the roving-blockade strategy they would use to keep people out of custody for as long as possible.

"We want to get maximum mileage out of civil disobedience," she said. "What worked during the antiwar shutdown was to establish a sit-in at an intersection, like we're going all the way to arrest. The police would respond by moving in the jail buses, and the motorcycle squadrons, and the bundles of plastic handcuffs. Then when they were almost ready to take people away, we'd stand up and march someplace else."

A few of the spokes whistled their approval.

"Lather, rinse, repeat," Meg said, and got the laugh she'd aimed for. "It tied downtown up in knots."

"But it didn't stop the war," someone called out.

Christopher winced.

"Not yet," Meg said. "But nobody's here because they've given up on street protest."

Next up were "new angle actions," affinity-group plans outside the blockade-arrest model. The Left Coast Wingnuts out of UC Davis would conduct mutant organism inspections in downtown restaurants, Meg explained. Doctors Who Do The Math would hold a press conference on the steps of the International Public Health Institute to propose ten measures, each promising to improve one hundred times as many lives and cost a hundredth as much as a single bioengineered drug. Local chapters of Raging Grannies would conduct mock hostage-takings along Market Street to call attention to the Percy Schmeiser case.

"Who's Percy Schmeiser?" whispered a woman to Christopher's right.

"A Canadian farmer," he explained. "Monsanto's suing him for 'technology fees' after their seeds blew in from a neighbor's field."

The room was buzzing by the time Meg reached the end of

her slide deck. In an unscripted moment between agenda items, Nora stood on her chair.

"That was a great overview, Meg," she said, her voice piercing the hubbub. "But I'd like to see people sit in a circle for the rest of the meeting—that would be a better fit for a coalition of affinity groups."

"I'm not sure that's the best—"

Nora turned up her volume as Meg tried to break in. "What do the other spokes think about meeting in a circle?"

"—way to get through the business—"

"Yeah, circle up."

"Spokes are made for wheels!"

"Let's do it!"

"—in the little time we have," Meg was saying, but people were already up and at it. The rubber report and metal clang of folding chairs being dragged across hardwood drowned out any prospect of imposed hierarchy.

Christopher returned Nora's thumbs-up as they joined in rearranging the room. Very good, he thought. An auspicious start.

TWENTY-EIGHT

Brendan showed up at the ER an hour and a half behind the ambulance. Jonah sat between Zac and Allison at the far end of the waiting room, hunched and miserable.

"How's he doing?" Brendan asked as he joined the others. "Have I mentioned that I hate hospitals?"

"Get in line," Zac said. "Buzz'll be fine if he quits trying to kill himself. They're making sure he doesn't go back into OD when the Narcan wears off."

Allison stood to examine Brendan's forearm through the slit Luke had opened in his jacket. "Is that okay?"

"Lucked out, it's a clean cut."

"Silver Star," she said, her voice catching.

"C'mon, Al, you know it wasn't like that. So they release him once the naloxone runs its course?"

"If his mom shows up," Zac said.

"You should have the nurse take a look while you're here," Allison said.

"It's nothing."

"If it takes much longer to find Buzz's mom they're going to call in Child Protective Services," Zac said.

"Have the cops been by?"

"No sign yet," Zac said. "I bet the hospital's going to call them in when his family shows up, so they can scare him straight. The city doesn't have cell space for what they've got on Buzz."

"He didn't have anything on him when they carried him out of Luke's place," Allison explained. "Not even works."

Zac winked. "Lord knows how that happened."

"An immaculate overdose, eh? So what about reaching family?"

"Everybody's trying," Zac said. "Us, the hospital staff. The number Buzz gave gets an answering machine."

"And now he's not talking," Allison said. "As if that'll convince the hospital staff to let him go."

Jonah couldn't contain himself any longer. "What happened to Luke?"

Brendan pulled up a chair. "I think we did the best we could, Jonah. He jammed the front door like we talked about, and wouldn't let the cops in. Then his dad got home."

"Mr. Conners let the cops in?"

"No way. From the look of their place it wouldn't surprise me if Luke's folks have duffle bags of bud stashed in a closet. That would explain how pissed off he was, at Luke and at me both."

"Why you?" Zac asked.

"Because I kicked his front door in, maybe? Didn't Allison tell you?"

"Oh, we told him," Jonah said.

"Right," Zac said. "They also said something about a jujitsu move you pulled when Luke went ballistic."

"Hardly."

Allison smiled through deepening worry lines. "It looked pretty superhero to me."

Embarrassed, Brendan just shook his head.

"So what happened?" Jonah pressed. "With Luke's dad?"

"I guess we worked it out between us, me and Lucas the

Elder. Basically, I'll patch up the door frame." Brendan glanced over to Allison, inquiring. He didn't want to aggravate Jonah, but Allison nodded, encouraging him to continue. "That wasn't enough at first," he said. "I wasn't telling tales on Luke, and his dad wasn't getting how the whole thing went down. But when Luke 'fessed up about how I got cut, his dad broke out the first aid kit and rewrapped my arm. Then he grounded Luke for the rest of his natural life, and assigned him to be my apprentice fixing the door."

"So he's in trouble," Jonah said, slumping deeper into his chair.

"Hell yes, he's in trouble. Six ways from Sunday. But I did explain he was trying to head off a copfest in the house. At least Luke was aiming for damage control."

Zac shook his head sadly. "Mr. Conners must have been proud."

"How come?" Jonah asked. His lip trembled, caught between outrage and tears.

"There was a certain awkwardness to it, Jonah," Brendan said. "It's hard to get around the fact Luke invited kids over to shoot heroin in the Conners' living room. And that he held you hostage with a lethal weapon."

"Just one kid ever shot heroin."

"Be that as it may." Allison placed a hand on Jonah's leg.

Zac cleared his throat. "We need to figure out about Buzz's mom," he said. "Allison got the address, when Buzz gave his info to the paramedics. I think we ought to go over. Maybe the phone's turned off."

"Maybe," Allison said. "Or maybe she's not home. Or maybe there's something more complicated going on."

"Jonah, you know *nothing* about his family?" Brendan asked.

"Not really." Jonah shifted uneasily.

"Have you heard stuff from other kids, from anybody?"

"A guy from school said his mom's boyfriend used to be in prison. The boyfriend's name is Vince."

They all mulled over what that might mean.

"Okay," Brendan said. "I was in prison too. Did this guy say anything else?"

"I don't think it was the same thing," Jonah said, without a trace of irony. "He said Vince is a bully. When the guy joked about Buzz getting beat up and stuff, he went crazy."

"Buzz hit the guy, you mean?"

Jonah nodded. "He was really mad."

"Do you remember what the other kid said, exactly?"

Jonah shrugged. The adults exchanged glances.

"Maybe we've had enough heroic saves for one day," Allison suggested quietly.

Zac looked up sharply. "That boy is not going to the Youth Authority."

Jonah hid head in hands. Nobody spoke.

"How deep are we prepared to get into this?" Brendan asked after a long pause. "Tuesday's awfully close."

Bursting out of his seat, Jonah shouted him down. "Who cares about a stupid protest?" he wailed. "Buzz almost died!"

Allison pulled Jonah into her lap. "It's not an either-or," she said, stroking his back. "We're going to help Buzz, the only question is what's the best way."

On the other end of the room, a Latino family was gathered around a grandmotherly woman in a dark blue dress. Somebody turned up the sound on a television set mounted in the corner.

"Jonah's right," Brendan said, under cover of a blaring promo for *¿Quién Quiere Ser Millonario?* "I can ride over." Buzz's back-story was about to come clear. Brendan dreaded the prospect of having his nose rubbed in ugliness that would drive a seventh grader to mainline, but Zac was right too: letting Buzz get caught up in Child Protective Services, the Youth Authority, any of that—they couldn't sit it out on the sidelines.

Allison looked up, her face drawn. "Don't go by yourself," she said.

Zac stood slowly. "Guess that puts me in harm's way. We'll take it easier than the ride to Luke's, right?"

"Um, sure. What did Allison tell you?"

"Seriously," she said. "Let's keep this low key."

—

Brendan came to a full stop at every signed intersection as they puttered west into the Mission, then up into the neighborhoods behind Civic Center. He was in no rush, and Zac wasn't urging him on. The streets in Buzz's neighborhood were named for trees—Hickory, Linden, Birch—but broken glass littered the barren sidewalks: pebbled car windows and shattered forties. Brendan edged the motorcycle to the curb and Zac climbed off.

"What are the chances of unqualified success here?" Brendan yanked the bike onto its kickstand.

"Nil," Zac said, peering dubiously into the parking lot at the heart of Buzz's U-shaped apartment complex. "But I always see the bright side."

The slab stairs shook on spindly steel-pipe columns. Lit by bare bulbs, the exterior walkways were strewn with baby carriages, plastic trikes, and a ripe abundance of leaking garbage bags. Edging along a balcony, Brendan and Zac hugged metal railings that quivered at their footfalls.

"I thought our back stairs were in bad shape."

"No shit. Like walking on a trampoline."

An elderly man trudged back from the dumpster to his apartment across the way, carefully oblivious.

"This is not a happy place."

"Check," Brendan said. Tlaxitlán was a happier place than Buzz's home turf. No wonder he'd never invited Jonah to visit.

At the interior end of the complex, apartment 3F faced the street. A wire milk crate, upended, had been set beside the door. On its makeshift tabletop, a tin can brimmed with cigarette butts. A television squawked at high volume inside.

Brendan knocked.

No one answered. Blue light played across a flannel sheet that stood in for a curtain.

Brendan knocked again.

"Go 'way!" barked a voice from inside.

"That would be the boyfriend."

Brendan knocked a third time, louder and more decisively. "It's important," he called through the door.

The barker mumbled something and the television went quiet. Then the door jerked open. "What the fuck!?" Vince towered over the two younger men, fists clenched, tattooed biceps swelling out of his shirtsleeves like melons.

Zac stepped back.

"It's about Buzz," Brendan said, holding his ground against all better judgment. "There's a problem."

"What problem? Who the fuck are you?"

"Name's Brendan. This is Zac. We live with a friend of Buzz's from school, a kid named Jonah—maybe Buzz has talked about him." The hulk in the doorway let Brendan's pause hang. "Anyway, Buzz is in the hospital. We've been trying to call. If his mom doesn't show up they're going to put him in juvie and send the cops out to find her."

"She cain't leave the house. What'd he do?"

"OD. Smack. They took him to General in an ambulance."

Vince stared balefully, weighing the news. "Wait," he commanded before stepping back and slamming the door.

They couldn't make out the words, but it sounded like Vince

was talking to a woman. Zac spoke softly into Brendan's ear. "No cozy homecomings here."

"I'm thinking Buzz'd be better off in foster care."

"Or staying with us," Zac said.

"Best if the boyfriend stays home, right? That leaves the most wiggle room."

"Yeah, but how do we—"

Vince yanked the door open again, filling the space, a lamp's light shadowing his coarse features. "Who says the cops'll come lookin'?"

"He almost died of a heroin overdose," Zac said.

"Shut up! I'm talkin' to him."

"My friend is right. Buzz was clean when he got to the hospital. No points, no dope. But they can't just let a kid his age walk after pumping him full of Narcan. If it's not the cops, it'll be a social worker with cops at her back."

"You're the one did time in Mexico," Vince said.

Brendan let a long moment pass. "Maybe I am."

Vince gestured vaguely behind him. "She's messed up. Fell down taking out trash, a few drinks to kill the pain. And I ain't about to walk into shit for that punk."

Brendan heard an ex-con's evasive whine beneath Vince's belligerence. His abdomen tightened. "It's your call," he said. "We came by so you'd have a chance to give Buzz a break—and keep the heat off. If she can clean up we'll take her to the hospital. Might want to make sure there's nothing lying around the apartment, you know? In case the police come by anyway."

Vince crossed his bulging arms. "So what's your angle?"

"We're helping Jonah's friend. And the Youth Authority's a shithole I wouldn't wish on my worst enemy."

"Fuckin' right." Vince stood in the doorway, thinking it through. "Wait here," he said, and went back inside.

"Was that a kinder, gentler slam?"

"She's going to be a sight," Brendan said.

"He beat the shit out of her."

"I'm guessing. Can you get her over to General in a cab? I'll follow on the bike."

"Not a lot of options. The question is what happens after. Can we get her into a shelter, or what?"

Brendan shook his head. "I got a bad feeling."

—

At the hospital, Cheryl wouldn't take off her sunglasses, but that didn't keep anybody from noticing the bruises. Nora arrived soon after they returned with Buzz's mother, and Christopher soon after that. None of them could talk Cheryl out of returning home. In a flurry of whispered side conversations, they agreed to take Buzz in, but that got nixed too. "Vince wouldn't like it," Cheryl insisted. The social worker allowed herself to be persuaded that extended family could put things right.

At four the next morning, not six hours out of the hospital, Buzz showed up on the landing outside Jonah's room. Brendan and Allison were both roused from sleep. By the time Brendan got to the third floor, Jonah was sitting up, groggily entangled in his blankets.

Allison opened the back door. Buzz stood with his head hung down, as if ashamed. His left eye was swollen shut, and a gash on his forehead was seeping blood. "Come inside," she said after a short, shocked moment.

"God damn him," Brendan swore. "Vince did that?"

Buzz didn't answer.

"Leave it be," Allison said quietly. "Buzz, come into the kitchen. Let's get you fixed up."

Brendan swallowed his rage and dug a tray of ice cubes out of the freezer. Even sitting down, Buzz looked as if he might collapse any moment. Brendan rolled up the cubes in a dishtowel and pounded them with a rolling pin. The stir drew Nora upstairs, in her bathrobe and slippers. "What—oh, God. Oh, Buzz."

Jonah watched from the bedroom doorway as Allison set the ice pack against his friend's bruised eye. Nora fetched first-aid supplies from the second floor, returning with hydrogen peroxide and a supply of bandages left over from dressing Marty's head wound. "This is going to sting," she warned, then gingerly touched a peroxide-soaked pad to Buzz's forehead.

"Ow!" He flinched, but submitted stoically to the women's care. "They were fighting," Buzz said.

"You don't need to talk about it unless you want to." Allison guided his hand to the icepack. "Hold it gently. Don't press too hard."

"Yeah," Buzz said, then looked to Brendan. "You saw him."

"I did. Allison's right, tell us what you want to, but you don't owe anybody an explanation. We get it about Vince. Al, Nora—where can we set up a place for Buzz to sleep?"

"We can put a futon in my room," Jonah said. "There's that foam one in the hall closet."

TWENTY-NINE

Chagall tugs an access panel into place over his head, lowering himself flat against the cold concrete. Parallel runs of PVC and copper tubing dig into his ribcage on either side. He's closeted in a pitch black, steel-skinned plenum beneath third-story laboratory space at the University of Nebraska's Center for Agricultural Genomics. He and Romulus have pushed their target date to its limit: since his last visit, the formal name of the AgBio complex has been carved into a stone marker erected at the gate. Construction is nearly complete. The corridors are lined with wooden pallets bearing costly electronic instruments.

Switching on a headlamp, Chagall plays its beam over the field of battle.

He is flanked by rows of pedestals supporting the laboratory's raised floor. The concrete underfloor is also the auditorium ceiling. A single beam supports the massive, heavily reinforced slab on which he lies. Eighteen inches of meaty, A36 carbon steel, according to the engineering diagrams. Ventilation ducts breach the structural floor where bolts attach the beam to supporting columns. The girder is isolated from the plenum by a scrim of sheet metal.

Moving slowly and carefully in the constricted space, Chagall pats himself down, confirming his gear is correctly pocketed and secured. It's zero-one-forty by his 24-hour watch. He underestimated how long it would take to snip through ductwork under a lab on the opposite end of the I-beam. Still, there's plenty of time. No reason to rush.

Chagall infiltrated the AgBio complex through a service door at the west end of the loading dock. He never intended to break in through the entrance Romulus used a few nights before. The cable spliced by the hacker is irrelevant, the camera in question of no importance. Romulus broke, entered, and performed as instructed; all Chagall needed was to see evidence of a physical crime.

It's easy enough to slip in and out of the complex. At this stage of work, inner stairwells and doors are left unlocked for construction crews. Chagall's target is a prairie state research facility, not a Las Vegas casino. Drug addicts, high school dropouts, the weak-willed, and the poorly conditioned break into buildings every day and night, commercial and residential structures alike, all across the continent. Never mind what locksmiths would have one believe. There's not much to it.

Like Romulus, Chagall has come to augment the building's inventory. The thermite he'll leave behind is stable at normal temperatures, but throws off hellish quantities of heat when ignited, heat well above the critical temperature of carbon steel. The powdery stuff is easy to make. The simplest binding agents allow it to be formed into bricks, cylinders, or coins. Thermite contains its own source of oxygen. It will happily blaze away in a vacuum.

A seasoned autodidact of the pyrotechnic arts, Chagall has refined recipes for thermite suited to ignite overbuilt homes in exurban subdivisions; to burn through the engines of heavy machinery; to cut locks, fences, and cages; and, germane to the occasion at hand, thermite to weaken construction-grade beams. In initial experiments he tested a variant used in the Allied invasion of Normandy. What's good for fouling artillery, he had reasoned, might prove first-rate for compromising structural steel. In practice this was not the case. Thermate-TH3 failed to cut deeply into Chagall's sample girder. The customized material cooked up in its stead, packed in open, flanged ceramic coffins, is a simpler mixture of aluminum and iron oxide. The loads placed tonight will burn fiercely for about a minute and a half, reaching maximum heat some twenty seconds after ignition. They are more than sufficient to prime the building for collapse.

On padded knees and elbows Chagall crawls through the inky dark, his cyclopean light casting shadows that swing in wheeling wedges through the ranks of floor supports. He inches forward deliberately, sliding a nylon kit bag before him. There isn't much room. From his entry point beneath the access panel, he turtles along a wall above the auditorium's northern edge. The tight quarters induce a mild claustrophobia, and when he reaches the ventilation duct Chagall is sweating heavily.

He pulls a smartphone, sister to the one procured for Romulus, from a zippered pocket. Images relayed at twenty-second intervals show the guard at his post on the grainy screen.

After a short rest he lays out tools, sets the kit bag aside, and hikes himself into position. He exchanges latex gloves for a heavier cotton pair, with leather finger pads to protect against roughly cut sheet metal.

Chagall decouples the ventilation riser from a network of horizontal ducts that spider through the plenum. Turning, he extracts another set of screws from the vertical end of the elbow, removes the piece, and sets it aside. Tapping lightly along the inside of the riser, he sounds out the concrete slab's thickness, then punches a starter hole with a short, sharp hunting dagger. Chagall takes tin snips to the sheet metal, cutting as wide as the space allows. He clips several inches down each side, and pulls back a thin strip of ducting. A moonscape is illuminated by his headlamp, gypsum fireproofing sprayed directly onto the girder. Chagall completes the cuts methodically, using pliers to fold the sheet metal back as far as he can reach.

To catch debris Chagall tapes a plastic bib in place. Then he begins to pry gypsum from the beam. Once a small section is exposed the going is easy.

He checks again on the guard. The figure on the smartphone screen is stationary in his chair. It's impossible to tell for sure, but Chagall has a hunch it's nap time.

Now he unzips the nylon case and arrays elements of the incendiary in easy reach, along with a digital multimeter to test the trigger's hookup. He smears the ceramic coffin's flanges with high temperature epoxy, then slathers more onto the I-beam itself. Dotting the tips of several bundled sparklers, the kind anyone can buy at any fireworks stand on the continent, he inserts the ready-made fuse through a hole drilled in the enclosure, deep into the thermite charge. Chagall maneuvers the assembly into place. Carefully mating epoxied flange to sticky steel, he holds it steady until the goop begins to set.

Silicon sealant fixes the triggering rig to the I-beam. Chagall wires up the fuse, checks the connections, and flips a switch. A flashing yellow LED goes steady and green, then blinks off.

His smartphone now shows the guard absent from the booth. Cycling through the surveillance cameras, Chagall sees only empty parking lot.

It's just past three. The construction crews will start to report as early as five.

Chagall switches off his headlamp. He'll lie low while the epoxy hardens.

—

Suspended in darkness, Chagall drifts through his punch list. There's a roundabout drive immediately ahead. South into Kansas, west into Colorado, a backroads zigzag up into Wyoming. Past the outskirts of Cheyenne, then northeast into the Black Hills. He'll park the quarter-ton he's driving tonight, and pick up a box truck garaged outside Rapid City.

The plan is to deadhead across western Nebraska, carrying an almost-legit contract for hauling fertilizer out of Norfolk. In Meadow Grove, a hundred twenty miles from his target, Chagall will load the empty truck with eight tons of bagged and palleted ammonium nitrate.

He has set up a way station some fifteen miles from the research complex, in a barn on fallow property near Staplehurst. A motley collection of propane cylinders, acquired secondhand for cash, is cached in a grain bin there. Blasting caps and automobile batteries are buried near the rented property's fence line. In the barn's rafters he has concealed steering and accelerator motors, a GPS sensor, and a modified laptop to govern the bobtail's last-quarter-mile approach.

A metallic thud interrupts Chagall's reverie.

It sounded from nearby, perhaps the fire door at the floor's northeast corner. Now there are footsteps.

Another door opens and shuts, this one not so massive. The guard is in the lab overhead. Chagall scarcely breathes. What did he leave showing? Why would the guard turn in from the corridor unless he has seen something amiss? Above him, heavy boots pace from the door to the windows beside the hinged panel Chagall used to access the plenum. A pause. Chagall silently counts off ten seconds. Twenty. He is unarmed, and can hardly move in the tight, underfloor space.

Wait.

The guard is stepping back toward the door. Was it just a routine walkthrough? As the laboratory door shuts, Chagall resumes breathing; the guard's footsteps recede. Now the fire door, echoing heavily as it slams shut. Time passes. Taking care not to make the least sound, he checks the smartphone. The booth is still unmanned.

He waits ten minutes by his watch, and checks again. Still empty.

Seven minutes more.

Now the guard stands outside, having a smoke.

Chagall's heart pounds with release and relief. He stretches in the confined space, then pokes at the silicon ooze with a screwdriver, at the epoxy that bonds thermite to steel. Neither is fully set, but each seal is stable enough.

He wrestles the cut sheet metal straight. Duct tape is enough to mask the incisions. So long as light doesn't shine through, there's no need for cosmetics. He screws the elbow joint back into place.

Chagall packs and pockets his tools, then begins a retreat toward the access hatch.

THIRTY

T he drivers killed their headlights as they rolled through the predawn darkness and turned into a little-used parking lot, some two miles south of the Berkeley campus. Eddie's junkers idled wheezily along the east side of the staging point, overlooking Highway 24. The chatter-valved wrecks had survived their second trek from Sebastopol—they'd caravanned in for the rehearsal too—but it seemed a better bet to squander gasoline than to risk a balky ignition on the morning it mattered.

The lot boiled with muted activity. Zac stood with a clipboard at the curb cut's edge, directing drivers as they arrived. Others worked the crowd, making sure everybody found their assigned vehicle. Eddie and some of his Mendocino County pals divvied up leaflets to be distributed on the bridge. There were freshly minted "I Sat in Traffic to Stop Frankenfood" buttons too, meant to mollify trapped drivers by suggesting they were part of a Historic Occasion.

Christopher stood in a faux-commuter's suit and tie with Allison and the tower crew. They'd clustered by the cargo vans that would transport the banner, and, optimistically, getaway bikes for the climbers. "Everybody's set to channel three?" he asked, checking his own walkie-talkie in light spilling off an adjacent overpass.

Marty was nervously fingering carabiners clipped to his harness. "Sure we are, Chris. But say again how we're supposed to remember the sequence when we're swingin' in the wind?"

Allison chided Marty with a wink. "Three, five, eight, thirteen, twenty-one. If a math retard like me can do Fibonacci numbers . . ."

"That's it," Christopher said. "And the code to switch up is 'boost the volume.'"

"You've got spare batteries?" Phil asked.

Christopher patted his jacket pocket. "Somebody made sure about the color codes, right?"

Phil nodded. "I triple-checked. Orange rope for the Golden Gate side of the banner, blue for San Jose."

"Please God," Allison said, "don't let us pull it up backwards."

"What do we hear from the coalition?" Marty asked.

"Too early for the phone net to go live," Christopher said. He shivered, only partly from the cold. "Nora checked in a few minutes ago and said there's nothing since Meg's e-mail to Tactical."

Zac broke into their circle. "Everybody's here, everything's loaded," he said. "Eleven minute warning."

"All for one," Phil said.

"Jayzus." Marty clasped his fellow climber's hand. "We're really gonna do it."

Allison took Christopher's arm as he turned to find his place. "Did Nora say whether the boys are awake?"

"She didn't," Christopher said. "They're going to be okay, Al. We've got your back."

"I know. I know that. You look sharp. Like somebody's lawyer."

"Sheesh." He shook his head, momentarily tongue-tied.

"I'm not saying you should make a habit of it."

"Not to worry," Christopher said. "Good luck out there."

"To all of us."

———

When Nora and Brendan took their posts at half past five, the thermometer by the bay windows read fifty degrees. They shut the library's pocket doors and ran space heaters at full throttle. Nora wore fingerless gloves as she worked the phone. Brendan sat beside her in a watch cap, keeping an eye on webcams run by a local network affiliate. Light glimmered up on the westbound deck, silhouetting sparse traffic.

"I just started that Kerouac novel," Nora was saying to a long-time antinuke activist with a downtown day job. The woman on the other end of the line—they were careful not to call each other by name—was standing by to blast-fax press releases as soon as blockaders controlled the bridge.

"You're going to love it," the downtown conspirator read off her code sheet.

"I know I will," Nora replied. "I'll call as soon as I can get away for coffee."

"I'll be ready when you are."

Nora disconnected the call. "That's it," she said to Brendan. "Now we wait."

"If this thing comes off, it'll top ripping up the railroad tracks in Concord."

She smiled. Trains carrying weapons bound for Central American dictatorships took them back a lot of years. "It's good to have you around," she told her compadre. It was true, despite his caginess. The warmth she felt wasn't just nostalgia. There was something immutable about being on the barricades together at a tender age.

"I'm glad to be someplace folks'll put up with me."

"For a while, anyway." The Embarcadero webcam refreshed its image. More of the same. "Seriously, though," she said after a silence. "Are you going to stick around this time?"

Brendan looked up, then away again. "I can't say."

"Nobody's caught you nosing around Allison," Nora said. "And she hasn't been complaining either. A girl's got to figure . . . maybe something's up?"

"Christ."

Nora was amused to see him blush.

"Nothing's—it's just—I'm not there yet," he said. "That's all. Not Al so much as the whole of humankind."

She nodded. "I know. I can't even imagine." She couldn't. None of them had ever been dumped the way his Chiapas comrades had dumped Brendan. "Leaving Allison aside," she said. "If Buzz ends up adopting us, he could use a role model with your—what? Your chops. Your cred."

"An ex-con who's not a wife beater, you mean?"

"Well, yeah, you can put it like that."

Brendan took a pull of coffee from his mug. "Y'all are the stable influence around here. I never was. Anyway, the kid detests me."

"That's where you've got an advantage." The cell phone's ring cut Nora short. She snatched it off the table and thumbed the device open in a single move. "Headquarters."

As Nora spoke into the phone the hallway door swung wide. Brendan jumped out of his chair.

"What's going on?" Jonah asked. Buzz's skunk-striped head gleamed in the hallway behind him; on Sunday he'd gotten Zac to shave off his mohawk.

"Roger that," Nora was saying into the cell phone. "Everything's a go on this side."

Brendan held up a hand, silencing the boys. "Give us just a second."

"Roger. Waiting for your signal from Isengard."

"Ice and guard?" Buzz was rubbing the sleep out of his eyes. "What the fuck's that?"

"*Lord of the Rings*, dude."

"Good morning, fellas." Nora snapped the cell shut. "You're up just in time for today's top story."

———

Accelerating out of the toll plaza, the drivers merged to form two single-file columns with three lanes of traffic between them. Speed and density were building gradually toward the clog of a weekday commute. There were no highway patrol on the road, ahead or behind.

Mount Tamalpais stood crisp against the sky's rising backlight. Approaching Yerba Buena Island, Christopher glanced at a banner over the entrance to the tunnel, touting electronic bridge toll devices. During the first Gulf War, he and Marty hung a hand-painted sign in exactly the same place. It didn't last an hour. Caltrans had rolled up, workers tromped down the steep slope, and the plea for peace was history. Traffic hadn't even slowed. It'll be a different story this morning, he thought as they emerged onto the western span.

With choreographed lane changes, the caravan converged into formation. A Vanagon, the one that was running rough when they were up at Eddie's place, kept enough ahead of the pack to allow straggling commuters an escape flue up the middle lane. With innocents purged from the wedge of activist vehicles, Eddie's wrecks maneuvered five abreast behind the cargo vans. The Vanagon remained slightly ahead, positioned to fall back into the front row at the last moment. As they crossed the center anchorage, the buffer vehicles aligned.

Christopher's dashboard clock read 6:38. A pearly light suffused the air and the sun had nearly cleared the East Bay hills. Alone in a borrowed Subaru, acutely conscious of his surrounding comrades, Christopher gripped the steering wheel, knuckles white against its pleather cover. His eyes were glued to the rusty Monte Carlo directly ahead. Its shocks sagged under the weight of a half-dozen activists and a trunk full of agitprop. A woman from the Friends Committee to Stop the War had the wheel of a red Accord to his right; Dennis Chu from Agritech Watch drove a black Toyota quarter-ton in lane one. A fellow he'd met that morning—Roy? Randy?—one of Eddie's recruits—followed in a late model Acura.

The Monte Carlo drifted toward Christopher's left lane line. The Vanagon slowed and slipped into the space straddling lanes two and three. Christopher held his breath and edged slightly rightward, as if preparing to scoot around a slow driver, corking the gap between the vehicles in front of him. They coasted to a halt in sixteen-part harmony. An apparently random, fully premeditated stagger across the bridge formed a three-layer dam against the commuter onslaught. Traffic silted unhappily behind them.

Christopher looked to either side, and back in the Subaru's mirrors. Marty had been right. If the blockade were left to the front rank alone, even six cars across five lanes, somebody would have tried to slip by. A thick blare of car horns blanketed the bridge. Christopher leaned on the Subaru's horn, joining in. He'd forgotten to count down, but the front row hadn't. Fifteen seconds after Eddie's junkers came to a stop, their doors burst open and blockaders spilled onto the deck.

Heart in his throat, Christopher tried to see the action with fresh eyes, as a stranger might, or a news camera. Purple-dreadlocked college students, gleeful and resolved; back-to-the-land veterans of movements past; hipsters wearing flesh plugs in their ears and caps to keep their shaved heads warm; a startlingly tall woman, six months pregnant, majestic in a bulky down jacket; an old fellow, white hair glowing in the light from the east—all of them scrambling in disciplined disorder.

Melissa Khachaturian, the pregnant woman, carried a mesh sack of short, fat PVC tubes to the south side of the bridge; the old guy, Freddie Millman, was her mirror on the north. As Melissa and the retired longshoreman took their places, the rest of the blockaders chained adjacent wrecks together by their window frames, ran webs of bright yellow tape across the span, and set oversized stop signs atop the vehicle roofs. The cardboard hexagons were the first explicit notice of what was up. "Frankenfood Kills," the signs proclaimed.

Through the bedlam, Christopher caught glimpses of the banner team under the tower. The gate to the ladder on the north side of the structure swung open a few seconds ahead of the one on the south. Becca and Mickey would be tearing across the tarmac to stash borrowed bolt cutters back in the vans while Allison and the drivers unloaded banner and bikes. Christopher couldn't see the climbers themselves, on the far side of the monumental beams, but Marty and Phil were probably getting underway. Keith and Laura would wait until the leads ascended twenty rungs up, then follow.

Now Allison stood on the running board of the lane-four Econoline, holding a pair of binoculars. She hung insouciantly off the van, glassing the stopped traffic as she spoke on a cell phone. It looked like she was arguing with the other end of her call.

His walkie-talkie crackled into life. Keith's voice, barely recognizable. "South support reporting all climbers are on the tower. Repeat. All climbers on the tower."

Christopher depressed the talk button on the device beside

him, and spoke into a headset. "Groundside lookout acknowledges, all climbers on the tower."

Clipping the headset into his rented phone, Christopher speed-dialed Brendan and Nora back at the Triangle.

—

"There are exactly zero cars moving west into the city," Allison said into her cell as she surveyed what amounted to a long, absurdly narrow parking lot. She clung to the Econoline's frame, alert and relaxed, lent a martial air by a faded corporal's jacket bought out of a surplus shop. A matter-of-fact ponytail snatched bright gold out of the morning sun. "Yep . . . that's right. . . . The blockaders are safe because there's a solid wall of friendly vehicles between them and the commute. . . . Leona, the point is not about tactics. That discussion has been preempted. . . . No. . . . Hell no! Look at where we are right now, in this moment. You can bet the farm that a battalion of SFPD are going to be diverted out here to deal with us."

Allison watched Becca and Mickey adjust the set of the furled banner, tracking their progress as they screwed together sections of PVC conduit to stiffen its top and bottom edges. Melissa and Freddie were distributing their shorter, fatter sections of PVC on the blockade line. "Listen, Leona . . . No, I won't tell you how we did it, not now. . . . Because I'm out of time, we've got work to do, and media calls coming in."

Allison jumped down from the van to let the driver climb in. She gave a thumbs up, and turning, signaled the second Econoline clearance to pull out. "Adjust to it, Leona, this is what's happening," she said as the cargo vans accelerated toward the city. "You're about to see some massive confusion among our uniformed friends at Moscone. I recommend you take advantage of the facts on the ground."

She began to walk eastward, toward the row of chained vehicles.

"Okay, Leona. Fine. Leona—okay. We'll talk about it in jail. . . . Okay, then we'll talk about it afterward. Seize the day, sister, before somebody snatches it away from us."

THIRTY-ONE

P ast Valentine the light falls away. Twilight, dusk, then the full-on rural night of north-central Nebraska. Chagall passes a huddle of low-slung buildings. Johnstown, population fifty-three. He keeps to the speed limit. A high-pitched whine coming from someplace deep in the trannie doesn't concern him. Only a few hundred miles to go.

He sits upright in the waffled vinyl seat, eyes prickly, willing himself to stay focused. Seven hours' sleep in Rapid City didn't even the books on the all-nighter outside Lincoln.

National Public Radio is playing through the truck's cheap speakers, pulled down into the Niobrara watershed with a satellite receiver. A captain from the Office of Naval Research is describing Silver Fox, a surveillance drone that weighs in at twenty-some pounds and can be launched from a catapult. Chagall is intrigued. Several years ago he outfitted a pair of Hobby-Zone Super Cubs with digital cameras and souped-up power trains. The buyer was a sadistic-looking skinhead, fresh out of supermax solitary. Chagall never asks, but he figures whatever the skinhead was looking for wound up destroyed or stolen, and would have with or without a model airplane's assist.

Vast fields of monocrop lay quilted across the nightscape.

Here there's nothing to surveil. He drives past corn sown for miles on end, then alfalfa for miles and miles more, field edges still in his headlights. Grassland lit by the waxing moon between Ainsworth and Long Pine, road straight as a plumb line. Straight as the run up to the AgBio complex. This would have been good country to exercise his autopilot rig, but it's stowed in the barn outside Staplehurst. Then again, there's precious little for the electronics to fix on. Just the road's faded center line.

Money dipped out of ill-gotten gain, like the wad he was paid by the Brotherhood skinhead, is what funds Chagall's work. Robbery, extortion, predation on weakness. These are fuel, at perilously thin remove, to his exploits. He harvests from evildoers to prevent another evil's fruition. In some ways he is distant kin to the navy captain on NPR, Chagall supposes as the radio report wraps. The naval officer is funded by compulsory taxes; Chagall shakes down the nation's sad underbelly to finance his own arsenal. They are equally convinced of their own ultimate goodness. Neither employs pure methods to influence the course of history. At their best, he and the captain each aim toward principled ends. Their ends differ, of course. But a greater gulf is the chain of command, behind which a military man can take cover. Chagall bears full responsibility for his choices.

Rock County passes underwheel without a stop. Well into Holt there's a stretch of circular, pivot-irrigated fields, like God's own change purse emptied out, great earth-coins laid edge to edge in moonlight. Then the dark houses and shuttered businesses of O'Neill. The Elkhorn River glints from time to time between shadowy stands of cottonwood and willow.

The scales are open outside Clearwater. A sallow attendant emerges from the cinderblock shed as he pulls in. Chagall maneuvers the bobtail into place, cranks the window open, and dangles a messy sheaf of paperwork out for inspection.

"Whas' your destination, cowboy?" the sallow man asks.

"Norfolk," Chagall says. He gives the papers a rustle.

"Nor*fork*," the man corrects. "Leastwise if you're from 'round here."

"That right?" It's a lonely job, and Chagall understands that he's a chance to relieve profound monotony.

"Yep. Eighteen-eighty-somethin' the US Post Office mucked up the name. Jes' like government." He's scanning Chagall's forgeries in the beam of a flashlight. "Big ol' bank holdup there."

"Catch 'em?"

"Hell yes. Killed four tellers and a little ol' lady, two years back. Came barrelin' up this road right here, caught 'em up in O'Neill. Mexican pricks, high on drugs."

Chagall withholds comment.

"Johnny Carson, he's from Norfork."

The scale attendant is a font of wisdom. "Never knew that," Chagall says.

"Do now. 'Pears you're deadheadin' tonight."

"That's right."

"Comin' in early for this here load. Tri-County Farm Co-op."

"Yup. First run for these fellas. Sleep up, take a day in town. See what the other drivers say. Maybe sign on regular."

"A'right. You come in town, angle right on Market Lane, find you some motels with plenty a parkin'."

"'Preciate it."

"Never mind that." The sallow man hands back Chagall's papers and waves the truck along.

He pulls back onto the road.

Only a half hour now from Meadow Grove. It would have been better if the scales were closed. There's not enough business along this route to blur the attendant's memory.

Chagall considers keeping the look he's wearing all the way through. If he skips a planned makeover at Staplehurst there's longer to sleep, which has its advantages. If anybody spots a scruffy, crew-cut middleweight fleeing the AgBio complex, their description will match what the sallow man saw. The wig he'd planned to wear out of Staplehurst can come into play later on.

He's clean and America's wide. Once the building goes down there'll be time to reach the city before sunrise. He has more unlikely vehicles stashed along back roads and side streets than he'll need under any circumstances that still allow a chance of escape. An eighteen-speed racing bike, a tractor and cargo cart, a gleaming hearse, a skateboard, a Harley. Once he slips into Lincoln the cops won't have a chance.

Chagall rolls up his window and drives on into the moon-dappled dark.

THIRTY-TWO

Christopher watched Gregor, Natalie, and Zac load up with shoulder bags full of leaflets and buttons. Melissa and Freddie would work the two outside lanes. On the other side of the blockaded vehicles, a cordon of activists stretched across the span, hands interlocked inside the PVC tubes distributed a few minutes earlier.

He couldn't help but worry. On the one hand, that was his nature. On the other, he had a point. Something always goes wrong. They didn't know what it would be this time, and that kept Christopher jittery. Traffic had stopped, but there were still plenty of opportunities for trouble—beginning with the banner crew performing gymnastics a hundred feet up in the air.

"South support reporting climbers in position and ready to haul," Keith said over the walkie-talkie.

"Banner ground south to north and south towers, you are cleared to haul," Becca radioed back. "On your mark—"

Christopher half-stood in his seat to watch. Seconds before liftoff, he spotted Beat Gordon cycling up the empty lanes from San Francisco, escorted by Deb Harris from Turnabout. "Yes!" he exclaimed out loud. The KGRB reporter had been sworn to silence in exchange for the day's premier scoop—he'd been told only where and when to meet. Deb's timing was perfect. Christopher wondered whether the Channel 4 crew was going to get through traffic in time to film the money shot.

The banner rose at speed. He switched in the walkie-talkie. "Groundside lookout reporting banner lift at fifteen percent. North, you're slightly higher, slow down just a bit."

Zac approached and knocked on the Subaru's window. Grinning through feigned outrage, Christopher lowered the glass. "What's going on here? Are you people insane?"

"There's a convention on genetic engineering this week at the Moscone Center," Zac said, swinging into the role play. "They're here to figure out how to trick people into eating genetically altered food—Frankenfood, as in Frankenstein. Have you heard about that? Did you know that medicines these days are brewed up in huge vats of mutant germs before they're injected into the veins of old people and kids?"

"Yeah, whatever," Christopher said. "What does that have to do with jamming my commute? And who elected you conscience of the nation?"

"Take a look at our materials, sir. We'll be out of your way real soon." Winking, Zac pressed a leaflet into the hands of its principal editor, along with an "I Sat in Traffic" button. He moved on to Randy—or was it Roy?—and from there into the ranks of truly irritated commuters. The furled banner was thirty feet up, and Beat Gordon was leaning into his microphone. Christopher switched on the radio.

BEAT: —a single row of protesters, Mike, standing next to each other in a line that stretches straight across the Bay Bridge. Like demonstrators at the WTO protests in Seattle, they're linked together arm in arm, with wrists and hands hidden inside of plastic tubes. When the protesters grab onto each other like this it's very difficult for the police to make arrests.

The studio DJ, Mike O'Malley, cut in.

DJ: Have police arrived on the scene yet, Beat?

BEAT: No, Mike, they haven't. I expect it won't be long, but any way you cut it, we're looking at the mother of all traffic jams. Between the protesters and literally thousands of stalled commuters there's a barricade of cars across the width of the upper deck, with their doors spread open like stumpy metal wings—

DJ: Very poetic.

BEAT: I need to tell you, Mike, these cars are not poetry to look at. They're scrapheaps. They could have been bought out of a junkyard. It's hard to believe they even made it here this morning. But with those wide-open doors locked and chained together, they're likely to be here for a while.

DJ: Beat Gordon live on the Bay Bridge, locked down by protesters at the start of this morning's commute. Beat, can you give any kind of estimate when traffic will begin to clear?

BEAT: This is an incredible mess—traffic is stopped dead across the span. Westbound traffic on the Bay Bridge is going nowhere, and it's impossible to say when the situation is going to change—

Christopher lowered the volume. "Groundside lookout reporting banner level," he said into the walkie-talkie. "Two-thirds up, looking good, and the story's live on KGRB."

When he called back to the Triangle, Nora answered. "I've got Channel 7 patched through to Allison," she said. "They say they've got a 'copter on the way."

"Banner's two-thirds up the tower," Christopher said. "Beat Gordon's live on KGRB. What's with Channel 4?"

"They're hiking through the backup. It took the camera guy a while to give up on his truck. We're listening to the radio. All else okay?"

"So far it looks great. I'll call when the banner drops."

"If Gordon reports it, you don't need to—we're leaving him tuned in. Jonah and Buzz are up and they volunteered to help monitor the media. You keep an eye on those climbers."

"Excellent, Nora, you know I will. Over and out then."

"Keeping our fingers crossed."

—

Thirty-five yards above the upper deck, securely harnessed to bridge infrastructure, Marty focused on steel's solidity. It was a long way to the tarmac, and an even dizzier plunge to the cold, gray chop of the bay. The view started to wobble whenever he looked down. The practical solution, he realized, was to stop looking.

After securing the haul rope, Marty worked at anchoring the banner to ladder rungs above and below his position. First he clipped a quickdraw looped around the top rung to a carabiner on the banner rig. When he couldn't pull the second quickdraw into the hardware's open gate, he tried the other way around. No go. The setup worked for either quickdraw singly, but clipping one in meant coming up short on the other.

Ascending another rung for purchase, Marty strained against the banner's weight.

Still no good. He didn't have enough hands to manage the weight, fasten the carabiners, and hold on at the same time. Easing off, Marty fingered the equipment on his rack. Maybe a pair of 'biners with their gates opposed would do the trick.

Feeling for the next rung down, Marty set his left boot against the horizontal bar, then braced against a massive bolt with his right. From the upper quickdraw he fingercrawled to its loose end, and clipped in a pair of asymmetrical Ds, triple-checking that the gates faced opposite ways. Again, retrieving the banner's top rope, he attempted to close the circuit on the weight-bearing rig. The first of the anchors proved an easy hook. He had to sweat over the other, but after several tense seconds he had it. Marty hugged the metal rungs and reached for a rip cord Velcroed to the anchor rope. "North top is securely anchored," he said into his walkie-talkie. "Sorry for the delay, fellas. Quickdraws came up a little short. Used a pair of 'biners to make up the distance."

He gathered himself for the last push. In a few minutes it would be all about descent, and the slim hope of escaping the bridge while the police were getting organized.

"Groundside lookout understands south and north anchor ropes are both secured." Christopher's voice sounded fuzzy over the walkie-talkie. "Lead climbers, announce when you're ready to rip."

"South tower ready to rip," Phil said.

"North tower ready to rip," Marty echoed.

"Support climbers, announce when you're ready to reel."

"South support ready to reel."

"North support ready," Laura said from her roost ten yards below.

One last time, Marty tested the set of the rigging.

—

"Hang on, San Francisco," Christopher said, steadying the arm holding his binoculars against the Subaru's steering wheel. "One thousand one . . . one thousand two . . . free fall!"

The fan-folded Tyvek seemed to hang in midair. Then the weighted sheet dropped slowly, swelling as it caught the breeze. Support climbers pulled in bottom cords as the banner opened. On KGRB, Mike O'Malley cut away from interviews at the Moscone Center to put Gordon back on the air. Christopher, spine tingling, felt for the radio's volume control and clicked it up a notch.

BEAT: —the banner is very large, Mike, very large—maybe fifty feet wide, stretching across the tower. I'm guessing thirty or forty feet high, but it's hard to get an exact fix.

Allison had stopped taking media calls. Working the line with Deb, she alternately looked back toward the tower and attended to the rank of activists, steadying the blockaders while the climbing crew tied down. Scott Cavenaugh, arms committed to comrades on his left and right, was staring fixedly out into traffic. When Allison reached him, her eyes narrowed, following the direction he indicated with his chin. Christopher craned around to see what the matter was. The support team was reeling the banner in flat against the tower, slowly, to balance the pull of the ropes against the release of wind pressure through dozens of half-moon flaps cut into the fabric. Allison fumbled for her binoculars.

BEAT: —taking in the last few feet of rope at the bottom corners. The banner is visually stunning. It has a border of helixes shaped like DNA dollar signs, and the slogan across the top reads 'GMOs = Poison for Profit.' What's stunning—or maybe I should say revolting, Mike—are enormous images of grocery store mutants plastered across this ginormous thing.

DJ: Genetically modified organisms, GMOs. Beat, can you describe the visual?

BEAT: On the left there's a—what should I call it?—a disemboweled apple, a green apple with a wedge cut out to expose a bloody tangle of intestines spilling from the fruit. Then there's a big, juicy red strawberry. But instead of seeds this thing is speckled with dozens of fishy, mucus-dripping eyeballs, staring out of it every which way.

DJ: I'm seeing that scene out of *Brother from Another Planet.*

BEAT: Yes! Just that nasty! Only multiplied like the monster from *Alien* was hatching 'em out back of the supermarket.

DJ: Yuck.

BEAT: Last image, Mike. On the right there's an ear of corn, with the husk pulled back to reveal pills and capsules in place of kernels, all crawling with fat, stubbly gray maggots.

DJ: Maybe a little too visual there, Beat.

Christopher couldn't see what was catching Allison's attention. He wanted to know, but his job was to watch the tower. Gordon's coverage was brilliant. Any moment now he expected to hear helicopters, and the banner would go live on national TV. Somebody stuck in traffic had probably posted cell cam images to the internet by now. The Channel 4 crew would be filming from farther back on the deck, for broadcast later in the day. Thousands of Eddie's dollars, hundreds of hours, the likely arrests and heavy-duty charges—their high-stakes gamble looked like it was about to pay off.

What the hell was Allison looking at? Again, Christopher craned around in his seat.

"North tower support ready to secure bottom line. Requesting visual confirmation."

"Ground support to north tower support," Christopher

answered. "Looks good so far. Wait for south tower before you tie in."

"North tower support, roger that."

The banner looked better than anyone had dared to hope.

"South tower support ready to secure bottom line," Keith announced. "Ground support, can we get a final visual?"

Christopher let a few seconds pass, watching for the breeze to vary. The Tyvek sheet rippled only slightly when the wind slacked off. "Ground support confirming the banner looks great. Go ahead and tie down."

"South support, roger."

"North support tying down."

The banner curved like a taut sail. Truly, a photo op for the ages. The walkie-talkie squawked again. "North tower support announcing bottom line fully secured. We'll be on our way down when south confirms."

Beat Gordon's voice brought him back to the bridge deck.

BEAT: Mike, I'm hearing sirens approaching—

Christopher hiked up as tall as he could in the bucket seat. The dashboard clock read twelve past seven. Thirty-four minutes in.

"South tower support announcing bottom line secured. Let's get the hell off this thing."

"North support descending."

"North tower descending."

"South tower coming down."

Beat Gordon was describing the cavalry's arrival.

BEAT: I can see what looks like five—no, six police motorcycles proceeding cautiously up the span. They're hugging the edge of the roadway and moving pretty slow, but it looks like law enforcement has joined the party at last.

"Ground support to tower crew, you guys are champs," Christopher said into his microphone. "Stay focused, ignore the cops arriving on the bridge. Your job is to get down safe. No shortcuts."

"Damn straight," Marty said. "Still listening, but will not respond unless there's a problem."

"Roger, assuming the same for all tower crew."

—

The tac squad approached, like giant insects in their bulbously visored helmets, flak vests bulging under a carapace of motorcycle leathers. Allison didn't turn around. She didn't see the sergeant wave Beat Gordon away, and wasn't listening to the pulsing thwack of a helicopter arcing in from the southwest.

Her attention was glued to a beefy, middle-aged trucker facing off with Zac. Scott had gotten a bad feeling as soon as he saw a driver, outfitted in Dickies and a Peterbilt cap, away from his vehicle. Allison didn't take long to get there herself. "I only caught some of what he's shouting about," Scott said. "Lettuce wilting in his truck, maybe?"

The man had been dressing down Zac with escalating urgency, his gestures becoming wilder, now almost convulsive. Zac was steadily retreating toward the blockade line. As the rest of the leafleting team noticed, they began to follow at a careful distance.

The SFPD's advance guard was clustered at the base of the tower when the trucker lifted his shirt and pulled a tire iron from his waistband. Waving it recklessly, he clawed the air like an enraged beetle.

Zac backed into the space between two cars. Gregor shouted from the next lane over, trying to draw the man's attention.

Allison panicked.

First ducking under the blockaders' linked arms, she vaulted over a chained pair of car doors like O. J. Simpson before the fall. Allison sprinted past Christopher, hurtling toward the nascent brawl. Gregor and Freddie were converging on the trucker from the opposite side. The man hauled back, on the verge of manslaughter. Gregor and Freddie closed in. His face contorted with fear, Gregor lunged, catching the weapon at the apex of its swing and snatching it out of the trucker's hand. In the same movement he pivoted the lethal thing around, as if to bash the life out of Zac's attacker.

"Gregor, no!" Allison screamed. Correcting her bearing a fraction of a degree she flew to intercept irrevocable tragedy, blocking Gregor's strike with an instinctive *morote ude uke*. He dropped the steel bar, stunned, bending at the waist to cradle his roughly checked arm; but momentum and fury still propelled the driver's fist forward.

As if the absence of his club hadn't even registered, the trucker drove an overhand punch hammer-hard into Zac's temple. The smack of flesh on bony flesh cut through a haze of running engines, sirens, and helicopter blades.

Zac staggered back.

The driver stumbled forward.

Everybody else stopped, as if time itself had seized up.

Zac wavered, then buckled. He hit the tarmac headfirst, with a heavy, crisp-liquid thud, like a cantaloupe dropped to the sidewalk.

———

She can't move. Allison sees her life flash by like a shattering window—everything crashing into chaos—and can't twitch a finger in response. Blood begins to pool beneath Zac's head. Now she understands what it means for scales to fall from blindered eyes. The world as it stands is revealed. The real and the raw sink like a pickaxe into yielding turf.

Their banner ripples in the ocean breeze.

The climbers descend into the tac squad's waiting cuffs.

Zac lies inert on the roadway.

Jonah. She can see him before her, frantic, and knows sure as daylight that she'll be in jail when he hears. Then Buzz. What will this be to him, this violence snaking into a home they assured him is safe?

Sirens. She's hearing sirens. Has she been paralyzed, or has only a fraction of a moment passed?

Meg will crucify them, and the coalition will pile on. The driver's aggression will be painted inevitable. And their inability to guard against it.

Zac's blood, pooling.

Freddie squeezes past the man who struck Zac down. Kneels. His white hair shining.

This is it, she thinks, as if she were watching someone else's calamity. All these years on borrowed luck.

Today is the day the piper collects.

THIRTY-THREE

Christopher turns at the sound of his name. Loosened tie askew, he stands and opens his arms.

Nora has found him staring at the hospital waiting room's wall. She has Jonah and Buzz in tow. Buzz looks away as the others embrace. "This place creeps me out," he mumbles.

"Where's Zac?" Jonah asks.

Christopher thumbs over his shoulder, toward the swinging doors. "There's a nurse, Jennifer something. She said Zac's got some pretty bad hemorrhaging where his head hit." His voice catches. "They have to open him up to stop the bleeding."

"Jesus God—"

"Will he be okay?"

"We don't know yet, Jonah. The doctors won't know until they can see the internal damage."

Jonah blinks.

"Have you eaten anything?"

He shakes his head. "I can't, Nora."

"Not okay," she said, laying a hand on his arm.

Buzz drifts off to a corner of the waiting room. He throws himself into a chair and fires up a handheld game console.

"Can we see him?" Jonah's voice has gone smaller.

Christopher registers the shift. "Not yet," he says. "Not for a while." He sits, and gestures the two of them into chairs beside his. It feels wrong that he is the adult here. He is the adult and Jonah is the child. Zac is in mortal danger, and he has to explain. "Tell me who got arrested." He's stalling.

"All four of the climbers," Nora says.

Christopher is glad to talk about anything else.

"Allison too," she continues. "Some of the blockaders dodged their way to the island, and got rescued by Eddie's crew when they circled back to the East Bay. You must have seen the CHP take down names and license plates before they let the drivers go."

"I did," Christopher says. "With ride-alongs. Just escorted them off the bridge. And they never caught on to the buffer rows. That we were in on it. Twenty minutes after Zac's ambulance took off I was on my way here."

"Gregor's working with Brendan to find the three blockaders we haven't accounted for."

"How's Gregor doing? And who's not accounted for?"

"Gregor's okay. Freaked out, but who isn't? Sherri Baldwin, David Kahn, and one of the USF kids are still missing. They're probably at Moscone, lost in the crowd. So you saw Freddie take over negotiations with the cops?"

"He did good," Christopher says. "I really didn't expect the police to let that many perps leave under their own power."

"They had a serious mess on their hands, especially with—everything we didn't plan on. CHP wanted the bridge open." Nora shrugs. "So Freddie gave them options."

"I could see it in his body language. That hunker down, strike-'til-they-fold thing."

"Union guys."

The waiting room vibrates when they fall silent, a low hum of hidden machinery punctuated by Buzz's electronic game. Christopher's tongue curls at the acrid aftertaste of Nora's words: *everything we didn't plan on.*

"Becca and Mickey and two other girls rode the bikes to get away," Jonah says.

Christopher nods. "That's good." He isn't really sure what he means. His pocket chirps.

Nora murmurs something in Jonah's ear as he fumbles for the cell phone. Jonah shrugs, then slouches over to sit with Buzz. Christopher squints at the cell's display and lifts it to his ear. "Dad? How did you get this number?"

"Brendan," Nora says under her breath.

Christopher nods. His father is saying just that. "No, I'm fine. . . . Yeah. . . . Yeah, it was. Zachary. . . . No, you've met him. Zac—tall, very skinny. . . . We're at SF General. . . . Could be better. Subdural hematoma is the preliminary word. . . . Not yet, just the surgical nurse."

Nora crosses over to the boys and leans in to whisper. Buzz offers a noncommittal smirk.

"No, Marshall didn't call. . . . Not since I saw him, maybe a week after I was over for dinner. He e-mailed a few times."

Christopher can barely pay attention. He closes the phone when his father is satisfied, and stares at it for a moment before sliding the device back into his pocket. He isn't used to being so reachable. It's not so bad, he supposes. Today, at least. He's grateful to be reachable today.

"He saw the news?" Nora asks from across the room.

"Radio," Christopher says, startled to remember he's not alone. "Worried it was his nogoodnik son got carried off in an ambulance. They didn't give Zac's name out?"

"They have to talk to his family first," Jonah says.

"Probably so."

Buzz remains deeply involved in his game.

"Any luck reaching Kansas?" Christopher asks. He crosses over to the others.

Nora shakes her head. "Not yet. Why was your dad asking about Marshall?"

"He's been away," Christopher says. "Doesn't explain himself. Dad wondered if he told me anything."

A young nurse in scrubs pushes through the swinging doors and all but Buzz turn toward her expectantly. Christopher introduces Zac's local clan. Her manner projects gravitas, a little at odds with her rosy cheeks and earthy solidity.

"I'm sorry we have to meet in these circumstances," she says softly.

"This is Buzz," Jonah tells the nurse, since Christopher hadn't. Buzz looks up but doesn't return her understated smile.

"Mr. Coyle has been stabilized for surgery," she says, "and the doctors are scrubbing up now for a craniotomy."

"What does that mean?" Jonah asks.

"They'll find the source of your friend's internal bleeding and try their very best to fix it."

"He's not my friend," Jonah says. "He's one of my dads."

"I'm sorry," the nurse says. "I didn't know."

Nora wraps her arms around Jonah. "How long will the surgery last?"

"We can't say exactly. Ninety minutes to two hours is average, but there might be delays for any number of reasons."

"Can we talk to the doctor?"

"Yes, of course. The presiding surgeon is Dr. Gupta. He's very skilled, both careful and experienced. He'll come out to explain after the operation." She turns to Christopher. "Have you contacted Mr. Coyle's parents?"

"Nora's been working on that."

"We left messages," Nora says. "Zac's family lives in the Midwest, in Topeka."

"It would be good to reach them as soon as possible."

Christopher stops breathing. When he sees Nora's eyes fill he looks away quickly.

"Thank you," he manages. "We'll keep trying."

The nurse turns and slips back into the hospital's interior. The susurration of rubber gaskets beats a fading rhythm as the doors swing after her, then still.

THIRTY-FOUR

H is digital watch vibrates. It's two o'clock in the morning, and Chagall wakes instantly. He stills the alarm and lies motionless in the cab, pressed against the seat, listening through rolled-down windows. Tree frogs and crickets. A rustle in the rafters of the Staplehurst barn. An owl, perhaps, or a nest of insomniac swallows.

The long drive has left him stiff. Daytime sleep followed by hours of shoveling and hauling hasn't helped. After he dug ignition matériel out of a fallow field, each of the ammonium nitrate pallets had to be torn down, then rebuilt around a propane cylinder stippled with blasting caps. Chagall pulls himself upright, feels for the keys dangling from the ignition switch, finds the truck's pedals with socked feet.

The engine catches, stutters, roars to life when he gives it gas. He boots a laptop loaded with autopilot and trigger-decision software. While the computer executes test routines, Chagall steps into his shoes and climbs down into musty darkness to stretch, methodically working kinks out of his back, arms, and legs. The truck's cargo doors are padlocked shut. Limbered up, Chagall sweeps the barn with a flashlight. He confirms that a hinged electric scooter stowed behind the driver's seat slides easily in and out of its cubby, then fastens a strap securing the first of his escape vehicles to the back wall of the cab. Chagall unbolts and opens the barn's wooden doors. He dons a thick watch cap, a ballistic vest, then a leather jacket to hide the body armor.

Over his own engine's noise he makes out the diesel hum of a tractor-trailer hurtling south, a couple miles distant over flat fields. Chagall steps up and into the driver's seat, pulls the truck forward, then dismounts to close up the crude building. All he hears now is his own bobtail. The roads are forsaken at this hour, in this sparsely peopled place.

Not inclined to prayer, not given to ceremony of any kind, Chagall pauses to take stock nonetheless. The next time he touches ground the truck will be seconds from impact, lumbering toward its destiny. Everything he knows and has is bound up in the next hour's performance. By four o'clock the deed will be done or his mission aborted. By six he'll be holed up in Lincoln, or captured, or dead.

He climbs aboard and lets out the parking brake. The transmission engages with a lurch, and tires bite the graveled road. Chagall pauses at a screen of cottonwood that borders the property. There's no traffic approaching, right or left.

He inches onto southbound blacktop, flicks on the headlights, and builds up speed.

—

Between Staplehurst and Valparaiso he encounters six vehicles. Two commercial semis, a late-model Caddy with tinted windows, two half-ton pickups, and a police cruiser. Nobody gives him a second glance, not even the state trooper. Near the Lincoln airport, clusters of residential tracts punctuate dark stretches of farmland. Runway lights stretch away to Chagall's right like garish strings of jewels. The next exit is his.

He swings north, away from a housing development through

which he has mapped multiple, forking escape routes. Harvest Springs. Lawns and swimming pools sucking down the aquifer. Chagall would be glad to see its McMansions razed, but he can't pull all the weight. Past vacant lots and shabby warehouses, he turns into a freshly paved straightaway. A half-mile ahead, metal halide lights illuminate his target, hard white stars against the empty surrounding acres. There are no fences. Concrete bollards meant to stop the likes of him come standard issue now on new construction, but none will be placed here until next week. Romulus ferreted out quality intel.

Chagall douses his lights, pulls over, and retrieves the autopilot kit from beneath the passenger seat. Two electromagnetic motors, a rangefinder mounted on a lusterless black box, and a system of rods, joints, clips, and bolts. With agility sharpened by meticulous rehearsal, he fastens the apparatus to anchor plates set into the dashboard and ceiling, then braces its frame against the seatback. One motor controls a rod attached to the gas pedal. The second steers. The laptop governs both, responding to signals from a fiber optic gyroscope enclosed in the box. Control panes on the backlit screen show all but one connection green. Chagall patches into the last wire, the one branching back to the payload.

His bomb-on-wheels is ready to roll. Using a cell phone, he establishes contact with the thermite devices barnacled to the AgBio structure's great transfer beam. A cryptic sequence tapped on the keypad primes their triggers.

Opening the door, he reaches behind the seat to release the scooter, pulling it out just far enough to telescope the frame. If he's nervous, he doesn't know it. At this stage of an operation Chagall is all about procedure. He knows exactly why he's executing this plan, but to think about that now would only dull his concentration. He works his hands into a pair of leather gloves, and straps pads over elbows and knees.

A second cell is configured to disguise his voice through a software filter. He punches in a speed dial code. The phone rings once. Twice. On the fifth ring a man's voice answers.

"Security."

It's the smoker, Chagall thinks. Must have taken time to snuff his cigarette. He punches through trigger codes on the first phone. The thermite will light up in a matter of seconds.

"Listen carefully," he says. A success signal flashes on the trigger phone's screen. "The research building you are guarding has a bomb in it. The bomb will explode and the building will be des*royed in three minutes. You must activate the fire alarm to clear the building immediately."

"Who the hell is this?!"

"Even if you believe the building is empty, activate the fire alarm now. Then run away from the building as fast as you can. Take cover."

"Is that you, Connolley?"

"Pay attention if you want to live. This is not a joke. The trigger cannot be disabled. This warning will not be repeated. Run away now. The building will blow up in two minutes and twenty seconds."

He disconnects the phone, tossing it onto the floor of the truck. Reaching around the autopilot linkage, he shifts into gear and the vehicle edges forward. With the rangefinder he aims for the center of the building's glass façade. Chagall locks in and engages the software. The laptop reads a distance of five hundred eighty yards and dropping. The truck trundles along at nine miles per hour, slowly gaining speed.

At sixteen miles per hour the laptop emits a shrill bleat. Its screen is showing divergence, just shy of two degrees between target and trajectory. Chagall shrinks back in the driver's seat, assuring that no unintended touch is skewing the equipment. A few seconds pass. Twenty-one miles per hour. The trajectory is still off. Chagall gingerly takes hold of the steering wheel and nudges the truck back on course. Three hundred forty yards to target. Two hundred eighty. Again, leftward drift. The laptop bleats its alarm.

Two hundred forty yards to target. Chagall overcorrects this time. He should have jumped by now, but if he leaves the truck on its wayward course it'll miss the auditorium, perhaps miss the building altogether. Feverishly he recalculates angles of drift and survivable bail speeds. A hundred fifty yards at three percent puts impact five yards off his mark. He has to go closer. A hundred yards max. Leaning over braces and rods to reach the keyboard, he throttles back the speed, choosing accuracy and escape over penetration and broken limbs. He'll have ten seconds to impact, thirteen until the blast wave.

The readout shows a hundred sixty yards to the building. He cracks the door, scrunching low as the guard's kiosk comes into view. Through the engine's rumble comes an unmistakable pop. Pistol fire. That's good, he thinks. The smoker understood the threat was real. One last, careful overcorrection. He pulls the scooter free, lowering it as near to the road as he dares before letting go, pushing away so it won't bounce under the bobtail's rear wheels. He sets his stance and balance. At the sound of another pistol shot, Chagall jumps into a forward roll.

Three, four, five times tumbling head over heels, he curls and scrapes into the roadside weeds. He waits a long moment after coming to a stop, then feels for arms and legs. Right. Left. Upper and lower. He can move. His limbs still bear weight. The sound of plate glass crashing gives him only seconds to spread flat.

When the blast comes he lets the concussion wash over him. Then he stands, a little shaky at first, and squints into the darkness, scanning for his scooter.

THIRTY-FIVE

Jonah and Buzz are up for school. The collective's adults are at the hospital, or crashed following an all-night vigil outside the ICU. Marty is still in jail. Allison was released from custody early enough to see the boys to bed the evening before. Her return calmed Jonah, though his mother warned that she would be away this morning, taking a shift in the waiting room at SF General. Buzz seems less skittish too, as he begins to comprehend that arrest in his new household doesn't foretell sadistic anger or long absence. Jonah plods sleepily down the hall to check weather on the internet.

What he finds are the smoldering ruins of the Bailey Center for Agricultural Genomics, streaming live out of every news site from Fox to the BBC.

Jonah watches for a few minutes, gape-mouthed, then flies down the stairs. Nora has been asleep for an hour when he wakes her. Christopher stumbles from his room when he hears the ruckus. Buzz joins the three of them upstairs, gathered around a computer screen to watch CNN's somber coverage. Christopher surfs print-news sites on his laptop. It takes a few groggy minutes to think past the onslaught of photos and video clips. The coin drops when he finds a link to the "Nebraska Bombers' Screed" on the *Guardian*'s home page.

Only now does he check e-mail. Chagall's manifesto has been delivered to both his *Reporter* mailbox and a freemail account he keeps as a spam sponge. It's the draft he wrote, barely edited. He looks up to watch CNN's talking head.

> The bombers' communiqué was posted on the White House website for about half an hour earlier this morning. Hackers doctored the site to portray the president applauding political positions espoused by the terrorists. Fraudulent links on whitehouse-dot-gov sent thousands of visitors from the trusted site to the Canadian Institute for Environmental Responsibility, a research group affiliated with the University of Toronto . . .

Christopher can practically feel his personality rupture as he throttles an impulse to confess. He continues to news-surf. "Reuters says the *Chicago Tribune*'s site was hacked too." He's not hyperventilating, but only by force of will. "Eight and a half minutes before they took it down."

The news anchor reports that no one is believed to have been in the building when a truck rammed its lobby, shortly after the single security guard received a phone call warning him to flee.

> Authorities say it will be hours until forensics teams can begin to sift through the rubble. Though the bombers' communiqué made no reference to suicide, the security guard is said to have seen a driver. Police declined to comment on rumors that the vehicle was operated by remote control. A three-state manhunt is underway, with federal

agents and staff fanning out from an Emergency Operations Center in Lincoln, according to a spokesperson from the Department of Homeland Security.

On the *Washington Post*'s site, Christopher sees the Justice Department is calling the attack "an unprecedented convergence of conventional and cyber-terrorism." The obvious comparisons are drawn across the spectrum of media: September 11th, McVeigh, the Unabomber.

Christopher's father calls. Nora holds out the phone, but he retreats to the third-floor kitchen and picks up there.

"This is despicable," Professor Kalman says. "Despicable! Do you agree or do you not?"

"I'm barely awake, Dad."

"This communiqué, whatever they're calling it—it's an apology for terrorist attacks on basic science. I'm ashamed to see that the excuses these hooligans offer are indistinguishable from the nonsense you and your friends were spouting yesterday."

If there had ever been a moment ripe for reciting the rosary, this was it. But his mother had skipped instruction in the Catholic aspect of his mongrel heritage. He didn't even know how to start. "I haven't read it all the way through," he says.

"Chris, tell me yesterday's stunt on the bridge has nothing to do with this insanity."

His stomach sinks. "Nothing, Dad. Nothing at all."

After a minute or two more, Professor Kalman lets him go. Christopher hangs up the phone. He wants nothing more at that moment than to catch a ferry and ditch his laptop in the bay. He returns to the others. "We need to get back to the hospital," he says to Nora. "We need to talk, all of us."

"What about me and Buzz?" Jonah asks.

Nora sighs. "Guys, this is happening two thousand miles from here, okay?" She speaks in a near monotone. Her face is slack, her eyes puffy and red. "You both missed school yesterday. We'll catch you up this afternoon."

Christopher is certain the police will look for a connection. Nora begins to herd the boys toward breakfast, but turns back at the library door.

"You're right," she says quietly. "But I can't string two thoughts together without more sleep. Let me get Buzz and Jonah out the door. I'll crash another couple of hours, then come to the hospital."

"Don't make coffee. I'll grab a cup on my way."

"I'll call Allison to let them know you're coming."

Christopher scrounges fresh clothes from his room. He clears his head under a cold shower. He's going to be telling a lot of lies in the coming days. Not just to his father, and not only over the sheltered distance of a phone line.

He has to get his story straight.

———

Trudging up the hospital's broad, concrete stairs, Christopher is blind to the seasick-green of thickly painted walls, the worn safety treads edging the steps, a whiff of thwarted hope lingering in the wake of those who trekked this way before him. None of the hospital's institutional ugliness registers. Nora relieved him from duty outside the ICU less than six hours ago. It feels as though he never left.

He leans into a fire door's push bar. The door absorbs his weight, prolonging a moment suspended between worlds. Alone, and then among. Christopher steps into the hospital corridor.

Will his comrades be better off warned, or safer in the dark? However indirect and blind his part, every person he tells anything will be implicated. Conspiracy after the fact. On the other hand, as soon as police draw a line between yesterday's protest and the Nebraska communiqué, the Triangle will be tossed from top to bottom by every agency with a stake in thwarting terrorism. Every demonstration they ever organized, every name on every list they ever compiled will be swept into the FBI's maw.

His father saw the connection immediately.

How can the government miss it?

———

In the waiting room Brendan sits glued to the TV. A woman in a powder-blue hijab rocks a dozing toddler beside him. Standing ramrod straight to the woman's right, an old leatherneck watches with arms folded, mouth puckered as if he's about to spit. Allison faces away, poring over the *Chronicle*.

Brendan turns when he walks in and gestures to the screen, inquiring. Christopher nods, and crosses to sit beside Allison.

"Hey," she says wearily. "You look like I feel."

"It's not a feel-good kind of a week. Any change?"

Allison shakes her head. "Jonah and Buzz got off to school?"

"Nora's making sure." Yesterday's elation collapsed into impossibility. This morning the ordinary is surreal.

They sit quietly. "Zac's got one fucked-up family," Allison says after a while.

"Worse than he warned us. Like he was born into a cult." Christopher wonders whether California evangelicals forgive their errant little lambs any more readily, or if he's just predisposed to despise their brethren in Kansas. "His sister's flying out?"

"This afternoon. The rest won't even pick up the phone."

There isn't a lot to say to that.

"Nora talked to Therese for the better part of an hour. She says their parents have spoken about Zac in past tense for years."

Allison sighs. "When they speak about him at all. The brothers are worse."

Brendan joins them. "Can you believe this shit? CBS says this 'manifesto' could reach a hundred million people."

Christopher opens his bag and pulls out a freshly printed copy. "E-mailed to my work account."

Allison skims over Brendan's shoulder. Christopher paces the room while they read. The news moves on to Iraq, where Marines have attacked insurgent forces in Fallujah.

"Jesus," Brendan exclaims when he finishes.

"It's solid," Allison says. "Not what I'd expect from somebody driving kamikaze into a building."

Christopher nods. "How 'bout we take a walk around the block?"

———

A park opens out behind the hospital's main building. Stepping off the sidewalk, Christopher breaks their silence. "This conversation never happened," he says.

"Sure." Brendan strikes a match and lights a cigarette.

He needs more than that. "I mean never ever."

"Chris, you have our word," Allison says.

"I don't mean to be dramatic." The park is poorly maintained. Gopher holes pock the lawn, crabgrass pushes out of red-gray dirt in knotty clumps.

"Go on," Brendan says.

"That e-mail." Christopher aims for a neutral tone. "Their manifesto. Did anything about it seem peculiar?"

"I—" Allison stops herself. She waits for more.

"My dad called the Triangle, about an hour ago. It made him livid."

"And?"

"He said it looks like 'the same nonsense you and your friends were spouting yesterday.'"

Brendan and Allison exchange a glance.

"We've spouted a lot in that vein over the years," Allison says carefully. "So have a lot of other people."

The three of them stand in the middle of the open lawn, watching each other.

"I had no advance knowledge whatsoever about what happened this morning," Christopher says. "So help me God."

"Then we're here because? . . ."

Christopher shakes his head, deflecting Brendan's prompt. "The text can't be tied to me. Not directly. Not definitively. But if my dad detects a resemblance the government might too."

"This is not our politics," Allison says. It's a question. A challenge.

"No. This is not our politics. It's extremism of a kind we would never endorse."

"Let's be clear." Brendan's voice is strained. He grinds his half-smoked cigarette into the mangy grass. "It makes a pickup full of Kalashnikovs look like a Sunday school picnic."

"The point is that cops hell-bent on a culprit aren't going to draw subtle distinctions."

"Okay," Allison says. "This thing is going to get full treatment, you're saying. And we'll be on the short list."

"Isn't this how they found Kaczynski?" Brendan asks.

Christopher swallows. "Ted Kaczynski was *actually* the Unabomber."

"And a brother figured out his manifesto was Kaczynski's writing. The Feds were handed their man's head on a plate. Am I right?" Brendan glares, his jaw working. If he's trying to mask his hostility, he's not trying hard. "How pissed off is your dad, Chris? And let's not leave Marshall out."

"Look, there's no point tying ourselves up in paranoid knots."

Christopher's throat is parched. "I don't want to invent a connection—"

"Then why are we standing here?"

"Because if a witch hunt is in the works there are steps we can take. Individually and as a group. For one thing, we need Marty to sanitize our computers. Industrial strength."

"Once they let us bail him out," Allison says.

Christopher can't get a read on what she's thinking.

"The climbers will be out today or tomorrow," Brendan says. "But the computers? That's the first thing that comes to mind? What about a book burning while we're at it?"

"What's with you?" Christopher snaps. "Why not scrub lists that lead to everybody we've ever worked with?"

"The kids downstairs deserve a heads-up, wouldn't you say?"

"Look—"

Allison interrupts. "Where are you going with this, Brendan? Why are you throwing weight around?"

"The Feds are going to show. One day after another, same issue. They're going to look into whether there was contact. And I take it back about Marty. Maybe they'll keep the climbers locked up for weeks."

"Was there contact?" Allison asks. She looks Christopher dead in the eye.

He forces himself to hold her gaze. Ruined. He has ruined them. "If there was, it would be a very bad idea for anybody to know."

"We're not anybody." Brendan isn't speaking now, he's hissing. "You're not alone on the wrong end of this thing."

Christopher looks back and forth. Allison is as beaten as he's ever seen her. Brendan is ready to pounce. "There was an e-mail," he says hoarsely. "Months ago, to my address at the paper. Nothing explicit. An invitation to communicate anonymously."

"And?"

"Let's say I ignored it." Christopher clears his throat.

"Goddamn it—"

"Let's just say that I deleted the e-mail. If that was a trail—I can't know if I didn't follow it—if that was a trail, it ended there. We can count on that." Can they? He hears his own words as if from a distance.

"Can we?" Allison asks.

Brendan is trying to extract another smoke from his pack. His hands shake visibly. "Fuck me, Chris. Are you out of your fucking mind?"

"I can't control who sends—"

"Bullshit! What the fuck were you thinking?"

"I knew nothing about this . . . thing until I saw the news." His voice quavers now. "Nothing until this morning."

"Tell it to the Gestapo." Brendan faces away, sheltering his cigarette while he lights it.

"Slow down," Allison says. "We need a couple hours to think, to figure this out."

Brendan whips around. "There's nothing to figure. And we might not have a couple of hours."

"Why do you say that?"

"Listen to me, Al. I'm out. Sorry for the shitty timing. I can't get caught up in this."

"That's—"

"—a done deal."

"You don't need to disappear," Christopher says.

"I'll decide what I need."

"You're running again, Brendan. Same as ever," Allison says.

He steps forward, leaning into Allison as if daring her to strike. "Nothing will ever be the same, Al. Chris is right to keep what he knows to himself. I've heard enough. Bottom line is the government's going to pull out all the stops, and the Triangle is right smack in their crosshairs."

Christopher tries to speak, but can't. It hardly matters. He's no longer in the conversation.

"Think," Brendan says. "Think where I was last year. What are they going to do if they find me in the middle of another armed fucking struggle? What conclusions do the cops draw if they find you sheltering me?"

"Don't go."

"I'll be in touch. Eventually. But I'm not going to be crashing at the Triangle when they bust down the door."

THIRTY-SIX

Nora wakes anxious, the place strange to her.

"Mrs. Tanner?"

Whose voice is that? And who's Mrs. Tanner?

The florescent lights and the rough, colorless carpet bring her back to the hospital waiting room. It's the night nurse speaking. She's sitting in the opposite row of chairs, beside Therese, waiting for Zac's sister to slog her way awake.

"I—Yes. Oh—yes, I'm sorry."

Therese's makeup is smudged, her eyes unfocused. Nora is still surprised to find Zac's sister so amply fleshed, so dramatically opposite from his beanpole skinniness.

Allison had been with Nora at the hospital when Therese arrived. The three of them parked Therese's red suitcase in a corner and began to poke at the strangeness of Zac's present meeting Zac's past. Therese quickly showed her warm heart, as open and empathic as her brother. She was ashamed that no one else from Topeka would acknowledge him. That had been awkward. They told her how kind Zac was to everyone he met, but omitted the yoga, and the Buddhist theology, and the nights danced away in bars along Polk Street. Therese hadn't asked about politics, not even about the protest on the bridge, and neither Nora nor Allison pressed. Now, watching her stir, Nora recognizes family resemblance in a blank uncertainty Zac shows when he wakes.

"Mrs. Tanner, I'm sorry to have to disturb you."

Nora stands, and takes a step toward the other two.

"What is it?" she asks. The night nurse meets her eyes.

"It's . . . it's fine," Therese is saying, still fighting her way into the present. The clock on the wall reads a quarter past two. A quarter past four in Topeka.

"I'm afraid I have unwelcome news," the nurse tells Therese, placing a hand on the other woman's arm.

"Oh, God—"

"I'm so sorry."

"How did—when?"

"Your brother suffered a severe seizure about twenty minutes ago. The doctor was by his side immediately, but . . . he didn't linger. We did everything we could to bring him back. I am so very sorry for your loss."

Nora feels herself sinking into a blackness at the edges of everything. Not just what she can see, but around the words she's hearing too, and the sense of her feet on the ground. She feels wobbly, as if she might fall away into deep, irrevocably deep sleep. She steps back, uncertain of her bearings.

"My colleagues are preparing him now. Please take whatever time you need."

Nora sits, a barely controlled fall into her chair.

Is it time to weep?

Her eyes are dry and her ears are buzzing. She has no idea what to feel, how to feel, whether she can feel anything at all.

THIRTY-SEVEN

It isn't as though Zac used to make a particular racket meditating in his room, or cooking to the rhythm of Vedic chants, or shepherding Jonah toward his homework. But the teakettle's lonely churn in the Triangle's quiet marks his absence nonetheless, reminds each and all of them that he won't step into the kitchen for a cup of chai, not ever again. No one has had the heart to enter Zac's bedroom since his sister left town with a plastic urn of ashes packed inside her suitcase. Brendan's insomnia, his late night orbits to the back porch, the brokenness his old friends wanted, somehow, to fix: all that is gone too.

In Christopher's imagination, the ticking clock marks increments of distance Brendan is putting between himself and the collective. The Kawasaki's whine, receding. Brendan no longer haunts the front room, and now it is he, Christopher, who seeks solace in poetry: John Milton, late into the empty nights. The blind bard is stern, certain, lending a longed-for solidity to Christopher's circumscribed pool of lamplight. Nora says she hears a ghost of Zac's boyish laugh behind every shut door.

The kettle warbles softly, threatening an all-out wail. Nora cuts the gas and the steam settles. Christopher idly riffles the pages of *Paradise Lost*. They're talking about Buzz.

"Rules and conditions would alienate him," she's saying. "He would never trust us. All we'd offer better than juvie is decent food and physical safety."

"Neither one trivial."

"No. Neither one." Nora drops a tea bag in her mug and pours water over it. A tart, floral fragrance fills the kitchen. "But it wouldn't be parenting, and we'd be naïve not to weigh the risk."

"Of?"

"Of exposing Jonah to . . . who knows what."

He sees that she is right, but can't find what to say. Even the smell of hibiscus tea is too much. If he stood, Christopher thinks, he'd probably puke.

"So do we become the bad cops? Put him through Narconon and pee tests and cell-phone roll calls? Or do we risk him dragging Jonah into the muck?"

"No happy choices." To his own ear Christopher sounds like the village idiot. All he can muster are platitudes.

"Meantime we wait for seriously bad cops to show." She sits opposite Christopher. "I've been thinking . . . it's like a race."

"What is?"

"Nebraska. Us. It's a race to see if they catch these truck bombers before we get served with a warrant. A bust is the only thing that'll keep the Feds off our backs."

Fear presses the air from his lungs.

If they find Chagall, he'll be next. Chagall knows who he is. If the police don't take down an actual culprit, he's in the line of fire on the manifesto front. If the government makes no headway at all they'll raid the Triangle because they have to do something.

No matter which way the wave breaks, Christopher can feel

he's going under. He woke that morning certain the only option he has is to walk into the local FBI office. Plead ignorance and beg for mercy. Now he isn't so eager. Is it rational uncertainty that holds him back? Or is he just scared?

He can't fathom the distance between a month before and now. Christopher called Suvali exactly once since everything happened. From a pay phone. She didn't pick up, so he left an elliptical message. What can you say in thirty seconds about the bottom falling out of your life? She hasn't phoned back, which he takes to mean that thirty seconds was long enough. She gets that she's better off avoiding him. It's probably what she wanted anyway.

Christopher can't explain any of this to Nora.

"Back to Buzz," he says, sublimating mightily. "He's not going home to Cheryl and Vince."

"Goddamn right he's not. Standards of proof be damned, Chris, there's no mystery about those two. Vince beats him, maybe worse, and Cheryl lets it happen." Nora looks up at the clock over the stove. "Allison's about to come on."

Christopher reaches for the radio. At that moment the front gate crashes shut. He freezes, then recognizes Marty's familiar pounding up the steps. Christopher presses the power switch. *Second Look*'s program signature swells out of the boom box speakers, then fades into Hannah Freedman's opening patter. Nora shakes her head wearily as Marty's messenger bag slides down the hallway and ricochets off a wall.

HANNAH: Last week April turned March on its head, going
   out like a whole pride of lions with nary a lamb in sight—

"Hey," Marty says breathlessly, stepping into the kitchen. He bends to kiss the top of Nora's head. "Did I miss much?"

"Nick of time." She turns up the volume.

Marty scoops a pair of beers out of the fridge and offers them to the others.

"Not me," Christopher says. Nora points to her steaming tea.

HANNAH: —protesters shut down the San Francisco Bay Bridge, hanging a gruesome and now iconic banner from its westernmost tower. A scuffle with one of thousands of drivers trapped behind their blockade resulted in an activist's fatal injury. The next morning, a truck bomb destroyed a genomics research center outside Lincoln, Nebraska. The bombers hacked and spammed their manifesto across the internet, calling for an end to the politics of destruction. Finally, on Wednesday night, CBS News broadcast photographs depicting United States military personnel committing acts of torture and sexual humiliation against detainees at the Abu Ghraib prison in Iraq. This is Hannah Freedman, welcome to *Second Look*. Today is Tuesday, May fourth.

Christopher shakes his head gloomily. "Hell of a lead."

"Hell of a week," Nora says. "She's setting up for compare and contrast."

"I don't like her leaving out Zac's name," Marty says. "He ain't just some protester."

HANNAH: In the studio we have Meg Wyneken and Allison Rayle. Meg heads the US arm of the activist organization Global Justice, and played a key role in protests against scientists and industry representatives attending the seventh annual GeneSynth convention. A mile to the east of Moscone Center, Allison was arrested on the Bay Bridge. As climbers hung their enormous banner, she witnessed longtime friend and fellow activist Zachary

Coyle fall victim to a driver's road rage. Meg, tell us: why genetic engineering, and why now?

MEG: Thanks for inviting me, Hannah, and for posing those key questions . . .

"First person singular," Christopher says.

Marty nods. "Maybe it's the only pronoun she knows."

MEG: —a situation where scientists see a convergence of mass die-offs, thousands of species each year, and the biosphere being taken over by freak life-forms whose DNA is corrupted and patented by major corporations. Nobody knows what damage these mutants will cause. In Europe, in Japan, in Canada, issues posed by genetic engineering are getting a full public airing. Global Justice insists that Americans have a chance to participate in that dialogue.

HANNAH: Allison Rayle, tell us why your group left the fold to organize a dramatic protest on the Bay Bridge.

ALLISON: Thanks, Hannah. I wouldn't put it quite that way. Many of the people on the bridge took active roles in the coalition that Meg's group was part of. We helped to craft and fully supported the coalition's points of agreement. The drama of a billboard-sized banner hanging off the bridge tower broadcast our common message in a way that mass media couldn't ignore. The police would have stopped us if they'd known our plans, so we took it off the radar.

"Holding her own against the queen of spin," Marty says. "Through round one." Nora sips from her mug.

MEG: Unfortunately, the risks that Allison's group guarded

against weren't the ones that sabotaged our protest. Zac was a vibrant and committed activist. I can't claim Allison's close friendship, but all of us mourn his tragedy on the Bay Bridge.

HANNAH: Let's talk about an event that abruptly upstaged West Coast activism against genetic engineering. Allison, where were you when you first learned of the bombing in Nebraska?

"Christ on a cross," Marty says.

ALLISON: That was not an easy morning, Hannah. Zac was in intensive care after a three-hour surgery, and I'd been released from jail the previous night. So I heard the early news about Nebraska at the hospital. The first thing I thought was how awful it would be if anyone was inside the building. Thankfully, the facility was empty.

HANNAH: What was your political response?

ALLISON: I am unequivocally opposed, and everybody I work with is unequivocally opposed to this type of destructive tactic. No responsible person or group blows up buildings, whether they're empty or not. What is perplexing here is that the perpetrators issued a statement criticizing destruction as the worst possible way to advance a political agenda. As you put it a few minutes ago, the bombers' own manifesto called for an end to the politics they practiced.

HANNAH: Meg?

MEG: Terrorism hurts our work terribly, Hannah. Of course I'm as thankful as Allison that no one was killed or injured. But no matter how the bombers tried to color their despicable attack, they have now linked opposition to genetic engineering with reckless terrorism in the public mind. We will be years repairing damage done to a righteous cause.

"Twice," Christopher says.

"Twice what?"

"Twice she said 'terrorism' in twenty seconds."

HANNAH: —eclipsed by the Nebraska bombers, and a day later the media refocused again, this time on the Abu Ghraib prison. Meg, we all feel moral outrage looking at those photographs. How can opposition to genetic engineering be maintained when we're confronted with hard evidence that American soldiers are committing acts of brutality in Iraq?

MEG: There is no excuse for the inhumanity those images show, Hannah. But as these atrocities and the policies behind them come to light, we need to remember that never in the history of political activism has there been one single, all-consuming issue. Torture of human beings by American soldiers is inexcusable and it must stop, right now. Environmental rape by corporate-funded genetic engineers? It's beyond dangerous, and simply not tolerable. Truck bombs as a means of advancing political dialogue? Absolutely never.

HANNAH: Allison?

ALLISON: Meg is on point. I would add that these issues are part of a single fabric. We can only assume that Abu Ghraib happened when rank-and-file soldiers were thrown into chaotic situations, then ordered by ideologues to betray their own humanity. When we find genetically modified corn used illegally to make tortilla chips and soft drinks, that's the result of workers in our food industries being manipulated by agribusiness giants who aren't accountable to anyone. These issues share symptoms of an antidemocratic influence in our government. Profit and expedience have replaced morality and stewardship as a basis for deciding policy.

HANNAH: There are a lot of listeners out there who see November's elections as our opportunity to nip that influence in the bud.

ALLISON: The sooner the better, Hannah, but unfortunately we're well past the budding stage.

MEG: As an avid listener myself, I see November as a critical opportunity. What's going to work against us, though, is when terrorism like the bombing in Nebraska is associated with citizens who want to create change through constitutional due process. And with all respect to Allison and to Zachary Coyle's memory—

"Here goes."

MEG: —I think we have to acknowledge that dangerous and clandestine urban disruptions are going to hurt our cause as well.

ALLISON: I take exception to characterizing a traffic delay in such frenzied terms, Meg. Where would one draw a line?

MEG: Let me ask you, Allison, how our cause is advanced by overshadowing publicly convened protest with secretly conceived, unaccountable, mortally dangerous disruptions?

ALLISON: Exaggeration doesn't improve our credibility as a movement, Meg. Diversity of expression and style is our strength. We lack a government's power, it makes no sense to tie ourselves up in mock-governmental bureaucracies.

MEG: And yet a young activist paid with his life for your group's recklessness—

—

Christopher switches off the boom box the moment the interview is over, and silence seeps back into the kitchen.

"I dunno." Nora sounds defeated.

"She gave it a great shot," Christopher says. "Meg wouldn't let go."

Nora carries her empty mug to the sink.

"Did anybody talk to Zac's sister?" Marty asks.

"This morning," Nora says. "Nobody's speaking with her back in Topeka."

"Jayzus. And nothing yet from Brendan?"

"Not a word."

"I don't think he'll be in touch for a while," Christopher says. "Not until we see what happens."

Again, the quiet. A chair scrapes across the floor upstairs.

"Jonah and Buzz?"

"Just Jonah."

"Hmmm . . ." Marty turns his empty bottle idly. "I been thinkin', you know? About Zac's ashes."

Nora slumps against the counter. "I feel so weird about that. Ever since Allison said—"

"What?"

"We were talking about Brendan. She said he's got this idea that only your blood family steps up when things get really bad."

"Right," Marty says. "It's like we all believed that, letting Therese take him back to Kansas. As if Topeka meant anything to him."

"Well, I don't know about that last part," Nora says. "I don't think Zac would have cared one way or the other about the ashes. Body and spirit." Her lower lip begins to quiver. "But he was our family too. Why didn't we think about what it meant to us—" Nora can't hold herself in check. All the words and worries of the past week crumble, like a sand castle giving way to the tide. She collapses in breath-snatching sobs.

Marty steps across the room to hold her close. At his touch, the sluices open wider. Nora tries to speak, but Marty gentles her. "Let it go, girl. Let it go."

Christopher sits immobile. Lines he read in the dark hours of morning well up in his emptied mind:

> Which way I fly is hell; myself am hell;
> And, in the lowest deep, a lower deep
> Still threatening to devour me opens wide . . .

Nora struggles to contain her grief. Marty murmurs consolation.

He sees they both believe the worst is past. They imagine that even if the government were to invade, the Triangle is inoculated against its sting. Christopher bows his head to the tabletop, overwhelmed by the havoc yet to come.

THIRTY-EIGHT

The collective feels preternaturally vacant. It feels that way no matter how many of them—of those who are left—are at home. Allison floats through the Triangle like a widow. Like a widow's ghost.

The third floor pulses with blurred metallic chaos, music indecipherable to adult ears. She climbs the stairs and approaches the boys' bedroom. Up close the noise is excruciating. They're lying on the floor, all bottled up and staring at the ceiling, listening as though the stereo's distortions were the subtlest string quartet. She knocks sharply on the doorframe. Jonah turns his head.

"The music is too loud!"

"What?"

"Turn the music down, please."

Buzz looks over. "Bitter Rockets," he says. She has to read his lips because she can't hear over the frenetic guitar.

Jonah picks himself up reluctantly and turns the volume a notch counterclockwise.

"More," Allison says.

He complies, and resumes his prone position. Their sullen vitality doesn't fill her void.

At least Buzz seems to be giving heroin a rest. It relieves her that an Estonian thrash band is the most offensive mud Buzz has tracked into the Triangle. She leaves them to their music, then stops in the hall, not sure whether they've dialed the volume back up again.

Bitter Rockets. As if naming the band clarifies anything.

With all they've lost, her sense of hearing isn't Allison's top worry. She can't ask the boys to close their bedroom door. No shut doors, an adult always home to chaperone. They've spent a lot of parental capital to establish ground rules now that Buzz has joined the household. If she capitulates to mere noise, he'll count it a victory over shaky authority. She returns to the second-floor kitchen.

Allison blames herself.

The bridge was her idea.

She was the one who urged Brendan to stay. If he hadn't, Zac might have staffed the phones with Nora, and not been on the span at all that morning.

If she'd taken out the truck driver instead of checking Gregor's overhand assault? Zac would be alive beside her, helping to make dinner. Gregor would have held himself back, or not. If he hadn't, she would have suffered the tire iron. She could have borne a few broken ribs.

What she can't bear is reliving the moment. Warding off Gregor's attack on a man about to deal Zac his deathblow.

Allison rinses peppers in the sink, peels carrots, breaks a bulb of garlic into cloves. She lays a cutting board on the counter, and absently tests the edge of a blade pulled from the knife block.

It didn't console anyone to learn that Zac's prognosis topped out at major cognitive disability. Perhaps someday they'll find comfort in the knowledge—the conjecture, it will always be a guess—that no happy endings were possible.

A freak accident, people say. Hannah Freedman wasn't the first or last to call it road rage, but to Allison that's senseless chatter. There are no explanations. There will always be the vacuum where Zac used to be, empty as the hollow Brendan left when he disappeared.

Emptier.

She can't look full-on at photographs of Zac surrounded by medics on the bridge deck, but neither can Allison put the scene out of her mind. Then there are the images from that festering prison outside Baghdad. Bound, beaten Iraqis being attacked with dogs, stripped and stacked like cordwood. It's clear now that government-sanctioned torture has knocked genetic engineering off the public map. Hannah got that one right. Everything they've done—what Zac died for—has vaporized in the glare of Abu Ghraib.

Even the research center bombing has dropped out of the news. Too bad for the government, given keener motive than usual for pumping threat into the nation's tele-consciousness. At the Triangle, no one is reassured. As Nora keeps reminding them, the other shoe will drop soon enough, unless the Nebraska bombers are arrested first. Some wait with greater trepidation than others.

They have shredded and burned reams of paper, as Brendan sarcastically foretold. Marty offloaded data from their disks, hid what needed to be kept, scrubbed the hard drives clean. Motion-activated webcams now cling like cockroaches to the library ceiling, like red-eyed bats above the building's gated stoop. A neighbor's wireless LAN pipes their video streams to remote storage, circumventing a network cable likely to be cut when the Feds come calling. Allison argued the surveillance goes too far, but Nora is adamant. Recordings of sloppy search and seizure could prove a potent weapon in court. Allison has debated telling Nora and Marty what Christopher all but confessed outside the hospital. But they're taking all possible precautions; she sees no benefit to widening their legal risk. Or to poisoning the others with her own dread.

She sets down the knife. Allison has filled a mixing bowl with diced eggplant and onion, carrot and bell pepper, crookneck squash as yellow as sunlight. She tosses the bright medley with salt, pepper, and a generous pour of olive oil. Spreads the vegetables onto cookie sheets. Slides them into the oven to roast. A pot of tomato sauce bubbles on the stove.

Buzz and Jonah have eased up on the Bitter Rockets. An Indian raga floats gently down the stairs. Jonah's calmer tastes have prevailed, at least for now. But the music's plaintive swell and haunting fade change nothing.

When the doorbell rings, Allison starts. It's not like her to be so on edge. But perhaps Brendan hit that mark, too, in his fury outside the hospital. Nothing will ever be the same again.

She approaches the video screen Marty mounted in the stairwell, and sees a pair of trim, neatly suited women peering through the outside gate's metal mesh. Allison immediately recognizes the inevitable. One of the women is holding something flat in her right hand. A wallet.

Allison clutches the banister, but a moment later finds herself riding an absolute calm. They knew this visit would come. She tiptoes upstairs, calling out urgently. Jonah appears at the far end of the hall.

"I think it's the police. Don't go near the windows." She pitches her voice low. "Get Buzz, and bring him to the second floor, quick as you can. Listen carefully when I talk to them. If they're cops, call Nora at work. She'll know what to do."

Jonah's eyes widen. The doorbell rings again, long and insistent. "It's okay," she says. "Do as I ask, Jonah."

"Mom, be careful."

"You know I will." She summons a smile from some former

life, then turns and bangs down the stairs. "Coming," she calls out. As if she hadn't a care in the world. Allison steps onto the stoop. "Yes?"

Both women are wearing earpieces, audio tubes spiraling under their collars. Allison assumes there's heat carpeting the neighborhood, that anything she says will be recorded by a sound truck down the street.

The one with the wallet responds. "Is this the residence of Christopher Kalman?"

"May I ask who you are?"

"Agent Roedell, Federal Bureau of Investigation." She flashes an ID. "This is Agent McKinnock."

"FBI," Allison repeats, loudly, for Jonah's benefit. Without turning away from the agents she raps on the door to the downstairs flat, then steps forward, hands plainly visible, showing her palms. "I didn't see your identification clearly. May I see it again please?"

Agent Roedell snaps open her thin wallet and holds it to the cut steel of the gate. The partner's hand hovers by her hip.

Allison takes a proper look at Roedell's ID. "There won't be any trouble," she says, staring into the second agent's eyes. McKinnock. The door to the downstairs flat opens. Natalie peers out, blinking into the light. Gregor is standing behind her. "These women are FBI agents," Allison says. "I think you should listen in."

"Sure," Natalie says.

She was right to prepare them. Natalie is tough enough to pretend indifference. "You asked whether Christopher Kalman lives here," Allison says.

"And you haven't answered." Roedell continues to speak for both agents.

"Chris lives here, yes."

"Is he at home? We'd like to talk with him."

"He's not here now. It's not for me to say, but I can't imagine he'd want to talk without a lawyer present."

"Open the gate," Agent McKinnock says.

"I don't believe I have an obligation to do that."

"Mom?" Jonah is calling from the head of the stairs.

"Could one of you guys go see what's up?" Allison asks over her shoulder. Natalie rounds the wall and ascends, calling out softly. "There are children upstairs," Allison says to the agents. "Two teenage boys. I don't want them exposed to a police matter."

"We have a search warrant, ma'am." Agent Roedell pulls a document from her jacket pocket.

"May I read it?"

The agents exchange a frustrated glance. Upstairs the telephone rings.

"Nobody's going anywhere," Allison says. "If you have a legal warrant, we will cooperate. I understand I have a right to read the warrant before I let you in."

Agent Roedell unfolds the single sheet. Allison sees through the mesh that the paperwork cites the Triangle's street address, but not the downstairs flat. She makes a show of reading closely.

"Jonah, Buzz—come downstairs now," she calls out, halfway through the court order. She looks to Agent Roedell. "I want them with me when you go barging in."

Leading with a forefinger, Allison continues to read, stalling. She recognizes Jonah's step as he descends with Natalie. Only the two of them. "Where's Buzz?" she asks when they reach the stoop.

Natalie replies. "Leona just called. Chris was arrested at the office."

Allison's heart sinks.

Jonah leans to his mother's ear and whispers. Agent Roedell folds the warrant and replaces it in her jacket. Agent McKinnock tilts her head, pressing a hand to her earpiece.

"The other boy tried to escape out the back," McKinnock announces. "He's in custody. Open the gate, Ms. Rayle."

Allison hasn't given her name. "Nat, Gregor, go inside and lock your door," she says. "The warrant is for our address, not yours."

Jonah presses up against her.

Gregor takes a step back. "Allison?" he asks.

"Go inside." She speaks as if she has no doubts.

Allison drapes a protective arm around her son's shoulder. With her other hand she reaches for the latch.

EPILOGUE

August 2007

The AgBio bombing was a loss: empty, humiliating, a bitter defeat. Our impotence was laid bare. All the trouble I took, a lifetime of secrecy and dissembling, of positioning myself. All vanquished.

Everything I ever sneered at in my brother's openly activist life has come back to bite me. And if that isn't enough, Christopher has been collared by secret police. Eight days after the bombing, the government spirited him off to they-wouldn't-say-where.

I set loose a monster. Christopher is paying the price.

It's my fault our father spent his last years hovering on the edge of nervous breakdown. It's my fault that Christopher is strapped to a gurney someplace, someplace dark and infested with vermin, wired up for electroshock more likely than not. Maybe they're keeping him awake for days on end, maybe they're raping him with police batons. I can only imagine, because why would the government tell?

The government isn't telling, and nobody knows it's my fault. Does the fact that I'm to blame and nobody knows give me a card to play? Or does the truth that I haven't stepped up and confessed make me a sniveling coward?

Chagall has vanished.

I drove my father to hysteria and sent my brother to hell on Earth.

How's a man supposed to repent for that?

—

I am writing these words in late summer. The house where Christopher and I grew up is silent. Sold. Escrow closes in a few days, and I'll walk out our door for the very last time.

An extrajudicial cabal swallowed my brother whole on the sixth of May, 2004. How all that went down, what we know of events that led to his government-sponsored disappearance, everything we've tracked or deduced afterward—that's the puzzle I've been piecing together these past three years. It took patience, especially to win the trust of Christopher's house-comrades, who knew just how much my brother despised me. They thought it was family duty that brought Marshall Kalman to their door again, that I was acting out of unwelcome obligation. Only after months of common cause, of running into brick walls right alongside Allison and the others, did they begin to take me seriously. To tell me what they know and what they guess.

Leona saw it happen. She told how the men who snatched him flashed badges as they burst into the *Reporter's* office, but never named their agency. They drew weapons, she said, shouted the staff onto the floor, hauled Christopher up off his belly and made for the exit. Barry Bortman, the newspaper's publisher, tried to block the plainclothes thugs as they dragged Christopher away. For his trouble, they knocked the old man flat on his ass.

Meanwhile Duboce Avenue was crawling with FBI. As Allison had guessed, Roedell and McKinnock were only the advance guard. Marty's webcam recorded twenty-two agents coming through the front door in four minutes. Then one of the goons ripped the device off its mount. They scoured the place, turned it upside down, sealed off Christopher's room and the library, and confiscated every piece of digital media they could find. Computers, optical discs, flash drives, even Jonah's MP3 player.

Allison and Nora told how they found books scattered, desks emptied, dresser drawers dumped, closets upended, and the kitchen a disaster when the Feds finished late that night. Zealous lawmen had dumped Allison's tomato sauce into the sink, seeking evidence among the diced onions at the bottom of the pot. Marty's countersurveillance technology was ripped off the windows and walls. Buzz had gone missing after the Feds let him go. Days later, Allison and Jonah tracked down his friend Jaggery in the Haight. Buzz had come through the neighborhood frantic, he said, like his pants were on fire, desperate for a ride out of town. He might have hitched north, to Portland, Jaggery told Allison. Or maybe east, to Denver.

It's been three years, and Christopher has not been charged with a crime. Civil rights powerhouse Tracey Braun is his lawyer, but they're permitted only occasional meetings, under full surveillance. We know now that the government is warehousing Christopher at a high-security prison in Atwater. Braun isn't permitted to carry messages in or out, not even for family. He reports that my brother is gaunt, coherent, easily upset, and in solitary lockdown.

That's as far as it's gotten. A few compromised meetings. No charges, no hearings, no trial.

The Triangle has not faltered from the struggle to rescue Christopher. They engaged local activists; they got Amnesty International on board; they rattled the cages of newspaper editors in San Francisco, Seattle, Chicago, and LA. They made peace with Meg Wyneken, who has thrown her weight behind the media campaigns, the letter writing, the dead-end hearings in Federal District Court.

Until he died of a heart attack last fall, our father served as the family's face to media. Christopher's illegal imprisonment killed him. The doctors called it "stress-induced cardiomyopathy," but strip away the Latin and you're left with "the government took my son hostage."

They should have written exactly that on Dad's death certificate.

—

Some weeks after the kidnapping I received an e-card for Flag Day. Flag Day! If that wasn't strange enough, the name of the sender looked like spam scramble, something translated by a Romanian with terrible English. I nearly deleted it unread, but then the message came into focus: Fraturnel Catastrafee. This was the start of my reevaluation. Christopher wasn't nearly so helpless as I believed all those years. He must have scheduled the card between the day Chagall struck and his own arrest. I opened it and found a cryptic payload, literally. Two hexadecimal strings and concise instruction: "Keep carefully, keep secret. More to follow." Christopher had also squeezed in reference to an obscure event from our past, to prove the communication was his. I won't share that. Some details are best left a little vague.

More electronic cards followed, months apart, like slow-release breadcrumbs. They promised a key piece of information to be delivered through his attorney, but Braun had nothing.

I didn't tell anyone about the e-cards. I tried to be a friend to Allison and Nora and Marty, and did everything I could to help keep Christopher's plight in the media and the courts. I corresponded with Brendan. I met Leona. I was trying to get to know who my brother had been, way too late. Eventually the e-cards stopped. Brendan agreed to meet me in a bar out in Concord about a year after everything went down. Allison arranged it, and Marty drove me there—Brendan didn't want me to know the location beforehand. He described late-night walks with Christopher, and their drive up to Eddie Bourgeaut's place, the hinting around Christopher did. Brendan put pieces together after the fact. He feels bad for my brother, not so angry anymore. He spent long enough in Tlaxitlán to know a thing or two about captivity. About betrayal. And he knows, as we all do, that Christopher's got it worse.

Two years into my brother's incarceration I stumbled across an 80mm mini-CD folded into a recipe clipped from an old newspaper, in our mother's recipe box. It was labeled in Christopher's handwriting with a blue marker: *Chagall (1 of 2)*. A quick spin-up revealed the disk was filled with images of work by the eponymous artist. A single file—deceptively named ParisWindow.jpg—was actually just half an image. Half an image and then some. *Paris par la fenêtre*, the painting whose reproduction hung above our kitchen table all the years of our childhood. And, grafted onto a rootstock of digitized art, several megabytes of encrypted data.

There was one other file on the disk. It was simply named "brother," and it was also encrypted. When I ran the file through an MD5 generator it yielded one of the hexadecimal strings Christopher sent in that first e-card: an MD5 hash. That proved that the same person who sent the electronic greeting had planted the CD. The e-card's other hexadecimal string was a key that decrypted "brother," but didn't unscramble the data hidden behind *Paris par la fenêtre*.

Much of the history Christopher detailed in "brother" is—how to put it?—dramatized in the account you've just read.

Christopher described how he was contacted anonymously, and enumerated exchanges with the correspondent he nicknamed Chagall. He laid out conditions established in his dealings with the saboteur. Christopher speculated, in brutally self-critical retrospect, on ways the government might tie him to the Nebraska bombing: the Triangle's bridge action, analysis of his writing style, intercepted communications correlated with surveillance video. Or maybe a call to the FBI tip line from Suvali, uncertain of whom she really met in that Marina café; or from Buzz in a fit of fear and anger; or from Buzz's humiliated mom.

The rest of "brother" was a set of instructions. Christopher had thought out how to offer a ransom to his abductors. Again, a deeper game than I knew to expect from him. The mass of data fused to ParisWindow.jpg is a scrambled half, he wrote, of e-mail and chat transcripts he kept to document communication with Chagall. He held onto them as insurance, protected by software that renders the transcripts indecipherable unless a strong key is applied to both halves of the data at once. Christopher didn't explain how to find the other half of the communication records. I assume that's a message he intended to convey through his lawyer.

My brother anticipated an information blackout while in custody. He expected that if and when I read his missive there would be a lot I knew and a lot he didn't. His instructions were therefore provisional. Christopher delegated considerable authority when he lobbed his message into the future during that panicked week of 2004, an admirably levelheaded call.

There are a number of things he didn't foresee. For one, Christopher didn't expect that I would find both of the disks he'd hidden, the second as I cleaned out our father's university office the month after he died.

—

It's remarkable that Christopher entrusted his rescue to me. Humbling too. But remarkable not because he and I have a contentious history between us. I know my apparent materialism and self-absorption annoyed him. I cultivated that façade carefully. Did he get that the futures we foresee are similarly dark, that we differed all those years only on questions of what's to be done, and how? Yes, I did think Christopher was whining from the sidelines for most of his life. But what he was whining about matters. How well did he understand that I know that? Perhaps this manuscript, and the bargain to which it is a preface, will reveal what I failed to show when I could have.

The remarkable thing about appointing me to steward his secrets is that I stood outside the circle of Christopher's chosen family. He followed a script that played out in Brendan's imprisonment, a script in which brothers prove steadfast. Yet everything I've learned from those who remain at the Triangle points to Christopher's commitment to his collective, and to his distance from blood family—including yours truly. His housecomrades have been more than steadfast. Vigils, blogs, petitions, interviews, testimonials, legal motions, even a congressional inquiry initiated through the slowest of roundabout channels. So the only sense I see in being appointed his proxy is that Christopher had no idea who at the Triangle would get caught in the government's net. Though none of them had anything to do with Chagall or Nebraska, he couldn't predict what police might suspect.

There's an excruciating irony here. That irony is the second thing Christopher didn't foresee. It is, of course, the question of Romulus.

—

So to say it straight out: I, Marshall Kalman, am Chagall's hacker. I am Romulus. It was my suggestion to Chagall, in direct violation of boundaries set by the saboteur, that drew my brother into our conspiracy. When I proposed his name, I imagined I was doing Christopher a favor. I thought I was giving him a shot at acting consequentially for once, and at long last. I thought encryption was enough to protect us all. I proceeded with our plan after wrongly concluding that Chagall chose someone else to write our manifesto.

And now I am staggered by the insidious route treachery took, through a labyrinth of indirection, anonymity, and stupidly arrogant rivalry. My treachery. Humbled, I am called to extraordinary acts of penitence.

As it became clear that the government would hold him indefinitely, I began a secret negotiation with my brother's captors, in the persona of the hacker who conspired with Chagall. I did not reveal my true identity, but demanded Christopher's release as a token of the government's honest dealing. He is, after all, innocent of anything more than expressing ideas. I gave proofs of my role in the Nebraska bombing, and promised more. Negotiations have been inching forward. They are ongoing as I type these words. If you are reading them, however, I have failed to trade my imprisonment for my brother's freedom.

This manuscript is plan B.

———

It no longer makes sense for Christopher to call the plays. Three years into this debacle, the terrain has shifted. It's time to use the authority my brother delegated in that excruciating week before the government took him.

Consider that Christopher can no longer point to either of the CDs he hid. I have them both. Christopher can't give up the data even if the government waterboards him into compliance.

Consider that my brother has found no way to strike a deal with the badge-flashing gangsters who hold him captive. He has no position from which to describe information he could produce, and then refuse to give it up. But from deep hiding—which is where I'll be by the time these pages see the business end of a printing press—I have position to burn. Having possession of both disks, I'm the one withholding evidence now. Not only Christopher's, but my own. Having told as much as I have, my only choices are to surrender or to disappear. Disappearance gives each of us far greater leverage.

And so, the bargain I propose:

If the government wants to fuel its stalled manhunt with records of Christopher and Chagall's communication, the first thing they'll do is permit my brother to read this account in full. Then they'll permit him to confirm that he has done so by posting a message synthesized from fragments he and only he will recognize as "Easter eggs" scattered through the text. He will know how to reach me.

In response, as a token of seriousness and proof of possession, I will publish the contents of the second CD in a publicly accessible location on the internet. Christopher can prove the data's authenticity. I won't say how. The government can then work at deciphering the encrypted fragment. So can anybody else who wants to take a shot, but be warned: it's only a fragment. Nobody can turn either mass of gibberish into cleartext without its complementary half. I know because I've tried.

Next, Christopher must be freed into the care of his house-comrades—his chosen family, the only family he'll have in the wake of Dad's death and my own fugitive status.

Only then will I publicly release the other half of the dataset.

Last, with the Nebraska bombing data made public, narrowing the government's impunity should they try to throw him back in the hole, Christopher may choose to retrieve and publish the encryption key that unscrambles it. Will he do so? Perhaps, if he believes his freedom is secure.

I do not expect Christopher's records will lead to Chagall's capture. I'm confident Chagall is smarter than that. He'll have had a long head start on his trackers. On the other hand, the Feds would be fools to pass on the best evidence they've been offered in their dead-end pursuit.

If I learn Christopher has given up the encryption key under duress, before his release, the deal's off.

—

What no government can guarantee, by taking my offer or spurning it, is an end to struggle of the kinds just recounted. This has nothing to do with Chagall's ability to elude capture. It's not bound by the Triangle's political analysis, or Meg Wyneken's, or anybody's tactics. The question of a right path out of the mess humans have made of the world, of how one can make an actual difference, will remain active and open. As Laura Whitehorn put it in *The Weather Underground*—again, as I had Christopher quote to Suvali the last time he saw her—people never stop struggling to change the things that make life unlivable. This is the core of what my brother got right in his life and work. That the government has paralyzed him these past three years won't prevent fellow travelers from pushing that work forward.

To what end?

It's too soon to say.

Allison has come around from the despair that followed Zac's death, and now clings resolutely to her optimism. She insists no good act is wasted, whether history appears to be moved or not. Leaving Nebraska aside, she maintains the bridge blockade helped frame public understanding of hubris among molecular biologists; hubris that is just as toxic as efforts to install neoliberal "democracy" with tanks and torturers, or wrecking ecosystems to fuel criminally excessive consumption.

Unmoved by her sunny outlook, I remain focused on the defining characteristic of pendulums, history's included. They swing both ways. Back and forth and back again.

Progressive theories of social evolution are wishful thinking. The truth is that it's always easier to wreck than to build. To wreck on a planetary scale, never mind using a truck full of processed manure to set back somebody's construction schedule. In the big picture, Śiva the Destroyer will always have a leg up on the competition. Those who see through a secular lens call this advantage *entropy*.

Which is not to say that pessimism excuses anyone.

In the manifesto that I, as Romulus, sent careening around the world, Christopher concluded with this:

> Living beings, human and nonhuman alike, all lose when our nations and institutions inflame unnatural greed. We have allowed abstractions about property—about stuff, about the right to own and consume—to count more than anything that actually matters. Gluttony clouds our vision and judgment, corrals our morality, tempts us into cowed silence as our only Earth is savaged.
>
> Every day we fail to resist—every day we go along because it doesn't hurt us personally, not too much, not yet—every day we let ourselves be dazzled by cheap distractions and enthralled by manufactured cravings— every such day that passes we fall deeper into debt. Every such day we creep closer to the hour when it will be too late to turn back and mend what our own apathy and sloth have broken.

That we can't see how to overcome the power of human weakness doesn't let us off the hook. That the other fellow isn't making sacrifices doesn't give us license to scorch and poison and hoard.

History will be determined by those who act, whether the acts are charitable or self-serving, whether they are loving or hateful, honorably empathetic or twisted with distrust.

The damned in every human theology are those who fail to act righteously, whatever their excuse.

I couldn't have said it better myself.

ACKNOWLEDGMENTS

Consequence has benefitted from the help of many readers, advisers, and editors throughout its gestation; any errors that remain are my own. With apologies for any inadvertent omission of those who lent their attention and expertise, I am grateful to Alice Bell, Dan Berger, Chansonette Buck, Stephanie Carroll, Larry Cohen, Lewis Cohen, Nancy Cooper, Mary DeDanan, Quinn Dombrowski, Andrew Eddy, Kristina Eschmeyer, Stuart Fisk, Susan Giles, Lindy Gligorijevic, Bill Harrison, Rebecca Hemphill, Liana Holmberg, Lisa Jakelski, Steven Long, Leslie Mikkelsen, Kate Raphael, Dorothy Reller, Richard Ruby, Ryan Ruby, Patrick Schmitz, Danielle Seybold, Michael Stack, Matthew Felix Sun, Michelle Wolford, and Steven Yi. Thanks are also due to Bertha Sarmina for gently parrying the least helpful of my suggestions as she translated the words of Subcomandante Insurgente Marcos included in Chapter 11. I hope that friends, former housecomrades, and fellow activists find that *Consequence* does justice to the community I have been privileged to share with them, over many years and through much unfinished struggle.

Though countless books, articles, film documentaries, lectures, and discussions informed the political and scientific landscape of *Consequence,* two books merit particular mention as sources. *Our Word Is Our Weapon: Selected Writings,* edited by Juana Ponce de León, enriched my understanding of Subcomandante Insurgente Marcos, and of the nature and aims of the Zapatista movement for which he spoke. *A Different Universe: Reinventing Physics from the Bottom Down* by Robert B. Laughlin illuminates relationships between scientific concepts of emergence, complexity, and reductionism that helped me to undergird the worldviews that drive this novel's characters.

Lines from "No Second Troy" by William Butler Yeats are taken from *The Green Helmet and Other Poems.* Lines from Giuseppe Verdi's *Il Trovatore* are excerpted from Act IV Scene 1. Lines from John Milton are taken from Book IV of *Paradise Lost.*

About the Author

Steve Masover is a native of Chicago and lives in the San Francisco Bay Area. His short fiction has appeared in *Five Fingers Review* and *Christopher Street*. He co-wrote the screenplay for *Soweto to Berkeley*, a documentary film of the mid-1980s anti-apartheid movement. *Consequence* is his first novel.

www.stevemasover.net